HUMAN

PART ONE OF THE IVY CARTER ADVENTURE SERIES

HAYLEY CAMILLE

For Alex.

ISBN: 978-0-9945491-0-5

ASIN: B01CUP83TC

Published by SpearPoint Press

PO Box 1799

Sunshine Plaza 4556

Queensland Australia

PART I
EXTINCTION

CHAPTER 1

IVY

Ivy's footsteps rang out through the cloistered stone, echoing off the great sandstone walls that surrounded the grassy courtyard.

She glanced at her companion as suits hurried past, shooting furtive glances their way. Ivy ignored their curiosity. Her companion Kyah though, stared back with keen interest. She was always excited to escape the confines of her cage.

Grand archways threw light across Kyah's face and the bonobo's eyes closed for a moment as she savoured the fresh air.

"You okay, Ky?"

Ivy received a squeeze of her hand. Taking that as acquiescence, they continued on their path, navigating service roads and buildings for another ten minutes.

Most of the staff were well acquainted with the sight of the fiery-haired archaeologist and her 'chimpanzee' ward strolling through the grounds after hours. But whenever visitors first came across them, Ivy was always plied with the same questions.

"Is it dangerous?"

"Where does it live?"

"Can it touch it?"

With polite predictability, Ivy always rolled out the same answers.

"Not usually, but only because she trusts me."

"In the Behavioural Research Laboratory."

And *"Absolutely not."*

When she had the time and patience for it, Ivy also enlightened most of them on the difference between a bonobo and a chimpanzee, the former, like Kyah, being smaller and with a more altruistic and gentle temperament among other things, and that Kyah lived in the university as a permanent guest and was treated as such. The bonobo's life had been a difficult one, and now Kyah was afforded every comfort they could offer her. This was enough to satisfy most visitors' curiosity, and they usually continued on their way, giving the odd couple a bemused smile and a wide berth.

Ivy preferred a wide berth, for her own sake as much as Kyah's. She certainly didn't consider herself a 'people person'. A cat person, possibly. A dog person, sure. A bonobo person, certainly. But a 'people person' - goodness, no. In fact, until quite recently, Ivy had never considered spending much time with anyone, other than Kyah.

That was, until she'd met Orrin.

Ivy gave Kyah's hand a squeeze of reassurance, and quickened her pace.

The buildings dedicated to Physics were imposing steel and glass and reached far higher into the chilled blue sky than the sandstone walls Ivy was familiar with. She didn't come to this part of the university very often. She supposed it was pretty, with its angular art installations and water fountains running down glassy sheets. Very modern. A bit intimidating.

Kyah loped contentedly beside her. The bonobo's dark eyes sparkled as she watched the fountains throw rainbow prisms of light as they passed.

Ivy liked this time of day most, when nightfall was almost

touching. Most students and staff had left for the day and the monumental campus was quiet. A gust messed Ivy's hair into her eyes. She tucked it behind her ear.

Building 246. This is it.

Adjusting her satchel, Ivy opened her arms and the bonobo climbed into them like an overgrown child, balanced comfortably on Ivy's hip, arms wrapped around her neck.

In front of them, the glass doors and floodlights illuminated the foyer of a sleek building. She adjusted Kyah's weight and walked through past an unoccupied administration desk toward mirrored elevators. With a loud *ding!* the elevators doors slid open, then closed with her inside. She hit Level One, scanning a departmental map secured to the wall.

A twinge of jealousy caught her. Ivy imagined the dozens of laboratories hidden within these walls. Gleaming equipment and state of the art technology.

What we could do with that level of funding in the archaeology department. It seems I'm fraternising with the enemy. She smiled despite herself. Interdepartmental rivalry didn't usually rouse her, that was Jayne's, forte. Her laboratory partner took any opportunity to harangue the board about their ageing equipment and repurposed furniture. The Archaeology department looked almost as decrepit as the artefacts they studied within it.

The elevator chimed once again, and Ivy stepped out, hugging Kyah close as she navigated the long corridors scanning door plates.

Laboratory 179. Dr. Orrin James, Astro-physics.

"Okay Ky." Ivy pulled her face back a bit, to meet the bonobo's sparkling eyes. "Now, I know it'll be tempting with all the bright, shiny buttons in there, but behave yourself. We're trying to make a good impression, remember." She tried to straighten her cardigan, but Kyah's weight held it crooked. She hadn't thought to look in a mirror before she came. "I hope I don't have anything in my teeth." She glanced around for a reflective surface but saw none close. "Damn. Well, what do you think? How do I look?"

Kyah's lips formed a gentle grin and she hooted. There was no doubt in Ivy's mind that she understood every word. Whether Kyah was in the mood to put on a good show, was another thing altogether. The bonobo pushed Ivy's face away with her long fingers, then dropped her own head back laughing.

"Oh, don't tease me," Ivy grinned. "You like him as much as I do."

Ivy smoothed her unruly hair behind her ear then sighed as it sprang loose. "Alright. We'll have to charm him with our wit then, I suppose," she grinned. "Ready?"

Kyah gave a soft grunt and adjusted herself on Ivy's hip.

Ivy turned the silver door handle.

Stepped into the laboratory.

And disappeared.

Streaks of lightning clawed at her. Ivy's skin burned. She jerked her head around, searching frantically for the room she had expected.

White walls had become swirling grey.

No walls, no ceiling. *Nothing.*

A blue sphere pierced with vertical white stripes trapped her eyes like a blinding sun somewhere in front of her. The shape shattered into a haze of colours and something screamed, deep and broken, as if the light itself was in agony. It dissolved into the swirling dark.

"Please help us," implored a man's voice. It sounded warped and distorted from far away, but right behind her.

Ivy spun, terrified, but found nothing but the same swirling haze.

Suddenly, a suffocation of harmonic noise filled her head. *Singing?*

"*Help!*" She thought she screamed, but no sound came out.

Instead, hysterical screeching pierced her eardrums.

Kyah!

The bonobo's lips were pulled back in terror and her eyes were wild. She clung to Ivy's neck. Beyond Kyah's face, was nothing.

Kyah's scream was the only solidity left. Ivy's knees buckled. She gripped her friend's back, struggling to envelop her.

Something was tugging at Kyah. Ivy gripped harder. Her heart was pounding as if it might burst. Ivy's feet were slipping. *On what? Where was the floor?* Her skin was agony now, as if on fire.

Ahead of her, a pinprick of darkest black expanded in the grey. It swirled as it grew toward her.

No. This isn't real.

The harmonic singing intensified. The sound distorted, deafening. The vortex was bigger now. It reached her, touching Kyah's back. *Please, god no!* She was being dragged from Ivy's arms. Kyah screamed again and clawed at Ivy's cardigan with her fingers, drawing lines of blood under the wool as she was torn from Ivy's grip. Ivy wrenched her back in, screaming into the hurricane pitch. Fighting for her friend. The swirling black vortex won.

Kyah was gone.

"*No!*" Ivy's scream was lost. Her hands flung forward, disappearing into the black, desperate to follow Kyah. She felt nothing ahead of her, not even her own fingertips. The vortex swelled again toward her, desperate to swallow her inside. She spun. There was no way out. Nothing behind her. The inevitability swirled ahead in slow motion. Time seemed to freeze.

Ivy's veins shot with adrenaline. Her muscles burned within her skin. Like lightning, clarity broke the chaos of her mind.

Then I'll do it myself.

She made a choice. So simple and pure, it broke her fear in one swift blow.

Ivy leapt forward.

The black void engulfed her.

Existence was shred from her bones.

CHAPTER 2

IVY

*O*ne week earlier: *Archaeology Department, Melbourne University.*

Ivy's brow furrowed in concentration as she peered into the microscope eyepiece. A twist of long, bright red hair fell across her face; she scooped it up absentmindedly and tucked it behind her ear. A moment later, it escaped again, forcing her to break meditation of the small arrowhead illuminated on the stage.

She blinked in the dim light. Ivy's green eyes were shadowed with dark circles. Textbooks and research papers lay scattered on the desk around her, scribbles and notes adorning many of the open pages. Her previous night's research had reached into the early hours of the morning and a second coffee had not yet entirely woken her.

The small office in which Ivy sat could easily be mistaken for the storeroom of an old museum. Artefacts from long-forgotten cultures ornamented the shelves, once integral pieces of human lives, now collecting dust. Shards of pottery lay in piles, each imprinted with the signature style of its maker, like ancient jigsaws waiting patiently to be reassembled. A chipped coffee mug brimming with colourful African beads acted as a paper-weight for a large pile of photocopied journal articles on the floor. Good intentions to organise the ever-expanding piles of notes were always lost to feverish attempts to keep up with new research.

Ivy's laptop buzzed quietly. Its corner rested on the cover of a leather-bound journal; fat and well-loved, stuffed with thumbed pages, loose additions and a soul's worth of thoughts and sketches. Two photographs had slipped out. The first was of a teenage boy with grey eyes and a carefree laugh, his arms wound around sixteen-year-old Ivy's waist as she twisted to meet his smile. The second was a fading portrait of a middle-aged woman with runaway red hair. Her mother's wide smile and shining eyes were mirrored in Ivy's at rare moments of relaxation; when Ivy's intense concentration dropped to reveal a wicked sense of humour. Such occasions seemed rare these days and the woman in the photograph, gone nearly eight years, would have been worried at the growing isolation of her daughter. As it was, Ivy's dedication to her work went largely unnoticed, which suited her perfectly.

Ivy peered once again into the eyepiece, her fingers shifting the fine focus ever so slightly. An arrowhead on the microscope stage zoomed into clarity. To the naked eye it was simple and smooth. An axiom of days long gone. However, as Ivy stared intently, the pencil in her right hand was busy creating the story of the arrowhead's last use. Spectacular blood striations swept across the blade from some deadly impact long ago. Above that, a layer of dirt it had accumulated since it had been discarded. Later, Ivy would analyse the dried blood to identify who - or what - had died, but for now, she was engrossed in preserving the markings on paper.

Carefully finishing the last detail on her sketch, Ivy pushed her pencil back into the crowded jar.

She stretched her legs out and grimaced at the pins and needles she felt, then stepped gingerly to her small office window and yanked it open. A chilly autumn breeze finished the caffeine's job.

For a few minutes she gazed down at the sprawling grass courtyard below the Social Sciences Building where students were eating and sleeping between lectures.

A loud laugh drew her attention to a familiar face below. Jayne Williams had spent long hours over the last month assisting Ivy in the Molecular Archaeology lab. As the department's newest postgraduate, she'd been bounced by overworked staff and had finally landed under Ivy's wing.

Ivy's feverish late night attempts to make progress on her PhD research were now frequently accompanied by Jayne's spirited assistance. In return, Ivy offered copious amounts of chocolate.

Ivy watched Jayne chatting below. The woman's olive complexion seemed to soak up the sun's watery rays. Ivy drew her hand up her own forearm self-consciously. Too many hours under the fluorescent laboratory lights had taken their toll and Ivy wondered if her scattering of freckles and quick make-up attempts were the only thing that kept her from disappearing altogether.

Jayne always manages to find the cute ones, Ivy thought.

She watched the scene below with grudging admiration, as Jayne gave animated directions to a disoriented and possibly smitten teenage boy. Jayne tossed her honey-blonde hair with a laugh, fully aware of the effect. The boy left somewhat reluctantly, a smirk playing his lips until the corner of the sandstone wall stole his attention. He ducked away with a red face.

Ivy leaned out of the window as Jayne turned once again for the building entrance.

"He's a bit young for you isn't he?" Ivy teased down.

Startled, Jayne stopped and looked up. Her blue eyes were all innocence, but an impish grin tarnished the facade.

"No such thing, Ms-twenty-four-going-on-fifty!" Jayne yelled back. "It's about time you got your eyes off the microscope and onto some of the scenery!"

Ivy laughed. By now several people were looking up at her with curiosity. Their long-distance exchange was rather loud. With a pink face, Ivy dismissed Jayne with a wave and made to bend inside the window frame again.

"Hey, wait!" Jayne called. "I've just been up to Lab Six. *You're wanted.* Apparently I'm second rate…"

The words hit the empty window as Ivy grabbed the brown woollen jacket slung over her chair, and swept from the room.

CHAPTER 3

IVY

"Match-stick!"

Ivy was grinning before she even turned around. As predicted, the unruly mop of blonde curls calling out to her was waving a beer glass in one hand, while the other clutched a handful of poker cards. A dozen undergraduates were crowded around him in the refectory beer-garden. Some held playing cards but all carried boisterous enthusiasm and glassy-eyed veneration for the man in the middle.

"Come hither and join the revelry - a celebration is afoot! Tonight we raise ale in thy honour, M'Lady." The man stood up and bowed theatrically, knocking the wine-barrel table with his knees and sending the cohort of poker players around him into a tirade of good-natured abuse. "Grace us with thy flame-haired beauty that doth eclipse the setting sun and shame it to hiding, this eventide," he called with a flourish. "What say you?"

"Methinks not," Ivy laughed. "Thou art a cheat and foolish drunkard, My Goodman. In times past I've had but naught a coin after your trickery at the table. Besides," she winked, *"I've got a date."*

Liam Kent's face fell in mock offence. "Me? Cheat? By my

troth, I would never! Thou woundest mine honour, fair maiden!" He dropped back onto his bar stool with a thunk. Liam tossed his curls insolently. "A curse upon you then, Match-stick. I hope thy date is hairier than I am." His companions laughed. Behind Liam, a couple of first-year girls scowled toward Ivy.

Ivy smiled and turned to continue on her way.

"Ives?"

She turned back to face him. The others resumed their rowdy poker game but Liam's eyes were momentarily clear.

"She needs her meds." Liam's carefree, roguish exterior had been dropped entirely. Ivy nodded, exchanging a look that spoke more than words could. Moments later, he re-joined the poker match with a cheer of "Wench, beakers all round!"

Ivy kept walking.

She had always appreciated that Liam was, well, incorrigibly *Liam*. They'd begun university at the same time, seven years prior. From the first day, he was renowned in their undergraduate zoology lectures for amusing students and testing lecturers' patience. Igniting and fuelling animated debate about ethics in science research, his conviction in first year had led to a mass student boycott of laboratory dissection, forcing administration to decree optional participation. There was no doubt of his talent though, and his progression to research saw him employed as lab manager in the Animal Behaviour department.

Ivy ran her fingers along the sandstone and looked out across the grass. Modern glass and steel constructions towered beyond the traditional sandstone. In recent years, university progress had been marked by new headquarters for engineering, biomedical science and contemporary arts departments, among others. The juxtaposition of old against new was welcomed by most. Private bequests gave an elite group the opportunity to have their names forever adorned on new buildings in the prestigious university. It was a small price to pay for the eager chancellors to extend their academic prestige. The monumental institution now sprawled across the better part of an entire suburb. At its fringes, developers exploited ageing residential properties for mass student accommodation. An entire life could be lived sheltered within this cocoon.

This inner court of sandstone and greenery was the heart though, and was more a home to Ivy than anywhere else in the world. After eight years navigating its corridors daily, she felt as much a part of the walls as the gargoyles adorning them. In the vein of true medieval architecture, the grotesque ornamental heads had been fixed to convey water away from the masonry and prevent erosion of the sandstone walls. During tropical summers, Ivy loved to hear the rain gargling as it streamed through their stone throats. She was actually quite fond of them, to the point of giving them names.

"Hi, Mendel… Darwin… Leakey…" she nodded to their blank stone eyes as she passed by.

Ivy turned her back to the sunshine and passed through the open doors of the Biological Sciences building. An expansive reception area and gleaming desk was flanked by wide staircases. She took the stairs two at a time. Slipping behind an unmarked door, she corridored through the building, passing countless laboratories of students peering carefully over Petri dishes and microscopes. The strong smell of formalin assaulted Ivy's nostrils. *Dissection.* Finally escaping into sunlight at the back of the building, a heavy metal door held guard to a second building. The words Behavioural Research Laboratory Six were marked in red. Ivy frowned, hating the implication of cold steel as she pulled a key from her jeans pocket.

Mice were the secondary occupants of this area; a row of monitoring cages stretched the length of the room. Scribbled whiteboards filled the walls above them. Once deep inside however, the room gave way to a partially open ceiling. The huge enclosure was filled with trees and shrubs, climbing ropes and trusses like a hidden Eden, separated from the surrounding gardens by a strong wire wall and ceiling. It was colourful and comfortable, like the messy tree house of a child.

The untidy occupant, Kyah, was a ten-year-old bonobo, quite small for her age, and currently stretched out across an overhead branch, one long black arm dangling apathetically, while the other picked at a spot on her chest. Her brows were furrowed.

"How's my girl?" sang Ivy as she unlocked the enclosure and let herself in. Kyah let out a hoot, swung down and reached out to Ivy, gently stroking her arm. "Being a bit tricky today, are you? Poor Jayne, you know she loves you… and it sounds like you've given Liam an earful too. I'm sorry I'm late. Forgive me?"

Kyah hooted softly and lifted Ivy's right hand, placing it gently against her own cheek. Her deep brown eyes locked onto Ivy's green ones, searching for a moment. Then, satisfied that she had her companion's full attention, Kyah turned and scooted back to her branch and picked up an orange that was lying on the floor under it. She sat down with her back against the wall, and proceeded to peel the orange and eat it.

With her long arms and gracile build, Kyah was smaller than a common chimpanzee. Her petite ears were set aside a curious, black face and high forehead with long, fine black hair neatly parted in the middle and gleaming with care.

Ivy looked around the enclosure. As expansive as it was, she still felt restricted by its wire walls. Ivy couldn't help but remember the day, two years before, when Kyah had first arrived.

"You there, Liam? I got you soy chai-" Ivy had called down the corridor as she walked. The laboratory was unfinished, with empty shelves and new furniture piled with boxes.

For the past few months, Liam had overseen the construction in anticipation of his newest arrivals. Three chimpanzees had been transferred from a rehabilitation centre the prior week, and another was due to arrive.

A crash echoed up the corridor. There was a cacophony of ear-splitting screeches and the sound of something thudding against metal, over and again.

"Jesus Christ! Get back! Give her some space!"

Ivy rushed toward the noise. A handful of overalled men surrounded a transport carrier against the far wall of the enclosure. One had a tranquiliser gun cocked toward the carrier. Liam lunged toward him.

"Just get the hell away! You've done enough damage dropping the damn cage!" Ivy had never seen him so furious.

Inside the carrier, a black chimpanzee was screeching hysterically and banging its head against the steel bars. The door hung open. Its chest was scratched and bleeding. On the playground of ropes and branches above, three more were jumping and screeching in agitation at the goings-on. It was chaos.

"'Scuse me, Maam." A man pushed into the room from behind Ivy and quickly surveyed the situation. He strode toward the one with the tranquiliser gun and passively directed the barrel down to the floor. "I'll meet you fellas outside."

"What about the cage?"

"Leave it." As the others made their way out, the newcomer turned to Liam who was trying desperately to calm his newest charge and held out his hand.

"Paul Nerov, Resource Management," he said. "You Liam Kent?"

Liam eyed the hand before shaking it.

"*Resource management*," Liam repeated. "You deliver post-it-notes too?"

"Hmph," smiled the man, "That's a good one." He pulled out a clipboard of papers. "Just out of quarantine, in good health." He shot a dubious look to the animal in the cage. "Well, physically, at least. You signing for her?"

"Yes," Liam growled, "and dealing with the fallout of those idiots dropping her crate." The chimpanzee inside it was still hysterical.

"Sorry mate, new recruits." Nerov scanned the enclosure while Liam signed the documents. "I heard you were the man that brought Cosmitech down. That's no mean feat. The board of directors in that place were well connected. I worked for them years ago. Bunch of bastards if ever there were." Nerov looked down at the screaming chimp with a furrowed brow. "I'm surprised this one's still alive after what they did to her."

"She's the only one left," Liam scowled. "The others had to be euthanazed - chimps, dogs, cats, rabbits - they went through hell, each and every one. The AEC guidelines for the management of pain and distress were routinely ignored."

"Mmmm." Nerov clucked sympathetically. "Like I said - bunch of bastards." He was quiet for a moment. "I remember this one you know. From when I worked for Cosmitech. I brought her in."

"You what?!"

"A job's a job, Kent. Had to feed my family. " Nerov ignored Liam's scathing look. "I remember her because she was so quiet. Barely a year old, shipped over from some research facility in the US. Probably black market before that. Tiny little thing- I had her in a dog carrier and not a peep from her the whole drive. Just those big eyes looking right at me." Nerov scratched the back of his neck. "Couldn't sleep for a month after I left her there."

"Good," Liam said. His jaw was clenched.

"What did they do to her?" Ivy asked, stepping forward. Liam looked surprised, having not noticed her in the doorway. He shot Nerov a dirty look.

"Let's see shall we?" Liam pulled the clipboard from Nerov's hand and flipped through the pages. "For her first year, she was a candidate for RSV research." He looked at Ivy. "Regular general anaesthesia to collect swabs and tracheal irrigation samples to monitor her resistance to the virus." He looked grimly at Ivy, who had her hand over her mouth. "Three cardiac arrests in twelve months."

"But she was still a baby-" Ivy said.

Liam nodded. "Since then it's been hepatitis and malaria research as well."

"What did-" Ivy began.

"Isolation in a sterile bio-containment facility," Liam said through gritted teeth. "Serial blood draws, inoculations - biopsies as often as they wanted to. Surrounded by technicians in a lab, firing tranquilizers through a dart gun to immobilize her any time they wanted," he said grimly, "more often than not hitting vulnerable body parts as she struggled to escape it. Eight years of terror in complete isolation. No wonder they couldn't rehabilitate her." Liam finished his rant with disgust and handed the clipboard back to Nerov. "The very sight of a human is terrifying to her."

"Never wanted to do it Kent," Nerov muttered.

"I bet *she* didn't want you to either." Liam crouched down, intent on calming the caged animal. "What's her name?"

"Whatever you want it to be. The form says she's called K32."

"K32?" Liam shook his head. "Not here, she's not." He looked up at Ivy. "You name her, Match-stick. Pick something nice."

Ivy was taken aback. "You want me to name a chimpanzee?"

"Of course not. I want you to name a bonobo."

Nerov left. Compelled to stay, Ivy watched as Liam quieted the three chimpanzees above with some food. He created a temporary divide to keep the others from the bonobo's cage and spent hours trying to entice her from the tiny prison. Every time he got close, K32 would scream and bash the open cage door against the wire enclosure wall. She hit her head against the bars and scratched at her chest until it bled freely. As each hour passed, Liam grew more desperate. He stood outside the enclosure, well past dinner time, raking his fingers down his face.

"I just don't know what to do. She's terrified of me, the chimps, everyone. I thought she'd be alright here, but she needs so much more."

"Isn't there a rehab facility she can go to?" Ivy asked. "Somewhere better equipped?"

Liam's expression was grim. "There's no room anywhere else and no funding even if there was. It was me or the needle."

"Go home Liam. You need rest."

"I can't leave her. Look at the state she's in."

"Well, I'll stay then. All night if I have to."

Eventually, Liam left.

There was something so disturbing, so *human* about K32's anxiety. Academia had taught Ivy to look at the animal scientifically, detached, and never to project her own human thoughts and emotions into its behaviour. Never anthropomorphise. But as Ivy stood there, watching it rock and stare in its prison of fear, broken beyond repair, her instincts screamed *human*. This creature knew only fear and pain, and silently, Ivy understood that fear. Humanity sometimes seemed too painful to be a part of. There was loneliness in it. And loss. Ivy shivered, suddenly cold.

Very slowly she stole over to the far corner of the room and sat on the concrete floor next to the enclosure wall. Cold steel bars were between them. K32 shrieked, backing into the crate.

All night Ivy sat on the frigid concrete, occasionally making soothing sounds, but mostly just sitting quietly, sharing in her isolation. When Liam returned the following morning, the bonobo was still withdrawn, but at least no longer hurting herself. Over the following week, Ivy only left to teach and sleep, returning early each morning to tempt her with fruit and water, mostly unsuccessfully. Liam busied himself with the unpacking and care of the others, grateful that Ivy was willing to stay.

Gradually, the bonobo became accustomed to her presence. As Ivy daydreamed against the steel bars on the fifth afternoon, she realised that K32 had left her open crate. By dusk, the bonobo had moved closer still. It was so gradual, Ivy barely noticed. Finally, there was nothing between them but unforgiving metal bars. Ivy reached her hand up to grip the steel. Painfully slowly, with her eyes to the ground, K32 copied her. As the bonobo's long fingers curled over Ivy's, the metal underneath seemed to melt away.

From a memory long buried, Ivy finally found it. The perfect name.

"Kyah," Ivy whispered. "You aren't a number anymore. You're Kyah." Ivy repeated it softly, over and again. Eventually, Kyah looked up. An immense sadness within her deep brown eyes made Ivy's heart ache. Kyah pushed her fingers through the bars towards Ivy's face. Ivy covered them with her own.

For the first time in what seemed like forever, she wasn't alone.

From that moment on, they had been inseparable. For two years now, Ivy had become surrogate mother to the bonobo who had been orphaned so many years before. Her socialisation and behaviour had improved dramatically. Now ten years old, Kyah was Ivy's clandestined companion around campus, occasionally seen loping by her side through the grounds at dusk and spending countless hours playing together in the enclosure. Others found refuge here as well, as an intermediate hospice between rescue and retirement. Long-term placement in rehabilitation facilities and zoos were scarce, so a small number of chimps stayed as permanent residents, observed for behavioural studies. Working closely with dedicated keepers, they learnt symbols and words with varying levels of success. Kyah quietly observed their lessons, sitting apart while the humans invaded her living space. Although she was never taught the lexicons directly, Kyah knew many of them and frequently drew them on the concrete floor in chalk to emphasize what she wanted from Ivy. *Sandwich, tickle, yellow rope, quiet...*

With years of abuse still etched in her memory, her shy and

anxious manner would trust no one but Ivy. Her head twitched sharply to the left, a nervous habit she had developed in her solitary infancy. This was accompanied by a tendency to pick at her chest, leaving tiny scratches scarring her heart.

"You'll need antiseptic on that," Ivy said breaking out of her reverie, as she watched Kyah picking once again at her now inflamed skin. Ivy retreated to the locked first aid cabinet where she found not only Kyah's medication, but also a small parcel wrapped in brown paper. The word *'matchstick'* was scrawled on the top. Peeling it open, Ivy caught her breath. It was a book. Ancient, fragile and well read, but solidly bound. *'On the Origin of Species'* was printed in faded gold lettering down the spine, *'1883 edition'*. A lump caught in her throat as she touched it reverently. *You're too much sometimes, Liam,* Ivy thought. She tucked it carefully inside her jacket and walked back into Kyah's cage.

Leaping above her in the maze of ropes and ladders, the three other residents hooted playfully to each other. Kneeling on the floor, Ivy smeared antiseptic across Kyah's scratched chest. The animal stiffened with the sting but she didn't strike out. Of all the staff that cared for her, only Ivy was trusted to administer her medication.

Kyah curled affectionately into Ivy's lap. After a moment she changed her mind. She picked up a yellow stick of chalk lying nearby. In wide strokes on the concrete floor, Kyah presented Ivy with her request. *See birds now. Tree.*

"I'll get you out of here this afternoon Ky," soothed Ivy taking her hand, "I promise I'll be back as soon as it's safer for you."

Ivy got to her feet and Kyah followed her to the wire door with her head down and eyes shining. The bonobo trailed long, sensitive fingertips over the steel bars as Ivy locked her within them. An aching heart dogged Ivy's steps as it always did walking away, with little consolation gained by knowing that her promise was sincere.

CHAPTER 4

NEIL

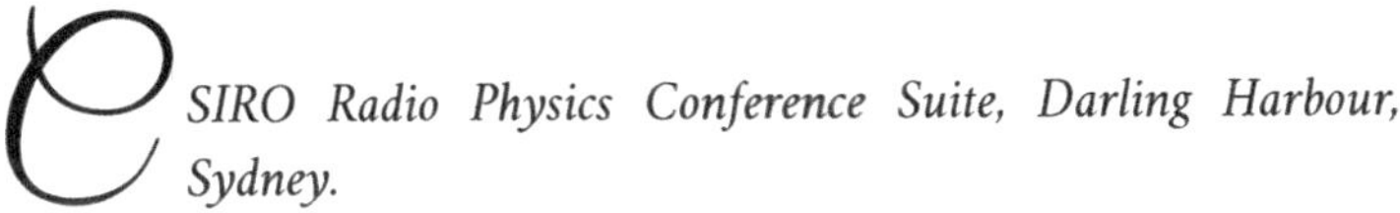

CSIRO Radio Physics Conference Suite, Darling Harbour, Sydney.

A thousand kilometres away, overlooking Sydney harbour, Dr Neil Crawford scowled into his scotch. Slamming it on the table he turned from the sheets of glass that walled the sleek hotel room from the traffic-jammed streets below. The blue banded sphere emblazoned on his coffee mug was splashed with amber liquid. He flicked his hand in irritation. The map of Australia in the centre of the logo seemed to mock him. He butted his cigarette into a marble dish of complimentary mints.

"This is bullshit," he growled. "We've been hanging by our toenails trying to analyse these readings – I need some answers!"

No response. Neil pulled at the knot in his tie and took a deep breath. In his younger days, being stuffed into a laboratory at the beck and call of his superiors had rankled his ego, but now he wondered if he'd actually had the upper hand after all. It was at times like this, that being on the ground floor was the only cure to insufferable incompetence.

"What- is- this- thing- and- why- the- hell- can't- you-track- it?"

The conference phone crackled with the awkward shuffle of bodies in chairs. He pictured their eyes darting as they silently jousted from the responsibility of bearing bad news. Finally, a woman's low, calm voice sounded through the speaker.

"Director, it's only a matter of time, the readings were getting stronger day by day. Forty-eight hours of corrupted data is just a hiccup – and Dimitri's working on a recovery. We'll have it-soon."

"Soon? Not good enough and you both know it." The danger inherent in Neil's reply was effective.

Her smooth voice faltered. The excuses kicked in. "Look Neil, our equipment isn't sensitive enough. If we could just get more data- a stronger source point – then we could isolate this ... anomaly. We *need more* data."

"We *need* to be discreet!" Neil spat back. "Whatever the hell we're picking up here needs to stay in that room. I can't afford to draw attention to this by opening communication with NASA yet – we'll lose the ball and any rights along with it. I've already got the board breathing down my neck, so we've got to get this *right* before we hand it over. Do *you* want to explain to the NASA Board of Directors that we fucked up *again*?"

He pictured Cassandra Chevalier pouting on the other end of the line, Dimitri Angelis hiding behind her skirt. Both were digital systems engineers under his umbrella in the CSIRO Division for Astronomy and Space. In his opinion, both were quickly becoming dispensable.

At least Cassandra has other assets. Neil smirked lewdly to the benefit of no one. Since she'd arrived at the sprawling ITC Centre, Cassandra had elevated rapidly to senior research level at the Radio Physics Headquarters. Twenty kilometres north-west of Sydney, the Marsfield Laboratories were home to one hundred and eighty researchers managing data from the CSIRO Australia

Telescope National Facility, ICT Centre and Anglo-Australian Observatory. Cassandra was confident, intelligent and shrewd. She knew how to play the game.

He exhaled into his fist. Neil had seen twenty years in office, a game of arse-kissing he played with the same affected interest he had paid his ex-wife. This discovery was *intrinsic* to his plans. He knew he was already on thin ice. *Johnston did it, they set me up, the bastards. And now the inquiry with NASA... Jesus Christ, I need this one.*

This energy mutation – potentially capable of powering an entire city, was the perfect fix. He wasn't going to let this minx and her pet nerd screw it up for him.

"Okay kids – we need a new plan," Neil said. "This data stays with *us*. Dimitri – keep working on that recovery, as soon as we're back online *I want to know about it*. If we're right in our predictions, we've got less than a week before we get a major energy kick up the arse. *Less than one week, got that?* I want to be onto it – *first* with the press, publicity, interviews – this is *our* game. Both of you – get your shit together and get on the next flight out. Meet me at The Dish."

CHAPTER 5

IVY

Stretched under a tree in the vast quadrangle, the late afternoon sun filtered through low-hanging leaves. The grounds were nearly deserted. This was Ivy's favourite time of day, when she was allowed to give Kyah a taste of the freedom she yearned for. Now, the bonobo explored the branches above, dangling one-armed and hooting softly. The few straggling staff and students still leaving were familiar with seeing Kyah around the campus, and either ignored her or smiled as they passed. Confident that the bonobo was occupied tormenting a line of ants that trailed the jacaranda tree above her, Ivy stretched out and closed her eyes, silently revelling in the soft breeze. She tucked her earphones in and scrolled through her favourite playlist on her phone, settling back on the grass. Ivy's thoughts drifted lazily from Kyah to her research, then to familiar and new faces around campus. A fleeting figure with dark wavy hair and a boyish grin swept through her mind. Her thoughts strayed, completely unaware that she was being watched by two separate individuals.

"Ivy!" Jayne came hurrying across the grass, blonde hair whipping her face. *"Ivy!"*

Ivy sat forward as Jayne approached, pulling out her earphones.

"What's up?"

"The first artefacts have arrived! They're amazing, covered in red blood cells and cellulose, starch, fibres…. seriously hon, we're going to be looking at these for *months*. I don't even know where to start! They've sent charcoal and calcite as well; Eli's running it through the system. We should have a radiocarbon date confirmed within a few days…."

Ivy could feel Jayne's excitement in her own veins.

Morwood's team had been pushing for excavation approval in Indonesia for years, fuelled by the growing realisation that Aboriginal culture in north-west Australia bore resemblance in sophistication and style to those in Borneo. This discovery pinpointed Indonesia as a prime suspect for funnelling the first migrations of humans to colonise Australia from Asia.

It made sense. Migrating from mainland Asia to the joined continent of New Guinea and Australia would have been akin to an epic prehistoric game of stepping stones. There were a handful of potential pathways through the 13,000 islands of the Indonesian Archipelago to navigate. Each progressive island situated close enough that it could have been seen from the one before. However, it wasn't an easy trip.

Dangerous currents still isolated the string of volcanic islands from greater Asia by a menacing division known as the Wallace Line. In their tropical seclusion untouched by humans, the islands had flourished, tempered by seasonal monsoonal rains and harsh, dry winds that left the earth thirsty. Birds and animals grew bizarre in their isolation and each island became a game board of nature's experiments.

Then fifty thousand years ago with a burst into sea-faring technology, modern humans finally broke through the perilous water break. They had populated the volcanic necklace of Nusa Tengarra and forged new homes throughout South-East Asia, island-hopping all the way south to Australia, leaving tantalising archaeological evidence of their trip. Morwood's team needed proof – and a place in Indonesia to begin the task of sifting through time, unearthing the origins of the first Australians.

Propelled by the potential of a known Stone Age site at Mata Menge in Flores, a small team had broken off to perform an exploratory dig in the cave of Liang Bua, near Ruteng. After months of careful excavation, they'd been greeted with fragments of animal bone and charcoal in caves; tempting evidence of fire-making hunters long gone. The questions they raised far outweighed their scant evidence.

Still the digging went on, wearing resources, optimism and funding thin. But hidden in that deep, dark cave, a secret lay six meters underground. A secret so shocking, that it turned the scientific community on its head.

Sophisticated stone tools had finally been recovered, over 450 of them - in itself, a remarkable find. But the hominid bones they were associated with were extraordinary. First a tiny skull and then the petite skeleton of its owner had been uncovered. At only three feet tall, LB1, as she came to be known, was proving to be an evolutionary enigma. With a brain cavity three times smaller than a modern human, LB1 should not have been capable of producing the tools she was found with, those same tools that were now sitting on Ivy's desk. LB1 appeared two million years later than expected in the fossil record. She looked more ape than human. She created fire, tools, and survived to a time when modern humans had already begun invading the Nusa Tengarra islands. And she had friends.

More partial skeletons were found, twelve individuals in total. How they had arrived across the impenetrable sea hundreds of thousands of years before modern humans was anyone's guess. The implications for early human evolution and migration patterns into South-East Asia were potentially enormous. All that had been considered fact was suddenly thrown in a heap and archaeologists were scrambling to pick up the pieces and re-align them in a race that Ivy desperately wanted to be part of.

Ivy's specialty, molecular archaeology, was a new and contro-versial discipline. Still, she had lobbied the controlling institute for a chance to analyse the stone tools. Organic residues on the tool surfaces could indicate evidence on the diet and lifestyle of this strange addition to the human family. So tuned were the methods she used, Ivy could now determine between bird species based on a single shaft of feather. She used DNA sequencing to determine the species of plant or animal that had been cut, pounded and butchered by the tool.

To her astonishment, permission had been granted for preliminary analysis of a sample of tools. She and Jayne had been anxiously waiting the impending arrival for weeks.

"How many have we got?"

"One box so far, twelve artefacts inside," Jayne replied. Her eyes were shining. "More in a few days, we've got some seriously late nights ahead of us..." Her enthusiasm was contagious. "I've had a quick look already; we've got bi-facial flakes, points, perfo-rators, hammer-stones and scrapers. Volcanic material by the looks of it. Just brilliant. I've left them on your desk with a little surprise -"

"Jayne! I told you not to-"

"Couldn't have asked for a better day for it!" Something caught her attention. "Ooh, *someone's got a visitor...*" She winked. "Catch you later." Jayne gave a quick wave to the person approaching as she left. Ivy lay back on her elbows, anticipating Liam's arrival.

"How's it going?" The voice was deeper than she expected and carried an Irish accent. *Not Liam.* Ivy glanced up and into the sun, losing her balance and falling backward. She felt her face burn with embarrassment.

"Orrin, hi," she said, sitting up awkwardly. Ivy hoped her face wasn't as flushed as it felt, but she couldn't hide her grin. "I wasn't expecting… I mean, it's great to see you again. How are you settling in?"

Orrin James flashed Ivy a wide smile. "Grand. The usual delays with I.T. access of course, but the lads are onto it."

He gestured to the grass.

"Mind if I join you?"

"Of course not," smiled Ivy. "We were just getting a bit of fresh air." She nodded toward Kyah, who was now sitting a few feet away. The bonobo's nimble fingers were twirling as she dug for ants in a small mound at the tree base. Her brow was furrowed in concentration.

Orrin's hair caught the sunlight as he lowered himself onto the grass. Black framed reading glasses complimented his strong jaw line and flecked brown eyes. He looked over curiously at Kyah.

"You keep unique company."

"This is Kyah," Ivy laughed. "She lives in the Behavioural Research Lab. Liam Kent runs it, I think you met him at the interfaculty mixer the other night – tall guy, crazy mop hair… a few too many beers…"

"Oh, yeah I recall, nice guy." Orrin glanced sideways at her. "Actually I think I've seen him down at the union baths."

"Baths?"

"Swimming pool," Orrin corrected himself. "Sorry, I forget your Aussie lingo." His eyes shone with confidence and good humour that seemed effortless.

Against her better judgement, Ivy had let Jayne drag her to the last two interfaculty social events. Her blonde assistant had argued for it relentlessly.

You're meant to be showing me the ropes here, woman! Besides we need to be more visible so we can fight for funding. I heard they're funnelling some of our resources into Sociology…'

'No way!'

Although Ivy thought the sly grin on Jayne's face was a little suspect at the time, she couldn't argue with her logic. So Ivy spent the evenings forcing herself to mingle amidst the canapés whilst feigning disinterest in gossip about the new member of staff who was now watching Kyah intently. And there was plenty of gossip to be had.

Appointed a month ago, Orrin at only 27, had become the youngest of the lecturing staff at Melbourne University and was fast gaining popularity with the students for his infectious enthusiasm to 'think outside the quasar'. He was Irish, clearly, but when and why he'd transferred to Melbourne, Australia seemed generally unknown. More curious though, Ivy had decided, was the blaze he'd ignited in the Physics department. The younger staff and research students seemed to orbit him like electrons, impressed by his growing renown in scientific circles while he encouraged their efforts to push boundaries on scientific theory. Older staff members skirted the edges of the fray, disgruntled and eyeing him with envy and distrust.

Now, Orrin nodded towards Kyah, his hand shading his eyes from the sun. "Is she the only chimp here?" he asked. "I mean, are there others in the lab? Are they part of some sort of biological research?"

Ivy's pleasant thoughts quickly left her. She scowled. *Here we go.*

When she didn't speak, Orrin continued, "It's just that I've been looking to extend my own research parameters and would love to incorporate -"

Ivy sank with disappointment. She cut him off, her voice uncharacteristically harsh as she sat forward. "Firstly, Kyah's a bonobo, not a chimp. More importantly – she's *retired*, they all are. She's already had a lifetime of invasive research done on her. She's only here because she hasn't got the social capacity to survive in a wild population. Her rehabilitation has already taken years." She glared at him. "Kyah's not going to be anyone's new lab rat." Perhaps it was time to go.

Silence fell on them for a long moment. When she looked back, Orrin was watching her with an unreadable expression, his confidence momentarily shaken.

"I'm dead sorry Ivy, really, I didn't realize," he said. "Of course I wouldn't want to hurt her, really I'm sorry…"

"Well if you're sorry then you're a minority. The biochem and pharma labs have been trying to get their hands our bonobos for over a year. Liam and I go through hell keeping all the vultures at bay." She looked to Kyah as she spoke, the words rushing out angrily. "Most of our bonobos have been traumatised in the name of research since they were infants. They're traumatised by the time we get them. They need rehabilitation, not more fear." With her mouth set, Ivy pushed up from the grass, making to leave. "Most especially Kyah."

Orrin caught her wrist. "Hold it, please, I didn't mean to… I had no idea. Please stay."

Ivy's defensiveness ebbed away as she saw the sincerity in Orrin's eyes. She took a deep breath and sat down again.

"Sorry. I guess I'm a little over-protective."

"It sounds like you have cause to be."

"I really do." Ivy offered a smile, which still didn't quite reach her eyes. "So, what is it that you're working on, anyway?"

Orrin brushed grass off his hands. He looked at her for a long moment, deliberating. Then, he seemed to decide something. He returned her smile.

"I would like to tell you about it actually," he said. "But my newest research is still unpublished, so I'd prefer to keep the details between us, if you don't mind. What I've discovered is not a big problem *yet*, but there is definite potential for concern in the future. I don't want to be considered an alarmist -"

Ivy sat forward, intrigued.

"My lips are sealed."

"Alright. Well, it actually started as a side project with a couple of my research students," Orrin leaned forward with child-like enthusiasm. "It's a bit complicated."

Ivy held her hands up. "Fair warning then - this isn't my area of expertise. How about the 'astrophysics for dummies' version?"

"Sure," Orrin grinned. "Are you familiar with the magnetosphere surrounding the earth?"

Ivy shook her head.

Orrin looked thoughtful. Reaching out, he combed his fingers across the grass, raking in two small rocks and some pine needles. He placed the smallest of the rocks on the grass in front of Ivy.

"This is the earth," Orrin began.

"Why do I feel like I'm in kindergarten again?" Ivy laughed.

"Humour me," he winked. "So *this* is our earth." He pointed to the rock in the grass. "The outer core of the earth is made up of liquid iron, which rotates along with the rotation of the earth. This rotation of metal in turn creates a convection current, an electrical current per se, which is what gives the earth its magnetic field. So just like a bar magnet, the earth has a north pole and a south pole which incline about 10 degrees to the rotation axis of the earth. Between and around them, there's an area of magnetic field surrounding the earth. Are you following me?"

Ivy nodded.

Orrin carefully shaped the long pine needle into an elongated tear shape, twisting the ends together to keep them in place. He placed it around his rock earth. "Right, well, the outer limits of this giant magnetic field surrounding the earth, is sort of shaped like a bullet. We call the magnetosphere." He gestured to the pine needle surrounding the rock. "It acts as a shield for the earth, protecting the ozone layer- protecting life on earth- from *this*."

Orrin held up the second, larger rock. He dropped it near his model earth, outside the rounded end of the pine needle shape. "This second rock represents our sun."

"Got it."

"Now as you probably know, the sun emits a continuous stream of charged particles into space in all directions. We call this phenomenon the 'solar wind'. These particles are mostly protons and electrons and are so highly charged, that they break away from the sun's gravity and shoot towards earth. This solar wind is capable of making the earth entirely uninhabitable. The Ultraviolet radiation from the sun could heat up the earth and strip away our atmosphere. Without the magnetosphere protecting us, there'd be no life on our planet – it would be way too hot."

Orrin paused to catch his breath and his eyes sparkled. *It's no wonder his students are so drawn to him,* Ivy mused. *Even a topic as dry as solar radiation was suddenly intoxicating.*

"Okay," Ivy interjected, anticipating that he was heading somewhere she might not follow. "So in a nutshell, our earth is surrounded by a giant magnetic shield, sort of shaped like a bullet, which protects us from the radiation of the sun. Is that right?"

"Bang on," Orrin said. "But this magnetosphere is a changeable, fluid shape. The earth's magnetic field, in conjunction with the shape and strength of the solar wind, can influence it. If the sun emits a massive solar flare, for instance, the size and shape of the magnetosphere gets temporarily distorted. We might get geomagnetic storms on earth. These storms create massive electrical ground currents, making a right mess of satellite equipment and global positioning systems, causing blackouts and surges in power grids; they can even stuff up the migration patterns of wild animals."

Ivy nodded again as Orrin barely paused to breathe.

"Normally there's no problem at all though. After all, our magnetosphere is pretty stable and deflects any radiation that we would consider to be harmful." He raised an eyebrow to her conspiratorially. "*But* this is where it gets tricky. It's been known for a while now, that the magnetosphere surrounding the earth is weakening in places. There are places even now, that satellites have to shut down as they move through, to avoid being affected by the intense solar radiation."

Orrin lowered his voice. "In the last one hundred and fifty years, the earth's magnetic field has decreased by ten percent," he said. "Now, it may simply be the case that earth is preparing for a reversal of its magnetic fields. Every million years or so that happens and there don't seem to be any serious repercussions to life on earth when it does."

His smile faded and Orrin looked pensive. "The thing is Ivy; I'm not convinced that's what's happening this time."

"What do you mean?" Ivy asked.

Orrin's tone had changed. Before where he had been relaxed, now he sat straight and tense, frown lines burrowing into his forehead. He looked *burdened.* He sat his fingers on the rock model he had made in the grass, deep in thought. Ivy felt a strange compulsion to place her own hand on his.

"You can trust me, you know," she said.

Orrin looked up, surprised.

"I know," Orrin said, frowning. "Thanks. I just- I think something a little more sinister is affecting the magnetosphere. I can't quite put my finger on it, but the patterns I'm detecting suggest it may have something to do with the elemental rock here on earth. I think, perhaps, that *we* are causing this phenomenon. And if we are, it's not going to fix itself."

"From what you've described to me, surely we'd have to do some serious damage to the earth's magnetic field to impact the magnetosphere working properly? How could we manage something like that?"

"Look, like I said, I don't want to be an alarmist. Even if I'm right, the repercussions for what I'm talking about might not show themselves for hundreds, hell, maybe even thousands of years. But still, it's worth worrying about. Because if we are doing something wrong, and we accelerate our efforts, we could pass some point of no return before we even realise what we've done."

"How can you know if you're right about this?" asked Ivy.

"That's what I'm trying to figure out. I've just started a series of experiments to test my theory. I'm bombarding different rock elements with high voltage electricity and electromagnetic fields to create changes of state within their atomic structures. Basically what I'm getting are measurable shifts in magnetic pulse when they're ionized. I've got a couple of PhD students analysing the data with me. The patterns are concerning to say the least. Certain fluctuations in their weakening magnetic fields are almost identical to those reported from the National Space Weather Program in the magnetosphere. I can't prove anything yet. They're just… *tendencies*. I could be over-reacting." He offered a humble smile. Orrin was passionate about his work, no doubt about it, but Ivy didn't think he seemed the type prone to over-dramatisation.

Ivy considered his timescale. Prehistory had taught her to consider life on a much larger scale than normal. In her eyes, even a few thousand years would pass in the blink of an eye. "So hypothetically, if we *are* creating this problem, in a few hundred years, or even a few thousand like you said- what could happen to us?"

"I don't want to dwell on that. Like I said, this is still just a theory."

Ivy rolled her eyes. "Of course, but *hypothetically*."

He frowned. "Okay, do you remember what I told you about the earth's magnetosphere?" Orrin gestured to the pine needle on the grass, still twisted into a teardrop protecting its pebble earth. "If it's weakened too much, high energy radiation from the sun breaks through to earth." He removed the pine needle, leaving the pebble alone. "The earth heats up. Our atmosphere breaks down." He held her gaze intently. "So that's it. Life is no longer sustainable on our planet."

"Jesus." Ivy sucked in a breath.

"Yeah."

She shook her head in disbelief. "That's not a good prognosis. I sure as hell hope you're wrong about this."

"Believe me, so do I."

A few minutes passed in silence as they both considered their conversation. Ivy felt unnervingly lonely. She watched Kyah picking at an orange on the grass. *At least I have Ky,* she thought. She looked up to find Orrin watching her intently. Embarrassed, Ivy restarted the conversation.

"So what was it that you wanted Kyah for anyway? In your lab I mean. Although the answer is still no, obviously." This time Ivy's smile was genuine.

Orrin's mood seemed to lighten. "Obviously. Well, we're looking at this idea of recreating the ionisation patterns of elements under controlled conditions. Firstly, we generate different magnetic fields using high powered lasers, then use high voltage electricity to create measurable shifts in the magnetic pulse. We try to anticipate different conditions- changing the properties of the waves. It's often unstable though and unsafe- no, no, hang on!" He floundered at the appalled look on Ivy's face. "The chimp would never have been subjected to this part of it!"

"Bonobo," corrected Ivy.

"Right. Bonobo." Orrin hurried to explain further. "No, no. Our data modelling is mostly theoretical- on computer. But we also take measurements and monitor the effects on different substances within the lab during and after the experiments; minerals, plants, animals- ourselves included- essentially trying to establish what sort of effect the magnetic fluctuations have on life forms. Nothing sadistic- just heart rate, growth patterns, blood pressure, that sort of thing." He leant back on his hands, nodding toward Kyah. "That's what I meant, when I asked about Kyah. Nothing invasive at all, just physiological measurements. But I entirely understand your aversion to it." He winked. "And I'm perfectly happy to keep using myself as the guinea pig."

Ivy frowned at the term of reference. "How very *Pierre Curie* of you."

Orrin grinned. "Yeah, I suppose it is. The things we do to save the world, hey."

At that, Ivy chuckled. Now that she knew more about his research, Ivy regretting thinking the worst of him so quickly. And the accent was growing on her, to say the least. She liked Orrin. But her heart was tainted. Loss coloured her memories just enough to keep the walls around her heart opaque. She'd learnt long ago, that clear glass could shatter.

Kyah made a gentle noise in her throat and eyed Orrin warily. She shuffled behind Ivy and sat down, picking at her chest again, now bored with the greenery. Kyah prodded Ivy in the back with a toe. Her head twitch was almost imperceptibly quickening, but Ivy noticed. Its frequency was a signal that the bonobo had grown tired. It was almost dark now and the grounds were deserted. Ivy stood up smiling, a little less gracefully than she would have liked. She turned and took Kyah's hand, pulling her up too.

"I think I'd better take this one home," she said, "or we're going to get caught in that." Ominous clouds pulled in above them. "Thanks for explaining your research to me. It sounds - potentially devastating. I only hope you find out you're wrong."

"In this instance, I'd love to be wrong."

"And here I was, assuming it was all pretty boring in the physics labs," she teased, "what goes up must come down, apples falling on heads, that sort of thing…" Ivy tried to tear her eyes from Orrin's. She squeezed Kyah's hand and shivered, despite the warm air. "It's been… interesting."

"So it has," Orrin said. "In more ways than one." His eyes danced over her, reflecting the lights that were flickering on throughout the gardens. "I appreciate you listening, Ivy. I don't usually discuss it out of the lab."

"Understandably." Ivy made to turn away, but hesitated. "Can I ask you a question?"

"Of course."

"Why did you tell me this stuff? I mean, I'm glad you did, but why?"

Orrin sat up straighter. He pushed his fingers under the bridge of his glasses, letting them fall askew momentarily then ran his fingers through his hair. He shrugged.

"I honestly don't know. But I'm glad I did too." He took a deep breath. "Maybe you could swing by the lab sometime? I'd love to show you around. Kyah too, if you like," adding hastily, "as an honoured guest. No strings attached."

"Thanks. We'll think about it."

As Ivy walked away smiling, she could feel Orrin's eyes following her. Which made her smile more.

CHAPTER 6

IVY

*W*alking down a narrow street in the fast-fading light, Ivy quickened her pace. The air was getting colder and she longed for a hot bath. Jacarandas lined both sides of the road, their arms reaching bare into the sky. A few weeks ago, they were ablaze in a riot of lilac blue flowers that marked the heat of summer. Now the flowers were a dry, scattered carpet across the road and rooftops, so deep that the footpath was barely visible. Ivy turned into the small brick apartment block where she had lived for nearly six years. As usual, Tom Chapman, her landlord, was out the front raking the masses of fallen leaves into piles. His rake was as much a walking stick as it was a tool. He rubbed his brow and stored the rake neatly into his garden shed, then picked up a small pile of daisies he had left near the shed door. *For Iris*, Ivy knew. Tom's late wife had loved the bright white flowers. Although she was no longer alive to receive them, habit ensured there was always a bunch in Tom's hand each afternoon when he retired for the night.

"Hey Grandpa Tom," Ivy said smiling, kissing him on the cheek as he turned to face her.

"Ivy, love." Tom's weathered face and bright eyes wrinkled with affection. "I was hoping I'd catch you today."

Although they were not biologically related, Tom had insisted Ivy call him Grandpa when she'd moved in, and still beamed with satisfaction each time she did.

"I have something for you, my dear," he said. "Just a little trinket." Tom's eyes sparkled in the flickering porch light. He placed his handful of daisies on a low wall then fumbled in his pocket with knobbly fingers, searching for the object he had been so carefully carrying around all afternoon. He placed it into Ivy's palm and patted her hands closed gently between his own, with a slight tremor. "I must say, you get prettier every year."

A wave of sadness swept through Ivy as his hands clasped her own. *He looks tired today. He does too much.* Ivy had seen the effects of Parkinson's disease creep over him the last few years and it pained her to see him suffer. She tried to hide the recognition of it from her face. *I've neglected him lately.* The guilt fell heavy.

"Oh, don't you fret," Tom said, his face crinkling into a smile. "I'm as fit as a fiddle."

Ivy furrowed her brow, surprised by his admonition so close to her own thoughts. "Of course you are."

He nodded, his tartan drivers cap shifting. "Well, that's that then, isn't it?" Tom's mouth twitched and his eyes dimmed momentarily. An aching loneliness suddenly overtook her, and Ivy felt frail and tired to her core, almost *ancient.* Tom's eyes washed with confusion and looked down to their still-joined hands as the first of the raindrops began to fall.

Ivy followed his line of sight. She let his hands go gently and held the object he'd given her up to the light. It was a smooth, elongated black stone, shaped like an oddly flattened teardrop, about two inches long. It had a small hole drilled through the top end. The glossy surface had dulled in places with age and wear, but even in the dim light Ivy was touched by its strange elegance.

Initials of *I.C.* swept the rounded side in cursive lines. On the back, five circular indentations were scattered across the stone.

"This belonged to Iris," Ivy said, dismayed. Tom's late wife had worn it everyday on a chain around her neck, no matter the outfit or occasion. "I couldn't possibly -"

"I want you to have it," Tom insisted. "It was very special to her and you are very special to me. Sean sent that amulet to her in a letter not long before he, well, *you know.*"

Ivy *did* know. She'd heard Tom's stories many times. While serving in the Vietnam War, his son Sean had disappeared. Dishonourable discharge, the official letter had said, on account of desertion. Tom however, had refused to accept it, as did his late wife. But still, the young man had never returned home and was never seen again.

"Iris missed Sean so much, but this amulet seemed to give her some comfort," Tom continued, "She was forever hoping our boy would come home one day, just walk in the door whistling like he always did." Tom looked down. A lacework of sad memories set on his face.

The old man squeezed Ivy's fingers closed over the black stone and patted her hand. "So, it's yours now. I'd only give it to you my dear," he said, "because I know Iris would want you to have it. She thought you were something special too. And look, you even share the same initials, see?"

Ivy sat alone on a kitchen stool, her fingers moving fluidly across the strings of her cello. The dull thud of heavy rain fell outside her window. The scales Ivy played were reflexive and her eyes were closed as she felt, rather than noticed, where her fingertips pushed the fingerboard. The wooden body of the cello was resting softly against her left knee like an extension of her own. Eventually, Ivy graduated to playing pieces she knew by memory. The bow in her right hand chased the strings leaving a few long hairs broken and hanging from the tip. She had drifted so far into the music that it took three knocks before Ivy realised someone was at her apartment door. Reluctantly, she placed her cello in its stand next to the bench and ducked through the tiny lounge room swinging the front door open without checking.

"Tom?" *Oh. Not Tom.*

"Hey, Ivy." *That damn accent.* Blood rushed to her face.

"Orrin." Ivy covered her mouth with her hand briefly, not sure whether to smile or hide. *Too late to hide.* She quickly drew her hand back across her undoubtedly messy curls and pushed them behind her ear instead. "Um, well, this is… unexpected."

"You're upset. I'm sorry, I shouldn't have stopped by." Orrin turned to leave, his face a little flushed and his hair and shirt clinging to him from the deluge outside. He was holding a bedraggled bunch of flowers in one hand. He turned quickly back, passing the bouquet to a stunned Ivy. "I almost forgot, these are for you. And this." He pulled Ivy's phone from his pocket. Orrin placed it in Ivy's free hand, leaving her skin tingling as he stepped back. "You left it on the grass and then I ran into Jayne in the car park as I was leaving. She told me it was your birthday today. Then she gave me your address, she sort of insisted actually- didn't think you'd mind if I dropped it back to you. I couldn't lave a message for you, because well -" he gestured to the phone helplessly, "you wouldn't have got it. But I can see that you're busy so I'll just, I'll go. I'm so sorry to-"

"No!" she spluttered. "Sorry." Ivy took a deep breath. "Please, stay a minute, you're drenched."

"It's lashing out there," Orrin shrugged.

"Come in. Really, I don't mind, you caught me by surprise that's all."

"I keep doing that, don't I?"

"It does seem to be your thing." Ivy stepped back, turning the slim mobile over in her hand. She hadn't even realised it was missing. Orrin followed her into the lounge room. Ivy looked at her books spilling from the coffee table and photocopied notes strewn on the floor as if she was seeing them for the first time. "I'm so sorry, it's very messy. I wasn't expecting anyone-"

"It's nothing to the mess I'm making on your carpet," Orrin said, apologetically. It was true. Water was dripping from his shirt to the floor and his shoes had mud puddles beneath him. He sneezed.

"You're freezing," Ivy realised. "Let me grab you a towel." She disappeared up the hallway for a moment leaving the flowers in the kitchen, and returned with a towel, almost tripping through the doorway in surprise.

Orrin's wet shirt was already draped over her old oil-heater, leaving him in an undershirt that clung a little too perfectly to his chest. His muddy shoes were now beside the front door. He seemed entirely at ease with his state of undress and if he noticed Ivy's flushed cheeks and slightly manic grin, he didn't mention it.

Instead, he turned to her incredulously as she passed him the towel. "Are those *human* skulls?"

Ivy smiled self-consciously and followed his gaze back to the overflowing bookcase against the wall. Twelve macabre looking skulls peered down from the top shelf.

"Yes, well no, they're casts actually," she clarified. "*Australopithecus africanus*, *Homo ergaster*, *Homo habilis*, *Homo floresiensis* and a few modern primates and other hominids. They're exact reproductions of fossil finds. I use them for my research from time to time. Mostly, I just love looking at them, to be honest." She bit her lip at his wide eyed expression. "A little creepy to non-anthropologists I'm guessing?"

"No, not creepy. Just…unexpected." Orrin raised an eyebrow then grinned. "Okay, maybe a little bit creepy."

Ivy laughed. "You're lucky I donated Lucy to the archaeology museum then."

"Lucy?" Orrin gave a puzzled smile.

"An articulated skeleton of Lucy, the first nearly complete *afarensis* fossil found. She was 3.2 million years old. Well, not my cast copy of course, but the original Lucy. She used to hang in the corner there with a wig and robe on." Ivy watched Orrin's eyes widen, amused. "I'll admit it was a forced relocation on my part. She caught me off guard when I was sleepwalking one night and scared the hell out of me. I do miss her though."

"I won't even pretend to understand that sentiment, although-" Orrin feigned concern, "I'm sorry for your loss?"

Ivy laughed. "Thanks. And thank you for the flowers too." She wandered toward the kitchen, Orrin trailing her. "Can I get you a drink then?"

"Thanks, sure, whatever you're having." A minute passed in silence while Ivy busied herself with coffee to avoid staring at the half naked man drying his hair in her kitchen. *It's been* way *too long.* She looked up to find Orrin studying her cello.

"So that was you playing before then? I thought it was the radio."

"You heard?" *Of course he heard.* "I was just practising."

"Will you play for me, then?"

"Hell no."

Orrin's mouth opened in surprise. Ivy's face burned.

"What I mean is," she stammered, "I don't usually play for anybody."

"I see. And why's that, then?" he asked, his accent and eyes disarming her simultaneously.

Ivy faltered. *Because nobody is ever here.*

"I don't know."

How it was that ten minutes later Ivy found herself playing the cello for her guest was beyond her. Orrin leant against the doorway with his coffee as Ivy took a deep breath, resting the tall wooden body of the instrument between her legs and adjusting the end pins slightly. She let her hand fall from the scroll to the strings and then pulled the slender bow across them in one long stroke, soothing and mellow. Ivy pressed her lips together and closed her eyes, shutting out the self-consciousness that threatened to overwhelm her. Immediately she was alone again, lost in the music. The tone was warm and deep, almost like a human voice as it rose and fell. Ivy felt the harmonics course through her. She played a bittersweet melody of sorrow and love that drifted from one note to the next, her bow arm extending fully before sliding back in a continuous melancholic expression. Her fingers shimmered the strings with vibrato, anticipating their next movement without conscious thought. It was Ivy's favourite piece. The melody consumed her. She imagined a swan, the inspiration of the composer, gliding effortlessly through water as each note took form.

"Deadly," Orrin whispered as she finished. His eyes were soft and dark. Ivy cleared her throat, blushing. She'd forgotten he was there. "What was that called?" he asked.

"'Le Cygne'- *The Swan*. It's part of a progression of movements composed in 1886 called The Carnival of the Animals. My mother used to play it for me as a child on an old record player."

Orrin nodded. "It suits you. It's beautiful, haunting almost. It's strange. I feel like I know it somehow. But I don't really listen to classical music so I don't see why I would. My best friend plays piano. I should probably appreciate his talent more."

"Probably," Ivy smiled. "You've probably heard that piece before though somewhere; it's the most famous movement of the suite it belongs to." She stood and placed the cello back on its end pin in the stand, leaning against the elbow of the bench to face him again. "I think it may even be responsible for my ultimate descent into the archaeological pit, so to speak. This piece sort of- *spoke to me*, I suppose." Ivy stopped abruptly and looked away.

Orrin regarded her thoughtfully. "In what way?"

She dismissed him. "No. You'll laugh at me."

"Scout's honour, I won't."

"Were you even a scout?"

"No," he laughed. "But seriously, what do you mean?"

Ivy sighed. *In for a penny.* She picked up her cold coffee and put it in the microwave. "I first heard *The Carnival of the Animals* as a child. It's really written for children, you see. So much so that the composer, Camille Saint-Saens, wouldn't even let anyone play the suite until after he'd died- he didn't want to ruin his reputation as a serious French Romanticist."

"And?"

"Well there are fourteen parts to it altogether, each one based on a different animal - the swan, which I just played, the donkey, elephant, tortoise, lions, one is even inspired by an aquarium. And the whole classical suite just tore into my imagination. All of the animals did, but one of my favourite movements is called 'Fossiles'. An American poet later wrote words to match the music and recorded it with an orchestra. It's meant to sound like a dance of dinosaur bones at midnight in a museum. It really got to me as a kid; apparently I used to recite it on a daily basis. It appealed to my overactive imagination, I guess. Mammoths and pterodactyls with rattling bones and prehistoric ghostly wails - all entirely bewitching to an eight-year-old. Hence," Ivy gestured through the door to the shelf of skulls, "the archaeology obsession." She recovered her warm coffee cup and leant back against the elbow of the bench, glad she once again had something to hold onto.

"It must be some poem to inspire an entire career. Do you still remember it?" Orrin put down his coffee cup and leaned forward in anticipation, smiling at her. The simplicity of the movement brought him a touch closer, and a rush of warmth and nervousness gripped her chest. She couldn't help but return his smile. Ivy's nose wrinkled as she twisted the smile on her lips nervously, trying to ignore the enticing scents of oak moss and fir from his aftershave.

"Not much of it. But for what it's worth, I think I was an easy target," Ivy laughed, her eyes sparkling. "I spent most of my childhood daydreaming in trees and digging up dirt."

"And you managed to make a career out of it." Orrin pursed his lips, biting back a laugh. "That's impressive."

"You promised not to laugh!"

He held up his hand in surrender. "Scout's honour."

"Thank you." Ivy jutted her chin forward in mock indignation. "I did say it was for children. Anyway, there you have it - the origin of my obsession with bones and very old food implements. Still keeping me entertained, twenty years later."

"It's a good story. It's, um, how do I put it-? *Unique*." Without either of them realizing it, he'd moved closer. "Just like..." Orrin's fingers grazed hers where they were pressed around the edge of the bench and he stopped still, all trace of humour gone. His brow furrowed for an infinitesimal moment as he studied her face. His eyes flicked down to her mouth then back up.

Ivy suddenly felt too warm. Her breath was too loud. Her fringe shifted into her eyes and she had a fleeting desire to stay hidden behind it. Orrin's fingers brushed hers again as he lifted his hand hesitantly toward her face. *So close.* Ivy felt his breath stutter and his fingers pause halfway there, a silent question in his eyes. *Too close.*

Ivy reached up slowly, curling her own hair back behind her ear and met his eyes more boldly than she felt. *It would be so easy.* His lips were only a moment from hers. Loneliness and longing tempted her forward. *But I've been here before.* She could still feel heartache, just below the surface. Another, more recent loss compounded her self-preservation. Ivy closed her eyes, turning slightly away.

Orrin's voice broke the silence, a little rough and deeper than usual. "You know, I think I'm finally starting to get inside your head Ivy Carter."

Ivy straightened, offering a smile tinged with regret. She slipped sideways along the bench, out of reach. "In that case, I think it's probably time for you to go, Orrin James. My head is the last place anyone should be."

As Ivy sank into a hot bath later that night, her mind buzzed with the events of the day. She pictured Tom in his little apartment downstairs, making himself a cup of tea and going to bed. The amulet he had given her was sitting on the dresser. Although she didn't usually wear jewellery, she quite liked its unusual shape and colour. Its unassuming nature seemed to want to deflect interest, but somehow it drew her eye.

Something else had held her eye today, she thought begrudgingly. She didn't know what to make of Orrin, which irritated her. Physically, there was no denying it. He was charismatic, sexy, and intelligent. His easy confidence, that mischievous grin, the way his eyes sparkled as they danced across her and then something… something *behind* those eyes. Something that seemed to know her, or see into her. Something that had the potential to break through the wall she had so carefully constructed around herself to preserve and protect.

No, absolutely not. Ivy splashed her face with warm water. Orrin was right. He *was* getting inside her head. Resisting the warm feeling that was creeping through her body, she pushed the thought of him away and changed the scene in her head like a movie. *'Is she the only chimp here? It's just that I've been looking to extend my own research parameters…'* Orrin's eagerness to use Kyah as a lab rat fell on her again like a dead weight.

"He's just another guy with an agenda", she said aloud, aggravation flushing her face as she searched through the bubbles for the soap. "You have your research, you have Kyah, and you have your job. If you want to get anywhere in life you can't get distracted." The chastisement sounded like a parent berating a wayward teenager; only in this case, the teenager was willing to listen. Hauling herself out of the bath with renewed singularity of thought, Ivy dressed quickly and worked furiously until the early hours of the morning, when sleep finally took her.

CHAPTER 7

IVY

Ivy sat up, cursing that once again her mostly sleepless night had ended in sweat-drenched horror. Different dreams, different threats but they always carried the same desperation to protect someone. Planning an escape, creating diversions, hiding places, shielding others, carrying them. And it was all to save herself from losing them over and over again. Ivy could live with death, as long as it was only her own. The nightmares had been the same since she was a child. Vivid, extraordinarily real, terrifying.

The masked killer had a single purpose. To take people from Ivy's life. *To bring loss.*

A teenage boy with grey eyes faded from her mind. *Jasper.* Some nights, water rushed through her dreams, dragging her back to the place she'd lost him. It had been her idea to go swimming that day, she'd teased him as they kissed until he'd relented and dived into the river. The storms had shifted rocks beneath the surface. It was a whole day before they recovered his body.

That was the day that walls began creeping up around her heart. A year later, Ivy's mother lost her battle with cancer. Ivy's father, stricken with grief, had eventually moved away. *More loss.*

Ivy buried her face in her hands and took a deep breath. The dreams never disappeared when she woke; they haunted until her mind found a distraction. Ivy was used to them now, repetition had dulled her senses to their potency and she no longer dwelled on them when they woke her at night. Sleep was elusive.

Thankfully, Ivy had decided that she didn't need much sleep to function and a heavy duty study schedule benefited from the insomnia quite nicely. She was only betrayed by somewhat tired eyes and a dream journal fit for a box-office premiere. Yawning into the mirror, Ivy let a hot shower wash the memories away.

She rummaged through her jewellery box for the only silver chain she had. It was cheap and had a faulty clasp, so Ivy resolved to get a replacement as soon as she could. She threaded the amulet on and closed it behind her neck. It felt warm against her skin, despite the cold morning. Skipping breakfast, Ivy ducked down the concrete stairs. Her palm brushed across the mass of daises at the letterbox as she passed.

She was late. She pushed into the Residue Analysis Lab and pulled on a stained laboratory coat. Jayne was already preparing blood samples for DNA amplification.

"Morning!" Jayne was far too chirpy for pre-coffee conversation. "I've done a preliminary analysis of the first blade from the Flores dig. Red blood cells all over it."

Ivy returned Jayne's victory smile, settling down on a nearby bench. "Brilliant. Let me know if you need any help." Surreptitiously, Ivy noted Jayne's slow and methodical progress. She was pleased. A small collection of control samples were already waiting to her left. Soon, Ivy would spin tiny vials of solution in the centrifuge to filter particles from the genetic soup-mix. DNA replication would follow. Finally, Ivy would be able to identify the animal that had fallen victim to the blade.

The samples were tiny, but the implications were huge. Using these ancient stone tools, Ivy could determine the subsistence patterns of the extinct, tiny hunter *Homo floresiensis*. The organic residues on the stone gave away what animals had been butchered with them, which birds were killed, what plants had been chopped, which roots and tubers cooked and then eaten.

Archaeological residue analysis was an emerging specialisation with a complex methodology. In small laboratories across the world, scientists raced to uncover its mysteries. Competition was fierce, academic criticism was rife and the stakes for success were high. Ivy was one of the best.

Flicking on the radio and pulling on gloves, Ivy peered into the cardboard box. Within it were a dozen clear bags, each holding an oddly shaped stone. Each bag was labelled with an identification number corresponding to the stratigraphic layer in which the tool had been found. Ivy pulled out a large flake of black chert and took up her position at the electron microscope. An image of the roughly triangular stone flickered up onto a large screen above her desk as she focussed. She was surprised by what she saw. Although the excavating team had given her a description of the tools they had found - suggesting they were comparable to those of much more modern *Homo sapiens*, she couldn't help being cynical. But the technology of this tool *was* modern, or at least, too modern for *Homo floresiensis*. It was not what she had expected.

It was widely accepted that stone tools got more sophisticated, technically and functionally, the further up the evolutionary tree they appeared. It made sense. From nearly two million years ago, early hominids had started using crude stone choppers to break into marrow and sever the flesh and joints of their prey. Culminating with modern *Homo sapiens*, tools had progressed to delicate instruments and finely formed stone blades. Each tool became specialised for its use in processing vegetation, meat or decorative functions, skinning, carving or fighting.

The stone tool magnified on Ivy's monitor was supposedly created by a tiny-brained, chimp-like hominid, surely as evolutionarily distant from their modern large-brained cousins as humanly possible - yet the similarity in technology was remarkable. Ivy checked the box label again, looking for a mistake. *Liang Bua Sector IV; Layer 8; Section E (12 items).* She definitely had the right box. It seemed the evolutionary tree was about to be severely uprooted.

Ivy began photographing the microscopic hills and valleys of the stone. They were littered with remnants of ancient blood cells and the flesh of chopped plants. Cellulose plant fibres draped like miniature desiccated ropes. After a while, a detailed pencil sketch accompanied the photographs and notes. Ivy began another as the hours ticked by unnoticed. The third tool was larger; a core that had first been stripped of smaller, sharper flakes that were useful for slicing through flesh. Instead of being discarded however, the core had also been used. There was a grainy polish along the worn edges, likely the result of a back and forth motion of scraping raw animal hides. Ivy scribbled in her journal as she worked.

Marvelling at the tool maker's skill, she examined the next artefact. This stone had been progressively and deliberately chipped away along two parallel edges creating a crude and strong needle point. Perfect to perforate through tough hide and bone.

"A perforator Jayne…my god. I wonder what they used it for?" she pondered aloud, staring into the microscope eyepiece. "Decoration of clothing? No, surely not… too primitive…."

"Help us…" A deep voice whispered behind her neck, soft and guttural.

"What?" Ivy's heart raced as she spun around. *There was nobody there.* The laboratory was empty. The hair on her neck tingled, sending a shiver down her spine. The lab door was closed. Jayne's chair sat empty, her row of test tubes lined neatly against the wall. A cold rush crept up Ivy's arms.

"Talking to myself - the first sign of madness," she muttered.

The word *LUNCH* was scrawled across the whiteboard with a happy face drawn underneath. *P.S. Don't forget your two o'clock tutorial.* A radio presenter introduced another song as Ivy stared blankly at the whiteboard.

"Crap!" A glance at the clock as she ran out of the lab told her that she was already ten minutes late. Ivy took the stairs two at a time. *Late again.* The small class of undergraduates hadn't appeared to notice. Chatting and texting with their feet and coffees on desks, the group was typical of second-years. It was early in the semester with exams still a distant concern and the confidence of their first year behind them.

"Sorry guys, important meeting," Ivy lied as she strode in, wondering if they ever actually believed her. It seemed they didn't.

"Nice meeting glasses," laughed a boy with unwashed hair.

"Yeah thanks Travis." Ivy rolled her eyes good-naturedly, trying to brush off her embarrassment. She rubbed the red rings around her eyes left by the microscope eyepiece. "Lost your brush again?" Travis chuckled and took an aim at the over-flowing bin with his empty coffee cup.

"Alright, what's on the agenda today?" Ivy asked.

"Chapter three - migration patterns," offered Kathryn passing a textbook forward. One of only three mature-aged students in the class, Kathryn's attentive barrage of questions frequently channeled their discussions off-topic. Ivy didn't mind, though some of the younger students found her irritating.

Ivy perched herself on the front desk.

"Right, so we're looking at the migration of early humans across the continents. Who, when, where, why and how. Did anyone do their readings?" A few mumbled apologies, a few "yeahs" and a handful of blank faces were thrown back at her.

"Come on guys," Ivy admonished, "keep up or you'll be cramming in a few weeks. Don't come crying to me when Professor Emery whips your backsides in the exam." A scattering of appreciative giggles followed Travis's impromptu demonstration.

"Okay, let's get into it then. The line of modern human evolution is based in a pretty complicated tree. We've got branches here and there and evidence from many different fields – archaeology – *obviously*, but also palaeoecology, geology, palaeobotany, climatology, and genetic phylogeography. We'll look at each of these methods in detail as we progress through this section. What we are most interested in here, is the spread of anatomically modern humans across the continents, particularly South East Asia, including the *Sahul continent*." She noted some quizzical eyebrows in the audience. "For those of you who didn't do their readings, that's us - *Australia*." Someone at the back gave a patriotic whistle.

"So," Ivy pushed on, determined not to lose their train of concentration so early, "who's going to give us a rundown on traditional theories?" Kathryn raised her hand.

"The floor's all yours." Ivy leaned back surveying the room and the students shuffled in their chairs. Kathryn looked around a bit imperiously and cleared her throat recounting her exhaustive textbook analysis with perfect recollection.

"Brilliant," said Ivy. "So, in summary, we've got anatomically modern humans, skipping out of Africa within the last 100,000 years, which happens to coincide with some significant social advances and innovations in tool making. As we all know, innovation allows for the manipulation of new resources and environments; migration encourages change through adaptation; change leads to innovation in technology... it's a classic case of which came first - the chicken or the egg? Migration or Innovation? But, we'll dive into that mess tomorrow."

Ivy heard a few groans.

"But first," she held up her hand, "let's talk about a much earlier migration from Africa. Pre-humans originally left what is now considered to be the 'cradle of humankind' at some point between 1.8 million years and 300,000 years ago. We have numerous subspecies of Homo erectus that span Europe to Indonesia during that time." Ivy grabbed a whiteboard marker and began scribbling notes on a timeline.

"Let's look at all the fossils we've dug up so far. We've got the sexy 'Java Man' excavated in 1893 and 'Peking Man' as our celebrity *Homo erectus* poster boys." She grinned at the anticipated wolf whistle. "But there are many more sub-species out there as well. Our smaller cousins *Homo erectus georgicus* from central Asia at 1.75 million years young. From China we have Nanjing Man, Lantian Man and Yuanmou Man. In Java, Indonesia, we've got Solo Man and then there's Tautavel Man who lived in France nearly half a million years ago." Ivy shot Kathryn a wink. "Ironically, at least half of those fossil 'men' were actually female, but what's in a name, right?"

"Moving on, let's not forget *Homo erectus palaeojavanicus*. More commonly called 'Meganthropus'," Ivy continued, turning back to the whiteboard, "which is a seriously misunderstood fossil who was believed for a long time, to be a giant." Ivy faced the group with a grin. "No fairytales here though - it turns out that this species is just the Schwarzenegger of hominids. Tall guy, big muscles, funny accent."

"*Come with Meganthropus if you want to live*," called Travis in a terrible impersonation. A few students groaned and Claire kicked the back of his chair.

'They couldn't talk, idiot," said Claire.

Travis looked affronted. "Says who?"

Oliver turned to face Claire. "He's right, for once. Erectus had to have spoken in some capacity because they co-ordinated hunts, made complex tools and cared for sick family members.

They used fire by 800,000 years ago and cooked their meat. Erectus also had a larger brain capacity than earlier hominids and the part of the brain linked to speech was already developed. Right?"

Oliver turned to Ivy for confirmation and she nodded, impressed.

Travis shot Claire a dirty look. "*See. I'll be back.*" Claire scowled at both of them.

Ivy began pacing the floor. "One thing we need to keep in mind is that Homo erectus populations were extremely successful; in Africa, the 'old world', it's generally accepted that Homo erectus became Homo sapiens and eventually anatomically modern humans- that is, you and I."

"In the so called 'new world' of Europe and Asia, we think they gave rise to archaic Homo sapiens and Neanderthals," Ivy tapped at the wall map with her fingers, "and new research suggests at least one *erectus* population may have actually co-existed with modern humans in Indonesia up to 40,000 years ago. In evolutionary terms, that's as good as last week.

So, the question begs to be asked; could there have been even *more* descendant species of Homo erectus that haven't been discovered yet? How big was this branch of our evolutionary tree?" Ivy stood in front of the class, animated, her eyes bright. "In those dark, hidden forests and caves of the new world, what *other* types of humans existed before we arrived from Africa? How did they evolve? And most intriguing of all," Ivy paused for dramatic effect. "*Why* did they die out?"

Ivy lay her cello gently back into its case. She stood up, stretching and pulling at her aching neck and shoulders. Once again she'd lost track of time. She crossed the small tutorial room, leaning out the shuttered window before pulling it shut. The sky was darkening outside and Kyah would be waiting for her to visit. As Ivy bent to pick up the cello case, there was a knock on the door. Without waiting for a response, Orrin's head popped around the corner.

"Found you." He winked at her.

Ivy raised an eyebrow. "Apparently so, although I'm not sure how-"

"Jayne again."

"Aah." *Damn that girl.* Ivy pushed her fringe behind her ear, balancing the cello case on her foot.

Orrin looked around the room curiously. "No audience?"

"Just me. It's a good place to practice," Ivy replied. She felt awkward. The last time she'd seen Orrin, she'd all but rejected him. "The acoustics are great," she continued, trying to fill the otherwise silent room. "And there's an audio recording facility set up for tutorial sessions. Students use it so they can slacken off in class and download the lectures later." Orrin laughed. "When it's empty, I record my cello practice so I can play it back at home. It helps me pick up mistakes."

"I bet there aren't any. Mistakes, I mean."

"Of course not. I'm a regular *Offenbach*." Ivy rolled her eyes good-naturedly. *Damn you Jayne.* She changed the subject. "You were looking for me?"

"Oh yeah." Orrin took a deep breath. "The other night, I think I might have given you the wrong impression. Well, not entirely wrong maybe, but, I didn't mean to mess you about, if that's what you think. You just don't know me yet, so I thought maybe we could-" he paused, his eyes hopeful. Ivy felt a familiar twisting in her stomach. *Don't go there. You've been down this road. It's messy. It hurts. You'll hurt him. Just stick to work. You have Kyah-.*

"Kyah. Kyah! Sorry Orrin, I really have to go." Ivy pushed past him, ignoring the heat that came when her shoulder grazed his arm. She felt blood rush her neck and face and cursed having such pale skin. "I just remembered I was meant to call into the biology lab earlier – Kyah's, um, medication. Damn it. I just- I really have to go. We'll talk soon, okay?" Ivy waved apologetically over her shoulder as she carried the unwieldy cello case, lugging it down the stairs to avoid the risk of getting caught with Orrin in the elevator.

CHAPTER 8

NEIL

The Dish, Parkes Observatory, New South Wales

As Neil pulled into Parkes Observatory he never failed to be impressed by the sixty-four metre radio telescope. As the largest of its kind in the southern hemisphere, "The Dish" as it was affectionately known, had become an Australian icon. The facility had become legendary for its role of receiving the images of the first Moon Walk in 1969. Now, over 120,000 visitors travelled the vast emptiness of Western New South Wales to marvel at its distinctive shape each year. The receiver was constantly upgraded with cutting-edge technology and remained a vital tool for astronomers. Decades of achievement hung in the visitor centre, complete with educational theatres and paraphernalia for tourists. As an added bonus, sightseers could even ogle the giant rotating dish from below, over a cup of coffee and sandwich from the café.

Primarily, the dish was used to measure the radio energy

produced naturally by stars, galaxies and clouds of gas and dust within the universe. Tracking and receiving the data sent by space probes was a minor directive, as well as receiving radio transmissions from space craft during exploration missions. A team of twenty engineers and astronomers lived and breathed its glory, 24 hours a day, every day of the year.

Neil dropped his silver cigarette lighter into his pocket; the engraved nautical helm wheel on its front caught the afternoon glare. It was engraved with a single word, *Benjamin*. Neil bypassed the straggling holiday makers as they shuffled back to their cars, ready to resume their journeys along the epic Newell highway linking Queensland to Victoria. The sun was setting a rich red across dead-flat sheep paddocks. A hot wind blew through the dry grass toward the distant Goobang Range. Kangaroos dotted the horizon. Neil drew on his cigarette one last time, heeling it on the pavement.

They were waiting for him in the observers' quarters. Dimitri was attacking his laptop with lightning fingers, apparently still trying to resurrect the corrupted files. Cassandra paced the small living room flicking her fall of ebony hair as she turned. Her blue eyes were glued to the monstrous, polished white dish dominating the window frame. She startled as Neil strode in, loudly discarding his overnight bag to the tiles.

"Chill out Cass," Dimitri murmured. "You'll wear a hole in the carpet." After a wary glance at Neil, the younger man resumed his focus punching keys.

Cassandra raised an eyebrow. "You can talk. Christ, passive-aggressive tendencies perhaps?"

Neil studied the younger man's tense shoulders bent furiously into his work and the sweat shining from his pores. *Good.*

Cassandra turned to Neil. "So how did we get in here so fast? I thought the La Trobe team were working on the Pulsar Timing Array." Her smooth voice failed to hide an undercurrent of apprehension.

Neil moved to the centre of the small room, demanding Dimitri's attention. "I pulled some strings Ms Chevalier. Damn expensive ones. So you'd both better make this happen. Yanking the PTA team out will raise questions – and piss them off." Neil's 'Target of Opportunity' proposal had overridden scheduled observations, effectively cutting out their competition. The proposal was rarely used. It had been created solely for situations where astronomical events of extraordinary scientific interest cropped up unexpectedly. *I'd class this as extraordinary.* "We've got the Dish for the next five days – no questions asked, under the Time Critical Clause – but it won't last." Neil scowled, to emphasize his point.

"Data Proprietary?" As chief number cruncher, Dimitri was all about data security.

"No deal. Cutting the scheduled observations kills our right to the eighteen-month period of data privacy. Whatever we learn here will be open to the public in seven days. Hell, what does it matter, in a few days it'll be all over the news, anyway."

"*We'll* be all over the news..." Cassandra began.

Neil met her assumption with silence and a clenched jaw. *Correction – I'll be all over the news.* Cassandra's eyes flashed at the unspoken reproach. Her sycophantic facade returned.

"So when can we get in there, *Director?*"

As distracted as he was with this mess, Neil still considered watching Cassandra a leisure pursuit. *A few days stuck here and she might be willing to reconsider my previous offer.* "We get in there now, kids. Get your stuff, John's waiting."

From the outside, the base of the dish resembled a clay windmill with three levels of small square windows. It seemed scarcely strong enough to support the massive parabolic receiving dish above it. The high precision wave-panel dish had been extended over the years by aluminium plate and steel mesh, culminating in one thousand tonnes of engineering precision.

The grounds were now deserted. The operations manager

greeted them, running through the usual reminders before retiring for the night. Well experienced with the equipment, they each listened with the patience of school children waiting for afternoon bell.

The control room was a cramped circular cave lined by white desks, cobalt monitors and high racks of equipment. Flashing lights and tons of electronic cabling connected sensors and experiments, giving the impression of organized chaos. Neil hunched over the motion control console, the familiar smell of country air lingering on his tastebuds.

Astronomical navigation had always been Neil's strong point at university but the nitpicking of detailed research had irritated him. The money was bad and the food chain placement even worse.

He'd decided that his science career would only be worth pursuing if it *paid*, as it were. So, years ago Neil had bypassed the nitpicking in favour of corporate management. He'd exceeded his goals, and not through diplomacy. On rare occasions like this however, he enjoyed the moments of pure science. It had always called to him. *Like a sailor following stars...*

With a rush of key strokes, Neil focused the master equatorial telescope hidden in the heart of the dish structure to the co-ordinates of their last known readings. The giant receiver began to slowly shift its gaze as the tiny guide tracked a new course across the sky.

Neil got to his feet. "Okay kids, fourteen hour shifts - you two can start. You'd better have something for me by morning." Neil smirked, flipping his hard hat back onto his head as he pulled the door closed behind him.

Dimitri scaled the thirty metre tripod-leg that ascended to the sky from the centre of the dish, thankful he wasn't acrophobic. He watched Neil enter the observers' sleeping quarters far below him, like an ant on the ground. *Good riddance.* For a moment Dimitri contemplated the rumours. If he hadn't overheard two of the board members himself, he mightn't have believed it.

He's giving the institute a bad name Charles.... the women, the booze.... It's got to stop, it's time.... he's just gone too far... the media are just waiting for another slip-up.

A shuffle of feet. A sigh. *I know, I know. But think of what the poor bugger is going through, Frank... his only son...*

We aren't the bloody AA, and since when has Neil ever given an inch? And the poor kid, it's bloody awful, I'll give you that. But, well, I'm not sure it matters anymore...to him at least. And this debacle with NASA... Jesus Christ, Charles, we can't afford another mistake.

Dimitri had left then. Too much information would only make his job harder. He hated politics.

Now, Dimi sucked the warmth into his lungs with relish, immersing himself in the still night air. Up here, it was just him and the infinite night sky. His insignificance in its immensity was comforting. Below him the dish glared into the darkness, an acre of white metal, lit up like a fallen Ferris wheel. Of all the telescopes he worked with, this would always be his favourite.

At the ladder's end, Dimitri pushed through the door of the suspended focus cabin. Inside, a revolutionary thirteen beam receiver collected, amplified and fed data to the control room below. Custom designed by the CSIRO, the Multibeam provided unprecedented efficiency in large scale radio surveys – ideal for their current dilemma.

"How are you going, old girl? Miss me?" Dimitri hummed tunelessly as he adjusted the gleaming silver receivers with the finesse of a concert pianist. "Alright, let's see what's out there..."

Sixty straight hours of observation and modelling were ruthless enough, but the results were crippling. Neil stood, gripping the back of a chair. His knuckles were white.

"Holy shit."

"Yeah."

"Where is this data coming from?" Neil's face was as shadowed with fury as the others' were with exhaustion. Even Cassandra had lost her charm. Dark rings flawed her perfect eyes and her voice cracked with fatigue.

"All the usual readings for deep space energy waves. In addition, we've been picking up electromagnetic radiation through the two closest probes. That's four magnetometers all up - one space probe that's currently orbiting the moon and a satellite over South-East Asia. Both are consistently giving us two different patterns. Dimi has run them over and again and I've analysed the data through as many models as I can think of. It's definitive." She stood aside to look at Dimitri expectantly. The red digits on the atomic wall clock blurred. Dimitri knuckled his red-rimmed eyes. It was 4.45am.

"She's right," Dimi said. "Both sources have their long booms deployed to minimize emission interference. The two outboards are bringing in this Extra Low Frequency band here – we've got constant low frequency electromagnetic fields at hotspots around the globe. We've got one in North Africa, Bosnia, Indonesia, Mexico, Tanzania, Croatia, China... the list goes on. Very specific co-ordinates - all emitting photons in random phase. They're all increasing in strength by the same rate every 24 hours. We'll have to get more data but the pattern is there. It's a natural field, so they must all have something in common... no idea what."

Neil's jaw clenched. "But this one... are you sure about this?"

Neil ran his index finger down the bright monitor, leaving a trail of sweat. He glared at Cassandra, willing her to deny what he saw. She didn't.

"Positive," Cassandra sighed. "This second pattern was picked up by the inboard magnometer from both spacecraft as well as our sensors. A stream of high frequency energy. Pulsing; almost Gamma level. Dimi was able to retrieve our corrupted data - it fits the pattern. It's getting stronger. It's putting out a massive amount of power Neil, and each night is stronger than the last. The readings are saturating our equipment. It's going to peak… soon. This field – it's like a giant finger reaching down to us – it's almost reached the earth's atmosphere."

"How soon?"

"24 hours… 48 maybe. I don't know. There's no precedent here."

"*24 hours?* What the fuck? Not good enough! I need clarification on this. *Now.* What is it?" Neil licked his lips, caught between the inherent danger of the situation and its potential. He needed more time.

Cassandra groaned and pulled on the back of her neck. "I've never seen anything like it. Well, not close to earth anyway. There was a case in the seventies when military satellites detected radio bursts like this flashing all over the sky. They turned out to be massive star explosions, supernova, collapsing and forming a black hole. Same pattern, but stronger… but this is weaker and much too close."

Neil knew the consequences of high energy magnetic fluctuations. If this energy mutation reached the electron–rich layer of the earth's atmosphere, *the ionosphere,* it would be breaking through the earth's safety net. At the very least it could destroy electrical power distribution grids and interrupt radio signals and global positioning systems across the continent. And at the very worst… so much for harnessing its power. *Shit.*

"What's the point of origin?"

Cassandra met Dimitri's eyes quickly and turned away, straightening her shoulders.

"That's the weird thing Neil. There seem to be two origin points. It's like they are reaching for each other, attracting each other – one from space and one on earth. The strongest field – the one pulsing as it increases in strength each night, is coming from the light side of the moon in the general vicinity of the Clavious crater. The other one … well, it's very specific."

"Where?"

"Here - Australia. I don't know what is creating this Neil, but I don't think it's natural. The location is… suspicious."

"I asked *where* Cassandra."

"Okay, Australia – specifically Melbourne. Actually, more specifically… the exact co-ordinates for Melbourne University." She looked to Dimitri for support but got only grim silence. She shot him a scowl.

Neil was taken aback. "Melbourne University? Are you sure? The bloody *university* is drawing this thing towards us? What the hell are they doing down there?"

"I don't know, but it's something big."

It's something big alright. The corner of Neil's mouth twitched. *Fine. They may be creating this surge, but I'll be damned if they're going to control it. This is my game.*

Dimitri shuffled uncomfortably but Cassandra didn't falter as they waited his instruction.

Neil's eyes narrowed. "Well kids, in the words of Sun Tzu, 'Opportunities multiply as they are seized'". There was no humour in his tone.

For a moment no one breathed. The first blinding rays of morning sun hit the dish and reflected, dazzling their eyes. Neil jumped to his feet and strode for the door.

"Where are you going?" Cassandra followed.

"Stay! Keep working! I want as much on this thing as you can get."

"But where…?"

"Where the hell do you think I'm going? To the airport! I've got to get to Melbourne University to find out what the hell is going on."

CHAPTER 9

IVY

"*H*elp us."

"Mmm?"

"Help us.... It is time."

A jolt like lightning pierced her heart. Ivy clawed at the bed sheets, struggling to pull them higher as she lurched forward. The pitch black was blinding. Her pupils narrowed, straining to make out shapes in the room. The voice had been gravelly and hot against her face. *Someone's here, someone is in my room. Oh my god. I'm going to die.* For a moment she was afraid to breathe, afraid that the sharp, shallow breaths would alert the intruder to her consciousness. Hasten them to act. But she had already moved and there was no attack. Just blackness. Terrified of exposure, Ivy reached out and flicked on her bedside lamp. The room was empty. But the radio was on. Soft music was playing. Ivy smacked her fist over the sleep button to turn off the false alarm. *What the hell? It's the middle of the night.*

She rubbed her face with clammy hands and pulled her knees up high. She had been having a typical nightmare until that voice had broken through her dream. Louder than her own thoughts – it had seemed... *present.* As if the man had been next to her, breathing in her ear. *I'm going insane – there's no one here. It was just a dream.* The vivid imagination that brought her nightmares had always been a curse. Ivy chastised her fears. She wiped her eyes. *It's nothing. Just me and my stupid brain. It's nothing, nothing.* But it wasn't until the first rays of sun crept through branches at her window, that Ivy finally relented once more to sleep.

She was late. Again. A tantalising aroma greeted Ivy as she passed the coffee stand but it would have to wait. She dumped an armful of heavy books in her musty office, scattering the cup of pencils. Ivy cursed, rustling through her bag and pulled out a scrunched leaflet. 'Palm Oil murders' blazoned the front cover. Stuffing it into her jacket pocket, she rushed back down the hall to the elevator. After an agonizingly slow ride, she leapt out. Rounding a sharp corner, Ivy skidded, attempting to make her jog less awkward for the benefit of the professors sharing a coffee and almost toppling a display of South American tribal masks. The professors pressed themselves back against the walls to let her through, straight-faced in their ties, eyebrows furrowed disapprovingly. The only exception was a round man with a brightly coloured shirt and long silver hair tied back in a pony-tail. She waved at Professor Karl Ellery as she passed and he saluted her with his cup, then chuckled into his coffee.

Tucking her unruly hair behind her ears, Ivy joined the growing throng of people gathered in the great courtyard. Plastic tables were being set up by volunteers, bright orange and green banners hung between trees. The air was thick with anticipation. In her pocket, Ivy's hand closed around a crumpled flyer. Hundreds of the same papers were being passed through the crowd by volunteers in orange shirts. An outlined artistic impression of an orangutan face with sad eyes adorned their backs with the words 'Systematic Genocide' in bold print under-neath. Busloads of students arrived for their lectures and watched with curiosity as they wandered through. Some stopped and joined the crowd. More flyers were quickly dispersed.

Spying Liam, Ivy pushed towards an information stand. Nearby, a student in a giant orangutan costume lay on a rusty old hospital stretcher in the middle of the throng. A bloody bandage had been wrapped around his head. Ivy paused, surprised. *A little macabre,* she thought, *but he's certainly drawing attention.* A second costumed student was handing out flyers in the west archway, drawing more attention from commuters. A dozen orange shirts carried posters through the crowd with photos of endangered animals behind prison bars stamped *'Green or Gone?'* and *'Orphaned'.* Reaching the information table, Ivy was greeted by the smiling faces of volunteers, eager to hand out information. She looked back through the milling crowd in front of the empty podium. Liam was nowhere to be seen.

A few hundred students and passers-by were now jostling around the information booths. Orange shirts called out provocatively. Cheering followed. Anticipating trouble, a few police officers roamed the outskirts of the crowd.

"It's genocide! Systematic slaughter by multi-national corporations!" yelled an orange shirt near Ivy sporting a large banner. "Hold them responsible!" Cheering and clapping resounded as the crowd closed in. "Once the forest is gone, how will the indigenous survive?" his voice rose angrily, "No forest, no food! Where will the corporations be then? Counting their money!"

The crowd again roared, eager to support this new champion to their cause. They jostled back and forth and Ivy felt bodies closing in around her. The chanting of the crowd became rhythmic, almost harmonic in intensity. Eager to escape the throng, Ivy turned away.

It is time. The voice that had broken her nightmare, suddenly whispered warm in her ear. Ivy spun around, terrified, to find only a woman cheering the orange-shirt.

Come to us. The voice came again, heavy in the space behind her neck, menacing in its soft promise. With a shriek Ivy spun around, wide eyed and frantic. A misplaced foot in the crowd tripped her. She fell awkwardly, grabbing at people as she hit the ground hard.

"Damn it!" There were gasps as people strained to look. The menacing voice was gone. Her panic was broken. Humiliation washed over her as she lay sprawled on the grass surrounded by feet. On this rare occasion that Ivy had chosen to wear a skirt, she now found it failing to cover her. For a split second that seemed like agonising hours, the large strawberry coloured birthmark high on her left thigh glared back at the students looking down at her. Feet around her shuffled and someone heavy stood on her fingers as she groped for her skirt.

A hand broke through the dense crowd, briefly grazing the ivy leaf birthmark as it sought out her aching fingers through the jostling feet. Ivy grabbed it, struggling to regain her footing with stinging eyes. One-handed, she pulled her skirt across her thighs. Her face burned with embarrassment as she looked up into the eyes of her rescuer.

Orrin. For the third time in a short morning she cursed her overactive imagination as he led her through the crowd to a space beside the empty podium.

"That was quite a spill, you all'right?" Orrin asked. Ivy cringed at his sympathy; he'd obviously seen the whole thing. The *whole* thing. His eyes seemed to linger on her skirt.

"Yeah fine, I'm fine, thanks..." The crowd had escalated their feverish chanting and cheering, but Orrin seemed oblivious.

"Jaysus," he muttered vaguely, still staring at her skirt.

"It's a birthmark," Ivy offered unnecessarily. As if caught with his finger in a jar, Orrin quickly looked up. "An ivy leaf... *Ivy...* my parents weren't very imaginative," Ivy said. As much as she refused to entertain the thought, this was not the way Ivy had hoped he'd find that birthmark. She could almost see Orrin consciously regaining his composure, pulling his casual charm on like a suit. She, on the other hand, wanted to crawl into a hole and die.

Orrin smiled. "You sure you're alright, didn't break anything?"

"No I don't think so, just my self-respect..." she muttered, smoothing her skirt down and tucking her hair behind her ear again. *Damn fringe.*

"Not on my account," Orrin said gently. He cleared his throat, pulling his hand from his pocket. "Actually, you might have broken something; this was on the ground where you fell." Ivy's silver chain hung through his fingers, the black stone swinging. "Seems okay now." Orrin studied the stone for a few seconds. The initials IC stood out in sharp relief under the morning sun. The warm amulet fell between their hands as his fingers grazed her palm. Her body reacted instantly to the touch and for a split second she saw herself as something else entirely. *Beautiful. Wait, no- I didn't think that.* The emotions that coursed through her were overwhelming. Orrin wanted her. Ivy was suddenly sure of it. But it felt all wrong - she felt easy, confident, enamoured, even intrigued... by herself? Conflictingly, Ivy felt racked with humiliation at the same time. *Just breathe.... What?* She took the amulet, dropping her hand from his.

The grass beneath her feet suddenly became very interesting as Ivy fumbled to clasp the chain behind her neck again. By the time she looked up again, Orrin stood straight and poised with a crooked smile.

"Can I get you a coffee?" Orrin asked. "Seriously, you look like you need one, or maybe something stronger? I've a throat on me and I really need an excuse." His eyes danced as he held out his hand to her once again. Ivy offered him a smile, confident now that she looked slightly less manic. Her fringe brushed against her eyelashes and she pushed it back.

"I'd love to Orrin, but I -"

Orrin interrupted. "No again? Seriously? Please, just grant me the pleasure of a single, terrible refectory coffee. Just one. I saved you after all." He gestured back to the crowd.

Ivy looked around, suddenly conscious of the burgeoning

rally. The protestors had driven the crowd to fever pitch with their war-cries and now the people were growing restless. They were waiting for a speaker to ignite their passion and direct it. The orange shirt, his sales pitch complete, directed his attention and banner at the empty podium. The eyes of the crowd followed expectantly. Silence fell.

Yes, god damn it. I deserve this. Ivy nodded. "One terrible refectory coffee then, I promise." She drew confidence from Orrin's boyish victory smile. "You'll have to wait though." A flicker of confusion clouded his eyes as she turned away.

Ivy took a deep breath and stepped up to the podium.

CHAPTER 10

IVY

A sea of eyes washed over her as she stood before the hushed crowd gathering her thoughts. Finally, inspiration took Ivy by the shoulders, as it always did, and directed her voice.

"Insatiable."

Ivy drew her eyes across the multitude, gathering strength from their collectively held breath.

"Think on that word, because that is what we are facing. An *insatiable appetite* for Palm Oil. If we do nothing, then within a decade - that's in *your* lifetime," she pointed for emphasis at the middle of the human sea, "... *ninety-eight* percent of the rainforests in Borneo and Sumatra will be burnt to the ground and replaced with Palm Oil plantations." Ivy's eyes were aflame and her long hair whipped her shoulders with each movement. Her reclusive nature had been temporarily evicted. She was vibrant with passion.

"Every hour, *three hundred* football fields of primary forest are destroyed in South East Asia alone. Over twenty-two million acres are already gone. It's an epic loss, but I guarantee you, we have much more to lose. Production is set to triple within ten years." Ivy paused and took a moment to look directly into the eyes of audience members.

"So let's put a face to the destruction. *Elaeis guineensis.* A seemingly innocuous palm tree which is mass cultivated to create the most widely produced vegetable oil in the world."

"In the last 24 hours, *every one of you* used palm oil. But you didn't know it, because *they* don't want you to know it! It's been a part of your *cooking,* your *chocolate, snack foods,* your *cosmetics, soaps, detergents* and maybe even the fuel in your car. But you don't know what you're buying because it's labelled as ambiguous, generic 'vegetable oil'.

Ivy took the microphone from its stand and stepped in front of the wooden podium instead. There was now nothing between her and the swelling crowd and just for this moment, she wanted it that way.

"So," she called bitterly, "considering a lot of us here didn't know what palm oil was a few minutes ago, I'd say it is high time we gave it some attention!"

The microphone rang and cheers of support from Ivy's orange-clad crew sounded through the crowd. A rush of applause and affirmations rose to the podium. She let a moment pass.

"There are at least two and a half billion acres of abandoned land around the world that could be used for palm oil plantations with nearly sixteen million in Indonesia alone. Enough to cover the projected need our world has. So why burn our forests and take the homes and livelihoods of the indigenous people that need them?" Ivy's jaw clenched. Her eyes were hard and cold.

Ivy turned and threw her fist onto the podium. "I'll tell you why! Because it's cheaper to burn forest than to resurrect ruined land. And after the forests are ravaged and sold off as timber, they're cleared in great blazing walls of fire as far as the eye can see." She paused for dramatic effect but her audience didn't need it. "Massive amounts of carbon dioxide are released, pushing climate change. The lands suffer with drought, soil erosion and these uncontrollable fires. Toxins drain into the ocean bleaching the Great Barrier Reef."

Ivy let the words flow from memory. She never worried she would forget what to say anymore, only the consequences of saying nothing.

"*This* is unsustainable. *This* is criminal. And to compound the problem, these plantations are financed by major international banks. *Your* banks, *your* money. Flowing to the pockets of a handful of people with strong political influence -and because of their influence, it's almost impossible to enforce laws on them."

From the crowd below the podium, Liam jumped up onto the platform. Ignoring the microphone in Ivy's hand, he yelled toward the audience.

"Ten years ago, these villagers had the most biodiverse forests in the world to provide their food and shelter! Now they work for pitiful wages under dangerous conditions. They're angry!" Liam's voice rose provocatively. "The *legacy* they leave for their children will be ruined land and a broken economy." His face was red and sweaty. Ivy ushered him back off the stage with a minute shake of her head and a glare.

"This is about more than employment," Ivy replied evenly, moving back behind the podium. "Pesticides are being leached into rivers, killing fish and leaving no fresh water for drinking and bathing by indigenous communities. There are chronic illnesses and breathing problems in plantation workers and brain defects in newborn children."

Visions danced before Ivy's eyes of violence and sacrifice and the most innocent of victims. The fire within her mellowed. This was always the hardest part.

"Setting the forests alight is the cheapest and fastest way to clear land. But these fires destroy everything in their path. Animals that try to escape, like these Orangutans," Ivy threw her arms wide to the wall of the photographs in the information stands, "Flee to the only remaining trees for food and safety. *The plantations.* But there's a price on their heads. Palm oil workers are *paid extra to murder.* Orangutans are beaten and attacked. Burnt alive in their desperation to escape, when they have nowhere else to go. Any infants that survive are captured, only to be sold into a life of misery in the illegal pet trade. There is no escape for them."

Ivy drew her eyes slowly across the courtyard; even the air seemed not to breathe.

"Not a single tree is left to shield these creatures from one of their closest cousins. *Us. Humanity.* A cousin that shares *ninety-seven percent* of their DNA. A cousin that has already murdered more than fifty thousand of them and leaves them clinging to the very edge of extinction. An endangered listing holds *no* weight against profiteering and industry." Ivy's voice rang out. Appalled silence caught even the orange crusaders, who were well versed with the horrors she spoke of. *When did humanity become so inhumane?*

Ivy's thoughts flicked to Kyah, whose wounds were reflected in the eyes of each orphaned orangutan plastered on the information booths. She imperceptibly shook her head and her voice dropped to almost a whisper into the microphone. "These creatures are gentle, benevolent and highly self aware. I guarantee each and every one of you, that if you look into their eyes, you will see a reflection of your own humanity." Ivy searched the eyes of her audience and tried to find her own.

She took a deep breath. It was time for action, strong and clear.

"These forests are the most biodiverse place on our planet. The cure for cancer could be hidden in those trees, burning as we speak. This loss is on *our* head; *we* must act now. *We* must take on this challenge! *We* must be their voice!"

Cheering erupted from the crowd and orange banners flew. The released tension of hundreds of protesters shot through the chilled morning air like lightning.

"We *cannot* leave this to the corporations that feed their own pockets first!" Ivy yelled. More cheers came. Banners waved. Those who had been watching from the sidelines surged forward to join the throng.

"We must make financiers accountable *for their impact!*" Ivy's fist hit the podium as she spoke and with each resolution came a resounding applause.

"We must ensure that sustainable resources are the *only* trade companies that we will accept!

"We must enforce environmental impact assessments, effective law enforcement and humane wildlife management *on the ground*!

"We are the consumers! We drive the economy! This is our money and we will decide how it's spent!"

The crowd roared. Ivy's heart thumped as she stepped down from the podium. Her audience began moving and the orange shirts set to work once more. They milled through the masses with banners held high, dispersing leaflets and sponsor forms, information sheets and a limitless supply of enthusiasm.

Ivy's eyes searched the crowd and quickly found Orrin. He was leaning against an information stand, staring at her with an unreadable expression. Ivy took a deep breath and walked towards him. *I don't care what he thinks.*

But she knew it was a lie.

CHAPTER 11

IVY

*O*rrin placed a latte in front of Ivy on the stained plastic table.

"So… that wasn't what I expected. Again."

Ivy smiled, hiding a pang of disappointment. "I keep doing that, don't I?"

"Don't get me wrong, you were actually - brilliant. Really you were." Orrin sat down opposite her with his own coffee, knocking the refectory table as he did so. The coffee cups wobbled precariously, sloshing across the table. Ivy jumped up but a large coffee stain was already blossoming on the front of her skirt. "Jaysus! Sorry!" Orrin leapt forward to help, knocking the table again. He groaned and clapped a hand to his forehead.

"Aah, shite. I've made a complete haymes of you now." His smile faltered as Ivy mopped up her clothes with serviettes. "That skirt of yours is really getting abused today isn't it."

"Don't worry. Refectory coffee is notoriously cold," Ivy said. "And to be honest, I'm not one much for skirts anyway." *Not after today's treachery.* This skirt seemed fated for the bin.

They sat back down to awkward silence. Finally, Orrin spoke.

"You really *were* fierce up there. The protesters were near scrapping over it for you. Those guys in costumes revving up the crowd at the end, well, I sure don't envy the guards; they looked like they were anticipating trouble." He leaned back in his chair. "Where are they headed now?"

Ivy's forehead creased momentarily with worry as she glanced toward the waiting buses. Streams of students were piling on, encouraged by the continuing war-cries of the orange shirts.

"The city," she said. "There's a multi-national corporation in Flinders Street that supplies palm oil to some of the big food manufacturers. The protesters have a petition to deliver. 'Make it sustainable or don't make it at all.'" The first of the buses pulled slowly from the curb. "Don't worry; I doubt there'll be any trouble. Liam's our head campaigner on the ground - he's enthusiastic for sure, but he can control the crowd."

"Enthusiastic? Bit of an understatement for that boyo." Orrin's framed eyes flicked to the buses, then back to Ivy's face as she watched them leave the turning circle one by one. Liam's mop of hair bobbed up and down as he herded more bystanders onto the buses, convincing them to skip class. Ivy grinned, familiar with his tactics. A campus party had undoubtedly been promised.

Orrin cleared his throat hesitantly. "Am I keeping you? I mean, shouldn't you be with them?"

"No. I've got a tutorial later and I'd hate to leave the newbies without their homework." Ivy flashed him a smile. "Anyway they don't need me, I just lay out the facts, and Liam leads the action. Yin and yang, you know? We're a good team." Her mind drifted back to the pulsing crowd, the claustrophobia, *that terrifying voice.* Falling. She felt the heat in her cheeks at that last memory. "I'm not much of a people person to be honest," she admitted quietly.

"The crowd loved you," Orrin said. "Liam seems pretty - uh, *enthusiastic* too. Are you...? I mean, are you and Liam... together?" Orrin seemed unable or unwilling to look at her. He ran a hand through his hair. "Sorry, none of my business...." He laughed nervously.

Ivy paused. "Um, no. *No*, not at all. Just friends, colleagues." She caught a flash of relief on Orrin's face before he masked it. "God no," she smiled. "I mean, Liam's one of my closest friends, but nothing more. He's practically got a conveyer belt of interested women at all times. All far more stunning than me and fresh out of high school." She raised an eyebrow. "They usually last about two weeks."

"Fair play," laughed Orrin, visibly relaxing. "Although, I doubt they could be more stunning than you, age regardless." He winked at her. Actually *winked*. Ivy snorted with laughter and hid behind her coffee cup.

"So anyway," she frantically searched for a subject change. "What brings Orrin James to Melbourne Uni, really? Not enough academic notoriety where you were?" This time it was Orrin that looked discomfited.

"Too much actually." He leant forward conspiratorially. "You know what I'm working on - how important it could be." Ivy nodded. "I just – I couldn't afford to have the academic board breathing down my neck as their 'up-and-coming promotional resource'. Their words obviously, not mine. I'm not a damn *resource*. I had to get out. To be honest I needed much better equipment and a wider berth anyway. No one's watching me here. At least not as closely."

They chatted intently for the next hour, oblivious to the people slowly drifting away from the refectory, heading back to lectures and work. Ivy explained the finer points of her research to Orrin, and was surprised to find he followed with rapt interest. Usually, she received vague, glassy smiles.

Orrin leaned closer. "So what of this 'usewear analysis' then? I mean, if you find blood on these stone tools you're working on, what can you actually do with it?"

"You mean, what *can't* we do with it?!" She leaned in. "The tiniest amount of residual blood blows our window into prehistory wide open. It's like… having a camera in the kitchen of a cave man - or on the end of a spear. What animals did they butcher? How did they cook their food? Hunt? Make clothing? I can literally recreate the daily lives of humans that have been extinct for thousands of years. I use everything I can find - blood cells, plant fibres, feathers, hell, I can even tell you what poisons they used to tip their arrows." Ivy's face was like a beacon of light, her green eyes sparkling. "Didn't you ever see Jurassic Park?"

"For sure. But I thought that DNA stuff was a hypothetical? Can you really get dino DNA, then?"

"Well, not quite," Ivy admitted. "Sixty-five million years is still a little beyond our reach for DNA repair. *For now*. But we're getting closer every day. You see, ancient DNA degrades the longer it spends in the environment. It fragments; breaks down into shorter sections like a microscopic jigsaw puzzle with missing pieces and jumbled parts. *But* we have managed to get DNA fragments of other prehistoric animals, not quite as old." Ivy leant forward, not even aware she had grabbed his hand on the table as she was speaking. "Woolly mammoths, cave bears, reindeer, musk ox…. We've also got genetic material from nineteen plants in Siberian ice cores that are over four hundred thousand years old!"

"That right?" Orrin was beaming.

"Yes! Just imagine - the earth was so different back then. Humans were still evolving, *Homo erectus* were walking the earth, and who knows who else? It's incredible stuff. Did you know that we've already mapped the genetic code for Neanderthals? My hope is that one day; we can use DNA to set our phylogenetic family tree in stone."

Ivy leaned back in her chair, her cheeks suddenly pink as she dragged her hand back with her. *Oh my god, did I do that?* She laughed nervously.

Slowly and deliberately, Orrin leaned forward, taking her hand again in both of his. They felt strong and warm.

"And?" he prompted. "What about your Flores blood, any

chance of resurrecting the little lads?" He let her hand go gently and sat back, shuffling his empty coffee cup instead.

Ivy felt suddenly lost. "Um. Flores? No - no such luck. *Yet*. The bones are pretty recent, maybe 60,000 years old, but they've been under some pretty rough chemical and environmental decomposition. They were like mashed potatoes during excavation apparently - it was a difficult process. The DNA breaks down under those conditions. But the stone tool residues were younger, so - maybe? That's what I'm here for. That's what I do."

When Orrin's questions finally drew closer to her personal life, Ivy stumbled on her answers self-consciously.

"So what's the craic for Ivy Carter, then? Outside of the little dead people, I mean."

"Work *is* fun. Did you miss the memo?"

"Apparantly so. All work, hey? So, no boyfriend hidden 'round the corner then? Waiting to knock me down for spilling my coffee all over you?"

"I could have done that myself," she smiled. "Still might."

Orrin laughed. "I don't doubt it. But seriously, put me out of my misery here-"

"It's been a long time for me," Ivy relented. "The longest. I'm not even sure if I have it in me anymore." She rubbed the coffee stain on the plastic table with a serviette. "I don't get close to people, if I can help it. The people I love always seem to..." *die...* "leave."

"That sounds like a story, right there."

"It's really not," Ivy deflected. "There's nothing much more to it. I'm quite boring actually."

"I sincerely doubt that," Orrin said quietly, eyebrows raised in amusement. "Help me out here Ivy. I know there's something you're not telling me. I just can't figure it out."

"Maybe there's nothing to figure?" Ivy smirked, looking away. But the smile didn't reach her eyes.

Orrin leaned forward in the plastic chair, his brow furrowed.

"Okay, here's what I've got so far," he said quietly. "You clearly don't trust anybody, but I get the feeling you'd throw yourself on a grenade for that bonobo, and vise versa, so you must trust her. You've got a head full of your own secrets, but you're digging skeletons out of prehistoric closets for a living and exposing them instead. You don't seem to like attention, but when the spotlight's on, you can incite revolution from a picnic crowd." He pushed on. "Any more contradictions I should know about?" Orrin smirked conspiratorially.

Ivy's shoulders stiffened. She swallowed hard. This man was dangerous. He wasn't just breaking through the wall she had so carefully built. He was smashing it down.

She laughed humourlessly. "I don't know Orrin; you tell me?" She tucked her fringe behind her ear and allowed herself a moment to stare right back at him. "Are you such an open book?" *Two can play at this game.*

He swallowed under her scrutiny. His jaw clenched slightly and his chin rose. Orrin's black framed glasses glinted in the sunlight and behind them, his eyes were amused and inviting as he considered her challenge. Ivy took the opportunity to rake her eyes over his body. Orrin's shirt was fitted across his chest, a single button open at the collar. She already knew that his hours in the university pool were working to great effect. Short, white sleeves fitted snugly around his biceps and his hand rested casually on the table, strong fingers cradling his empty coffee cup. Once more, she couldn't help but imagine those fingers finding her birthmark. And other places. Ivy bit her lip to keep from grinning as she brought her attention back to his face; she was surprised to see Orrin actually seemed impressed by her bold assessment.

He leant forward, lowering his voice to a hoarse whisper. "Oh, that's right. This last contradiction messes with my head the most." Orrin paused, arresting her eyes with his own. "You deflect me constantly, but I can't stop thinking about you."

Ivy's face burned as she looked away, inordinately pleased.

"I think you seriously underestimate yourself, Ivy Carter," he said. "You're captivating."

Oh God. Ivy had never considered herself one of those women that fawned over an accent before, but in this case, she couldn't deny that it made her toes curl.

"Yes, well, when you put it that way…" She shook her head at him, laughing at her own defeat. She needed to change the subject. "You're a long way from home, Dr James. Ireland must miss you. I'm guessing you moved to Australia alone then?" She drained the last of her cold coffee in an attempt to hide her grin.

She expected Orrin to roll his eyes at her perfectly executed deflection, but instead they dimmed.

"Actually, I did. I got divorced a few years ago." He tried to make his voice light, but Ivy detected an air of regret.

"What happened?"

"The usual, I guess." The sudden shift in Orrin's mood made Ivy regret her stupid mouth. "My ex-wife is a doctor in Dublin. Medical one, that is. We met at college not long after I moved there; she was a few years ahead of me. She had lots of night work as an intern, long shifts, and I was totally absorbed in my studies at the time. The first few years were fine, we drifted along fairly happily. Young love and all that. Didn't even notice that we were growing apart. Well, I didn't anyway." He laughed ironically. "It seems she'd had distractions other than work keeping her busy for quite a while. Another doctor – a cute hoor that one I tell you," Orrin said bitterly. "So in the end, she got the gaff and the dog, and I got the rest of it." His voice had lost its humour altogether. "I think I'd rather have kept the dog." The regret in Orrin's eyes was now unmistakable. He looked away.

"You have a dog?" For some reason, it was the only thing that stuck in her mind.

"*Had* a dog," Orrin corrected. "I left it all behind. I ran, Ivy." He stared across the cafeteria grounds, lost in thought for a few minutes before he spoke again. "It was just too hard you know. Seeing what I lost everyday. She stayed in our house. The langer moved in too. *Bastard.*" Orrin took a deep breath. "So I left. Started again. Most of my family are still home in Cork. But one of my sisters moved here about ten years back and married an Aussie. I just thought, 'Why not?' So I came over, finished my doctorate and got into research." He seemed to be talking more to himself than Ivy now, as he watched people pass back and forth through the refectory doors. His jaw clenched with some distant memory as a cloud passed overhead. "It might surprise you to learn that I don't trust easily either."

"I'm sorry," Ivy offered quietly, her face a mess of humility. "I didn't mean to pry, really. It's none of my business." She cursed herself again, watching his distant eyes.

Orrin glanced back at her. He shook his head as if escaping some internal darkness and seemed to pull himself together. He looked away briefly to take a deep breath then leaned forward across the table capturing her eyes with a beguiling smile. He reached out, grabbing Ivy's hand and wrapping it up in his own.

"Sure you do Ivy; it's totally your business." His eyes danced once more across her blushed face, unruly hair and coffee-stained skirt. "The thing is… I want you to have dinner with me this Saturday, and it's not going to work if you're worried about saying the wrong thing. I'll tell you anything you want to know. I'll even try not to spill coffee on you. So what do you say?"

Ivy bit her bottom lip and tried to look nonchalant for a moment. She failed. Despite the conflict in her heart, her shining eyes agreed before her lips did.

Back at the lab and buzzing with anticipation and coffee, Ivy tried to settle back into her routine of microscopes and research.

It didn't work very well. Her effusion of energy was soon put to good use in the first year linguistics tutorial, however. Blank looks and a distinct aversion to discussing the week's course material, told Ivy that old Harold had lost his students within the first five minutes. With a sigh, she started at the beginning.

A mountain of articles lay waiting for her after lunch and Ivy retreated to her small office. Jarring open the timber window frame with a book, the musty air was slowly replaced by a chilling afternoon breeze as she picked her way through notes with a highlighter. She distantly heard doors and windows being locked throughout the building. Other staff were escaping to their warm houses, families and lives. Ivy's life existed almost entirely in this small room, so there she stayed as it grew slowly darker outside her window and the full moon crept up.

What seemed like hours later, Ivy's frigid and tired body finally sunk into a hot bath. Steam fogged the wall mirror and the heavy scent of vanilla bath oil hung in the air. As she dozed, Ivy's mind was finally free to consider her encounter that morning with Orrin. Closing her eyes again and grinning, she sunk under the steaming water and disappeared beneath the bubbles, emerging a moment later and resting her head. She picked up her tired journal and pen from the old wooden clothes stand set next to the bath. Ivy propped it on her wet, bent knees and began to write.

Stepping out of the bath an hour later, she wrapped an over-sized towel around her body and dried her hair with another. As she pulled her pyjamas on, Ivy's fingers brushed over the large strawberry birthmark high on her left leg. As a child she'd despised having such a prominent blemish. Now it was just *her*. Through the fogged mirror glass, Ivy's green eyes sparkled as she imagined Orrin tracing that mark with his rough fingers. Shaking her head, she padded out to the lounge room in dressing gown and slippers.

Faced with another long night of reading, Ivy curled up on

the couch with a blanket and stack of papers. Orrin's face stubbornly flicked in and out of her thoughts. Ivy squeezed her eyes closed, trying to clear her mind. Within ten minutes, she was asleep on the couch, a journal article across her smiling face and the rest fallen to the floor.

CHAPTER 12

IVY

The stench of stale cigar smoke assaulted Ivy as she unlocked and pushed through Professor Chuck Ellery's office door. The carved nameplate *'the dungeon'* smacked the dark wooden door as she entered, echoing up the empty staircase behind her. The somewhat eccentric archaeologist preferred to hide down here between lectures to deter the onslaught of student inquiries and administration requests, smoking thick cigars and defying as many school regulations as possible. Chuck was a colourful, round Canadian with a neat beard and silver ponytail. He was perpetually busy, overloaded with students to assist, papers to mark, curriculum to write and a lavish professional interest in digs throughout South America. As such, Ivy rarely saw him, and even less got any assistance from him, but she never asked for any. This fact alone made Ivy his favourite, albeit entirely neglected, research student.

Although not strictly a dungeon - the rusty louvres at the top of the walls looked out into the shrubby gardens above - the large room looked dark and imposing. A cluttering of book shelves and bizarre artefacts filled every space. Ivy ritually took it upon herself to entice a bit of sunlight and fresh air into the room whenever she dropped by; more so for the feeble scattering of pot plants than for Chuck himself. Leaving a scribbled note and a stack of marked undergraduate papers on his desk, Ivy let herself out again.

The contrasting brightness of the green courtyard above was delicious. Ivy filled her lungs with crisp air. A fluttering lightness played within her as she wandered toward the Biology building. Although she still had a stack of work on her desk and an as yet, untouched, second box of artefacts from the Flores dig; it felt entirely criminal to be inside on such a beautiful afternoon. Being a Friday, with no classes to teach and only her faltering conscience to push her, Ivy figured a few hours of freedom with Kyah was in order. *I'll be working all weekend anyway. Except Saturday night...* Her mind wandered and refused to return. As Ivy rounded the great jacarandas with their fallen carpet of purple, grinning at her own disreputable thoughts, she smacked straight into someone.

Orrin stumbled, caught off guard and smiling broadly as he stuffed earphones into his jeans. Ivy could hear soft classical music finishing.

"Is that-?" She dismissed the thought. *Of course it wasn't.*

"I was hoping I'd run into you today," Orrin said, "Not literally maybe, but I'll take what I can get." His eyes were casually suggestive and Ivy blushed under the weight of them. "Actually, I'm lying," he said. "I saw you coming so I waited for you. Trying to fill my quota." He grinned.

Ivy ducked her head, laughing. "Catching me by surprise, right?"

"It's a full time job." Orrin's words teased, but there was a flicker of uncertainty in his eyes. "I actually wanted to confirm our date tomorrow night. You're not going to stand me up, are you?"

"Of course I'm coming. I said I would." Her fingers curled her long fringe behind her ear. "I'm looking forward to it, actually." *A little too much.*

"Brilliant. I couldn't decide where to go, so I thought… what about dinner at my place? It's not far from here - spectacular views of Port Phillip Bay. What do you say?" Before Ivy could answer, he added, "I'm deadly in the kitchen, well, I tell myself I am anyway." His eyes searched hers intently for an answer. Orrin shifted slightly, and Ivy became critically conscious of just how close he was standing. "No expectations, just pasta," he said, adding quietly, "Trust me." There it was again. *Trust.* Why did they always want the one thing she found so hard to give?

Orrin's breath touched her face. Ivy's chest felt tight. Her mind raced forward to the unspoken opportunities afterward, brushing heat underneath her pale skin.

"Your place… sounds great," she mumbled, barely breathing. "Dinner…"

Orrin held out a folded piece of paper. "My address, then."

She nodded, pushing it into her pocket with an odd frown. "Um… I'm vegan." Her chin rose and her arms crossed subconsciously in front of her waist. She fell back a step. Orrin grabbed her hand and pulled her gently forward again, deftly closing the space between them.

"That's okay," Orrin whispered with an amused smile. "I'm an Irish Catholic."

His eyes swept her face, suddenly losing humour for intent. Orrin's hand reached up at the same time as her own, hesitated and then pushed Ivy's aside. He swept the runaway section of hair from her face, tucking it behind her ear. His fingers lingered against her skin. Ivy's heart hammered in her chest as the outside world fell silent.

"So, my place then?" he breathed.

"Your place."

"Brilliant." With critical intention, Orrin trailed his fingers around the back of her neck. His touch burned the skin it traced and Ivy suppressed a shiver. The air between them felt heavy. The smell of eucalyptus drugged her senses. Orrin pulled her minutely closer. She could feel him there, behind the layers of clothing that suddenly seemed too much and too heavy. His neck, his chest, those arms. Under the veil of her own clothes, every nerve ending ached. The burn that danced under his fingers turned inward, rushing from her nape to her chest, then pooling deep within her. Orrin's eyes swept across her face, then down to her lips. Gravity tipped, drawing her in.

For an infinitesimal moment, Ivy felt as if she had nothing to lose. She leant forward, sealing Orrin's lips with her own.

His mouth tasted of coffee and spearmint. She felt his fingers across her jaw as he angled his head to the side, groaning softly. *Nothing to lose.* Draping one arm around his neck, Ivy pushed him very lightly with the other so that his back hit the tree behind. Her hand was flat on his chest. She could feel the firm line of muscle under his shirt, and beneath that, the steady, quick beat of his heart. She was enveloped in the scents of oak moss and fir. Ivy deepened the kiss, parting her lips and felt the soft intrusion of his tongue. She felt a hand glide up her side and grip tightly on her waist. *Nothing to lose. Everything to lose.* For the first time in what seemed like forever, Ivy began to lose herself.

"Ivy!" A loud voice called out from the other side of the courtyard, crashing the silence with a confusion of footsteps, talking and background noise. Ivy was suddenly aware of the busy footpath behind her and the chatting students across the grassy expanse. She looked over to see Liam standing on the far edge of the court with a handful of yesterday's orange shirted ambassadors. He beckoned her to join them.

Orrin pulled away, licking his lips. He ran his fingers through his hair, looking stung.

"Apparently you're in high demand."

"Apparently..." Ivy murmured, shooting Liam a scathing look. She offered Orrin an apologetic smile. "I'm so sorry. I'll definitely murder him later though. When there are fewer witnesses." She ducked her head, stepping back carefully. "I'd better go."

"Of course. Do me a favour though. Come by the Physics lab when you're done? I'd love to show you around."

"Actually, I can't," Ivy said regrettably. "I'm on my way to see Kyah. She depends on our time together, it's the only freedom she has." Ivy hesitated, chewing on her bottom lip and waving dismissively to Liam across the expanse. Her fringe escaped and Ivy longed for Orrin to touch her again, but the moment was too far gone.

Orrin shrugged. "Bring her then. I won't scare her with any equipment, she'll be entirely safe - scout's honour."

"Thought you weren't a scout?"

"Minor detail."

"I don't know Orrin, she's easily scared. I think it's best if I don't. Laboratories aren't great…"

"Trust me Ivy; it's not what you think," Orrin said. "No formalin smell, no cages. Just a room with computers. I'm setting up a new trial today and I would love for you to see. Come on; indulge me, one more time." The final thread of Ivy's resolve broke at the persuasion burning in his eyes.

"Why do I get the feeling you'll be nothing but trouble for me?"

"Maybe that's exactly what you need," he grinned.

Ivy gave in. "Okay. Later this afternoon though. At dusk. That's when I take her out - when everybody else has gone home."

"I'll be waiting."

PART II
DIVERGENCE

CHAPTER 13

ORRIN

Orrin rushed from his office into the laboratory, another man at his heels. As he pushed through the half-open doorway, a cold sweat pricked his skin. The scream that had scorched their quiet discussion was now followed by an electrifying silence. His eyes searched the room frantically. There was nothing. *Nothing.* Walls of equipment beeped quietly, methodically. The low frequency hum of computer servers was barely audible.

"What the hell was that?" Dale's voice was shaking.

"I don't know. It was here though; it was just here -" Orrin replied. "Woah! What the hell? The coil is discharging." Orrin dashed to the other end of the laboratory and quickly cut the AC supply, unconcerned by the sharp flicks of white blue electricity that crawled across the toroid reaching for his bare hand. "Dale, was someone here just now?"

The laboratory door was slightly ajar. Poking his head out into the hallway, Dale turned back, confused. "Nah, no-one there." He shrugged nervously. "Scared the shit out of me though…" He exhaled deeply and leaned against the door frame.

Orrin paced the room, his heart still racing. He drew his hand roughly over his face. Everything else looked normal, untouched.

What happened here? He replayed the last few minutes in his mind. He and Dale were completing the calibrations for their next test in his small, adjoining office. Nothing extraordinary there. Then, still etched in his mind, came that terrifying scream that had ended so abruptly.

A high pitched, torturous, animalistic scream.

Animalistic ...Kyah -

"Ivy!"

Orrin raced past Dale down the bright hallway and took the stairs two at a time. He passed the glass entrance, blinking as the setting sun suddenly split across the horizon. His gaze swept the concrete expanse. Empty and quiet.

"Shite!" He punched the door frame as he re-entered the lab. "I lost track of time. Ivy was bringing the chimp down here this afternoon. It must have freaked out when it saw the lab equipment."

He sank defeated into a chair. Orrin's eyes burned. He pushed his thumb and forefinger under his glasses in agitation. Dale stuck silent to the wall.

"She's gone, probably taken the chimp – *bonobo* - back to the Biology lab, it must have legged it on her when it saw the coil going off. I've made a bags of everything now. I shouldn't have even suggested she bring it here." Ivy's consistent reservations rung in his ears. '*She's had enough invasive tests to last a lifetime.*'

"God damn it! Why do I always push things too far?" Orrin knew that Ivy's over-protectiveness of the bonobo also extended more than a little to herself. He'd been *so close* to breaking that wall around her. Now he'd practically handed her the bricks to rebuild it and shut him back out.

"Eejit." He smacked his forehead with his fist and grabbed his mobile to dial Ivy's office extension. The refectory napkin it was written on was still folded in his wallet, her neat cursive hand-writing finished with a smiley face.

"I'm sorry, this number is not connected. Please check the number before calling again."

"Brilliant, just bloody brilliant." His heart sank. *Did she give me a wrong number deliberately? No. She must have copied it down wrong, that's all. We still have a date planned. She'll call me.* Orrin forced himself to his feet.

The screams had been *so* intense, more than scared. Spine-chilling. Agonised, even. Orrin dragged his eyes over the equipment as he stalked the room.

"That's not right," he muttered.

Glad to be reprieved of his attempt to become invisible, Dale darted across to join him.

"What?"

Skimming his fingers down the nearest computer screen, Orrin scanned the displayed stream of variables. "These calibrations," he continued, "they're all wrong." Orrin had often convinced himself that his near photographic memory was a blessing, at least with regards to his work. His relationships, of course, seemed cursed by remembering *too well*. Dwelling on past mistakes. There was a certain freedom to be gained in forgetting those details that punished the most. However, now his memory served him as he identified anomalies instantly. "And here, what's this? These aren't the calculations we set up." Orrin moved to the next screen, aggravation growing.

Dale nervously jumped into the nearest swivel chair and scooted to the keyboard. With fingers a blur, he began analysing the data. "Um, sorry Orrin, I'm not sure… just need a minute… shouldn't be… um… "

"Evening dudes, what's happening?" Phil Chan breezed through the door. He waved a pair of expensive sunglasses at them as he dumped his laptop case on the nearest desk. Tall and immaculately dressed, his carefree self-confidence was amplified by a combination of intelligence and a very wealthy family. He had the preened, adored look about him of an only son.

"Where the hell have you been all day, Phil?" Orrin's voice was uncharacteristically bent with anger. "Get yourself over here and help Dale. The systems have gone haywire. Someone's stuffed up." Phil's nonchalance faltered as he took in Dale's wide eyed reticence. He grabbed the stranded chair.

"I'll be in my office." Orrin turned and stalked away. As he neared his door a glint of silver caught his eye. He picked up a delicate chain from the floor. Ivy's necklace.

Broken.

With a sigh of regret, he shut the door behind him.

CHAPTER 14

IVY

*I*vy lay nauseated and broken; her ears still ringing with the high pitched scream that had followed her. She didn't want to move and didn't try. Perhaps she couldn't move anyway. Somewhere, her mind stayed connected. Her body, her *self*, didn't feel important anymore; it had ceased to exist to Ivy as anything but this manifestation of searing, agonising pain. Reality had become only the shredding that had torn at her bones, and the lasting heavy ache that consumed her now. She tried to surface, to claw past the pain, but the blackness suffocated and dulled her senses. Ivy struggled. A tiny part of her grappled bravely against this loss of control, desperate to make sense of the pain, sure that there was something more important to remember. Desperate to be *aware*. But there came no insight; she was not *alive* enough anymore. Her strength sapped quickly and easily and Ivy's distant mind only mumbled incoherent thoughts in offering as a wave of nausea hit her again. The pounding of blood through her ears washed away all sound. She forced open her eyes but only blackness greeted her, so she thought that perhaps she had not opened them at all. As the nothingness overwhelmed her again, Ivy sank into it willingly this time. Gratefully. Hoping the terrible ache would disappear in its embrace.

When she awoke for the second time, comfort greeted her. Black heaviness still filled her head, but there was no longer suffocation, no longer pain. This time, it was a quiet, dark place to hide. Ivy lay still with closed eyes, slowly becoming conscious of her arms, her legs and her face. She was curled on her side, with something hard under and around her. She was warm, much warmer than usual. A hand stroked her forehead gently. The soft fingers ran from her brow up into her hair, rhythmically. It had been many years since she'd felt the love and safety of such a hand. She lay contemplating this new knowledge. *Mum. I guess that means that I've died and that's why the aching has gone. I'm here, with her, and it's over.* This death didn't bother her. Memories of the shredding and its agonising, mind-numbing ache were so close by that they threatened to smother her again in fear. Death seemed like a reasonable price to pay to be free of it.

This is peaceful, I like it here. I won't be missed. Silently, Ivy felt the weight of her conviction. No one would miss her. She *had* been disappearing over the last few years, little by little. She had camouflaged herself into the backcloth of society, consumed by her research. To protect herself, she reasoned. There was no one left now to grieve her loss. No one would even know she was gone. Perhaps it was better this way, better to leave no mark on the world, and just disappear.

As a child she had been indomitable, entirely doubtless of her own impending imprint on the world. Now that life was over, Ivy wondered where that bravery had gone. What she had done to herself to let it fade.

Death was quiet.

Tantalising scents and long forgotten memories came flitting back. A shining Christmas tree with a lopsided cardboard angel, a thickly scented carpet of pine needles on glossy floorboards, over-sized gumboots full of rain, the coconut scent of her mother's thick red hair. The memories came faster, chasing each other as Ivy struggled to catch them. A flash of white teeth and the laughing eyes of a boy, a first kiss under the soft fall of snow, heartache. Memories of her father in his favourite chair, so many books, her beloved cello, blinding laboratory lights, daisies, chocolate and strongly brewed coffee, sheets of music, faces – so many faces, dark wavy hair, bright purple jacarandas towering above her, Kyah playing in their branches. *Kyah!*

Ivy sat bolt upright, her eyes bursting open as she grappled at the air around her for stability. *Kyah!* Ivy could not afford death, even such a peaceful one.

Something gritty and foul coated her lips and Ivy spat out dirt. She sucked the humid air fiercely, filling her lungs. Angular grey shapes violated her eyes and she blinked furiously, rubbing them with filthy fingers. In front of her, a familiar black face came slowly into focus, hand extended. Soothing, guttural hoots touched Ivy's ear. She was so grateful; the sound was precious. The bonobo's warm fingers again sought Ivy's forehead and this time they were met by a shaking hand. *It was you,* thought Ivy. *It was your touch that reached me in that dark place.* A tiny shadow of renewed grief arose as she realised. *It was only you.*

"But you're alive," breathed Ivy, holding the long fingers to her cheek.

Kyah's eyebrows creased and she gave another soft hoot, clearly pleased Ivy was finally responding. Strong arms encircled Ivy and she couldn't help but smile. She pulled away, studying the bonobo. There was a gash on Kyah's forehead which had bled and dried around her eyes. Her usually immaculate hair was filthy and the scab on her chest flamed with scratch marks. But the bonobo's onyx eyes were clear and responsive and her face showed no sign of pain. The cut wasn't life-threatening, a few grazes, no broken bones. Ivy exhaled with relief.

Finally appeased, she leaned back and looked around. She

immediately wished she hadn't. Her stomach flipped with vertigo as she realised she was sitting on a stony ridge, high above anything else in sight. Her left hand slipped as she startled and Ivy found herself staring down a sharp cliff face into an almost perfectly circular lake far below. The water was dark and red as blood. A death trap if she fell.

"Where the hell are we?"

Ivy shuffled back, terrified, grabbing Kyah's hand. The bonobo watched her, concerned. She lifted a hand to point to Ivy's right side and Ivy followed her line of sight. Two more lakes. The closest was bright blue, like a perfect cloudless sky. Beyond it, a deep green expanse of water filled the second. They were dug into the top of the mountain, like twin craters of a volcano. Bile rose in Ivy's throat. Squeezing her eyes shut, she tried to push the nausea away. *It isn't. I can't be.*

Her hands gripped a layer of loose dry dirt. Disorienting ridges and mountains stretched in every direction. Her vantage point was immense. Sickening. She could see for miles. The terrifying majesty of the landscape dwarfed her. Ivy didn't recognise this place. She didn't want to. *Those lakes? Kelimutu? No, it can't be,* she willed the thought away. It was insane. And she needed her sanity.

The pinnacle of an ancient volcano, she guessed; the humidity was like a living force pressing in on her. *I would remember this,* thought Ivy. *I don't remember this.* Her heart hammered. *How the hell did I get here?*

Trees. Kyah's hand signal left no doubt which way the bonobo felt was safer.

Below them, a few hundred meters down the side of the ridge, a forest was clawing its way upward. Every possible shade of green overwhelmed it.

"You're right. We can't stay here," Ivy said, biting back tears.

Ivy pushed herself up off the ground. White sparks showered before her eyes and a searing pain shot through her right leg.

Falling back down again, she ran a filthy hand across a dark patch on the leg of her jeans. She rolled it up. A deep cut sliced Ivy's right ankle an inch long, blood bubbling at the edges and a thin layer of white visible underneath. She pinched the edges together, biting her bottom lip hard.

"Damn."

Deep breaths. Come on. Think. Scanning the surrounding earth, Ivy spied her satchel nearby. She shook the contents one-handed onto the dusty earth. A stack of papers sprayed across the ground. She shook it again and the contents of her bag flumped out in a pile. Her hairbrush. A half-empty water bottle. Purse. Head scarf. A half dozen pencils. House keys. A chocolate bar. An apple. Finally, her mobile phone and heavy beloved journal.

"Brilliant first aid kit," she sighed. Grabbing the scarf, she wound it tightly around the cut and tucked it in. It throbbed, pushing against the fabric, now dark with spreading blood.

Where was I going? Minutes ticked by as Ivy dug into her memory, trying to resist the focus her leg was demanding.

Well, wherever we are, I'll need an ambulance, or at least some help getting out. Maybe a helicopter or the SES? The necessity for help grated at her. Grabbing her phone, Ivy saw the battery icon blinking as it struggled to find a receptive tower. No bars. No reception. Ivy looked around, her heart sinking. There must be a tower somewhere – how big could this place be? The enormity of space was suffocating. There was no road in sight, no humanity. Certainly no technology. She dialled emergency, knowing it was futile but still felt a pang of disappointment when the declining beeps signalled her failure. *Idiot mobile never works when I need it.* In fact, it usually did work, but acknowledging that fact felt like inviting despair. Ivy stuffed the mobile angrily back into her bag, along with the other useless belongings and spilled papers. Kyah watched her silently. She was, as ever, close to Ivy's body, lightly touching.

Ivy rolled her jeans back down. The denim was stiff with

blood and she realised she was filthy, covered in dust and grime. She groped her own hair and neck, flinging a crawling insect into the leaves. She felt wet soil matted into her hair. *Had it rained?* Her fingers faltered against her throat. Her amulet was gone. *Oh no. Tom will be upset...* A sinking guilt settled in her stomach. She raked the ground with her fingers, but the amulet was gone, and so was the silver chain that had held it around her neck.

Where on earth am I? Ivy looked around. She'd been at Melbourne University long enough to know that even the loveliest areas were artificially designed. There was nothing this massive, this *wild* near the university. *Breathe. Try to remember.*

"I took those papers to Karl's office. Then I ran into Orrin," she said aloud. Ivy caught her breath. Warmth coiled in her chest. It had been impossible to resist that boyish grin, the suggestion and humour in his eyes. Memories came flooding back, almost overwhelming her. He had leaned in close under the jacaranda, his intentions clear. But they'd been interrupted... and then?

"We were at the Biology lab all afternoon, right?" She asked Kyah. The bonobo was watching her intently. Kyah had been with her since then, that much at least, seemed obvious.

"We walked to Orrin's laboratory."

An involuntary shiver crept down her spine. In her mind's eye Ivy saw swirling grey mist. The black nothingness drawing closer.

"It took you. It stole you from my arms. And then - I leapt after you, didn't I?" Ivy searched Kyah's eyes, looking for an explanation. "Then that *pain* - I don't remember anything after that."

It had been a desperate ache in her bones. As if she was being pulled apart, limb from limb. Ivy closed her eyes and heard the echo of a scream.

"Did *I* scream? Was it you, my darling?" Filled with worry, Ivy pulled the bonobo into her lap and studied her face once again.

"Did you feel that agony in your bones like I did? How long did you sit waiting for me? How long was I unconscious?"

Fear welled in her chest. Ivy's breath came fast and shallow. Kyah's face swam as Ivy's tears welled. *Hasn't she suffered enough.* Ivy blinked them back and took a deep breath.

"What the hell happened to us Ky?"

CHAPTER 15

IVY

Kyah shuffled quietly around Ivy, making soft noises. Ivy scrunched her eyes tight shut, ignoring Kyah's attempts to placate her. It was the bonobo's instinct; to diffuse potential violence, to dissolve tension and distress with physical affection. Bonobos were the most altruistic and peaceful of any primate on earth. In another place and time, if she had been allowed to live free with her own species, Kyah would have offered body contact to dispel another bonobo's anguish. Ivy knew this. She understood. But instead, now Kyah sat behind Ivy, dragging soft fingers through Ivy's hair attempting to groom her friend with soft grunts instead.

But Ivy didn't want to be touched or consoled. *She wanted to punch something. To scream.*

Ivy focused on breathing instead.

In. Out. In. Out.

Anything to contain the panic she felt building up inside of her. She screwed a fistful of dirt inside her hand and felt her fist spark with pain as she smashed it down against the rock.

In. Out. In. Out.

Just breathe.

With utmost self control, Ivy relaxed her fingers. Bright sparks appeared behind her eyelids, but she kept them shut tight. She couldn't stand the thought of opening them to the mountains that invaded every conceivable space around her. *Where the hell are we? Isn't it bad enough that I'm stranded here in the middle of god-knows-where with nothing but a bag full of stationery and a screwed leg, but Kyah as well! Kyah's vulnerable. I've got no food for her. No protection. I promised her no more pain. I failed.* The thought was unbearable. Had Kyah felt that bone-shredding ache? *Who would inflict that kind of pain on another person?* Ivy tore her eyes open again and glared into the blood red lake below her, willing the culprit to come forward.

"Who did this?!" Ivy's scream shattered the air. In the forest below everything went silent. She shivered. The volcanic dirt where she sat looked undisturbed - no footprints or tracks; but then again, perhaps she wouldn't recognise them if there were. Ivy studied Kyah again. The bonobo didn't *look* like she had been in pain; maybe this situation hadn't affected her in the same way. Whatever this *situation* was. *What happened to them? Some sort of freak accident?*

Pulling her cracked watch off, Ivy tossed it into the satchel. It had stopped working at five thirty in the afternoon. Ivy looked around to find the sun. *What time is it now? Daylight – just before sunset? Or have we been here all night? Is this morning again?*

It was impossible to tell. She decided she would have to move regardless. They were still perched on the precipice of a mountaintop. Completely exposed to the elements. They couldn't stay here another night. Ivy needed to find shelter for them both.

Kyah pulled gently at the clasp on Ivy's satchel. Her eyes held a familiar request.

"You're so polite." Kyah could easily have undone the clip and helped herself. Ivy tossed her the apple. While the bonobo ate, Ivy pull herself up straighter, gingerly pressing her leg. The cut was tender but manageable. The makeshift tourniquet seemed to be working.

Ivy pulled herself up and threw the battered satchel over her head and shoulder. Defiance flooded every cell.

"We need food and water, Ky," she said to her companion. "And I need to know where we are." There seemed to be no obvious path but the one in front of her. The volcanic rift was folded against itself into a concertina of rocky ravines, all leading straight down into the jungle below. White flecks danced again before her eyes as Ivy tried to step forward. Kyah appeared beside her as she came close to the edge. "I'm going to have to slide down this on my backside. There's no way my ankle will manage on such uneven ground." She looked at Kyah enviously. "Times like this I wish I could knuckle walk." Kyah was already making her way down a fault line toward the treeline below. Ivy took a deep breath, sat down on the edge of the ravine and gritted her teeth. "Here I go."

As soon as she hit the trees, Ivy pulled herself back onto her feet, using their branches for support. She limped forward. Her jeans had taken a beating. Ivy flattened herself against the tree, and stretched as far up as she could. Her fingertips dragged back a strong, straight branch and she gripped and hung off it until it snapped under her weight. She quickly stripped it of twigs and leaves. With some weight off her ankle, they could travel faster.

"I think we should find a cave or something in case we need to spend the night," she said to Kyah, leaning on her stick to test its strength. "Maybe there's a village in the distance or a road to follow. Then I could find a phone. Any plan of action is better than nothing, right?"

Kyah was already on her feet again, ready to move.

"Okay Ky, I guess we're exploring." Ivy plunged into the undergrowth, walking stick first with her friend close behind.

It was Ivy who impeded their progress, ducking, scrambling and crawling gracelessly through the increasingly thick tangle. Her leg throbbed with pain, but she was pleased to find she was reasonably fit from years of jogging in the quiet streets near her apartment. It had become a routine. A safe, solitary choice of exercise.

In comparison, Kyah travelled gracefully. Ivy marvelled at the efficiency of her perfect balance and wished for just a moment she was even half as coordinated. Kyah leapt from one vine to the next with her long fingers and toes curled tightly, swinging and releasing just over an arms length away to grip again and propel herself forward. Sinuous muscles twisted mid flight to alight horizontal branches on all fours. With her knuckles slightly curled to support her own weight, Kyah navigated the branches like a tightrope walker. Her shrewd and curious eyes missed nothing.

Ivy watched her as she walked, oscillating between delight to see her friend so uninhibited and anxious that Kyah might become lost in the trees. If Kyah chose to explore, Ivy knew she had no hope of finding her again. Thankfully, she showed no interest in leaving Ivy behind. The bonobo called back playfully in high-pitched bursts as she kept pace with Ivy's sluggish progress. As the hours passed, darkness never came. *So I did spend last night on the edge of that mountain,* Ivy realised.

The forest was loud. Insects buzzed raucously and birds screeched. Ivy imagined hidden predators she had no hope of escaping. Fear threatened to overwhelm her. *Just deal with it,* she willed herself. *Find a way out.*

There was a shuffle at her feet. As she looked down, the bushes burst apart. A streak of light fur tumbled across her shoes. Ivy panicked, stumbled. She lost her balance and hit the ground hard. In the branches above, Kyah suddenly began screeching and pacing with fright.

"Shh, it's okay, Ky," Ivy shushed, waving her arm. "It's just a possum - or" *No.* She knelt forward, trying to get a closer look. The displaced ball of fur at her feet was dead still, with only its little chest heaving air to give it away. It seemed to be hurt and instinctively decided that playing dead was the best option for survival. Blood was smeared on its face and a hind leg was skewed oddly to the side.

"I think it's a rat," Ivy muttered. "But it's the biggest rat I've ever seen. I wonder if I can help it?"

As the words left her mouth, a shadow fell across Ivy. She looked up.

Oh. My. God. Her mouth fell open. But Ivy was too terrified to scream.

An enormous bird loomed over her, at least six feet high. With a slow predatory stare, it stepped toward Ivy on a long slender leg with webbed short toes and blunt claws. Still hunched on the ground, Ivy knew that even if she were standing, this bird would be far taller than her at full height. Its massive body was feathered in dirty white plumage and black coverts covered its wings. The bird crooked its neck toward her and lowered a bald, scabby head down, turning it sideways to stare at her with an unblinking eye. She froze. It's long, sharp beak suddenly clattered together in warning.

Ivy shrank back, horrified and mesmerised by its potential power. She didn't dare make a noise. She could barely breathe. A macabre parody of an enormous stork delivering a sweetly bundled baby to waiting parents-to-be, came unbidden to Ivy's mind. The size of this delivery stork fit the nursery rhyme. But this bird was more likely to eat an infant dangling from its beak. As if to amplify this terror, the stork suddenly snapped at Ivy's face. She scrambled backwards in the undergrowth, trying desperately to put distance between them.

It turned it's beady eye on the giant rat instead then tore at the shivering fur with a twist of its beak. The rat split open. The stork's beak thrust into its body cavity, tearing out flesh and gulping it. It collected the ragged remains of fur and threw it into the air, then swallowed them down a long, gangling neck. A strange sac of skin and air wobbled from its throat as it swallowed and the bird stretched its wings out for balance. They unfurled in great arcs, no less than eight feet across.

Ivy was still scrambling back. She pressed herself against the base of a tree as she stared at it.

"I know you," Ivy breathed. A crawl of icy fear crept under her sweat. She'd seen this animal before. In books. The bird's bald head was marked with ugly black spots of skin, now speckled with fresh blood. *No. It's impossible. You can't be.* The enormous stork ruffled its feathers, meal finished. With a clatter of its beak, it turned and strode back into the forest. Ivy clutched the tree trunk, her legs too weak to stand. *You're extinct.*

As she travelled up what seemed like the third mountain in her path, Ivy wondered if she would manage to find a clear vantage point this time to check her progress, though she had no idea where she was heading. The last two ascents had been too tree covered, even at the top, to glimpse the landscape clearly and the trees were ancient, massive and far too difficult to climb. Her stick sank into damp, decomposing leaves with every step and her lame foot dragged. Ivy knew she was leaving a trail through the undergrowth but didn't care.

I should leave more markers, she thought, scratching another large X into a tree trunk as she passed, *that way if anyone comes looking for me, at least they'll be able to follow it.* But there was no welcome sound of helicopters or sirens to give her hope that a search party was on its way. Disorienting greenery stretched in every direction. The forest dwarfed her. Far above, a weak sun broke through tiny holes in a dense canopy, shooting down dazzling pinpricks of light amidst a dank and shadowed ground cover. She was heading west, she thought, but couldn't be sure until she reached a bare peak and was able to see the sun properly again.

The humidity drenched Ivy's face and t-shirt. Her jacket and long-sleeved shirt were now a burden around her waist snagging vegetation as she travelled steadily upwards. Strong, pungent odours of fermenting fruit wove in and out of the thick air, sometimes sickening, other times appetising. Her stomach growled. She and Kyah shared the water bottle until it ran dry.

Her ankle began throbbing. Blood had soaked through the scarf now. Ivy pulled it tighter, cursing loudly and sending a handful of startled birds into the canopy.

"I need a break, Ky," she called. Ivy collapsed onto a fallen trunk covered in vines. "Crikey. Look at this thing." Kyah dropped down beside her, keen to investigate where Ivy was pointing.

Beside the tree trunk was a magnificent red flower that bloomed a meter across. Kyah reached out to touch it. "Wait." Ivy intercepted her hand. "It could be dangerous." A growing uneasiness settled in Ivy's chest as she tried to recognise it. Botany had become something of a niche skill for her, as plants usually ended up as food on the stone tools she analysed. Her reference library of drawings and descriptions numbered in the hundreds.

No. It can't possibly be... Ivy thought. Fleshy petals were curled back, each as big as dinner plates, boasting white decorative boils on their surface. The centre of the flower was enormous, like a bowl of spikes. It was incredible. *No. Definitely not. It can't be Rafflesia.* Ivy wrestled with the improbability. "Not in Australia. Wrong continent. They don't grow here." The back of her neck prickled. "Maybe it's been planted deliberately. An introduced species." She looked around. The jungle was far too expansive to be a private botanical garden. "An accident, then," she said to Kyah. "Or I'm wrong and it's something else. I can't know every plant in the world, can I?"

Kyah just raised her eyebrow then grinned. She leaned forward to poke the curious flower again. This time, Ivy leaned closer as well. She was so tempted to touch its squishy petal. It was the most bizarre plant she'd ever seen.

As she drew close, a stench like rotting flesh assaulted her nose. A haze of flies lifted from the spikes in the middle of it. They swarmed around Ivy's head, disturbed from their feeding.

"Holy hell!"

Ivy scrambled away, choking and dry-retching. Kyah coughed and snorted as she too, got a lungful of its foul perfume. The flower smelled rancid. They both spun, swatting around their faces, trying to breathe humid air without inhaling the flies that had suddenly filled it.

Grabbing her walking stick, Ivy laughed through her gasping as they both took off. It was a few minutes before the stench had left their lungs and the flies were left behind. They both slowed to catch their breath.

"Well, I think we learnt our lesson," Ivy grinned, wiping her eyes. "Don't touch *anything*." Kyah dragged her hand over tongue, apparently trying to remove a caught fly.

Hours later, nothing but pure exaltation swept her as Ivy finally found herself on the edge of a rocky outcrop with a faint breeze on her face.

She'd found a lookout. A *way* out.

CHAPTER 16

NEIL

D r Neil Crawford woke. A shaft of high noon sun broke through the leaves above him and pierced the forest, streaming his eyes. He lay between buttressing roots in a damp, earthy alcove on a steep slope. Mulch and broken branches covered his suit. He was completely hidden from view with the exception of the bright blue logo embroidered on his suit pocket –a sphere encircling a silhouette of the Australian continent, sliced by seven parallel pinstripes. *CSIRO.*

Reeling, Neil struggled to sit, but the twisting motion churned his insides and brought a wave of nausea. He emptied his stomach into the leaves around him and dove, dizzyingly back into unconsciousness.

Pain sought him out hours later. His shoulder burned and his left arm hung sickeningly low and limp by his side. In the now dim undergrowth, Neil shuffled up and back against rough bark. He struggled to place himself. Slowly, the pieces fell together in his memory.

"Now listen to me Chancellor, this is entirely unacceptable. One of your researchers is up to something. I need to know what the hell is going on here! "

An elegant glass office swam into view. Seated behind a chrome plated desk, a woman eyed him over reading glasses. The name Chancellor Reshma Thandi was engraved on a marble nameplate which sat neatly to one side. Her peppered hair was swept back and she was poised and calm in the face of Neil's increasing aggravation.

"I'm sorry Dr Crawford, but as I've said, all research conducted within our facilities are undertaken with the utmost care. All experimental practices are outlined clearly in comprehensive proposals by staff and students before they're undertaken. If there were any untoward activities, they would have been picked up immediately by the review board upon application." Her strange international accent, a bastardization of American, Australian and Indian pronunciation, grated on Neil's nerves.

"Well maybe your review board aren't tracking this one, Chancellor," Neil said. She raised an eyebrow at his insinuation of incompetence. Neil continued, "Surely you don't need me to remind you that a large number of your research students are funded by our scholarship opportunities..."

She leant forward, entirely unaffected. "And of course, you are most welcome to contact those students directly and review their research at your leisure, as per the scholarship guidelines," she said. "Regarding all other research within the Physics department, however, you have no authority or jurisdiction to request anything of me. Regardless of legalities, gathering this scope of information would require at least a week. Many of our senior staff are currently offsite visiting collaborative institutions."

"No, it's someone here. They are conducting their experiments here, now," Neil pushed her.

"Well, even if that is the case Doctor, I would still need a minimum of forty-eight hours to get even basic reports on what experimentation is currently underway within each office," she said. *"This is a very large department Dr Crawford; we occupy three separate facilities as well as a number of interfaculty areas. And with such little information from yourself... 'Experimental research involving energy field manipulation' – well, that describes a good third of our department. I'd like to help you, Doctor, really I would. I certainly wouldn't condone undisclosed research within my department..."* She smiled with closed lips. *"However, I'd need much more information to narrow the field of inquiry. If this is one of your scholarship projects, perhaps we can come to some sort of arrangement regarding intellectual property and media coverage?"*

Neil Crawford seethed. Antagonistic bitch. Even if you don't know what's going on here, you'd lay claim to it the instant it was worth something to you.

Neil's finger stabbed her glass desktop. "Begin your enquiries Chancellor, you will be hearing from me. I'll show myself out."

The elevator bell chimed softly and he stepped out. Neil surveyed the empty ground floor of the Physics headquarters.

Someone in this department is manipulating that lunar energy pulse. They're playing with fire. *His eyes narrowed.* My fire. I need to shut them down and use their data. If I could find out how they're controlling these field bursts - how to store them and direct them - it's unlimited energy. This is bigger than me; this should be a god-damn national resource.

The glass doors stood closed and silent, reflecting shards of light from the water fountain outside. Students chatted as they passed by, content in triviality.

It's time to make my own enquiries, *Neil decided.*

He slipped into the first empty room, finding nothing of interest. Quickly, Neil stole his way up the corridor, letting himself into any room he found vacant and searching the equipment for anything suspicious. When he'd exhausted his search on the ground floor, Neil took the fire stairs to Level One and kept going.

Laboratory 1-79. He let himself in. The silver door handle clicked softly behind him. Once again, Neil was faced with the sterile white walls of a laboratory. But this time, they were plastered with high resolution screens. Patterns flickered on them enticingly. Suspicious; that's a bloody understatement, *he thought.* Energy measurements, wavelength frequency, sound and light monitors - something isn't right here. Even the effing plants are hooked up. *Neil crossed the room silently.*

Behind a closed door on the back wall, he could hear quiet conversation. In the furthest corner, an impressive arrangement of spectrographic equipment was set up. A tesla coil took centre stage. Neil could tell that it was highly powered enough to provide a significant pulse of ionized voltage within the room. A lightning laboratory. Neil was only slightly surprised by its presence in the lab. He scanned the room again. A Faraday cage made of conductive mesh screening was against the back wall near the servers, just large enough to protect one or two men inside from the electrostatic charges released from the Tesla coil. But why protect the men, and not the equipment? *Intrigued, Neil looked closer.* Bizarre. *A silver trolley of labelled samples stood nearby. Cobalt. Iron. Nickel. Magnetic elements. The whir of server fans smothered his clicks on a keyboard nearest to him. Huge screens betrayed his prying fingers as he ran a search of the computer's data log.* What are they up to? *He reached into his pocket, searching for the usb cable he always carried.* If I can just steal another minute to download the data into my phone...

Suddenly, Neil heard the main door handle twist. Someone was coming in. There was no time to hide. Neil threw his shoulders back, preparing to greet the newcomer with his usual serve of intimidation.

A woman walked in. Long red hair. His scowl froze. Is she carrying a monkey? A fucking big one. *Its long, black fingers were gripping the dark cardigan she wore, pulling it down from her neck. Neil saw a flash of black stone against the white skin on her throat, before it pulsed electric blue like a neon light, stunning his eyes. There was lightning all around. Then the room drained of colour.*

The walls caved in around him. Screams followed him as he collapsed. He was falling.

And then there was nothing but pain.

The memory of that shredding pain, combined with the agony Neil now felt in his arm and chest were enough to send him again into a fit of nausea. He scowled at the infusion of green that surrounded him. The air was solid and oppressing.

"Where the hell am I?" Birds startled above at his sudden noise.

Huge trees surrounded him in all directions and dusk seemed to be falling fast. He leaned back against the tree trunk cradling his loose arm. Sweat glistened in his pores. With an almighty wrench, he pulled his dislocated arm out from his body, twisting and lifting it back into its socket. Neil grunted and cursed with agony and effort, then tucked it against his body. For a few minutes all he could do was breathe. Finally, he pulled himself up and staggered a short distance. There was no sign of human life.

"What the fuck?"

He searched his inner pockets. *Wallet, lighter, half a packet of cigarettes, mobile* – the screen was cracked across the top. *Shit.* Full battery but no reception. In the trees behind him a bird shrieked. Neil ducked, instinctively evading a potential threat. *Stupid bloody bird.* He straightened up.

"Where am I? What the hell is this place?"

Nowhere I've been before.

His survival instincts ran deep. Neil eyed the canopy, too high to climb with his damaged shoulder. But only meters uphill, it thinned into open air. Neil pushed his way through and found himself at the base of a precipice. He was on a mountain, nearly at the top.

Where the hell am I? I need a bird's eye view.

Carefully, he picked his way up the remaining twenty feet of rock to reach the top of the precipice. It was bare and dusty, a few meters of flat rock that lipped three enormous crater lakes.

Holy crap. I'm standing on top of a volcano.

The edge of the precipice fell away in all directions, sloping down in great rocky folds that were thickly forested from their shoulders down. *An extinct volcano, then.* Far below, jungle covered the land as far as the eye could see. *Blue, green and red lakes.* It was an awe-inspiring sight, but Neil was in no mood to be impressed.

He scrutinized the precipice floor as he explored further. *Someone's been here.* A space had been disturbed a few meters away, the ancient dirt churned up up and strewn about. Footsteps mottled the soil. Human. Small shoe, probably a woman or a child. Heading North-East. *The redhead?* She was the last person Neil had seen before he'd collapsed and woken here. *Lost and disoriented with a bloody useless arm and a gut full of nerves. Jesus Christ. That woman with the monkey? She barely looked at me. What could she possibly have done to knock me out so fast?* The pulsing neon blue that had radiated from the black stone at her throat burnt into Neil's vision once again. He reeled, clutching his knees. The nausea hit him again and he vomited at his feet, his anger rising exponentially with his own weakness. *Bastards!* Had there been someone waiting behind him, and the redhead was merely a distraction? Had they caught him snooping on their filthy little secret in the laboratory? Thought they'd be exposed? Shut down? *Well they're damn right they'll be exposed. I'll fucking hang them out to dry!*

But if that redhead is here now, Neil considered, *why is she on her own?* Had she been a threat to them too? *Why the hell did she leave me here alone, covered in filth on the edge of a volcano?* His arm ached. He glanced down the ravine to the undergrowth he had crawled out of. There were scuffs and broken edges on the rock. *Did I do that? Did I fall down there from up here?* If he did, it would explain his dislocated shoulder. Neil wanted answers so badly it hurt. But he wanted action even more. Whatever had been going on in that lab was way below board. And then this. *This is bullshit. Did they knock me out? Do they think they killed me? Did they dump me here to hide their control over this energy field? Well, the joke's on them. I'm not dead.*

Neil followed the footsteps a small way across the precipice. On the other side of it to where he had found himself, a track of loose dirt trailed down the ridge like a smudged fingerprint, leading into the forest below. At the edge of the precipice, soft, loose dirt was pressed into the mould of a shoe print, almost half the size of his own. Definitely a woman. *The redhead then.* He sat, clutching the rock with his one good hand as he slid from the edge, following the crack of folded rock until he reached the treeline beneath it. Dusting himself off, he resumed his scan of the earth. Here, the sharp end of a fat stick shadowed the right shoe track. *And she's hurt.* With night closing fast around him, Neil had no choice but to stay put until morning.

"They obviously don't know who they're dealing with", he said through gritted teeth. He traced the shoe print with his fingers.

I'll track her. Whoever she is, one way or another, she's going to tell me what she knows.

CHAPTER 17

IVY

*I*vy's heart plummeted. She stood on the pinnacle of another great mountain ridge, running a hundred kilometres across and dropping in sharp peaks and sprawling valleys. The midday sun beat mercilessly across a landscape ahead of her, that was so wild and untouched, it screamed prehistoric. In every direction, ancient volcanic rifts jigsawed the landscape into a blur of yellow ridges, rich emerald forest and dark barren earth. Narrow rivers snaked through the jungle mass. Through the canopy below, gargantuan hardwoods broke into the sky, propelled three hundred feet into the air and supported by massive buttresses. Epiphytes clung to them like parasites - lianas, vines and strangler figs all coveting the sunlight. Below, a suffocation of greenery competed for life-giving sunlight. Elongated crowns angled their leaves to best capture the sun's rays, rotating on swollen joints to follow it greedily across the sky. Ivy knew that under the canopy more layers existed. Beneath the tree mass, there would be ferns, orchids and fungi clutching the shallow nutrient surface.

Far into the distance, the volcanic peaks jutted a mist of thick white cloud. Beyond, a blue ocean glittered in all directions. Ivy's legs gave way beneath her.

"I don't think we're in Kansas anymore, Toto," she breathed. Ivy stared ahead, unseeing. "There's no way out of here, Ky. No civilisation. No help. I don't know what to do." Kyah crawled into her lap, curling close. There were no tears. Simply disbelief. They were unequivocally, undeniably *lost*.

Earlier, in her delirium as she had regained consciousness, the thought of death had seemed a mercy; a reprieve from agonising pain. But not now. There would be no reprieve in *this* death, Ivy knew. How easily mother nature could take her; a victim to the elements and an easy target for predators. Ivy imagined the cluttering beak of the giant stork slicing her own soft belly.

Despair tumbled out of her as dry sobs into Kyah's soft hair.

"At least I have you." Immediately, Ivy hated herself for the thought. *Kyah doesn't deserve to be here, lost in some god-forsaken jungle in the middle of god-knows-where. She's as easy prey as I am.* Ivy hated the human part of her that suddenly craved comfort from the very creature she was meant to protect.

"Surely someone will notice we're gone?" She sniffed. Old Tom would notice, thoughtful and lonely as he was. But would he report her missing? Or would her belongings collect dust, as he waited in vain for Ivy to return home as he had waited for his own son so long ago?

Her tutorial students might notice, but judging their lax efforts in finding her whenever she ran late, Ivy guessed they'd simply assume she had forgotten and take the opportunity to disperse. Professor Ellery would only notice when the unmarked papers began piling up. Jayne and Liam would notice her absence, but would they do anything? Their personal lives rarely crossed the boundary of seeing them outside of the university these days. She had let her friendships flitter away as she had prioritised her research.

I pushed everyone away. I did this to myself.

Suddenly, the prospect of someone coming to save her, or even just comfort her, seemed desperately appealing. Oddly, it was the thought of Orrin that hurt the most. A loss she had barely begun to possess. Orrin had been real. His interest in *her* seemed no longer just amusing or flattering – it was vital. The memory of his fingers curling the hair away from her face drew an aching sob. Ivy brought her fingers to her lips, tracing the kiss that had been interrupted. *I pushed him away too. No one is close enough to me to realise that I'm gone.*

Ivy stared across her island prison. For a long while she sat tall, her eyes searching desperately for a plane on the horizon or a ship in the distance. Any sign of help. She tried to rouse herself into action, but with no purpose, it quickly ebbed into self-pity. It was Kyah who finally forced her hand. The bonobo was hungry. She screeched and tried to drag Ivy back into the forest by her arm. When her attempts were ignored, Kyah chose provocation instead. The bonobo slapped Ivy on the head, grinning playfully, mouth open with lips pulled down over her teeth. Then she skittled back to the tree line and began systematically flinging rocks at Ivy's hair. When a particularly sharp rock found its mark, Ivy rewarded her efforts with a scowl, then a hopeless laugh. She stood up and took Kyah's hand.

"I'm being useless aren't I," Ivy sighed. "We're here, wherever here is, and we're alive. *For now.* Let's find some food and shelter. Then we'll figure out what to do. Let's just go."

Several hours of walking proved fruitful, in the most literal sense. A tree dripping with giant spiky fruit was on their path. The bonobo knocked a few to the ground and Ivy grabbed one. It smelt almost too bad to eat.

"Ouch!" She dropped it, then rolled it over looking for a better way to hold it. "I think this is a durian. Which means it's edible." The heavy weight of the fruit forced the spikes into her hands no matter how Ivy tried to pick it up, making it impossible to open. Her stomach ached with hunger and her hands had begun shaking. Dark blotches were beginning to invade her sight and a cold, clammy feeling flooded her skin. She recognized the precursors to unconsciousness and couldn't risk letting herself go. With unknown predators lurking in the forest, Ivy guessed she might never get the chance to wake up. "Damn it! How do I open this thing?" Ivy tried to pick the fruit up once again and dropped it, this time earning herself scraped arms and bruising her good foot. "Stupid thing!" She punished the obstructive fruit with a stick. Ivy grew more furious, kicking the thing against the base of the tree in the hope it might crack open. She kicked it again, punishing her own foot further. "Aah!" Ivy fell hard on her backside, half laughing and half crying in a fit of pure frustration. "I hate you!" she yelled at it.

Kyah dropped down from the branches beside her. The bonobo looked at her in apparent amusement, all white teeth and high pitched laughing then slapped her hand gently over Ivy's forehead.

"Alright then smarty-pants, you do it!" Ivy growled.

Kyah picked up the durian easily and carried it to a nearby rock.

"Your skin is thicker," Ivy muttered under her breath as Kyah perched herself beside the rock, and began smashing the fruit against the sharpest edge.

"Why the hell didn't I think of that?" Ivy sighed. She found a sharp stone on the ground and together they dug into the tough outer skin to the spongy layer underneath. "It's like cutting a shoe," Ivy grumbled after a few minutes. Eventually the holes were big enough to scoop white, fibrous flesh from the inside. Kyah immediately sucked on the large elliptical seeds she dug out, holding them still to scrape the sides clean with sharp teeth. The fruit smelled pungent, like vomit or over-ripe paw-paw with the consistency of a custard apple. It made Ivy's eyes water. Holding her breath, she ate some, expecting the worst. Miraculously, it wasn't too bad. A questionable blur of peach, mango and coconut flavours managed to overcome the overwhelming smell. "I suppose I could live on this," Ivy said begrudgingly. After a few minutes, her hands stopped shaking and her head cleared as they quickly emptied out the multi-chambered fruit leaving an empty shell. Ivy grinned, tipping the spiky casing upside down onto Kyah's head. "Viking!" She laughed. Kyah threw it off, knocked Ivy backward with a playful grimace and ran to get another one.

After what Ivy assumed was another couple of hours, they came upon a stream. It looked clear and cool, so Ivy tested the water with a sip, then, finding it fresh, drank as much as she could without making herself sick. She refilled her water bottle and washed her face and hands. Kyah drank and cooled herself, then they set off again, in search of somewhere safe to spend the night. The hopelessness of the situation needled at her. Insects needled at her and Ivy slapped her bare arms in irritation. The fear of never being found began to fester under her skin.

"Neither of us are equipped to survive here, Ky," she said, slapping a mosquito for what seemed like the thousandth time in an hour. She looked up at her friend. "Though you're doing a lot better than I am." Though Kyah could rely on a degree of instinct to guide her, the bonobo's survival skills were far less than they would have been had she been raised in the wild. Through no fault of her own, Kyah had spent her life in cages. She'd been reliant on humans for her food and welfare, never allowed the opportunity of learning the skills her mother would have taught her from infancy to survive. In this jungle, Ivy knew their mutual survival relied more upon their ability to adapt, along with a great deal of luck, than anything else. She slapped another insect and stumbled, shooting pain up her ankle. Ivy blinked back tears and pushed down the growing terror that threatened to over-whelm her.

. . .

As the sun set in a red blaze, Ivy realised how badly she had judged the time. Darkness was falling fast. With no cave or shelter in sight, she collapsed under a tree. Kyah climbed into a low lying branch, where she set about expertly making a woven nest of thick green leaves. Ivy eyed it enviously. She knew her own nightmares would throw her to the forest floor if she fell asleep so high up. The night air brought a sharp chill. Ivy shrugged further into her jacket. Her fingers curled around a paper, folded neatly in her pocket. She pulled it out. The sudden sting behind her eyes shocked her. *Orrin's handwriting.* She had tucked the note straight into her pocket when Orrin had given it to her, not pausing to look at what she assumed was his address for their dinner date. It was. *7pm - 25 Beach Street, Port Melbourne.* But underneath, were three more words. *Please trust me.* He'd completed the note with a single *O* representing his name. Ivy choked back a sob. *Please trust me.* She had been *so close.* But now she might never have the chance.

The birds fell silent, their chorus taken up by insects buzzing, whirring, chirping and zitzing, each one incessant and amplified by the resonant hollows of the jungle. Light from a waning full moon broke the canopy. Moving shadows became menacing shapes in the dark. The rhythmic, rasping sigh of some nocturnal beast was frighteningly close. Ivy shivered as twigs snapped in the darkness.

Eventually Ivy fell into a fitful sleep. Unaware that she was being watched.

CHAPTER 18

IVY

Squabbling of dawn bats woke them in a shower of leaves and fruit. Kyah dropped from her nest and salvaged, sniffing and then shoving bits into her mouth. Ivy stretched and felt the pull of stiff muscles. She wasn't used to yesterday's exertion. *Ouch!* She sucked air through her teeth. The fabric of her jeans stuck to her ankle with dried blood, and Ivy gingerly pulled her makeshift bandage away. The cut was pink and raw and her flesh swollen tight around it. *Infected, damn it.* Ivy felt a jab from her back pocket. She retrieved a small tube of antiseptic cream, beaming at her companion.

"We're in luck, I forgot to put your medicine away. Pity it's almost empty." Kyah stiffened as Ivy smeared the remnants of the medication across the bonobo's inflamed chest and grazed head then dressed and re-wrapped her own injury. When Ivy had finished, Kyah scraped the leaf litter away from their feet. She picked up a fallen stick and snapped it easily underneath her foot then dragged it across the bare soil. Ivy anticipated the symbol Kyah drew before she'd finished it. *Food.* The durian they had carried with them from yesterday's surplus proved a welcome breakfast. Kyah offered Ivy the last of the fruit, holding it out with an endearing toothy smile. When Ivy declined, the bonobo ate it herself with a soft grunt of appreciation.

"Come here, beautiful," Ivy said.

After all she had been through in the last twenty-four hours, Kyah's obvious joy in spending time together touched her heart. She pulled Kyah into a playful hug, running her fingers through the bonobo's hair affectionately. Kyah hooted softly and reciprocated, her fingers catching in Ivy's knots.

A loud snap startled them both. Leaves and twigs had cracked. *Underfoot? Close by.* Ivy stared intently into the shadows, but no animal surfaced. Invisible predators prowled in her imagination.

"Just breathe," she urged herself. "We're okay." She was suddenly exhausted of the constant danger. She rubbed her eyes, prodding them into vigilance. As much as she had wanted to rest, Ivy knew it was foolish to do so. Kyah fidgeted in echo of Ivy's stress and found the raw scratches on her chest again. Ivy gently pulled her hand away.

"I'm over-reacting Ky, it's okay. Let's just go." Ivy was keen to find a river, not just to quench her dry throat but for the cleanliness it offered. The sun rose crimson and gold as they set off again.

Two more days had come and gone with no sight of civilisation. Ivy's hope for being rescued was both more desperate and more desolate than ever. Days were spent doggedly pushing through the undergrowth. Night fell with tears and the terror of being eaten alive by unseen predators that she felt sure were stalking them.

Kyah's fingers curled into Ivy's hand as they walked. She bent down and kissed the top of the bonobos head.

"How are you going, Ky?"

A soft hoot and hand signal was given in reply.

Food.

Blinking back tears, Ivy opened her arms and the bonobo climbed into them like an overgrown child. She stood holding her, trying not to put too much weight on her ankle. They had run out of food the night before and Ivy was constantly on the lookout for anything that might be edible.

"I'm sorry, there's no durian left, you'll have to make do with what you can find in the trees."

If not for Kyah's relentless affection and motivation to keep moving, Ivy knew she would have given up. But she forced her legs to keep walking. Forced her mind to keep focus. And pushed on. She had still seen no sign of people. No houses or huts. No roads. Certainly no phones.

On the fourth day, salvation came in the form of a new vantage point. They had trekked up an enormous ridge that cut the land in half as far as the eye could see. Under the sweltering sun on its pinnacle, the western side of the range swept ahead of them for miles. In the heart of the forest laid far out before her, a large cave mouth was nestled high on a ridge overlooking a wide river terrace. It looked dark and uninviting, but fresh water was nearby and it would be nightfall soon. Ivy tried to judge the distance but gave up. *A few hours perhaps,* she thought. They set off again, desperate for the safety of shelter before darkness brought her terror back.

They were being followed. Consciousness of this fact had grown with Ivy's sense of unease over the past few days. Her skin prickled as she limped along. She felt eyes watching her.

She was sure they were being tracked by some predator that stayed camouflaged in the tangle of forest. But the fact it had made no appearance only served to send chills up her spine. *Is it waiting for us to die?* Ivy worried as she walked, throwing glances over her shoulder. She gripped her walking stick. *Like a vulture waiting to pick our bones? Why doesn't it attack?* She tried to walk faster but lack of food had left her weak.

"Stay with me, Ky." The bonobo dropped to the ground and continued alongside her. After a few moments, Kyah ascended again to the lowest branches. She clearly felt safer there. The danger in the air was palpable.

Together, they pushed on.

Ivy stiffened her neck. A shuffle here, a snapped twig there. The clues had become too consistent. *This can't be a wild animal. An animal would have shown itself. It must be something else. Or* someone *else. They want me to know I'm not alone.* Her palms grew clammy.

Kyah circled Ivy fearfully on the ground, fully aware she was being hunted but unwilling to leave Ivy alone. She screeched into the jungle din. *Another noise. Closer.* Ivy twisted slowly as she walked, desperate to catch a glimpse of the creature that hunted them. Cold sweat dripped down her back.

Is it human? Ivy wasn't sure a human was even preferable anymore. At least, not the sort that stalked her in a jungle. *Another shuffle, closer.* Ivy spun around. The clamour of the forest deadened in her ears as she strained to focus only on her pursuer. She heard the blood whooshing through her skull.

"Kyah, come to me." Ivy opened her arms. The bonobo was shrieking now, clearly petrified. They clutched each other, their eyes and breaths jarring frantically together. A shuffle to her right. A faint splinter to her left. *Oh no. There's more than one.* Ivy froze. She couldn't breathe. She was surrounded, dwarfed into the base of an enormous buttressing root. With an almighty effort, Ivy shoved Kyah as hard as she could up to the lowest branch.

Kyah screeched hysterically, pacing above her with desperate eyes.

"Stay Kyah! Stay up there, don't come down!"

In a frozen moment of fear, Ivy considered her options. She would run. Through her hunters, if need be. She would lead them away from Kyah and fight as long a she could manage. Her intentions built as she pressed up against the wood, preparing to spring forward. She felt the adrenaline coiling in her muscles.

A noise made Ivy's blood run cold. *Whispers. Talking.*

"Who are you?" She had tried to scream it, but barely a breath escaped with the words.

"What do you want from me?" Oxygen came too fast into her lungs and her head grew light. She was hyperventilating. Ivy pressed back into the wood. *Breathe, Ivy. Breathe.*

The whispers grew louder. The words were fast and confusing, in a language Ivy didn't understand. She shook violently, sweat running in rivulets down her face, neck and shoulder blades. Her heart tried to escape her body and she could no longer stand it.

"What do you want?" she screamed into the trees. "Just come out and get it over with!" Birds above her scattered in fright. A deathly silence entombed the forest.

The shadows in front of her broke. Someone stepped forward, into the light. A rush of ice ripped through Ivy's veins despite the warm air. Her knees hit the ground before her mind understood why. With eyes like saucers, she reeled.

It was a man.

The man staring back at her was in miniature, oddly proportioned, his features every bit as human as her, but not human at all. He stood waist high with strong sinuous muscles and a thickly shaped body. Tangles of grey hair contrasted against his coffee-coloured skin, lined with age. Pronounced brow ridges framed his face, shadowing a broad flat nose and wide cheekbones. He had no forehead and his skull was long and low beneath the matted hair. His head was lifted proudly. He watched, with an aura of quiet intelligence, appraising Ivy with piercing dark eyes. There was no mistaking what this creature – this man – was. Ivy had come across drawings of the fossils in her research. She had *pursued* them, in fact, diligently and passionately, aching to put a face to the bones.

"Homo flores-iensis." The words escaped her lips in whisper. At once, the pieces fit. It was horrifyingly real. The weight of it slammed the air from her lungs. *I know where I am.*

The jigsawed landscape, this jungled island - so over-whelming in its wild beauty - had a name.

Flores.

The fossils had been found nowhere else. The volcanic peaks and rifts that she had seen from the outcrops took on new mean-ing. She had seen this place in photos; but the reality of it was even more surreal, raw and dangerous and… *epic.*

… Reality… Her breath hitched. Maybe this wasn't reality at all. *Is this a dream?* Had she obsessed over the archaeological dig and its bizarre fossils so much that she'd become trapped in her own warped daydream? *I was unconscious for so long – how hard did I hit my head?*

Ivy squeezed her eyes shut. *Pain. If I pinch myself, I'll know if I'm dreaming.* She pinched her arm. It wasn't convincing enough. Ivy's fingers found the dry-bloodied patch on her ankle and she pressed hard. Her eyes shot open at the responding pain. Real pain. The man was still staring; but now concern seemed behind his eyes. Ivy grappled for an explanation. Her plans of escape had been overwhelmingly blind-sided.

Her mind raced, exhausting all logical thought and leaving her with… insanity.

If – against the laws of nature and physics – I was brought to this place somehow - why? Why Flores? And this man, Ivy stared in disbe-lief, *should be extinct! Have I stumbled on some undiscovered tribe so remote… so inaccessible… that no-one knows they're even here? And if*

I'm in such a place, how can I find help? The sudden realisation that humans - her own species of humans - lived in Flores as well offered a glimmer of hope. *There are villages on this island. People in villages! Towns with telephones and ships. If I can survive long enough to find them.*

Ivy looked into the man's eyes. He seemed to be waiting for something.

"Hello" she said out loud. The word sounded stupid.

His eyes were strangely round, not slightly elongated like her own. They tightened thoughtfully and after a moment, he whispered toward the shadows. Another man stepped into the light. He was also small, but younger and stronger with a scarred and twisted face. A thick wooden spear with a flaked stone point was held tight in his fist. He raised it swiftly to her chest. Ivy held back a choke. Adrenaline surged again and her bent knees began to ache. *There are only two of them and I'm taller. I'll run. Fast.*

They seemed to guess her intentions. As if melting into shape from the shadows, nine more of them appeared, surrounding her. Each clutched a weapon with varying degrees of distrust etched onto their face. Together, they were a menacing sight, even with their diminutive stature. This was their territory and although she was dubiously faster, Ivy knew she was defenceless. In fact, she knew it all too well. She had studied the deadly accuracy of those weapons they carried. Blood residues left on tools like those they held had suggested that their victims were often bigger and stronger than she was. *I've got no hope.*

"Please," Ivy whispered, "Don't kill me... *us,* oh no, not Kyah..."

Unable to stand the isolation any longer, Kyah dropped with a thud and scrambled into Ivy's arms, screeching. The hunters drew back, hissing and muttering at each other as Ivy clutched the bonobo, twisting to shelter her.

A brusque command broke through the hunters' circle. Weapons lowered. Still collapsed on her knees, bent over with

Kyah's weight, the old man that had appeared first, stepped past the others. She met his eyes.

"Hiranah," he said softly, beckoning to her.

I know that voice! Soft, guttural, warm against the back of her neck…Violent fear came with recognition. *It was his voice in my bedroom... at the rally... in my lab!* The voice suddenly fell into place. *He was calling me!*

The old man searched Ivy's face intently. Then he ushered the hunters back into the trees and turned to beckon her with a disproportionately long arm.

"Keecha.. sha sha kika monahta…"

"What?"

The man was insistent. He beckoned her again, repeating himself in a voice that might have been soothing, if it weren't coming from a stranger in a jungle surrounded by weapons.

Ivy got to her feet trembling, grateful for the strength of the buttressing trunk behind her. It suddenly dawned on her. *I have no choice. I go with them and risk everything, or stay here and die.*

A hesitant step forward brought a grunt of approval from the man. He took a few steps forward, glancing back to her. Hitching Kyah higher into her arms, Ivy straightened her shoulders and took a deep breath.

One foot after the other, still limping, she boldly followed tiny footprints through the jungle, unsure where they would lead.

It's time to live the dream. Or the nightmare.

CHAPTER 19

ORRIN

A wiry woman at the Anthropology reception desk turned to greet Orrin with a haughty smile. Her eyes quickly assessed his handsome face and athletic arms and she rearranged her expression into something she considered more flattering. Brightly painted lips offered her name and assistance.

"Good morning," said Orrin, tapping his fingers nervously under the counter frame. "I'd like the office room number for Ivy Carter please. She's a doctorate research student here. Archaeology."

"Carter was it? Mmmm, just one moment please." The secretary browsed a list behind the counter, batting her eyelashes as she looked up. "I'm so sorry; we don't have anyone here by that name. Perhaps you misheard it?"

"No, it's definitely Ivy Carter," said Orrin surprised. "Audrey, was it? Could you check for the name Ivy then, please? She's been here for years. She tutors undergrads."

"Ivy, Ivy, Ivy … noooo, so sorry sweetie, but I'm afraid there's no Ivy here. Perhaps you're in the wrong department? Sociology is just up the hall." A girlish wink and apologetic smile looked misplaced on her heavily made-up face.

Orrin didn't move. His fingers gripped the countertop. *Eight years in the department and no record of her? No office? This was all wrong.*

Audrey raised a pencilled eyebrow at his lingering presence. "Perhaps there is something else I can do for you?" Beyond the smoked glass partitions, Orrin heard muffled chortles. He didn't have time for this game.

"Listen, Audrey, I've *got* to find this woman. *Ivy Carter.* Can you cross-check her with your current tutor list? Or perhaps an old database? I really need her number."

Audrey's smile dissolved like sugar and her haughty lips returned.

"I'm sorry, but our records have no such person. I'm afraid you're in the wrong department … or perhaps you've been given a false name." A smirk settled onto her mouth and looked at home.

Shite. Orrin took a deep breath and tried again, attempting his most charming smile. "Perhaps if you could call…"

"I'm sorry sir," Audrey interrupted, "I have a lot of work to do. Good-day." She spun on her heel and disappeared.

This is bollocks! He knew Ivy was here somewhere and he *would* find her. Orrin's memory raked over their past conversations. She'd been in that department for over eight years. She did have an office, that napkin proved it. He just didn't know where. This receptionist was obviously new. Or just chronically unhelpful. *The residue lab.* Scanning the directory beside the elevator, Orrin located the most likely laboratory. He'd go there. *Jayne!* She'd have Ivy's number.

He followed the third floor corridor to its end and rapped on the door. Jayne whisked it open with a bright smile.

"Hey there, come in!" She stepped back into the room with her white laboratory coat billowing and seated herself behind a row of test tubes and pipettes. An airmailed box was open in front of her, its contents spilled across the bench. Music spilled from a dusty radio.

Orrin relaxed against the door frame, desperately thankful for her normality. He shook his head, smiling. *Not mental after all.* After a few seconds Jayne looked up, surprised by his lack of movement.

"You all right, hon? Am I in your way?" She looked around, confused.

"Of course not, I'm just here for Ivy. Is she around?"

Jayne winced apologetically. "Ivy? Oh jeez, I'm sorry! I'm new here; I just assumed you needed the lab."

Orrin frowned. "Why on earth would I need the lab? I work in Physics."

"Oh-kay. Well, I didn't know that. Anyway, as you can see, I'm the only one here today."

Orrin looked around the room. The other benches were clearly empty and a closed door on the far wall had a radioactive sign lit up above it. His own small office had been refurbished from a similar unused laboratory extension. In this case however, the glowing sign suggested radiation of biological samples was in process. No one would be in there.

"Right," Orrin said. "Well, can you tell Ivy I dropped by? I was worried about her – and the chimp, after they left my lab. I couldn't find her."

"Ivy, who, hon?"

"What do you mean?"

"I mean, I'm sorry but I don't know her. So, no can do. But you should check up the hall for another researcher to pass on the message."

"Jayne – Ivy's your supervisor!"

Jayne's smile faltered at her own name. She stood up, moving around the desk toward him.

"Sorry, have we met?"

"Have we- *of course* we've bloody well met! I'm Orrin, remember? Ivy introduced us at the interfaculty mixer."

"Ivy did?" Jayne shook her head. *"Ivy who?"*

"Ivy Carter!"

Jayne looked genuinely confused. "I don't think so; I don't know anyone by that name. I haven't been here long though, maybe you're confusing me with someone else-"

"Ivy Carter," Orrin repeated, slower this time. Jayne's face remained blank. "She's your supervisor, Jayne. Here in the residue lab. I saw you talking with her the other day in the courtyard. You're working on the Flores tools together." Orrin's patience began to wane.

"Look … um, Orrin, is it? I really can't help you. I don't know an Ivy Carter." Jayne frowned. "Professor Ellery is my supervisor and I'm working on these Flores tools alone. He organised it all for me." She gestured to the scattering of sample bags on the desk in front of her.

"But Ivy's been waiting months for these tools," Orrin said. "She told me all about it."

"Months? She can't have." Her blue eyes registered Orrin's annoyance and grew wide. "These artefacts were airmailed with a week's notice. No one else wanted them. They were pulled from a salvage dig before the mining began."

Salvage dig? Mining? Orrin dismissed their obvious miscommunication. It was Ivy he wanted. *Needed.* "This is crazy," he said. "I saw you in the courtyard just a week ago, Jayne. You were *talking* with Ivy - she had the chimp with her, up a tree - I mean *bonobo* or whatever - right out there in the courtyard. You even waved at me! I saw you again that afternoon- and a few days after that as well!"

"A chimp?" Jayne repeated. "Like a chimpanzee?" She looked embarrassed for him. She took a step back.

"Yes - Kyah. Black hair, up a tree…"

"Wow," said Jayne. "Okay, I really think you've got the wrong person, I haven't been in all week, I've had the flu. Honestly, I can't help you." She glanced surreptitiously to the security phone on the far wall.

Orrin's breathing came faster. *She thinks I'm nuts. This is mental.* This woman had spoken to him. Numerous times. She knew Ivy. Ivy knew her. *Would Ivy have asked Jayne to pretend she wasn't here? Was she avoiding me altogether?* He didn't see how that would work when they were both on the same campus. *Did I honestly upset her that much by scaring Kyah?* Orrin shook his head and rubbed his eyes under his glasses. *No, Ivy doesn't seem like the type to lie.* At a loss, he took one last stab.

"Look Jayne, if Ivy turns up here later, can you just tell her I'm sorry? I didn't mean to let the chimp get hurt, or upset. I should have realised - can you ask her to call me at least? Or leave a message at my lab?" He took a step closer to the bench and then scribbled his contact details on a coffee receipt from his pocket.

He held it out to Jayne but she had withdrawn further and made no move to reconcile the space between them.

"I'm really sorry, but I'm telling you the truth," Jayne said, eyeing off the paper on the bench. "I don't know this Ivy woman and I've never met you before or any chimp. Just take the number to the admin ladies upstairs or to someone else. *Please.*"

"I've tried upstairs and they said she doesn't bloody exist!" Orrin shouted.

He leaned forward, both hands on the counter. This was either a desperate ploy to get out of a date, or he was going insane. His eyes burned. Caught under his finger was one of the small plastic sample bags. He stared at it, his eyes toying with the black stone artefact inside as he tried to calm himself. A stone tool, he supposed. It looked oddly familiar but nothing that stirred his memory so he directed his attention back to Jayne. She had backed up a few steps more and was looking at him with panicked eyes.

Orrin lowered his voice and raised his hands in surrender. "I apologise; there's obviously been some sort of mistake here." *I'm losing it.* He took a deep breath. "Here's my number anyway… just in case." Orrin slid the scrap of paper across the bench and let himself out of the room.

He heard the lock click behind him as he walked away.

An insistent telephone ring greeted him as he hit home that evening, tired and angry.

"Orrin here."

"Big brother, I was beginning to think you'd disappeared," a woman's voice came down the line. "So how's the new job?"

Orrin's shoulders slouched. For a split second, he'd hoped.

"Sorry Bernie, it's been brutal. This month has been really busy."

"Nothing too bad I hope," his sister said.

"Nothing I can't handle."

"Mmm. That sounds ominous. Listen, I just wanted to check you were still coming next Saturday. The kids are dying to see you."

Damn. Jess's birthday party. He'd entirely forgotten.

"Sure, I wouldn't miss it."

"You'd better not. Hey… you can bring someone if you want," she ventured.

I'd have to find her first. "Thanks, but at this stage I'm on my own."

"Okay sure, well in that case, I've already invited Renee from work, with the short red hair remember? She's great, and she's really looking forward to meeting you."

Red hair. "Bernie, any more set ups and I will *disown* you."

"Ha ha, you wish it was that easy. Okay O, but seriously less work, more fun, hey. Hang on, Jess wants to say hi."

"Uncle Orrin?"

"Hey Jess, how's my favourite niece?" He tried to hide the tiredness from his voice.

"I'm your *only* niece Uncle O!

"No you aren't! What about Chrissy?"

"She's a *guinea-pig!*"

Orrin chuckled. Jessica had an endless supply of coddled pets, and insisted he hold them all at least once during each visit.

"Guess what, today for school we went on an excursion. *To the zoo!*"

"Zoo, hey? Bet that was fun, dote."

"Yeah, and guess what! We saw koalas and monkeys and kangaroos, and Leah and I got to touch a snake! And we saw the cougars and the elephants and the hobbits and the ..."

"The what?"

"The hobbits. They were in a pretend cave and they had a babby and everything. The zoo lady fed them for us!"

"Is that right?" *Must be some new cute and cuddly for the kids.* Orrin was used to humouring Jess, the first and only girl in his extended family. The handful of little boys occupied each other while eight-year-old Jess clucked over them and her endless animal 'babbies'.

"Yeah, the zoo lady gave them apples and roast chicken. But I didn't like them. They looked scary. The babby one was *sooooo cute* though. It talked to me and I patted it and Mum said if I'm good I might get one for my birthday!"

Talked... "What do you mean? Animals don't-"

"Ma says I have to go, Bye Uncle O!" *Click.*

CHAPTER 20

IVY

*I*vy gave up carrying Kyah after the first half hour. She was surprised to find the hunters paid the bonobo little attention. The part of her mind that ached to analyse and categorise and *understand* the minutiae of life forced itself above her fear. As Ivy walked, she studied the hunters. *Homo floresiensis.* The very sight of them thrilled her, despite the fact that they could be the last things she ever saw.

One female trailed her side, closer than the others. Ivy chanced a look down at the woman's face. Her eyes were filled with curiosity, not aggression, although a spear was still tight in her hand. Ivy swallowed nervously. The woman's wide cheekbones were shadowed by pronounced eyebrows, each side defined and arched separately like Ivy's own. Her face was far from the mono-browed brute she'd so often seen depicted in pop culture.

The woman's strong but petite jaw line shaped a relatively flat face with wide, thin lips and markedly human teeth. She looked enticingly familiar but for the distinct lack of a chin beneath.

Ivy couldn't help but recall the debate sparked in her tutorial only a week ago. She'd been dragging her students through the complexities of migration routes while trying to stifle a yawn and her own rumbling stomach simultaneously.

"Let's get an early mark, guys," she'd said. "And seriously, catch up on your readings to avoid that arse-kicking from Karl...."

Ivy had begun to pack up, considering her caffeine options.

"Actually, I have a question..." Claire called over the shuffling and scraping of chairs.

"Sure, Claire." Ivy had pointedly ignored the muttered expletives and groans around the room as the others were denied their early escape.

"Well, I've been reading about this Homo flor-es-i-en-sis species?" Claire stumbled over the name as the others took their seats again, interest vaguely sparked. "They call it the hobbit? Well, if you're saying modern humans got to Indonesia around fifty-five thousand years ago, and they're saying these tiny ape-men were still there until up to at least fifty thousand years ago... then, how does that work? They lived on the same island at the same time?" Claire looked doubtful. "How could those hobbit-people get across that big tidal rift you were talking about if modern humans didn't do it until so much later? I mean there must be a mistake in the dating - this little thing was like a chimp, it had a tiny brain...so, not that smart, right?"

Ivy inwardly groaned. She took a deep breath. Like a perfectly targeted missile, Claire had managed to denigrate Ivy's two favourite subjects in a single sentence.

"Alright," Ivy said, holding up her index finger, "firstly I have it on very good authority that chimpanzees are actually very intelligent, more so than quite a few humans I know," laughs peppered the room, "and secondly, from what we're discovering now, yes, it seems this new species of hominid, Homo floresiensis or 'the hobbit' as it's affectionately being called by the media, must have co-existed with modern humans on the island of Flores for thousands of years." Ivy jumped to her feet. "Who's familiar with the Flores dig? Anyone?"

A scattering of hands waved half-heartedly.

"Come on guys, this one is actually really exciting!" Ivy's eyes sparkled. "Smouldering volcanos, an exotic rainforest island, carnivorous dragons, tiny warrior tribes...this is real archaeology! Eat-your-heart-out Indiana Jones type of archaeology." Ivy's enthusiasm washed over the group like a wave, dragging them back to her. "Okay everyone, picture this. Six hundred kilometres east of Java on a remote jungle island - a place only accessible by water - a skeleton is found in a cave. She's only one metre tall. No chin, tiny brain case, narrow V-shaped jaws with paired roots on her pre-molars - all these features are prehistoric, reminiscent of our erectus and australopithecine ancestors. Ancestors who died out at least two hundred thousand years ago, some of them, two million years ago!"

Ivy was almost lost in her own story as she painted the scene, pacing up and down.

"But...we have new, modern features thrown in with this fossil too. Stone tools that provide evidence for group hunting of stegodon, an extinct dwarfed elephant - but still much bigger than these tiny hominids. Hunting stegodon would require communication and strategy. We've also got fire use, impressive stone tools. To even be there, they must have had the ability to get enough individuals across the ocean to make the founding population genetically viable."

"This is a total contradiction of old versus new in a single population. What we need is a date; some way to place this new species, if that's what it is, into our family tree. So we test." She paused for effect, scanning faces. "And we get totally floored! Radiocarbon, thermoluminescence - all bringing in dates of only fifty thousand years, maybe younger. Recent time, sapien *time."*

"So what does that mean?" Ivy looked around the class and was met by confused faces, all struggling to make sense of the onslaught of contradictory information.

"It means we have a spectacular, brilliant mess in our hands, that's what!" she exclaimed, landing back onto the desk at the front. "Now seriously, just imagine the massive environmental changes up to the last

ice age. These little guys fought for survival and they won for a really, really long time. This is a very tough bunch of cookies!" A few of the students looked impressed. *"So Claire is right to ask - where do they fit in? What are they?"*

Ivy paused to look around the room. Nobody showed any sign of wanting to escape the adventure she offered now.

"Maybe it was just a kid?" offered Claire. "A child's bones left in the cave by modern humans? That's why it's so small?"

"It was small, about the size of a three-year-old human," Ivy agreed. "But the cranial sutures are closed and its wisdom teeth are erupted and already worn down. So we are definitely looking at an adult. Anyone else?"

"I thought someone said these hobbits were dwarfed modern humans?" called Ryan from the back row. "That the bones were pathologically diseased? Micro - whatever?"

Ivy clasped her hands, grinning. Excellent, a devil's advocate.

"Microcephaly? Maybe. But we aren't just talking about one person here. More skeletons were found - so far there are up to twelve individuals represented from a single cave. That's twelve diseased people from a single population. Although, to be fair, we only have one complete skull so far."

"What's microcephaly?" asked Travis.

Oliver, the anatomy major, answered him. "It's a pathology where the brain case is a lot smaller than normal. It's extremely rare though. Usually the life span, intellectual ability, speech and motor function are pretty low in microcephalics due to abnormal growth of the brain. Even if these were microcephalic modern humans, I doubt they'd survive to adulthood, not in such a primitive environment."

"Yet," interrupted Ivy, "the archaeological evidence suggests these hunters required strategy and communication - pretty sophisticated brain functioning. Which is exactly what endocast studies are showing up now; the structure of their brains are beautifully formed with no sign of microcephaly. Just tiny."

"Pygmies?" suggested Travis.

"Well, there are some native Indonesian populations that have a small body size, even in line with pygmies, but their brain size is proportionately normal. Our Flores friends have brains significantly smaller in relation to their body size. Perhaps the microcephalic offspring of a pygmy... but twelve?"

"Some of their skeletal morphology takes us all the way back two to four million years ago to the Australopithecines like Lucy," Ivy continued. "Fully adducted big toes tell us they walked upright, but their feet are way too long for a modern human and totally flat-footed, believe me, you wouldn't want to go shoe shopping for these guys."

"Here's a thought for you all," Ivy offered. "New finds in Ethiopia are actually suggesting tool use might go as far back as 3.4 million years. The foundations for technology were already there, so maybe these 'hobbits' are an entirely new branch of humanity derived from Australopithecines that made their own way to Indonesia a million years ago? Two million years ago? Even before Homo erectus did?"

"Why not an offshoot of Homo erectus though?" asked Oliver.

"Could be," said Ivy. "They do have similar cranial characteristics to Homo erectus, and we know our erectus poster boys were nearby in Java."

"But erectus were twice their size," Kathryn interjected, "and had a bigger brain capacity. So they would have had to shrink - devolve."

"That's true. But even if they were descendants of an Australopithecine or smaller Dmanisi hominid, they must have still evolved into a separate species on Flores sometime after they arrived. Homo erectus arrived there by boat 800,000 years ago," Ivy said. "But in a limited gene pool like this, you could see massive changes in body and brain size over a relatively rapid period of time. In 800,000 years of isolation, it's possible."

"But why so small?" asked Claire.

"Aha!" Ivy clapped her hands, bouncing on the balls of her feet. "Because these islands are famous for their bizarre effect on evolution! We've already got massive komodo dragons, giant carnivorous birds and rats as big as a cat. On the other end of the scale are dwarfed stegodon

and tiny humans. In isolated populations like these islands, cut off from outside breeding, mutations emerge and flourish. Dwarfism is a common occurrence." She looked to Oliver. "Who can tell us why?"

"A larger body is an expensive resource," Oliver replied. "A large brain, especially so. It's just natural selection. A smaller body size is more efficient if you have limited food available - you don't require as much energy to survive. If there aren't any predators, there's less selective pressure to be bigger and stronger to compete."

"Correct. Who's heard of the experiments of the biologist Safi?" asked Ivy. As expected only Oliver raised his hand. "Okay well, Safi studied brain evolution in bats - he determined that brain size in bats grew bigger or smaller through evolutionary time, based entirely on the ecological niche the bats kept." Ivy drew some quick sketches on the whiteboard to illustrate her point.

"Bats hunting in heavily forested areas needed bigger wings for manoeuvrability and had therefore evolved a bigger brain to control their wings. But for bats especially adapted to eating fruit and flowers in more open spaces, well, flying was a simpler affair. They needed less energy to control their smaller wings, and therefore developed smaller brains to manipulate them. So," Ivy turned back to the group, "were the smaller bats stupid?"

Travis grinned. "Were they Gotham bats?" he asked. Claire kicked his chair.

"Maybe," Ivy laughed. "But they weren't stupid. They lived, flew and fed just as effectively as any others. They simply adapted to their natural surroundings, in this case, by shrinking - brain and all.

"But isn't mankind smart because we have a big brain?" asked Travis, looking confused.

"We're smart, yes," Ivy said. "But surely you've learnt by now Travis - it's not how big it is that matters, it's what you do with it." The women in the room laughed. "Mankind seems to have a disturbing obsession with size. Humankind though, did become smarter, unquestionably. But it's the ratio of brain to body size that's more important, and how you're wired together. The human brain became more complex over *time, not just bigger. The number of neurons increased dramatically as we evolved. The parts that help us learn, adapt, communicate, strategize and think creatively grew more connections as we faced more challenging environments and bigger social groups. It's these nerves - the number of them, and how intricately they're connected to one another that really influence our intelligence as a species." Ivy was vaguely aware of muted shuffling and chatting in the halls as other classes ended.*

"But, humans are not immune to natural selection," she added quickly. "Brain size can shrink. Diet, gestational period, social system, predators – all affect the body shape of an animal over time. These evolutionary forces act just as readily on the human species as any other mammals; we are, after all, just another animal and part of a complex ecosystem." She'd kept them long enough.

"As far as Homo floresiensis is concerned, the jury's still out. So do your readings, there are a few articles coming up in the next few weeks about this very topic and I want some good debates happening in this room about it." Ivy flicked through the loose leaf folder she pulled out of her bag. "Start with Morwood, Sutikna, Tocheri, Lentfer and Brown. We'll discuss them first up next week." The references were scribbled down as everyone packed up and started filing to the door, looking much more inspired than when they'd arrived.

Ivy trailed after them into the hallway.

"This may be the most important palaeo-anthropological discovery in the last fifty years guys," she had called after them, "it really challenges our understanding of what it means to be human!"

Ivy limped through the undergrowth, alongside her captors. The irony of her current situation was much more painful than her injury.

These tiny people were an evolutionary dream; Ivy's dream. Living, breathing fossils, now leading her through the vegetation like a trail of deadly ants.

The *hobbits*, their fossils had been dubbed by sensationalist media. *Hobbits.* Strangely, it suited them.

The hominids she followed wore only a utilitarian belt made of straps and folds of animal hide which seemed identical on both men and women. Aside from that, they were completely naked and unashamedly so. Ivy revelled in their unique physiology as they moved.

They were muscular and powerful and slightly pot-bellied. Ivy guessed they would be of a similar body weight to Kyah. The tallest was barely over a meter high. Their legs were short relative to their height but they walked with quite long strides regardless. Unusually long, flat feet extended each stride and caused their knees to bend slightly further backward than Ivy's own with each step, giving them an unusual gait. The hobbits seemed flexible and stable as they navigated the forest tangles with ease and familiarity.

The woman beside her directed Ivy through a fall of rocks in the undergrowth. Her shoulder blades were shrugged forward, giving a slightly tight appearance. Ivy knew that anatomically, her collarbones were relatively short as well, compensating for the potential limitation of manual dexterity either characteristic would offer alone.

Ivy bent forward, using the largest rock to support her ankle. Her palm slipped on wet moss and she skidded down, falling hard. The hobbit woman lunged toward her.

"No!" Ivy yelled, terrified. She scrambled to her feet as the woman stepped back again, frowning. The hobbit bent down and reclaimed the spear she'd dropped.

"Oh. Sorry," Ivy muttered. The woman frowned, tilting her head to the side. Her eyes narrowed at the blood stains on the bottom of Ivy's jeans. She gestured for Ivy to keep walking.

The hobbit's arms reached almost to her knees and were lithely muscled. Despite her size advantage, Ivy knew she was no match for the woman's strength. Or spear. She recalled articles suggesting that these unique forearms may be reminiscent of a more arboreal lifestyle. They were built for climbing trees.

It wasn't long before Ivy discovered it was true.

"Shirakan! Shirakan!"

A yell went up from the front of line. The first four hobbits leapt backwards. They split from the group, scattering to the closest tree trunks and pulling themselves upward. Their long, muscular forearms proved faultless for the task, as did slightly curved bones in their fingers and toes. For a split-second, their movements seemed unprovoked. All of the hobbits, as well as Kyah were now stowed high in the branches, looking down at her. Ivy finally saw what the others had sensed much quicker. A lizard of gigantic proportions lumbered forward, eyeing her coldly. It's long, deeply forked tongue flicked and tasted the air. *Komodo dragon.*

Ivy froze with cold fear. She was the only one left in its path. The reptile was nearly nine feet long. A row of serrated inch-long teeth were already coated in swathes of its own blood-tinged saliva in anticipation of feeding.

Thunk! A spear from above found its mark on the hind quarters of the dragon. *Thunk!* Ivy bolted, clawing up the tree closest to her, shoes slipping and sliding on the bark as she tried to catch grip. Behind her the great lizard charged, faster than its size should allow.

The Komodo dragon was nearly fully grown, with loosely articulated jaws and an expandable stomach. It looked easily capable of swallowing a hobbit whole. Ivy was considerably larger. But she'd heard the horror stories of tourists caught off guard.

Great chunks of flesh and bone torn away-

I can't grip!

The rest of a man's body rammed against a tree-

Slipping! Her ankle was agony.

Forced down the gigantic lizard's throat head first-

Rasping! Hissing! Too close!

Thunk! Thunk! Thunk! Thunk!

Spears pierced the Komodo as it charged behind her. Ivy screamed, struggling to clamber as high as the others. With unexpected strength, four tiny hands reached down and grabbed hold of her arms, wrenching Ivy up into the branches. Enraged, the Komodo bore forward at the base of tree. It lurched up onto its hind legs, using its massive tail to stabilise its efforts to reach her. Teeth scraped the sole of Ivy's shoe.

Thunk! Thunk! Thunk!

A spear found it's exposed chest. The Komodo dragon fell away. Before Ivy had stopped shaking enough to descend, a handful of hunters climbed down and sliced the dragon's throat. They retrieved stone flakes from the folds of their waist hides, and quartered and drained the animal, lifting the heavy carcass onto their shoulders with apparent ease. Within minutes the hobbits were continuing on their way. The predator had become prey.

Every so often, the hunters would glance back to Ivy nervously. Only the old man seemed untroubled by her presence. He kept pace with Ivy, eyeing her limp critically and occasionally even offering encouraging noises. He made no effort to talk to her again. Ivy's ankle throbbed as she struggled through the web of undergrowth, impeding their progress. Finally, the band descended onto a yellow grassland spiked with shrubs. The roar of insects and birds was replaced by the sound of gushing water. A hot breeze whipped her hair across her face and Ivy recognized the wide river she had spotted from high above. Desperation for a cold bath and deep drink suddenly hit her and she gestured to the old man, but was quickly pushed toward the hillside by a prodding spear.

It was Liang Bua Cave.

Ivy almost laughed out loud. Earlier, from far above in her despair on the ridge and obscured by trees and tears, she couldn't have seen the classic stretched mouth of the cave or the raised lip of its entrance that she knew from so many photos. Liang Bua Cave was a geological anomaly – a gift from the gods to archaeologists. The cave had allowed sediments to slowly build over millennia, trapping artefacts and bones inside like a beautifully layered cake. In this context it was obvious. Ivy had no doubt of where she was. Her heart raced.

The drier grass gave way once more to damp forest as the small valley turned upward. Ivy picked up her feet self consciously, her footfalls and stumbles elephantine compared to the silent bodies ascending around her.

A knot twisted in her gut. *What can they want with me? Were there people here with them? Scientists? Surely they'd been seen by now if they'd re-claimed the site.* Kyah climbed into her arms, uneasy at the dark, confined space looming ahead. Ivy chanced a look to the old man staring from beside her into the wide cave mouth. He called out, then pulled her inside.

For a fleeting moment, Ivy's eyes were blind in the sudden darkness. A gush of cool air licked her face as movement swirled nearby. Then darkness resolved into shades of brown and grey. Hidden shadows took shape. Ivy stood in the entrance of Liang Bua Cave, frozen with fear and delight.

The massive subterranean chamber rose imperiously in a great arc above her, one hundred feet high and descending far back into the dim light. The ceiling was crowded with long stalactites; petrified minerals dripping like ancient candle wax from every conceivable space above. They pointed sharp and foreboding into the great open cavern. Half-crumbled boulders crept down from the wall edges to a dirt floor rutted with rocks. The cool air tasted like damp earth on her tongue – musty and suffused with jasmine flower. There were no scientists here. There was no help.

Dwarfed in their stone fortress, a hundred olive-skinned hobbits closed in around her, alive with animated whispers. Not a single one stood higher than her chest. Some held the hands of adolescent children so small they would have seemed infantile were it not for the age in their faces. The old man raised his arms and greeted them all in a hushed voice. Then he stepped away, leaving Ivy exposed.

An explosion of voices broke out. Ivy was pushed deep through the crowd into the cave, clutching Kyah in her trembling arms. Spears and hands reached up to graze her skin as she stumbled forward. Small pitted fires scattered the earthen floor. Drawing close to the largest flames, the old man gestured to the dirt. Intimately aware of the spears that had slain a Komodo already, Ivy complied, hugging Kyah tight in her lap. The bonobo's head twitched convulsively and she picked at her scarred chest, her eyes darting, shoulders hunched. Ivy ran her fingers through Kyah's matted black hair, shushing her.

If these people wanted me dead, she thought, *surely they would have killed me by now.*

CHAPTER 21

ORRIN

"**R**ight, what's the craic?" Orrin tried to sound buoyant as he strode into the lab, an enthusiastic smile masking his frustration. His stormy mood had only worsened yesterday after Ivy's disappearance. Accelerated by the lack of progress in sourcing their hardware malfunctions, he'd given up early and left them to it.

Dale and Phil clicked studiously under a wall of flat-screened monitors. Phil raised an eyebrow.

"We're still working on it," Phil said. "The systems were stuffed up pretty badly."

Dale fidgeted in his chair and shifted closer to the screen. He seemed unwilling to meet Orrin's eyes.

Jaysus, I must have been a complete gobshite yesterday. Dale's nervousness tended to correlate with Orrin's mood. As did his habit of screwing things up. Dale was a good student, extremely intelligent and dedicated, albeit massively under confident. Dale was so dedicated that he'd transferred universities, along with Phil, so he could continue his research under Orrin's supervision. Dale's expertise in creating the mechanical components of their experiments made him indispensable. More than that though, Phil and Dale were Orrin's friends.

Orrin whistled casually and dumped a box of doughnuts and two coffees on the desk between them.

"Got you lads a couple of lattes. Sorry about yesterday."

Phil appraised the lattes, then grabbed a doughnut.

"Whatever," he said. "We can't all be as smooth with the ladies as the Phil-meister." He swallowed half a doughnut without chewing, waggling his eyebrows.

"Fair play to you, man." Orrin laughed, again resisting his rising frustration at the thought of Ivy's disappearance. Phil was an eternal bachelor that never-the-less seemed to have a constant flow of adoring women calling in on him.

Dale's shoulders relaxed and he smiled, reaching for a coffee.

"So what's the story?" Orrin sat down.

"We've been recalibrating the measurement software," Dale finally spoke. "It's all back up and running now. There were some pretty intense readings recorded yesterday. Most of them cut out automatically at the surge, but we've got data backups."

"Thanks to you," said Orrin.

Dale reddened under the praise and took a swig of coffee.

"Take me through it," Orrin said.

"Firstly, look at these diffraction patterns," said Phil. He scooted his chair across the room, stopping expertly in front of a wide monitor. Green and red graphs scattered the screen. "Yesterday, about six pm, the laser system went ballistic. We've got sensor readings suggesting a period of extreme wavelength changes, short, constant fluctuations for about 30 seconds, then wavelength irregularity for another few minutes. The light intensity patterns too, totally haywire." Phil pointed to a flashing graph. "There must have been a serious light show in here."

Orrin glanced around the room. A series of diode lasers were wired at regular intervals around the centre space ceiling. Rotary motion sensors held them in place, unobtrusively gathering background energy fluctuations. They looked undisturbed.

"We were in the office at the time, I'm telling you, there was no light malfunction," Dale interjected. It seemed as if he and Phil had had this argument before.

"The door was shut, remember?" Orrin said. "We wouldn't have seen it if there was. What else Phil?" Phil's speciality lay in coding analysis programs to measure environmental variables. He knew his stuff.

"Okay, look at the general systems," said Phil. He rolled back across the room and the others followed on foot. "Temp, increased by about 15 degrees, then straight back down to normal. That could explain why we had some shut-downs." His index finger tapped a blue graph. "Relative humidity went up 50% in 15 seconds. Like a greenhouse."

Orrin glanced around at the rack of plants on the wall, kept there for experimental response measurements. They looked greener, more vibrant. *Can't be*, he decided. He rubbed his fingers over his eyes.

"Gauge pressure – dropped," continued Phil. "Even the pH of our fertilisers increased."

Orrin glanced again at the plants. Next to them, a slick laptop collected real time changes in physiological response. Tiny wires were prodded into the soil and clipped to leaves. Jars of shaded liquid below sported metal measurement rods.

"Did you check the plants?" Orrin asked.

"Yeah man, respiration rates went right up and have been higher than average since then. I think they liked it. This is some crazy shit…." Dale and Orrin shadowed Phil as he moved between monitors, typing quickly.

"Sound sensor - off the scale," Phil continued with his back to the others. "I'm not just talking loud; I'm talking high range frequency, upwards of 80,000 Hertz. That's where we lost it. A god-damn dog couldn't even hear that. And it's localised in this room, the outer sensors didn't pick it up." He scooted to the next monitor, reaching for another doughnut.

"And here is the *pièce de résistance.*" Bent over the keyboard, a series of brightly coloured graphs appeared on his monitor, and then flicked to the wide flat screen overhead. "Check that out." Phil sat back in his chair and fell silent.

Orrin caught his breath. To his trained eye, the whips and plateaus of the giant graphs told a bizarre tale. The electromagnetic fields in the room had coursed and waned, increasing to dizzying levels, the axial and radial fields were both volatile and unnatural. It was unlike anything he had ever seen. Along the base, the earth's natural magnetic field held a steady reference, increasing only slightly in the centre.

"Holy Mary and babby Jesus," Orrin breathed.

Even Phil, who had uncovered the devastating anomaly, was speechless.

CHAPTER 22

IVY

Ivy sat, clutching Kyah in her lap. She was *surrounded*. Whispers echoed off the cave walls and pierced her like arrows.

The oldest man, who had led her to the cave, broke purposefully through the crowd. He reached out and tugged at Ivy's arm encircling Kyah. His fingers were thin and felt slightly curved in the bone. They felt familiar. Kyah's fingers, though more pronounced, had the same curve.

Ivy let him pull her hand toward his own chest where a black stone hung from a leather strip around his neck. The old man pushed her fingers onto the amulet, *her* amulet. Ivy felt its peculiar warmth against her fingertips.

"That's mine," she breathed.

"Yes."

Ivy jerked her hand back, eyes wide. *What the hell?* The words that came from his mouth were unrecognisable, but their meaning was loud and clear. *He spoke to me. Inside my head.*

Ivy scrunched her fingers deep into Kyah's hair, squeezing her eyes shut tight. *No! No no no! I did that. It was me.* Ivy opened her

169

eyes. She took a deep breath, then another. *You're braver than this.* She gritted her teeth, took another deep breath and reached for the amulet again.

"Welcome, Hiranah."

Ivy scrambled to her feet, hauling Kyah up with her. *This is insane!* She spun around, trying to find an escape route. *There are too many of them!* Most held weapons. She hugged Kyah closer.

The man reached up to her, and pulled her fingers back to the amulet with surprising force.

"You can't leave," he said.

"Why?" She whispered. Her voice cracked from lack of use.

"Because we need you," he replied.

A wave of goosebumps prickled her skin. His words out-loud, in that foreign, whispered tongue, were harsh and truncated, but those in Ivy's mind seemed whole. Like a repaired translation. Ivy struggled to remain calm. The man held her hand tightly against the stone.

How? How can I hear you? There were no words this time, only a desperate thought.

"The stone speaks for us," he answered.

"How?" Ivy said aloud.

"I don't know."

"Well I need to know!" Ivy yelled. She could feel the tingling of adrenaline racing through her blood. Her fingertips twitched.

The old man frowned. "Then you must find that answer yourself."

Ivy bristled in spite of the danger around her.

"You took it from me, didn't you? That stone was mine." Although the silver chain was gone, the amulet was most certainly hers. *He must have been watching me, touching me even, while I lay unconscious.* It felt like a violation.

"No," he said. "My people have carried this stone for many lifetimes, waiting for you to arrive." The man hesitated, narrowing his eyes. For a long moment, he just stood there, watching her. Ivy shivered. Around them, the whispers started again. Slowly, as if summoning trust he didn't have, the old man pulled the leather strip over his head and knotted it around Ivy's wrist. "But it is yours again, Hiranah. I believe it was meant for you."

Ivy pulled her hand away. *Many lifetimes?* Apart from the leather, the stone looked identical to the last time she'd seen it. Even her initials, or rather, those of Iris Chapman, were still engraved on the face.

The man gestured and Ivy reluctantly sat back down, clutching Kyah. The bonobo cried anxiously in Ivy's lap, twitching her head sharply.

"It's okay, honey," Ivy soothed, "I've got you." She gently held the bonobo's chin and pulled her face close.

"Sharp- sticks- Kyah- hurt-" the bonobo signed. Ivy dragged her fingers through Kyah's hair, down the side of her face, hushing her.

"I won't let them hurt you." But Ivy's own vulnerability burned in her gut. Who was she to be promising safety?

The old man curled his hand around Ivy's wrist, covering the stone and forcing the reconnection between them.

"We shouldn't be here," Ivy whispered. She reflexively used her free hand to pull the bonobo's fingers from the scar on her chest. The old man noticed.

"We won't hurt your friend," he said.

"You *stole* her," Ivy accused. "You've already hurt her."

"We called for *you*, Hiranah." The man lifted his jaw defiantly. "This one fell too. We did not call her. Only you."

"You stole *me*?!"

The man's eyes hardened and his chest drew wider.

"You should be here, Hiranah. You *must* be here. You may not know it yet, but you *chose* to come."

"I chose to save Kyah!"

Something about that statement made the old man's eyes soften.

"Of course you did."

Ivy didn't know how to respond.

"Who are you?" she asked instead.

"My name is Gihn." He gestured to the hobbits that pressed in around her, listening intently. "We saw you fall so we came to find you."

"I fell? From where?"

"The sky."

Ivy scoffed, looking beyond the hobbits to the darkening sky outside the cave. *The sky.*

Gihn tilted his head to the side. "Close your eyes, Hiranah. I will try to show you."

Ivy narrowed her eyes and looked sideways to the spears still held by the hunters that had led her here. The man just stood, waiting. Reluctantly, Ivy closed her eyes. For a moment, there was nothing.

Then an image melted from shadow to relief behind her lids, slowly, like a watercolour taking form.

"What is this?" Ivy whispered.

"My memory," Gihn replied.

She was standing at the cave mouth at dusk, slightly off centre, facing towards the East. The sun was setting behind her, creating a silhouette of the mountain crest above. A perfect white moon was rising.

Other people were around her, pressed close, all oriented at the same obscure direction she herself was. *I'm one of them. No - I'm him.* Ivy was seeing the tribe through Gihn's eyes. More so, she somehow, *felt* them there, familiar and comforting. Each silhouette in the fading light held her heart. *I love them. No, I don't,* Ivy corrected herself. *He loves them.*

They were all standing, except for a few bodies hidden in shadowed pockets where they lay curled, surrounded by feet. An aching rush of sadness swept through her as she looked down at the shape of someone lying nearby. *Something's wrong.* The pain was all too familiar. *Loss... Grief...* Ivy tried to push the memory away but the grip on her wrist tightened.

Somewhere in the centre of the tribe a resonant hum picked up. It spread slowly. Each new voice brought a single note to complement the others, weaving through the night, like an instrument. It pulsed down the valley rifts and echoed from the cave walls, warming her body.

From the mountain they were hidden in, across the grasslands and to the jungle below, the encroaching night stilled. The ears of the forest pricked toward them. The sun was sinking. The moon was climbing.

The harmonic singing gripped Ivy's heart. She felt disembodied, a voyeur on a sacred rite, compelled to watch the scene but ashamed for wanting to. It was exquisite. She could not bring herself to open her eyes and lose it all. Ivy was suddenly desperate to stay part of this memory and to hear the transcendent notes that seemed to ignite the night forest.

Then suddenly, the dusk-song broke. A brilliant flash of white ruptured the sky, pulsing iridescent blue at the centre of the tear. The blue light splintered and fell to land, far to the east beyond the mountains.

Where they found me...

Ivy shuddered as she opened her eyes. The spears now seemed of no consequence in the face of a far greater danger.

"Gihn," she began tremulously, "I need to know something. This is very important." Ivy searched the man's eyes desperately. "Are there others like me here? Tall people?"

Gihn's eyes grew hard. "Yes. The karathah."

Her heart beat harder. "Karathah?"

"The karathah are tall. But their skin is dark and their spears are deadly -"

Ivy slumped in relief and let out a breath she didn't realize she'd been holding. *The karathah are tall...* Gihn could only mean Homo sapiens, native Floresians living in villages near the coast. If she could get there, she could get a bus to Labuan Bajo, a plane to Bali. *Oh, thank god.* She ran her shaking hand along the seam of her jeans. *Their skin is dark and their spears are deadly... spears?*

"These tall people - these *karathah* people," Ivy said slowly, "They live in houses don't they? I mean...big shelters made of wood and stones? With - ships and planes and cars and..."

Gihn was shaking his head, looking confused. "The karathah live in the north caves at the edge of the sea. They are...trouble."

Caves. Modern Floresians didn't live in caves. Nor did they need long spears. They had agriculture and the tourist trade.

No! Ivy scrambled to her feet, pushing Kyah away. She bent down, grabbing her satchel from the dirt and rummaged through it. A spray of papers fell to the cave floor as she pulled out her journal and began frantically leafing through the pages. *No. No no no. This isn't happening. It's not possible.* Ivy stared at the excavation map of Liang Bua that she had sketched not more than a week ago. Beside it was a copied photograph of the cave itself, still held in place with a paperclip.

Ivy looked up. Her stomach felt like lead and her hands trembled. Liang Bua cave was eerily familiar. But not quite right. Where were the picks and trowels? There were no piles of sediment. No signs of excavation. The cave mouth looked taller than that in the photograph she held. The massive stalactites that she had seen so many times they were committed to memory, still hung from the domed roof. But now they were shaped oddly and at least two meters higher than they should be. Ivy spun around, searching for better landmarks in the afternoon dim.

The ash!

She ran to the entrance wall and dropped her journal to the ground. Using broken rocks and her bare hands, Ivy started digging. She scraped and pulled the hard dirt from the floor, leaving her knuckles bloody and fingernails black. *No. This isn't real. It can't be.* The stratigraphic layers of Liang Bua were as clear in her memory as on the pages of her journal. Ivy grew more desperate as the pit got deeper. But no matter how far she dug, she couldn't find the layer of white tuffaceous silts that she was so desperately searching for. It was the single geological finger-print that could assure Ivy that she was still on the civilised side of the fine, white volcanic ash that had suffocated so many species on the island twelve thousand years before archaeologists dug them up again. But the layer wasn't there. Ivy covered her mouth with a filthy hand. Her nausea was almost overwhelming. There was no ash. Because those volcanic eruptions hadn't happened yet. *Extinction,* by whatever hand, hadn't happened yet.

But these - Ivy ran her trembling fingers down the inside wall of the make-shift excavation pit. Even in the fading light, subtle differences in the colours and texture of the stratigraphic layers screamed their individuality to her. They were a fingerprint in time. These layers, these *living floors* of Liang Bua cave past, belonged to the time far before volcanos had suffocated the island. They belonged fifty thousand years ago.

Ivy had landed on the knife edge of extinction in a volatile land.

She picked up the discarded journal with trembling hands. The black and white pages stared back at her. Archaeological records, maps, photos complete with stratigraphic lines, theodo-lites, researchers and their tools. But the once thrilling images now felt displaced and entirely academic. The bare ground of those photographs were soulless compared to where she stood now. Or rather, *when* she stood.

A wave of nausea rushed through her again. Ivy ran to the entrance of the cave. She collapsed down to her knees and vomited into the dirt until her stomach ached.

She knew they were behind her, still watching, but she didn't care. The realization of knowing not where she was, but *when* she was, was devastating.

Ivy had known from the moment she recognised the cave that she was in Flores. How she came to be there was anyone's guess. But then, the hobbits found her. A lone, surviving tribe of ancient hominid, hidden from the modern world. An archaeologist's dream, however unlikely.

But this cruel reality was no dream.

This Flores was primitive, wild and untouched by civilisation. The humans that surrounded her had been extinct for 50,000 years. *Fifty thousand years.*

The realisation that she had been somehow displaced was absolute. Ivy was far removed from civilisation, both in space and time. The earliest stirrings of art were only just ghosting the globe. Homo sapiens were still far from the infancy of agriculture. Bands of hunter-gatherers were finally weaving their way across Asia toward Australia. Neanderthals and Cro-Magnons were competing for food in the glacial plains of Europe where the last ice age wouldn't begin to retreat for another 20,000 years. The great pharaohs of Egypt, the Roman Empire, the first Xia dynasty of China – were still forty thousand years ahead.

Ivy was numb.

She twisted around and looked at Gihn, who was watching her every move. He stepped forward; his eyes level with hers, even as she crouched in the dirt. Ivy held her wrist to him.

"What do you want from me?" she asked hoarsely as he pressed the stone.

"My people are dying, Hiranah."

"Yes," she said. *Of course they are.*

"We need you to save us," Gihn said.

"Save you?" Ivy repeated blankly.

"You *must* save us," Gihn pressed.

"I *must* save you?" Ivy could hardly process his absurdly simple words for the weight of the task they carried. She clenched her jaw. A spark of anger flickered, catching heat in her chest. "You stole me!" she said. "Now you want to *use* me to save yourselves, but my own life means nothing to you?"

A rush of adrenaline charged through her body. Ivy pulled Kyah onto her lap, clinging to the comfort of the only creature to whom her survival did matter. She felt like a hostage. The blue and white light that had torn through the sky now tore through her mind and she steadied herself against Kyah's warmth. She felt on the verge of vomiting again.

Concern shrouded Gihn's eyes, but there was no apology.

"You don't understand, Hiranah. You *chose* this. We cannot survive without you."

Ivy tugged her wrist from his grip, breaking the connection. *You cannot survive at all.* Her lips trembled. She covered her face with her hands, trying to *just breathe*. After a minute, Ivy took both the amulet and his hand in hers again.

"This was no choice," she hissed.

"It was your choice to make," Gihn insisted.

"No it wasn't! I need to go back."

This time it was Gihn who snapped his hand from the amulet. He looked betrayed. Then scared. For a long moment neither of them moved. Then Gihn's eyes seemed to harden with resolution of whatever thought he was hiding. When he finally clasped the amulet on Ivy's wrist again, his voice was impassive.

"There is no way back, Hiranah. I am sorry you came."

Ivy's heart sank. She looked away. As the sun disappeared entirely, she stared unseeing into the darkness.

Her anger was suddenly gone. *Everything is gone. My life. My work. Orrin.*

I'm gone.

She sat for a long time, staring but unseeing. At some point, Ivy heard shuffling and whispers as her audience moved away. She was barely aware of them.

Eventually, Kyah's warmth brought her back. Ivy blinked,

surprised to find Gihn still beside her in the dark with his hand curled around her wrist.

"What is it you keep calling me?" Ivy asked quietly. "*Hiranah.* What does that mean, anyway?"

A smile touched the man's face. He reached a weathered hand to touch Ivy's cascading red hair.

"*Hiranah* is the colour of fire. I think perhaps, *Hiranah*, you fell from the sun."

CHAPTER 23

NEIL

eil Crawford pulled his aching arm close to his body as he trudged through the undergrowth. So far the redheaded woman had eluded him. He'd tracked her for three days now, fury mounting with each step. She was the only link to both the physics lab and this godforsaken death trap he'd fallen into.

It was hard. Harder than he wanted to admit. As a younger man, Neil had always conquered any situation he was thrown into; in fact, he'd relished the challenge of proving himself. But nothing could have prepared him for this. The jungle was an unwelcome detox and the humidity was drawing alcohol from his pores in rivulets of sweat. His head ached . His hands tremored. His heart pounded. Neil ached for alcohol. At this point, anything would do.

The precipice had been his first victory. His dilated pupils found the fine rocky dust layering the cliff edge, her shoe prints glaringly obvious. Sweeps of disturbance marked where she'd sat, staring across the horizon. In an instant, he'd guessed the river in the distance would be her first point of call. His own mouth had been aching with thirst. Despite his failing body, Neil had thrown his head back and laughed. *I'm on the right track; she can't be too far ahead.*

He'd found the durian tree. There was still half-eaten fruit all over the ground with human bite marks, most of it further attacked by bats in the night. He'd found the tree she had slept under, wet leaves and mulch tellingly piled into a raised bed. A few times Neil had become lost, doubling back to scour for signs of her on the forest floor. Three days had come and gone. But he was still tracking her. And he was catching up.

God knows what's happened to the lunar energy field by now.

Three nights and Neil still had no contact with the outside world. He'd eaten rats, snakes and fruit that smelled like vomit. His cigarette lighter had become his talisman, the polished silver spun over and over in his fingers as he walked. A nautical helm had been engraved on it long ago and had rubbed almost smooth. There was also a much newer engraving, a name; *Benjamin.* His memory found a young boy in a hospital bed. Blinking lights, nasal tube, no hair. Neil swore at the rush of anger that caught him and shoved the memory back down.

He pocketed the lighter with a scowl. At least with the lighter he didn't have to eat raw.

Neil turned his mind briefly to his ex-wife. They rarely spoke these days, so Francine wouldn't have missed him. She'd grown distant years ago, resenting his travel and work commitments after her unplanned pregnancy. He'd never wanted kids, she'd known that all along.

She'd changed though, as women always do, when it happens. And she'd tried to change him too. It was Francine who had engraved their son's name on his lighter, as a constant reminder. But Benjamin, well…. it was bad timing really, when Neil was at such a crucial stage of his career. He was expected to work late. To travel. To put in the hours. He refused to throw it all away to settle down and play Daddy. His own father had had little time for him as a boy. You suck it up, become a man. Life goes on.

A phantom scent of disinfectant thrust the boy back into his memory. *Maybe life doesn't go on.* Anger flared again in his chest. *There's nothing I can do.* Francine already martyred herself by the hospital bed day by day. He wasn't needed. He pushed the memory back under.

For years now, Francine had found comfort elsewhere. It made no difference to him. Neil had been left with empty rooms, which had held little of his love to begin with. Whether she had been aware or not of his frequent indiscretions during their marriage didn't matter anymore. It was only now that he was lost in this suffocating green hell-hole, that Neil wished that she would notice him gone, and care enough to do something about it.

Surely Cassandra and Dimitri, as inept as they are, have reported me missing. They knew I was heading to the university. They knew what was at stake. If they ever want to work again, they'd better be raising hell.

Great, my last cigarette. Neil threw the empty packet into the trees angrily. *Fucking hell.* His black Armani suit was covered in filth. He'd wrapped his jacket around his waist in the stifling air. His tie had acted as a sling for his dislocated shoulder during the first two days, but now it was screwed up in his pocket.

Neil pulled his mobile phone from his back pocket and turned it on. The battery was precious so he used it sparingly. There was still no reception which simply confirmed that he really *was* in the middle of nowhere. Worse, the GPS signal was non-existent. This bothered him more. The energy field must have peaked by now. *So, they've taken out the satellites.*

Neil flicked the screen with his finger, avoiding the cracked glass along the top. The only useful operation left was the virtual compass programmed into the software. The image of a needle swung across the screen, locating magnetic north. *She's still heading North-East.* With a sharp stick he scratched a deep arrow into the nearest tree face. If he had to, he knew he could get back to where he started.

Many years ago, Neil had dedicated his leisure time to rogaining. Ironically, it all had started at The University of Melbourne during his own time there as an undergraduate. His interest in navigation had led him to the University Mountaineering club which had developed a new sport based on cross-country navigation. Long distance challenges were set each full moon, with contenders racing each other in small teams to visit checkpoints with the intent of maximising their team score. Endurance was a key factor in the long distances and high mountainous peaks traversed, and as the new sport gained popularity, Neil's competitive streak soared. The annual championships became too easy. Neil pushed harder, exhilarating in the mental and physical challenge of outstripping the competition. Over the years Neil's team members had dropped off, unwilling to push their limits as they got older. Eventually it was just him, navigating even by stars once daylight succumbed. He preferred his victory alone anyway. Man against nature.

Nearing sixty years old now, those days were a distant memory. Neil's body had become soft and slow. He grunted in disgust and pushed himself harder, ignoring the burning of his shoulder and the pounding in his head.

I need a drink. Neil thrust his trembling hand back into his pocket and found the silver lighter. Once more, he began spinning it slowly between his fingers as he walked.

Another hour passed. Then another. As the light in the forest dimmed, Neil watched the floor more closely. The woman's tracks were getting harder to find and soon he would have to stop for the night. *I should start looking for something to eat. Another rat maybe.* Last night he'd sat still for four hours waiting for something to scurry close enough to kill. He'd seen those documentaries about surviving in the wild. They made it look easy;

after all, it was instinctual wasn't it? Catch an animal. Eat it. Survive.

But it wasn't easy. Neil's shoulder had stiffened painfully and only defiance had kept him sitting there, waiting for hours in the dark. But he'd succeeded.

Keeping a fire going long enough to cook the rat had taken another hour. Afterwards, the insomnia and increasing anxiety caused by alcohol withdrawal kept him shaking all night, sweating profusely in the chill night air, his eyes darting wildly with each noise. But he'd survived. For nearly four days now, he'd survived.

Neil kept his pointed stick in his belt. Now, he re-sharpened the tip with a broken stone as he walked.

Something isn't right. Neil knelt in the fading light, intently focused on the forest floor. The woman's footprints had been getting heavier and sinking deeper into the mud as he progressed. *Was she running?* Footprints were stamped haphazardly into the soft base of a ladder like tree. *Back, forth, left, right, back, left, right.* Something had happened here. The leaves had been swept away with movement, revealing a dark muddy soil. *Round marks – knee prints?* And what were these marks, like human hand prints but smaller and elongated with a long palm and the thumb shifted too far down the side. *Not human.* He thought back to his last memory of the redhead in the lab. She had been carrying a monkey, hadn't she? *The bloody monkey was here too?*

On his hands and knees Neil traced the patterns with his fingertips. The woman had been facing west, butted up against the base of tree, fallen to her knees. A slice in the mud drew his eye. *Her stick.* The stripped walking stick still lay in the muddy leaves. He picked it up, twirling it in his hands. Blood was smeared on the top end where she'd held it in her fist. It was smoother there. She must have gripped it tight.

Neil surveyed the area. It was almost too dark to see now. If she had found a new stick to lean on, he'd never know; the forest was full of them. *But why would she?* Neil ran his fingers up the shaft; there was no sign of weakness. If it had been left by accident, then the redhead must have been severely distracted. Tell-tale holes in the soil suggested she'd leaned on it heavily so she must have needed it.

And then Neil saw it.

A single footprint, facing hers in the patch of mud. Barefooted and small, even smaller than hers. *A kid?* His eyes followed Ivy's path, disappearing North East into the surrounding trees. It was too dark to follow now; he'd have to wait out the night. *But tomorrow... tomorrow I'll find her and she'll tell me what's going on. Whatever it takes.*

Neil rested back against the ladder tree, surrounded by footprints. He rubbed his thighs in agitation and drew his fingers through his thinning hair.

Somewhere, despite the insanity of his predicament, the answers would come. Neil silently inventoried what facts he already knew.

She left me there, mangled and unconscious in the filth. She left me for dead. His fingers twitched. She went into that lab, so she must know something. If she knew what they were doing with the energy mutation, then she was either a liability to them like me, or an ally to their research. Bitterness coiled in his chest. Either way, I'll make her talk.

Neil glimpsed a minute shifting of the muddy leaves beside him. *Flick. Stab.* A small marsupial caught the sharp end of his sharpened stick. He grinned, leaning back.

Survival of the fittest.

CHAPTER 24

ORRIN

They had resolved that the anomaly was restricted to their lab. But that was where certainty began and ended. The cause of the electromagnetic explosion still eluded them, as did their ability to predict whether it might happen again. With over three hundred staff in the Physics building alone, Orrin couldn't take that risk. If there was any recurrence or escalation in severity of the incident, the consequences could be devastating. For hours, the three men worked in near silence, running scans and tearing through endless lines of code.

"Lads?" Orrin pushed back from his monitor, fighting panic.

Dale moved across to him immediately, but Phil merely raised an eyebrow.

"I've just run a data comparison on magnetospheric fluctuations for the last year against the records from THEMIS," he began, hesitantly.

Phil nodded expectantly. The THEMIS mission by NASA had been established to gather multi-satellite data on space weather events, in particular, the origins of substorms that could affect Earth. Magnetospheric fluctuations were measured by five orbiting satellites which relayed the data for analysis to multiple highly regarded institutions. Monitoring these data changes in electromagnetic radiation had been fundamental to the calculations that had led Orrin to the devastating conclusion that Earth's magnetosphere was incrementally weakening.

"And?" said Phil, waiting.

"And… there's got to be some sort of mistake in their data records."

"Whose records?"

"NASA."

Phil dismissed the notion with a soft laugh. "Don't be ridiculous."

Reading the monitor from behind Orrin's shoulder, Dale let out a soft curse.

"That can't be right?" He looked to Orrin for reassurance.

"Of course it's not right." Orrin's voice cracked. "If this data was correct, then our magnetosphere would be in critical flux. Our electrical grids and satellites would be on the brink of breaking down. Hell, the highest altitudes of the earth would already be experiencing enough solar radiation to destroy biological organisms. It would only be a matter of time…"

Phil offered a grim smile. "The Himalayas are feeling it. Still, that's why we're doing all this right? Searching for answers." He turned back to his screen and continued his analysis.

"What do you mean?" Orrin demanded. "'*The Himalayas are feeling it?!'* Phil, wait, are you saying these figures are correct?"

Phil turned back, confused. "Of course they are. You know that."

"Bollocks I do! Our predictions didn't bring Earth under this intensity of solar radiation for hundreds of years," Orrin replied. "With these measurements, the atmosphere could heat high altitudes critically within the next six months! Maybe even less."

"Chill, dude," said Phil, "How is any of this a surprise to you? We've been looking at this data for months. Why are you saying you suddenly don't believe it?"

"This data is wrong, Phil, wrong!" Orrin exclaimed. "I've never seen measurements like these. I have the figures we analysed only last week on my laptop. The correct ones, from the same source." Orrin disappeared into his office, returning with the laptop. "Dale and I were running analyses on it for the new experiments when this whole mess happened." Sure enough, Orrin pulled up an identical file name and displayed its content side by side with the NASA report.

"It's not even close," said Orrin. "Last week the readings were stable, relatively at least, but this - this is critical! Christ Phil, it has to be a mistake!"

Phil scowled. "What the hell is wrong with you, O? That data is why we're on the payroll here; to figure out how to stop the fluctuations from getting worse. Why on earth do you think we've been doing these experiments? For fun? Because, if it is for fun, I know some ladies that are way more fun than you two." He swivelled back in his chair.

"How can you be so nonchalant about this?" Orrin yelled, spinning the back of Phil's chair to face him. "If this really is the right data, I'm telling you the radiation could reach critical levels within six months!"

"And I'm telling you this is not new to me," Phil spat back. "Get a bloody grip, man!" Phil picked up his wallet. "I need a breather." He left the room.

Dale excused himself nervously and followed him out. For the next hour, Orrin tried to find some way of reconciling the devastating discrepancy he'd found. He was convinced the new measurements from NASA were a mistake but those saved on his laptop seemed to be the only record of an alternate truth. Orrin was almost glad for it. It took his mind off Ivy and his inability to find her. She still hadn't called and he was starting to think that perhaps she didn't want to be found.

Completing yet another analysis, Orrin once again came up empty-handed. Stretching back in his roller chair, he rubbed his tired eyes under his glasses as Phil and Dale re-entered. Dale was carrying a wrapped sandwich and a coke under one arm and a bag of doughnuts under the other, the former two of which he passed to Orrin.

"Here, you're falling asleep."

"Thanks, Dale." Orrin ate the sandwich, not realising how hungry he was until he had something to fill him.

Phil flicked through a newspaper, looking annoyed. "My stocks have dropped again." He pushed the paper aside and rolled back to his computer.

Orrin took the newspaper, desperate for a minute's distraction. He sat forward with a jerk.

"What the hell is this?"

"What's what?" Phil sighed.

"This thing on the front page?" Orrin demanded.

Phil looked over with disinterest and shrugged. Dale glanced up nervously from his computer and wandered over to read. Photos of a burning high-rise dominated the front page.

Hobbit Shame - Violent Riots Sweep Nation

Melbourne, Australia - Political pressure has increased this week as riots continue to plague capital cities around the world. Public outcry over the use of so-called "hobbits" for pharmaceutical research is at an all-time high. Wildlife conservationists are calling for a ban on all invasive research in light of the appalling conditions brought to light by the recent downfall of a Melbourne-based pharmaceutical company.

Cosmitech, the pharmaceutical giant behind the allegations, was in a state of receivership during the time of the investigation and has now been foreclosed. Yesterday, rioters in Victoria's capital ended a violent rally with the arson of Cosmitech's corporate headquarters. Two office workers died in the fire and six more casualties are in a serious condition at St Cantor's Hospital with burns and smoke inhalation. Fifteen protesters were arrested at the scene on charges of wilful damage and arson. Court hearings are scheduled for later this month.

"It's a storm in a teacup" quotes sacked Cosmitech CEO Darrell Mayer. "Animal research has been accepted in the scientific and medical community for decades. These wildlife crusaders are suggesting scientific advancement should take a backseat to subjective moral ethics purely because this animal happens to share some DNA with us. It's absurd. Research is needed for advancement of the human condition; there will always be costs to progress. This is just one of them."

However, allegations that Cosmitech had deliberately ignored regulations for the management of pain and distress in experimental practices have sparked outrage in the wider community. Spokesperson for the Animal Research Regulation Department, Mr Alex Kraymer, says the company had been under investigation for some time before the claims were made public.

"This is a case of extreme conflict of interest between key government and corporate players. Major corporate investors have corrupted the decision-making process for direct financial benefit. I believe manipulation of political procedure has resulted in the prolonged illegal suffering and abuse of these animals."

Regarded widely as a pest in their native South-East Asian islands, "hobbits" have long been targeted for experimental procedures due to their biological similarities with modern humans. The Homo floresiensis species is widely accepted as the closest genetic relative to modern humans and are controversially suggested to display a primitive social system. As the alleged inspiration for the iconic fictional characters in a famous epic fantasy series, the severely reclusive nature of Homo floresiensis has historically done little to promote a positive public image.

A leaked version of the damning report on Cosmitech was made public earlier this week. Although no claims have been made to the source, Government officials continue to deny the use of Homo floresiensis in illegal experimental procedures. Claims of practices involving the permanent removal of skull bone to allow electrode manipulation of sensory perception have emerged, sparking heated debate on the ethics of such severe physical manipulation on live and un-anaesthetised animals. Other common practices include cosmetic and poison irritation testing on eyes and facial areas, as well as injections of pathogens and cancer causing agents to develop vaccines and medication for human use.

Animal rights activists are pushing for a full-scale departmental inquiry to be launched.

For related stories - see page 4.

Orrin dropped the paper on the desk in front of him. Dale had finished reading and was standing back, looking confused.

"What is this thing, this 'hobbit' animal? I've never heard of it," said Dale.

Orrin looked up mystified. "I have no idea. An entirely new animal? They're saying it's genetically related to humans."

"But they can't be new, that article references fictional hobbits too as being inspired by these things. Those epic fantasy novels have been around for over 70 years." Dale shuffled self-consciously, "I took a few undergrad courses in English lit."

"Well this is mental - whatever this animal is, it can't have caused so much trouble so quickly," said Orrin. "Riots, arson, two people dead...it's desperate altogether."

Dale stared at him mutely.

"How could they find a new *Homo* species?" Orrin muttered.

"They all died out millennia ago. It sounds like a load of gaff to me."

"Well …" began Dale thoughtfully, then shook his head. "Maybe it's all a big publicity stunt gone wrong?"

Orrin nodded vaguely at his suggestion, confused into silence.

Phil ducked between them, grabbing a doughnut from the paper bag.

"It's just the damn hippies again with the same old crap about hobbits. They push it because they're *Homo* - barely - it always settles down. They've been arrested. Forget it."

Astonished, Orrin and Dale both stared Phil down.

Phil frowned. "What?"

"You've heard of this hobbit animal before?" Orrin pressed.

"Of course I've heard of it, why the hell wouldn't I?"

"Well what is it? When did they find it?" Orrin asked.

"What do you mean, *find it?*" replied Phil. "They've always been around. In South-East Asia. They're bloody pests."

Orrin stared, dumbfounded. *Pests? What the hell?* His mind searched for ways to accommodate its apparent inadequacies. Maybe Phil's Asian heritage accounted for his familiarity of these creatures, while Orrin's European background stunted it? *Not a chance.* Phil was born in Melbourne, as Aussie as the next guy and certainly not a wealth of traditional Chinese folklore. Or anything cultural for that matter.

Dale broke the silence. "I've never heard of this thing and my parents are… were, biologists. There must be some mistake…"

"Seriously dudes, there's no mistake," Phil interjected, "Hobbits have been around forever, Charles Darwin even wrote about them in The Origin of Species. Everyone studies it at school. Hobbits used to be all over the place, hell, my grandparents even used to eat them as a delicacy. Apparently they taste a bit like pork. Personally, I'll stick to steak, thanks."

A wave of disgust hit Orrin.

"You're joking!"

"No joke," Phil said. "They're as common as koalas– well, maybe not the best comparison these days, but you know what I mean. You guys need to get out more." He sauntered off, dusting sugar on the floor, doughnut in hand.

Dale retreated to his roller chair and stared into space, clearly grappling with the terrifying thought of being so uneducated.

"I don't care how common they are," Orrin said. "This is the most idiotic thing I've ever heard. You can't claim another species has been on the planet my entire life and I just wasn't paying attention. I'm a god-damn scientist." His earlier frustrations rose again. "Hold up - did they say '*floresiensis*'? As in from Flores in Indonesia?"

"Yeah man, *Flores*," said Phil. "The little flower people - according to the hippies and eco-tourism pushers."

"Then they're not real! I mean, they're extinct. Ivy told me all about them."

"They're definitely not extinct, mate."

"Of course they bloody-well are! Look, Ivy will know all about it then," Orrin said. "She's studying stone tools from Flores – from these *extinct* hominids."

"Whatever man, it's your funeral." Phil shook his head smirking. "Did you kiss and make up yesterday, by the way - after she took off with the chimp?"

Already upset, Orrin nettled at Phil's casual intrusion.

"No, because apparently Ivy doesn't exist," Orrin said. "I couldn't find her in her lab and no one seems to know anything about her. I couldn't even find her office."

"Serious? Man that sucks." Phil's mouth twitched. Then after a brief pause, "maybe she's ditching you."

Orrin threw the remainder of his sandwich back into its plastic wrapper. "Jaysus Christ Phil! It's a wonder you get any women at all, you're so god-damn tactless!"

"Woah dude, I'm sorry, okay," Phil rolled his eyes. "I'm sure she's not the sort to cut and run on you. I never even met her, man."

"Well Dale did, and she *does* exist whether she's ditching me or not," said Orrin.

"Actually, I never met her either, Orrin." Dale said apologetically. "I mean, you told me about her, but I never actually saw her or the chimp."

"She bloody well existed, okay!"

Phil and Dale exchanged a harried glance.

"Course she did, man," placated Phil. "She'll come round - chicks always do. Just go buy her something; jewellery works best." Phil turned back to his desk, busying himself with a new scan. "I didn't even know they had chimps here," he mumbled.

Orrin collapsed back into his chair with a sigh. "Yeah, in the Biology labs apparently, for behavioural research." Flashes of Kyah in the great court needled at Orrin's guilt. *Kyah!* He jumped to his feet.

"Jaysus! You're a genius Phil! All I have to do is go to the chimp lab - Ivy visits Kyah every day so I'll leave a message for her there!" For the first time since Ivy had disappeared, Orrin's smile was matched in his tired eyes.

Phil kept typing. "You're the doc, doc."

CHAPTER 25

IVY

$\mathcal{I}$vy's shoulders were stiff. Her mouth was set in a hard line as she followed a tiny hobbit woman from the cave the following morning. She had refused to speak after Gihn had offered her a sleeping mat and some water the night before and instead, lay awake all night staring at the hearth coals glowing in the dark. Cyclic imaginings of her quiet, comfortable life shattered by this dangerous primitive one had rollercoasted her through grief and fear until daylight found her exhausted again.

Her ankle throbbed and her eyes burned. An aching loneliness had settled in Ivy's chest, punctuated constantly by the sharp bite of loss and the memory of Orrin's voice.

Desperate to escape the smell of bodies, Ivy had let the woman coax her from the cave at daybreak. She kept her distance though, studying her guide with almost paranoid intensity.

The woman's wide face was haloed by a mess of glossy hair that reached her shoulders in a thick tangle, falling unevenly down her back. Her body was naked to the waist and she supported a heavily pregnant belly with her free hand as she moved. A utilitarian hide slung around her hips swayed as she walked, bulky with hidden objects stored within it. Despite her burdens, the tiny woman had an undeniable grace. Her long arms were muscular but lithe and her forearms covered with a dusting of hair. Her knees were rough and scuffed light with dirt. She walked slowly and flat footed across the grass, muttering soothing words that Ivy didn't understand. Ivy threw a glance over her shoulder, to make sure Kyah was still following in the branches.

The forest opened onto the grassland they had crossed the night before. A river terrace was cut into the valley. The morning sun flecked silver across the surface of the water as they approached and Ivy noticed a handful of hobbits already gathered by the edge. The stomach of some large animal was being filled with fresh water. A pile of roots and shoots sat on a flat edged rock. Ivy's pregnant companion walked over to them and spoke. After throwing wary looks toward the newcomers, the others gathered their provisions, knotting and carrying the distended stomach by its adjoining vessels and disappeared into the greenery.

The pregnant woman returned and gave a tentative smile. She reached out and tugged on Ivy's hand. Ivy allowed the soft insistence and lowered herself to the grass, finally meeting the pregnant hobbit at eye level.

They stared at each other. Ivy had never expected to see the bone structure of this species so fleshed and vibrant. In fact, this woman's face was the only feature of the Homo floresiensis *human* - as there was no doubt in her mind that this was indeed a *human* - that Ivy's imagination had never done justice to. The woman's face was a beacon of kindness.

"Sha-ahn." The pregnant woman's fingers touched her own short forehead. "Shahn." Her thick eyebrows furrowed for a moment at Ivy's silence. The woman touched her own forehead once more. "Shahn." She glanced at the amulet dangling from Ivy's wrist.

She's being polite. With the realisation, Ivy pulled the amulet into her palm and held it out, inviting conversation. The hobbit curled her petite hand over it.

"Hello Shahn," Ivy said.

Shahn's face lit up. She suddenly drew close, placing her hands on either side of Ivy's head and bringing their foreheads together. It was warm and intimate. Ivy flushed under the woman's palms. Shahn smelt of aromatic herbs. Her belly pushed into Ivy's arm, surprising her with a distinct nudge.

Shahn pulled back, apparently delighted. She took the amulet between their hands again. "My unborn child likes you, Hiranah."

"Apparently so," Ivy smiled. As miserable as she felt, it was hard to be rude to this woman.

"I thought you would like to wash," Shahn said.

"Definitely," replied Ivy, getting to her feet.

From the recesses of her pouch, Shahn pulled a small mass of pulpy plant material and took it to the river's edge, setting it on a flat rock. Cupping water onto it, she mashed it with her fist producing a lather of slippery juice then came back to Ivy. "I'll clean your hides while you bathe," Shahn offered. She looked up at Ivy, unsure how to begin peeling the layers of clothes away.

"Thank you, but I can do it. These *hides* get very heavy when they're wet and you're, well - " Ivy trailed off lamely.

Shahn laughed. "I carry fish heavier than that Hiranah." She ran her finger down the seam of Ivy's jeans curiously. "I've never seen an animal with this pattern though."

"They're um, made of plants," Ivy said, regretting it instantly. Denim was not exactly hobbit *couture.*

"Blue plants?" Shahn smiled. "I haven't seen those either." Shahn stepped back then stared up at her, waiting. "So, will you wash?"

Of course. No modesty required. Ivy took a deep breath and then stripped to her underwear. As she peeled the jeans from her ankle, she winced in pain. The cut was still weeping. In her peripheral vision, she noticed Shahn frown.

Ivy immersed herself in the chilled river with a gasp. She rubbed the pulp over her hair and skin, grateful for the friction. She carefully cleaned the blood from her swollen ankle. Shahn walked knee deep with Ivy's singlet, squatting to accommodate her round belly. She hummed monotonously as she scrubbed it and Ivy was reminded of the dusk song she'd witnessed in Gihn's memory. The note Shahn hummed was probably her part of the harmonic whole. Ivy felt a hollow ache for the loss of her cello and swallowed the lump in her throat.

Dragging her jeans into the water, Ivy scrubbed the blood stains against the rock using the rest of the soapy pulp. They weren't clean but they would do. She wrung them out and spread them on a rock to dry. The sun was higher now, warming her skin.

Her attention was interrupted by a rustling in the trees. Kyah dropped to the ground nearby. She picked around the base of a candlenut tree before settling down. From behind her, a small boy clutching a grass woven bag dropped to the ground as well. He scampered to where Kyah was sitting with a huge grin on his face. The boy began to climb into the bonobo's lap, his knees splayed to each side.

Kyah's lips drew back in fear. She tensed at the unfamiliar contact, letting out shrill barks of distress.

"No!" Ivy pushed through the water. "He'll get hurt! Kyah's not used to other people."

The boy looked infantile, only two feet tall, but leanly proportioned with none of the baby fat of an infant. *Five or six years old,* Ivy thought fleetingly, but it was almost impossible to tell as the size difference to a human child was so marked. The boy stared up at the bonobo then suddenly knocked his forehead onto hers, rubbing them together enthusiastically. Kyah's shrill barking stopped short. She stared at him warily.

The boy laughed again and reached high, dragging his little fingers down Kyah's face and resting them over her scratched chest where he stopped. He drew small circles around the mark with his tiny fingertip. Kyah growled uneasily, and looked to Ivy who was desperately signing the word "baby" as she scrambled onto the grass edge of the river.

Shahn pulled Ivy back gently as she made to pass by.

"I think Trahg is safe," Shahn said placidly.

"No, you don't understand," said Ivy. "Kyah doesn't trust people. She could hurt him very badly." Kyah was unquestionably intelligent, but ultimately instinctual. If she felt threatened, the bonobo could break the child's bones.

"Just wait," Shahn said.

Kyah pushed the boy off. Unfazed, the little boy climbed back on. He curled his spindly legs into Kyah's lap and pulled open his woven bag. He retrieved some fruit and handed it to Kyah, who sniffed it. Hesitantly, Kyah ran her own fingertips down the boy's face, poking him gently in the nostril and mouth and making him giggle. Then they sat, seemingly transfixed, considering each other for a long moment.

What are they seeing? Ivy wondered, still itching to intervene, despite Shahn's insistence. An abused ape and prehistoric child, so alien to each other across time, continents and jungles, real and concrete...

Still connected, Shahn answered Ivy's thought.

"I think they see a friend, Hiranah." She smiled reassuringly.

Trahg suddenly laughed as Kyah's fingertips found a ticklish spot under his chin. He knocked Kyah's hand away roughly.

Kyah's nostrils flared. Ivy's heart skipped a beat.

Oh no.

"Wait," Shahn said again, more insistently.

Kyah's response was instinctual, but not in the way Ivy expected. The bonobo gently brushed Trahg's hair back from his face. Kyah lifted her wrist and gently presented the back of her long hand to the little boy's lips. It was the reassurance of a mother primate to an infant.

"You were right," Ivy whispered. Her eyes pricked with emotion.

Did she remember? Perhaps, in that very first year of Kyah's life, her own mother had done it to her. Innate protection for the boy was cemented by a connection that transcended species and language.

Ivy wiped away a tear.

Shahn left Ivy alone by a smoking hearth. Dozens of eyes penetrated her solitude but no one else approached. Across the cave, she saw Shahn approach a grey-haired woman who shot furtive glances in Ivy's direction as they spoke. The woman quickly tumbled something into Shahn's hands and shooed her away, scanning the vicinity as she left.

Shahn returned with various plants. She set to work by the coals, plucking dark, heart shaped leaves from a vine and piling them onto a flat stone. She ground half of the leaves into a green mash and then scooped them into a shallow bone dish brimming with water. Shahn nestled the bowl on coals to steep. After a few minutes, Shahn picked it back up and stirred it with her fingers. She turned to Ivy, tapping softly on the leg of her jeans.

Ivy hurried to roll the leg of her jeans up, exposing the seeping pink cut.

"The juice will cool your wound and reduce pain," explained Shahn as she dribbled warm liquid over the wound with steady hands. "Lahstri is our healer, but Krue won't let her... well, I can do it for now." Ivy looked around. Lahstri, whom Ivy assumed was the grey haired woman Shahn had spoken to, was now nowhere to be seen.

Next, Shahn pulled an orange, segmented root from the bundle. She ground it on a flat rock, and then placed the separated fibres in tepid water over the coals, spinning the mixture as it warmed. When she was satisfied, Shahn used her fingers to scoop the pulp onto some leaves. The paste smelled strong and aromatic. Shahn placed the poultice against Ivy's skin using the dark leaves as a protective outer layer.

"The root will clean your blood," Shahn explained. Ivy recognised the leaves used to wrap the poultice, and also those steeped to wash the open sore as those of the betel plant. Betel juice, she had learned only recently, was a natural analgesic. The orange rhizome Ivy guessed must be turmeric, although Ivy would never have known how to find it herself. Its roots held antiseptic and anti-inflammatory properties and were used to cleanse wounds and stimulate recovery. Ivy's thoughts wandered to a memory less than a week gone. *Her old life.*

"Archaeobotany, guys." Ivy had begun as she walked in. "A veritable treasure trove of palaeontological gold. This is how we study the emergence of agriculture, changing seasons and ice ages and of course, the prehistoric culinary arts." Ivy was on top of the world; she had just passed Orrin in the courtyard and exchanged not-so-subtle glances. "So, who can give me an example of methodologies used to study prehistoric plants?"

As usual Kathryn's hand shot up first. "Palynology."

"Brilliant. Pollen is everywhere. We can use the presence of pollen in archaeological digs to reconstruct the environment at the time of site occupation. Pollen equals plants and plants can tell us what season and climate our ancestors were living in. Another one?"

"Shit," smirked Travis from behind a paper coffee cup.

"Charming." Ivy rolled her eyes. "But surprisingly astute. I assume you mean coprolites. If we look at the micro remains of plant matter in fossilised faeces, we can actually tell what plants the animal had been

eating. There's often a good collection of seeds, plant fibres, cellulose and nuts -" Travis chortled - "still present in faeces which we can identify to species level. If we're lucky we even get the date." Travis laughed out loud, spraying a mouthful of coffee across the desk.

"Dude!" Oliver growled, wiping the back of his neck with his sleeve.

Ivy sighed. "It's a surprisingly useful tool for those mature enough to handle it." She raised an eyebrow to the handful of others who were snickering appreciatively.

"Not something I'm gonna handle," murmured Travis.

"Okay moving on. What else can we use to identify ancient plants?" There were no takers. "Has anyone heard of phytoliths?"

"I have," offered Kathryn. She straightened up imperiously. "During growth, plants take inorganic substances like silica and calcium oxalate from the soil, which then gets deposited within their cells. After they die and decay, these microscopic, rigid and uniquely shaped secretions, called phytoliths, end up back in the soil and can survive in conditions that destroy most of our organic evidence. Each species of plant has a distinct phytolith shape. We find them in residues on food preparation tools, ritual offerings, in agricultural soil and even food build up on fossilised teeth." Kathryn sat back with a self-satisfied smirk as Ivy clapped alone.

"Perfect. And if you ever do post-grad Kathryn, you're mine."

A dreadlocked boy spoke up. "But there are so many species of plants in the world, I mean, how can you tell which phytolith is from which plant?"

"Excellent question Jace and it deserves a practical answer." Ivy smirked. "Come by the res lab this afternoon and I'll show you. I'm currently using modern plant samples from the Lesser Sunda Islands to create a catalogue of phytoliths that might be represented on stone tools from our digs there."

Ivy jumped up and grabbed a stack of photocopied reference charts, dropping them in front of him. "We've got lots of ethnographic data already on what plants are eaten by local indigenous groups, so that's our starting point. First we identify and collect the different parts of the *plants; then we isolate the phytoliths under a microscope and begin the stimulating and relentless slog of cataloguing them for future archaeological reference. Every type is unique, so we can use them later to work backwards and identify the plant itself."*

"For the record, if anyone would like to join Jace in this highly esteemed task for extra credit, feel free to volunteer. I've got five boxes waiting that have just arrived through customs." Jace groaned and sunk low in his chair. Ivy couldn't help but laugh at the faces in front of her, all but Kathryn, doing their best to look inconspicuous. "Come on guys! This is real archaeology for you. And don't forget - microscopes are so hot right now."

There were at least one hundred hobbits, probably more, divided between seventeen hearths. Ivy had been given a sleeping mat at Shahn's hearth, which was shared with her mate Xiou, little Trahg and Shahn's younger sister Leihna. Gihn also shared the hearth and Ivy had come to realize he was Xiou's father.

Shahn presented Ivy with the shoulder blade of a large animal serving as a plate, heaped with stewed vegetables. Pinang nuts, yam bean tubers and wild cow pea were blended with grassy herbs giving off a rich, savoury smell. Ivy ate it gratefully, and when she was done, Shahn passed her a stomach pouch of water. Although the idea of putting her lips to the vessel of a stomach to drink was horribly unsavoury, Ivy had no choice. Shahn had not seemed surprised by Ivy's request that her own diet not include meat, apparently accepting it as just another peculiarity of Ivy's version of human.

As soon as Ivy had eaten, Gihn insisted she follow him to the darkest corner of the cave. Ivy recoiled at what she found there. Four grown men and one woman lay tightly curled on their sides. Four were shaking violently and the last was morbidly still.

In the flickering firelight, their skin looked sallow. Their breath came weak and fast and their bodies were in various stages of wasting. One of the men heaved upward shuddering, as he threw up violently. A woman rushed to help and Ivy saw blood on her hands as she pulled them away from his face.

Gihn had shuffled quietly next to her. He placed his hand over the amulet.

"It begins with the vomiting," he said. "There is blood from the mouth and blood in loose bowel motions. Then the heart beat grows slow."

Ivy crouched down and turned to Kyah. "Go play with Trahg, honey." Kyah shuffled back to Shahn's hearth. When Ivy was satisfied the bonobo was a safe distance away, she turned back to Gihn, reflexively covering her nose and mouth with her trembling hand. She guessed that if this was an airborne virus, she was already done for.

"They all have the same sickness?"

"Yes." Gihn watched for a moment, his mouth a hard line. When he continued speaking, it was through his thoughts, keeping their conversation private. *We call it the Swift Death. The sickness attacks only our hunters, the strongest and healthiest of our family. Truen,*" Gihn gestured to what looked like the most hopeless case, a man whose shallow, rattled breaths seemed to be the only indication that was alive at all, *"was young and fast. Our best with arrows.*" The man's ribs brutally corrugated his skin and his limbs clung from an unnaturally bulbous belly. His joints looked severely swollen.

Ivy was horrified. "How long can he live like this?"

Gihn's eyes glistened. "I am surprised he is still alive now. He responds just a little to his mate Juna. I think he only lives because she pleads him to stay. It has been just over half a moon since he fell ill, the others have lived barely past a quarter moon."

Dead within a week.

"Not one has recovered?"

Gihn's expression was grim. He shook his head. "When Truen fell sick I knew we needed help. Our ancestors believed the life stone would bring you to us. I had to try. We called to you many times. I'd almost given up hope. But then you came." Gihn knelt down and pressed his hand to Truen's forehead. He whispered in the man's ear and then crouched for a moment with his forehead pressed gently against that of the dying man. Once again, Ivy felt like an intruder to the intimacy around her. When Gihn stood up and put his hand to the amulet on her wrist, there were tears in his eyes. "Truen is not just our best with arrows, Hiranah. He is the the youngest son of my mate. She died too, four summers past."

Suddenly, Truen's back stiffened and arched. He cried out and the back of his head hit the sleeping mat hard. A woman, presumably Truen's mate, Juna, came rushing over as the convulsion stuttered to an end. Truen's eyes rolled back in his head. He was gasping for breath, a wet crackling sound. As Juna lifted Truen's head and gently placed it on her lap, he lapsed into unconsciousness. The woman began stroking his hair, curled forward to hush him. Judging by the passivity of those around, it was clearly not the first time it had happened.

Panic rose in Ivy's throat. "I can't do this Gihn. I know you want me to save him, but I don't know how."

Gihn's eyes stayed fixed on his son. "You cannot save Truen, Hiranah. It's too late, I know that. But there are others. In four moons, we have lost nearly half of our hunters. Lahstri has no plant that can help them. Without our hunters, we will all starve." Gihn turned to her. His gaze was arresting. "But there is more, Hiranah," he said. "This Swift Death - it is just the beginning."

"More?" Ivy whispered, horrified. The wasting sickness of the hunters was hopelesss enough.

"Our family is dying, Hiranah." Gihn said quietly. "There are less of us each summer than the one before. Women are not bearing children as often as they used to. Babies are born sick or die before their time to arrive. We call it *the Slow Death*. If you don't help us, then soon we will all be nothing but dust and bones."

Ivy's stomach turned at the graphic premonition of his words. They were *meant* to be dust and bones. To her, these people were real, breathing emanations of the past. Fossils re-fleshed. Ivy looked down at Juna consoling her dying mate and tried to stifle her rising panic. She had been where Juna was. *More grief. I've done this before. I can't do it again.*

"I know *nothing* about this, Gihn," Ivy said desperately. "I'm not a healer. You called the wrong person. I can't save you, I couldn't save my mother, or Jasper -" her voice cracked. "I won't go through that again. I can't!"

"But you must! Please. Stop the Slow Death from stealing our children. Stop this Swift Death from slaying our hunters. Save our family Hiranah, I beg you!"

Ivy shuddered with emotion, finally giving in to the overwhelming anger that gripped her.

"How am I meant to help you when I can't even help myself? You are asking me to exist only as a means to instrument your own survival!" Ivy snapped. "You have stolen my life as surely as Truen is losing his. You don't think that's unfair?"

"We called for help and you came," Gihn growled. "You are meant to help us survive."

"Gihn, I *can't* help you survive!" Ivy turned away incredulous. She could no longer bear the gentle desperation in Juna's administrations, or the veil of grief through which Gihn watched his youngest son.

She ran out of the cave, desperate for the privacy of her own screaming thoughts. Ivy's hands shook. She struggled to swallow. *I'm hyperventilating. I need to breathe, just breathe.* But she was furious. *How can I explain what they have no hope of understanding?* She thought. *He wants me to manipulate the course of natural selection! He doesn't even know what he's asking. These people are meant to die out. They are meant to become extinct.*

Ivy squeezed her eyes shut, willing her emotions to reconcile. Gihn's blind faith in her ability was grossly misplaced. She didn't blame him for his desperation. Ivy understood grief and loss all too well. First Jasper, that perfectly imperfect boy that had woken her heart, only to drown her in sorrow with his death. Then, still grieving, Ivy had nursed her mother for over a year through the ravages of cancer, watching her broken father retreat into his work, only to inevitably lose both parents; one to disease and the other to a new, distant life where his daughter's face, so devastatingly similar to her mother, couldn't haunt his days with memories of grief.

Ivy had no idea how to give Gihn what he wanted. The Swift Death was clearly a virus or disease of some kind, quick and fatal. But the Slow Death seemed more sinister and complex. Stillborn babies and infertility across the entire tribe. It was too much. Ivy's shoulders shuddered as she stared into the trees.

I've lost my life, my everything, for no reason at all.

Ivy sat in the filtered light of a copse of sweetly scented rosewood trees. The previous night she had awoken to the keening wails of Juna. Truen had died. Ivy had slipped outside, feeling overwhelmed and suffocated again, and inexplicably full of guilt.

Above her now, Kyah rummaged through branches scattering leaves and yellow flowers, shadowed, as always, by little Trahg. Ivy couldn't help but be grateful for their strange connection. There was intelligence within the child that seemed almost transcendental. He was different to any child she had ever met, but no less beautiful or complex.

Isolation stung at her heart and pricked her eyes. The beauty around her was unseen. Her purpose in life had been torn away. Her distractions had been torn away. And she was left with the naked truth of an aching loneliness that she had spent years trying to cover up.

She turned to her battered journal for solace. Ivy's pencil raced across the pages and the word that seemed to fill them most, swollen with regretful tears, was *Orrin*.

CHAPTER 26

ORRIN

Twenty-eight hours of pure frustration drilled into his temple. Orrin rubbed his eyes beneath his black glasses as he made his way to the biology building. All he wanted was a chance to apologise. Or better yet, to pick up where they'd left off, before this ridiculous situation had come about. Ivy's disappearance haunted him and his gut twisted with frustration and concern for her. Maybe it was just guilt.

Orrin knew he shouldn't care as much as he did. Not knowing *why* he cared frustrated him almost as much as the fact that he did. Other women had come in and out of his life since the divorce. But Ivy… there was something there. Undeniable physical attraction. But something else. Something that tugged at his subconscious and drew him in. She was an enigma.

After stopping for directions three times, Orrin finally found himself outside again, in front of a thick steel door. *Behavioural Research Laboratory 6. Whatever they keep in here sure as hell isn't getting out.*

His knocks received no answer. Orrin tried the handle and was surprised it yielded. *So much for security.*

"Hello?" The dim room only answered with the scratching

and scurrying of mice. Scanning the walls for a light switch proved fruitless, so he pushed the door wide open.

Louder, then. "Hello, anyone here?"

The fading light illuminated a dozen glass cages along the wall. Hundreds of mice scattered at his approach. To his left, rows of tall cabinets stood as sentinels in the dark, an avalanche of paper work and books spilling from the shelves. The corridor ahead stretched into darkness. Tiny particles of dust hung suspended in the still air. Orrin didn't scare easily, but this place gave him the creeps. *She's obviously not here; I'll just leave a note and go.* He squinted at the messy desk, searching for a paper and pen in the dim light. A whiteboard was propped against the wall. *Even better.* Orrin found a felt pen dangling from some string and scribbled a note for Ivy.

He turned to leave. Something on the desk caught his elbow.

"Shite!" Crashing metal on concrete shattered the silence as a bucket load of chopped vegetables rolled into dark corners. Sighing, Orrin bent to gather them up. *This day's gone arseways,* he thought. Groping under benches, the gritty floor yielded more dirt than vegetable. He gave it up as bad joke. *She'll find my note. And the mess I left as well, damn it.* Orrin made for the door, disappointed again, picking through a minefield of potato. The silence was brutal.

Wait - a noise. Grunting and shuffling sounds filtered to him from beyond the corridor. *The chimps,* he supposed. He wondered vaguely if Kyah would remember him. He reached the steel door.

Wait - no. That isn't just shuffling... it's - whispering? Orrin strained to hear. *There's someone here, two people maybe. Ivy? Liam? Why didn't she answer when I called out? Is she seriously hiding from me?* Irritated, he edged down the dark space between cabinets and cages. *Maybe they didn't hear me.*

Orrin caught his breath as the sun hit his eyes. Ahead, the roof of the laboratory had disappeared and wire mesh walls were gated all around. A large canopy covered part of the cage, with giant potted trees and rocks carefully strewn about. He wasn't sure what he was expecting, but the bizarre implantation of this false jungle within university walls seemed comical and ugly. *They could do better.* He looked around. There was no one in the room. And nowhere to hide. *Brilliant. I'm away in the head. Hearing things now too.*

As he turned to leave, a slight movement caught his peripheral vision. Orrin looked closer into the shadows of the cage, expecting to find a chimp shuffling around. He stepped forward, a wary smile on his face.

"Kyah?" he called awkwardly.

As his eyes adjusted, Orrin realised something was returning his stare. His smile froze. His heart crashed. *This is no chimp.* A chill crawled across his skin and he stumbled backwards. He fell, scrambling back up, frozen in place, not daring to look away. Every muscle in Orrin's body arrested at the sight of the creature staring back at him from the shadows.

It stepped forward into the fading light. Upright. Walking. A woman - naked and tiny, with dark skin and matted black hair. Cold sweat ran down the back of Orrin's neck as he fought with himself not to run. More whispers. There were others, all huddled together in the shadows. *What the hell is this?*

Suddenly, there wasn't enough oxygen in the air. Orrin locked eyes with the tiny woman. He recoiled. She narrowed her eyes accusingly. *Defiantly.* Her lips rolled back in an ugly grimace.

"Ash-awa negitah!" Her voice came at him in a low whisper, suffused with hatred. The cold night air caught in his throat. She was speaking to him; *it* was speaking to him.

She hissed and looked down, twisting slightly and Orrin realised there was something in her arms. With macabre curiosity, Orrin focussed on the dark space, blood pounding in his ears.

A pair of eyes stared up at him from her arms. Wide eyes. *A baby.* Naked, perfect lips, olive face. Undeniably more human than animal. But wrong somehow – misshapen, alien. Its little fingers clenched and reached upwards, toward the light. Toward him.

His breath left him like a kick in the guts.

Orrin turned, stumbling and falling into the darkness, desperate to slam the steel door between himself and the aberration of reality behind it.

It couldn't be true.

CHAPTER 27

NEIL

Hidden in thorny bushes on the far side of the river, Neil Crawford spat. The small green berries he chewed were bitter and did nothing to placate his gnawing stomach. He scraped the grit off his tongue grudgingly. He wouldn't have eaten them at all, if he hadn't seen her doing it first. *I'm surprised she can stomach this crap.* Without her entourage of freaks, Neil was sure the redhead would have died already, starved, no doubt. *He'd* survived on his own, of course.

He'd been watching the woman for days. At night, he stuffed himself into the cavity of a decaying tree. The hollow trunk was wide and long and had previously been home for a nest of vipers. The slithering golden offspring had broken through their membranous casings only hours before he'd found them, their mother birthing them live and escaping into the dark forest floor. He couldn't have known that the three dark brown spots ringed in black and white that ran down their body identified them as one of the most poisonous snakes in the world. If he had, Neil wouldn't have been so quick to claim their home. As it was, he didn't know, and each of the eleven juveniles remaining in the nest received a swift stab at the base of its neck between the dark patches on each blunt temple. He'd sliced them open to find three of them had already consumed their less aggressive siblings. Each one in turn, was consumed by Neil. The taste was smoky and rubbery, like chicken left out too long. The snakes had placated his hunger for two days, and then his gut had grown sick and twisted in retaliation, tying him in agonising knots. For the past eighteen hours Neil had had nothing but water stolen from the river after dark. This morning he was hungry again.

His mobile phone had run flat days ago, robbing him of his compass and the only tangible link he had to the real world. *I never asked for this shit.* He let his resentment grow thick like a shield. Given his time again, Neil wouldn't have gone to the lab at all. *But who could have anticipated this?*

Nothing could have prepared him for it. His shoulder still ached, his feet were blistered and swollen with the heat and his ageing body felt punished. The chill night air of the mountains compressed his cigarette-damaged lungs. But he pushed through the pain, refusing to succumb. *They underestimated me.* There was pride and victory in that, at least.

When Neil first spied the redhead by the river, putrid and furious as he was, he very nearly broke his cover. After all, she'd left him unconscious with a mangled arm in the forest, for God knows how long. She *must* have. Anyone with half a brain would have searched the area before taking off into the forest. She *must* have seen him lying there, exposed to the elements and predators. She left him to die. Reason fled and he itched to show her that he wasn't so easily disregarded. That she'd walked away from the wrong man. That he wanted answers from her, regardless of the means he had to use to get them.

While tracking her, Neil's mental interrogation had replayed over and again, growing exponentially fierce.

Who the hell are you? Who did this to me? Terrorists? The University? Some damned private entity pulling strings on the world's energy supply?

What was going on in that lab? How did they control the energy field? What were they planning to do with it? Convert it? Redirect it? Who was their target?

And most importantly; how the hell am I going to get out of this shit hole?

Neil had finally found her, as he knew he would. He stepped out of the shadows, ready to shout. Within a heart-beat he'd changed his mind. Neil had thrown himself back into his thorny hide-out, his mouth dry and the stinging of torn skin unnoticed. Since that moment, nearly four days ago, only one question had become critical; *what the hell is really going on?*

Bizarre, tiny ape-men were constantly by her side, surrounding her, leading her, protecting her. They were freak-ishly small, half-man half-animal - like something you'd see in a National Geographic magazine. Neil could find no place for them in his expansive knowledge; they looked like an insult to humanity. Whether they were some sort of sick transgenetic experiment or a well-kept evolutionary secret, he could only guess.

They carried spears and arrows. Even from a distance Neil suspected he didn't want to be caught on the end of one. The creatures visited the river in small groups, at least seventy so far, although it was hard to tell. They all looked the same, like pot bellied children with abnormally long arms and misshapen heads. They were mostly naked too, and even more unappealing for it. In his hiding place, Neil learned to lie still. He gently flexed his limbs one by one as he lay there, discouraging the spasms of contracting muscles. The ape men were vigilant; he had to give them that. He'd been nearly caught twice already. Even the children lifted their eyes to the slightest movement in the trees. *Children.* He spat again with distaste. *Not children. Animals.*

So far, there were only three things he was sure of. *One, I'm outnumbered. Two, I don't know enough and three, the woman is somehow involved.* Neil never acted from a position of disadvantage. Ignorance was the greatest disadvantage. *Know thy enemy.*

So he watched.

And watched.

The redhead showed no aversion to the ape-men, on the contrary, she seemed almost deferential to them. Contrary to his initial belief, Neil now doubted that the woman had known he was even there, lying unconscious merely twenty feet from where she'd been herself. This woman wouldn't have left an injured, vulnerable man to the elements if she'd known. Anyone who could muster up enough sympathy to see these *whatever-they-were* as equals, was clearly a slave to their own emotions. Which made them that much easier to manipulate.

The woman's limp was nearly gone and she was frequently barefoot. She was quiet, but not submissively so. It seemed a more calculated quietness, like she was *observing* the goings on around her with an air of fascination and God forbid, *affection.* Neil wondered if she even knew why she was there. *Maybe not.* Regardless, she still knew something. This woman was the only link between the physics laboratory and the death-trap they were stuck in.

For now, her goal seemed the same as his own; watch and learn. The only difference was the object of study.

The redhead was watching the ape-men; Neil was watching her.

Each morning, she sat by the river with her macabre menagerie and drew symbols in the dirt, with what he had now realized, was actually a chimpanzee. Once, he had sought out those drawings after dusk, risking a burning torch to see them, only to find the geometric shapes and patterns made no sense. It wasn't long after, the ape-men started copying her and the redhead had become agitated and left. A couple of days later though, she began to teach them willingly.

It was infuriating. The woman was wasting her time, teaching shapes to imbeciles, while he suffered. He tried to look at it rationally. This was bigger than him. The civilised world had probably suffered at the hands of this conspiracy. No doubt there was a shitload of money involved somehow. And damn it, those hands could have been his.

A niggling memory chewed at Neil's brain and he tossed it around again. He had been stewing all night. There was something he couldn't quite place, his last memory of the lab, and of her…

A flash of black and a pulse of neon blue that burned white in his closed eyelids…

Damn it! There was something about that moment, something that seemed significant that kept slipping away. Neil needed answers and the redhead was quickly becoming dispensable if it meant getting them.

If I could just get her alone.

Justification was a beautiful thing.

CHAPTER 28

IVY

It was magic. Not the magic of spells and supernatural incantations, but *real* magic.

The magic of storytelling.

Ivy knew it was a trademark of all human societies, no matter the form it took. A story, a song, a folktale, a chant, a parable. A gift passed from generation to generation preserving history without pens or paper. The story embellished, reworded, broken and rebuilt like a string of Chinese whispers through time immemorial. But there was always meaning behind the words, Ivy knew, that had been saved for so long. There was always a truth, no matter how deeply buried, in the bones of the tale.

Bright stars glittered in the night, almost close enough to touch. A cool wind swept the cave entrance where Ivy sat amongst the tribe. Trahg was curled in her lap and Kyah pressed against her side, the odd pair now inseparable. All eyes were on an old, bent woman standing to Ivy's right. The woman's name was Phren. Her wrinkled hand clutched Ivy's, the amulet warm and pulsing between their palms. With a cry that cast the restless night into silence, Phren threw her free arm out theatrically and began her story.

Ivy looked at Kyah, momentarily sad at the bonobo's inability to grasp the inherent spirituality of the situation. But the hobbits surrounding her were different. They not only grasped their oral history, they embraced it. *How very human.* Was it *culture* that defined humanity then? Ivy mused. She considered the elements of culture that each of the three species of ape represented here tonight, shared. Each species had the capacity to learn behaviour from its parents, to use that behaviour and teach others. Each species recognised its allies and foes and formed lifelong relationships based on kinship and rank. They all solved problems creatively, they cooperated and they empathized, they anticipated behaviour and the reactions of others. Culture was a concept shared, by that definition.

But this - telling a story; this was different, Ivy knew. Using words as symbols to explain an idea that might be purely hypothetical, changeable or even completely ambiguous. *Is this what defines us as human? Our driving instinct to understand where we came from and our ability to recount it over thousands of years?* Story was a powerful tool for learning, where each word - each symbol - could possess multiple meanings and only through context and shared experience might become meaningful at all.

"Baby. Hug." Kyah signed and pulled at Trahg's arm. The boy happily shifted into the bonobo's lap and settled. Trahg was beginning to understand Kyah's symbols, a realisation that left Ivy a little uneasy.

Ivy raked her fingers gently across the bonobo's arm. *So what was the very first story?* Ivy wondered. What idea, what symbol, could have been powerful enough to throw the human species from an intelligence that already worked perfectly in its time and place, into a feedback loop of this new, different type of intelligence? The type that forced our lives and tools, our language and brains into increasing complexity. How had it begun, and how blurry were the lines between us really?

There was a tranquillity about Kyah tonight which suggested

that although she may not appreciate the meaning, she felt a certain reverence for the situation.

Phren paused in her story and the tribe began their dusk song again. This time, Kyah listened to it, spellbound, with wide eyes. The bonobo's face was still and her breathing deep and slow. For a moment, Ivy could see no sense of self in their depths. An interesting thought occurred to her. *Has Kyah lost herself in the beauty of the voices? Can she feel the intensity that hangs palpable in each note? How close to a spiritual epiphany could she come? And how close to symbolic thought, might she be, if not there already? A tiny fantasy conceived and acted upon that led to another and another, slowly changing the way she learns, the way she thinks... Is this how it all began?*

The dusk song fell silent and Phren began another story.

Ivy's story.

"Our ancients were travellers," Phren said. "On rafts of bamboo, they crossed the broken sea to rest on this island of flowers. They grew to feel the Life within the land and became bound to it."

"They made their home at the place where fire and water and wind all boil together under the earth, by the three great lakes." Phren took a moment to seek the eyes of her audience. "Our first home. *The Three Sisters.* One lake was bright blue, like the great sea that gives Life to the fish that swim. The second lake was green, like the forest that gives Life to the animals and plants born to earth. And the last lake was red, like the blood that gives Life to our body." Ivy shuddered. What Phren described was all too familiar to her. The Tri-Coloured lakes of Kelimutu. Even in modern times, their volcanic beauty was legendary. Phren raised her voice dramatically. "But the earth suffered. It cried in fire and rain and the great mountains trembled. Dust filled the sky. The ancients left to search for a new home away from the fire. They sang their Dusk Song, calling for protection as they travelled."

"The earth answered. Blue lightning broke the night sky, and struck the top of the fire mountain, where The Three Sisters come together as one. Only one woman, Natu, was brave enough to follow the blue lightning."

"When she got to the place The Three Sisters join, Natu found that the earth had split apart." Phren turned her attention to Ivy and continued. "And she had a vision."

"What vision?" whispered Ivy.

"Natu saw the sky itself shatter into pieces around her," Phren said. "Within each piece of broken sky, she saw a strange dream land. In some, she saw huge and terrible animals. In others, she saw great birds that flew without wings. In many, she saw tall people, like Karathah, with strange hides and strange language. But in one piece of the broken sky, Natu saw a tall woman with eyes that were green like the trees. Her skin was white like the moon and her hair was *red like fire*. She held the *Life Stone* in her hand. She reached out to Natu through the broken sky and spoke to her."

Ivy felt sick. *Was this vision supposed to be me?* Phren certainly thought so.

"It's just a story," Ivy whispered, failing to hide the tremor in her voice. "I was never there." But the iconic tri-coloured lakes she had stumbled away from when she had first awoken on that distant mountain swirled in her mind. To continue to deny to herself that it had not been the Three Sister Lakes seemed futile. The coloured crater lakes were iconic. Five days of walking due west had brought her to Liang Bua cave. It all fit. She had fallen from the sky at the crater lakes of Kelimutu.

"When their hands touched," Phren continued, "Natu saw in her mind, a cave far toward the setting sun," said Phren, "A new home where our people would be safe from the fiery mountains that shook the earth." The crowd murmured. "Then the woman with fire-hair disappeared. The sky healed. And in the earth at her feet, Natu found a black stone, glowing blue." Phren held Ivy's wrist in the air for all to see, exposing the amulet tied to it. "The Life Stone."

"No." Ivy didn't want to hear anymore. None of it made any sense.

"Natu brought the Life Stone back to her people," Phren continued, "and together they found our new cave, just like the fire-hair showed her. A new home. The ancients believed that when our people needed protection again, the fire-haired woman, *Hiranah,* would come again to the Three Sister Lakes. She would come to reclaim the stone and to save us. And so she has." Phren's voice dropped to a whisper. "We have always known you would come when we had need of you."

"But it wasn't me," Ivy said. Phren's eyes darted to Gihn. He stepped forward.

"This is your stone, Hiranah, you said so yourself," he said.

"No! I mean, yes, it's mine, but I don't know how to save you!"

"You will." Gihn's eyes flashed. "The Life Stone answered us, just as the story told it would. Skin like the moon, hair like fire; the earth gave us *you.*"

"But I'm not enough!" cried Ivy, forgetting her audience. "There must be more, Gihn, more knowledge or help or something! I can't do this by myself! There must be more to the story!" He shook his head faintly.

"There is nothing else, Hiranah," he stated.

Phren took Ivy's hand in both of her own. Her voice softened.

"Our lives are fading," she pleaded. "Once there were many of us, now there are so few. The Swift Death kills our hunters and the Slow Death steals our children." She paused for a moment and Ivy could see the old woman's lips were trembling as she took a deep breath. "But the earth still protects us. It sent us you, Hiranah, as once promised. You *will* help us survive."

"What you are asking me is impossible!" Ivy growled again, the following morning. "I can't save an entire species from extinction! Even if I knew how to, who am I to interfere? This is totally beyond my ability, Gihn. I'm just a human, like you." Ivy finished her tirade with an angry collapse on the ground, sitting cross legged in the bamboo thicket. A warm breeze whistled through the hollow stalks, leaving a chiming whisper in the air. Gihn sat gracefully beside her and covered the amulet again with his palm.

He looked her squarely in the eyes. "A human with power."

"No! I *have no power*. I don't know why the amulet brought me here, *or how*, but I honestly can't help you! I have no medicine to save your hunters from the Swift Death and I haven't the first idea what is causing this Slow Death you speak of. Out there," Ivy gestured to the uninviting jungle in the valley below, "I'm more vulnerable than you are. I have *no* power here."

"Then you must have knowledge."

At that Ivy refused to meet his gaze.

Gihn's frowned. "Show me." His hand tightened around her wrist, locking the warm amulet between their skin.

"What?"

"*Show me* what you know. About my people. You recognised us in the forest when you Fell. You have seen us before. So let me see what you've seen."

"Absolutely not. You don't know what you're asking." Ivy gritted her jaw and dropped her head into her free hand. "There are things you can't possibly understand about my world...things you shouldn't know!" Her skin flushed red.

"If you refuse to help us I need to know why!" Gihn argued.

"I can't show you why!"

"You *must* show me."

"But knowing will hurt you more!" Ivy pleaded. She felt like an animal, cornered and tricked into performing.

"We are already hurt. We are *dying*."

Ivy tried to pry her hand away, but her strength was nothing to Gihn's grip.

"Show me what you have seen, Hiranah," Gihn repeated, his voice dangerously low.

"Fine!" Ivy yelled at him. "Take it then, take everything I have left!"

Furiously, Ivy tugged memories from the recesses of her mind, uncovering and throwing them into light so that Gihn might share them. The explosion of colour behind her eyes nauseated her and she squeezed them shut, not knowing how to control the stream of thoughts spewing to the surface.

Orrin, the university librarian, a politician, laboratory mice, the Chinese food deliveryman, a street performer in Federation square, a baby in a pink hat, Kyah, her father pushing her swing, Orrin, a home-less woman feeding birds, Jasper, her mother kissing her goodnight... on and on they came, faces she hadn't seen for years, many she had forgotten, some she didn't even know, all filed away in the secret spaces of her mind. *Loss.* The faces overwhelmed her and she desperately wanted them locked safely away again. They were all irretrievable now. *Orrin.* Ivy choked back a sob as the memories drowned her.

She felt violated by her own purging memories. But Gihn had forced this on them both. He'd *stolen* her life from her. He deserved the heartache of seeing what she had lost as well as the futility of what he sought to fix.

Ivy struggled to pull her memories in the direction Gihn was seek-ing. Cave paintings in Lascaux, a steaming jungle in Maya, shell middens, frigid Scottish moors, the crumbling pyramid of Mayapan, an African rifted valley, Emperor Qin Huang's broken terracotta warriors... her passion, her research, archaeology of the world - on and on the memories came, so fast it made her dizzy. Ivy's free hand clawed the dirt blindly for support... the spider web rice fields of future Flores, photos of theodolites and trowels and strangely organized piles of dirt, the stratigraphic map of Liang Bua, clinical and cold – I don't want you to see anymore... *Ivy tried desperately to pull her wrist away but Gihn held tight has they drew closer to the devastating memories he was desperate to see... please Gihn, no!... stone tools in a plastic tub, florescent laboratory lights, piles of broken bones plastered back together, NO! a clear display case with a tiny human skull, the letters EXTINCT across a textbook.* You are nothing but bones.

Ivy wrenched her wrist from Gihn and fell forward. She buried her face in her hands. The images faded slowly, leaving residual scars behind her eyes, as if she had been staring at the sun. She had given Gihn what he wanted. The truth. But there was no satisfaction to it. Ivy felt hollow. Ashamed.

Of course they'll die, all of them, she thought. *Their future is in a box on a shelf. Nothing will remain of the warm, rich lives they've built here. Evolution doesn't work like that. Empathy plays no part in selection; there's only struggle, and constant change.*

Survival of the fittest.

Life wasn't fair. Ivy knew that well enough.

Gihn's eyes opened. They seemed dead already. His hand trembled as he reached for the amulet. For a moment, he reminded her of old Tom. With a sigh, Ivy covered his hand with her own.

"I'm so sorry," she said. "I didn't want you to see it."

Gihn nodded. For a long time, he said nothing.

"Do you think we deserve to survive?" he finally asked.

"Your mortality has nothing to do with what I think, Gihn."

"Perhaps not, but do you?"

Ivy looked away. Kyah and Trahg had climbed a candlenut tree further uphill. Three other children shouted up at them from below. Laughing, Trahg leapt daringly onto Kyah's back as she swung higher. Kyah caught Trahg's foot to balance him, screeching. Together they tore fistfuls of leaves from the branch, throwing them into the sky so that they fluttered and swirled onto the delighted little faces below. Peals of laughter erupted from the children as they jumped for the showering leaves.

They're beautiful, she thought. But they weren't *special*, Ivy realized, no more or less than any other animal on the planet. And that was the very reason they deserved the right to survive. For the innate miracle of existing at all, despite the odds already against them.

"I think everybody deserves the right to fight for their own survival," she finally conceded. "But it's not as easy as you think. Nature dictates your fate." Ivy repressed the modern variation on that law - *Homo sapiens dictate your fate.* She dropped her head back into her hands. "If we can't change with the world around us, then we die. But you cannot possibly understand how complicated that is."

Gihn looked at Ivy critically, as if seeing her for the first time. "But you do."

"I do what?"

"You understand. You have the knowledge that could save us, which is why you chose to come." He pre-emptively met her denial. "You *did* choose this, Hiranah."

Ivy's heart sank. "Even if I were to help you…." She bit her lip. She wasn't seriously considering it, but Gihn needed to understand her reasons why. "I can't guarantee you would be better off. The world where I came from can be cruel and dangerous. Much more dangerous than this jungle. Sometimes it is so difficult that I hide from it myself." Her own admission surprised her. Ivy faltered, forgetting Gihn was there. *I hid. I hid from the world. And Orrin knew it.*

Rallying her train of thought again, Ivy shook her head. "And for a person like you, with your differences and vulnerability…" Ivy trailed off. *How would Homo sapiens treat their hominid cousins, if they had to live side by side?* She looked toward Kyah, remembering that first day she'd met her. Ivy shuddered. "No, Gihn. It's just not possible."

Gihn jutted his chinless jaw toward her defiantly. "But that's *our* choice to make. We deserve the right to fight for our survival, you said that yourself." He followed Ivy's gaze over to the children playing under the rosewood tree. Together they watched the children in silence. Finally, Gihn spoke again.

"I will meet you as far as you can go then," he said. "If you cannot save us Hiranah, at least give us more time. So we can learn to save ourselves."

"Lahstri!"

It was late afternoon. Two young men ran into the cave, past Ivy as she sat at Shahn's hearth. The bigger of the two boys was carrying a third, older man, in his arms. He lowered the man as gently as possible at the old medicine woman's feet. Lahstri dropped to a crouch beside the man's body and lifted his eyelids, then swiftly surveyed his injuries as others crowded around. A single arrow pierced his chest. The shorter boy collapsed beside them, clutching his own arm. There was an arrow in it.

Without a word, Shahn dropped what she was doing and picked up a hide bag. She joined Lahstri at her hearth. Ivy, who had been playing with Trahg, carried him closer to the gathering. She pressed the amulet to the child's palm and heard their words through little Trahg's thoughts as he watched the events unfold with a quivering lip.

All around, there were cries of dismay as Lahstri closed the man's eyes. She looked grimly to Shahn, then found Gihn's eyes in the crowd. She pushed the medicine bag away.

"It's too late. Terap is dead." Lastri turned to the two young men that were still panting with exhaustion, slumped behind the dead man's body. Only then Lahstri seemed to notice the arrow in the younger one's arm. She rummaged through her bag on the cave floor. "Chew these Kiran," Lahstri instructed, giving him a clutch of betel leaves. "It will help dull your pain when I pull out the arrow." She turned to the other boy as Kiran's eyes fluttered closed. "Kari? What did you do?"

"Nothing!" The remaining boy exclaimed, sitting straighter, with tears in his eyes. "Terap was teaching us how to make bird traps. We were nowhere near karathah territory! They just appeared and began casting arrows before we knew they were there." Kari's mouth became a straight line and he blinked repeatedly, forcing away his tears. Lahstri nodded, indicating for Kiran's father to carry the now unconscious boy back to her own hearth to tend. "It is best if I do it now, while his mind is asleep."

A small group collapsed beside Terap's body. A woman began to wail. From behind them, an old man stepped around the body and walked directly to Ivy, who still stood shocked, holding Trahg in her arms.

The man leant close, twisting his lips in a hateful grimace.

"Karathah."

He spat at Ivy's feet and walked away.

CHAPTER 29

ORRIN

*S*unglasses did nothing to hide the dark circles under his eyes. Orrin adjusted the rear-view mirror and sighed. Hours of insomnia had bled into vague and terrifying dreams and he had awoken near midday feeling hung-over without the benefit of a night on the tear. Orrin was rarely unnerved. This stuff - whatever was happening, unnerved him. So he threw down a few painkillers and drove.

He needed to speak to Ivy. The biology lab, this insane talk of 'hobbits' and then those creatures, *people*, locked there in Kyah's place... *Ivy, please know what's going on.* Everything seemed to hinge on her, on finding her, on restoring his sanity. *I'm a scientist. There will be a logical explanation.* A problem was merely a process of deductions, hypotheses and eliminating the theories that tested false. He needed some hypotheses to test. He needed *her*.

Orrin drove slowly, surveying the houses as he went until he recognised the old brick apartment block Ivy lived in. He slowed to a stop under a barren jacaranda. Its carpet of flowers was mulch beneath his shoes as he crossed the road. Strangely, a group of men were gathered on the front lawn, surveying Ivy's building with tapes and plans. Bulldozers were parked on the grass, their wheels shadowed by torn trails of dirt.

Orrin bypassed the men, heading for the front door. He heard a shout behind him.

"Hey! You can't go in there." A man with half-rolled sleeves dashed across the lawn as Orrin turned.

"Just visiting a friend of mine, Ivy Carter." Orrin plastered a smile onto his face. "It's all grand, she's expecting me."

The man surveyed Orrin over his sunglasses and raised an eyebrow. "I highly doubt that."

Orrin lifted his chin slightly. "And who would you be to know that?"

The man seemed amused. "I'd be the owner of this building. This *vacant* building."

"Vacant?" All other thoughts fled. "It can't be vacant. I came here just last week…"

"Well, unless your friend makes a habit of squatting in condemned apartment blocks, I'd say it's a pretty safe bet you didn't." The man seemed to notice the fall in Orrin's shoulders. He shaved the edge of sarcasm from his voice. "Look, I'm sorry to disappoint you mate, but all previous tenants moved out a month ago. Dunno how they managed to stay here that long to tell you the truth, the place is falling to bits." A thick glove smeared dirt and perspiration across his brow.

Orrin looked again. The man was right. On closer inspection, the building was in a terrible state, neglected and derelict. His eyes drew up to a broken second level window. *Her window.* It was empty except for a fluttering scrap of yellow lace. He shook his head slowly. *But I was in that kitchen only last week.* He had watched her play the cello, agonisingly beautiful and lost in her own notes. There were books and skulls and coffee and peeling daisy wallpaper. *And suddenly she was never there?* This made no sense.

"I swear she was here just last week," Orrin muttered. It suddenly occurred to him that at least this man might know where to find her. "Wait, you're the owner you said? So you knew the tenants, right? Her name is Ivy. Ivy Carter. Did she say where she was moving to?"

The man looked almost apologetic this time. "Can't help you, I dunno where any of the previous tenants have gone. Although I don't think there was an Ivy amongst them anyway. I've only owned it a week though." He looked critically up at the building. "Been waiting for a while actually, I was hoping it would go on the market sooner, less work to do. Had my eye on it for years. Tom Chapman owned it, nice old bugger. Kind as you like, but not all there." The man shook his head at the broken window. "Tom let this place go to rack and ruin in the end. I suppose he just couldn't keep up with the maintenance, although a few years back he used to try. Not the same though since his wife died. He was all alone for so long. I guess he just gave up."

"What happened to him?" Orrin asked.

The man raised an eyebrow, seemingly surprised by the concern in Orrin's voice. "Oh, he's still kicking. Got no family though, I think he's off to a nursing home. Pretty frail now, old Tom. A good bloke though, good bloke." He clicked his tongue sadly and shook his head.

"So you're renovating?" Orrin asked. "Fixing up the digs then?"

"Nah, too much work now. It'll have to come down." He thumbed behind him to the bulldozer. "Going to put up some new apartments. Get a busload of uni students in, there's a good market for it here you know, being so close and all."

"Of course…" Something indefinable tugged in his chest. Orrin stared at the building, willing Ivy to appear.

The man cleared his throat. "Good luck finding your friend." He offered his hand.

"Sure. Thanks."

Back at the car, Orrin took a deep breath. He let his eyes close, resting back against the seat. *Another empty space.* Disappointment and desperation hit him in waves. He'd been so sure he would find Ivy and force some logic into the insanity around him. Instead, he'd found a crumbling pile of bricks and an absence more disturbing than before. As the men continued working across the road, the building began to break apart. It looked soulless. Hollow. Even the garden beds had been choked by weeds.

Except those ones. Hundreds of bright white flowers crowned the dismal entrance, catching the breeze. The daisies still had life.

Orrin eyed the rumbling bulldozers. Defeated again, he drove away.

The car park was packed when Orrin finally arrived at the university. Lunch had come and gone in the hours he'd spent drifting, unwilling to face another stretch of relentless testing with no answers. Phil and Dale would have noticed his absence; they were probably relieved. It was getting harder for Orrin to keep his temper in check with the abyss of frustrations opening up before him. *I'll just have to try harder. Think harder.* He forced his unwilling mind into logic again. *The answer is always there; it's just waiting to be found.* Orrin got out of his car. As he walked he counted theories, pulling the stitches apart slowly, trying to find the original tear. Something had gone wrong. Whether in his mind, or in the real world, something had gone wrong and he had to find out what it was. Where *she* was. Orrin knew there would be no peace and no relief, until he did.

Deep in his bones Orrin felt the constant, dull ache of the only undeniable truth he could count on. Ivy had disappeared.

Even if no one else knew or cared, even if it was inconsequential to the rest of the world; *he* knew. She had disappeared entirely.

Orrin found himself at the university entrance where a line of city buses curved the roundabout. Students teamed into the doors like hourglass sand, encouraged by a raucous group in matching green shirts. *Another rally.*

"Oppression!" they yelled.

"They're slaughtering our brothers."

"Damn the multi-nationals!"

"Who pays the price for genocide?"

"Human rights for Hobbits! Human Rights for *all* Humans!"

Hobbits again? Orrin stared at the spectacle. At least three hundred students were already crammed onto the buses. Green placards and banners were streaming from the windows. Orrin moved through the sea of backpacks, blue jeans and sunglasses. The buses began snaking away.

This animal was beyond anything he could have imagined. *But it's real. I saw it.* The curiosity of that tiny baby, *staring* at him through eyes that weren't quite human, but so far from bestial, had haunted him all night. The defiant ferocity of its mother who had accused him without words. Her rage hadn't been primal or instinctual, it seemed… resentful and *intelligent*. As if she knew what Orrin was capable of, and hated him for it.

As the last bus pulled from the curve, Orrin leapt through the closing doors.

War cries erupted from the rioters as they pushed through the city streets, twenty astride and hundreds deep. They grew as they marched, gathering day trippers and workers, swelling past the stone shop fronts and impeding trams of angry commuters.

Police watched the rebellion with wary eyes. They had come prepared.

Orrin thrilled in the pulsing human mass, searching for answers. The space around him ebbed and surged then grew hot and sweaty as the crowd thickened nearing their destination. Thumping music from somewhere set a rhythm for the adrenaline surging through his veins. Orrin soaked up the intensity of the scene as if his life depended on it. Beside him, a bearded man grew hoarse as he shouted, waving his green placard. On the sidelines, people chanted and stamped, crushing the rockeries underfoot. The rioters were getting louder. Feet stumbled over each other and smaller bodies disappeared under the crowd. No one seemed to notice when they re-emerged covered in blood, dragged above the rising tide by police.

A man rushed his young daughter past, desperate to escape the mounting promise of violence. She held tight to his shoulders, wide-eyed at the spectacle. "Where are they going?" she cried.

Where were *they going?* Orrin wondered. It had been far too loud for conversation on the bus, and the roar of the rioters was now overwhelming.

A monumental pile of blackened steel and concrete ahead answered his question. The crowd swelled around their destination like a single breathing organism. Shattered glass and twisted metal framing lay in great heaps across half the city block. Police tape kept the arson site clear from pedestrian violation, but the chanting crowd surged, tearing away the thin plastic strip. A cocktail of burnt chemicals filled Orrin's nostrils and he could almost feel carcinogens finding a home inside his lungs.

"Freedom from oppression!" the crowd screamed.

"Basic civil rights to *hominid*-kind!"

"Murderers! Capitalists! Butchers!"

Canvas banners waved in the air. Gruesome images of hobbits

were plastered across them, undoubtedly victims of experimental research. Metal electrodes protruded from uncovered brain matter with the desperate eyes of the victim still open and alive. Those holding the placards screamed their objections to the crowd. "Strapped down! Drugged! Beaten into submission!" The photos made Orrin's stomach turn. He pushed away, searching for space to breathe.

Liam! Orrin's knees faltered with relief. Ivy's rally partner was standing on the blackened steps. He seemed to be heading the insurgence. It was his laboratory that was meant to house Kyah but now kept the bizarre *hobbit* creatures instead. Orrin elbowed his way forward until he was only metres from the man. Sweat escaped Liam's mop of curls and ran in rivulets down his face and neck. He was shouting to the crowd into a cordless microphone, inciting revolution and punching his fist in the air.

"Is this how we treat our brothers?" Liam cried. "We murder them and steal their land and livelihood for the sake of consumerism? We strip mine their jungles for profit and then mass produce palm oil on the ruined soil?" Liam's skin was burning red. Concern gnawed in Orrin's gut at the sight of him. Ivy had said Liam could control a crowd, but there was an edge to his voice that seemed raw and unpredictable.

"Hobbits are rounded up like cattle and sold off to the highest bidder," Liam continued. He gestured to the blackened shell of a building behind him. "Sent into death traps like Cosmitech! Tortured for the sake of cosmetics and medical research! Sold to circuses for entertainment." Liam screamed above the frenzied crowd and the air grew thick with hostility. "They are not possessions! They are *human*!" Placards waved and fists came up as the mass cheered a deafening roar.

"Where does it end? How close to our own DNA deserves dignity? Who's next? Who else is 'different' enough to deserve this kind of treatment? Minorities? Indigenous groups? Religious groups? You or I? The hobbits have no rights - as a human or an animal. Who the hell are we to determine their value?" Liam's eyes wheeled frantically as he struggled to reach the deepest layers of the rebellion with his message.

"*We* are allowing this! Consumers! *We* are the pinnacle of this monster. *We* must choose our path. *We* must force our governments' hand! *We* must take control and bring civil rights to our brothers. I work with these hobbits - these *people* everyday. They *KNOW*, they *THINK*, they *FEEL* our abuse and neglect, they are *SCARED*! Even now – today – I'm fighting to keep them from being sold off as lab rats. In my own lab I can't keep them safe! So who will be their voice? Who will stand up and make a difference?" Liam's chest heaved with effort.

The crowd roared in support. They surged into the ruins of Cosmitech like a living wave, throwing the twisted metal into the streets behind them and disembodying the brick corpse piece by piece. Police wove through the people with batons and shields, pulling the more violent offenders away with impatient force. Orrin heard the smash of car windows smothered under a blanket of screaming. He pushed frantically through the protesters and bolted for the concrete steps where Liam was still standing screeching encouragement at the wild abandon of his followers.

"Liam! Liam, man! Where's Ivy?" Orrin yelled over the noise. He grabbed Liam's jumper roughly and jerked him around to meet his own eyes. "Ivy!" Orrin yelled again. "Where is Ivy? What in hell are these hobbit things?" Liam's face was thunderous.

"Bugger off or help!" Liam yelled back.

"But I don't understand what's going on!" Orrin shouted. "Where's Ivy? Is she here?"

"I don't have time for this," Liam yelled back. He turned away, focussed on a policeman dragging a particularly violent green shirted protester out of the crowd. Liam ran towards them.

"Liam! Stop!" Orrin called. "You know me, from uni, I'm

Orrin! Ivy's friend. Liam - *Ivy, I just want to know where she is!"* he yelled. "Where's Ivy? Liam, where is she?"

Liam rounded on him. "I don't know you! I don't know any Ivy. Now back off!"

Orrin stopped still. *You don't know Ivy? That's a lie.* Of course he knew her; they'd shared Kyah's care for years. Liam and Ivy were friends, maybe even best friends. They rallied together; she was the voice and he was the fist. She said so. *He's lying.*

Orrin rushed at Liam again, spinning him around. The deafening crowd was nothing to the blood rushing through his own ears. Both hands clenched Liam's shirt as Orrin shook him hard.

"You're lying!" Orrin yelled. "This entire damned place is insane! You must think I'm mental to believe that load of bollocks!"

"Get off!" Liam spat, pushing Orrin roughly away. He fell backwards and felt the slam of concrete steps into the back of his head as Liam turned back to the crowd, yelling again with fervour. Warm, sticky blood trickled down the back of his neck. Orrin struggled to his feet in time to see Liam rushing toward a police officer who was pinning a protestor to the ground. Liam grabbed a placard and held it high above his head, as if ready to strike. Orrin raced forward, wrenching the placard out of Liam's hands and pulling him down backwards, away from the officer.

"You *know* Ivy!" Orrin yelled, struggling under Liam's weight. "So *where-the-hell-is-she*, you bastard!?"

Enraged, Liam lashed out, rolling off him and punching Orrin square in the face. Orrin tasted blood in his mouth and his ears rung. He found his feet but Liam had already bolted out of reach.

The protestor on the ground was fighting against batons and both sides threw themselves into the fray. Liam ran past them this time, ducking uniformed guards. A blazing fire seemed to erupt from his hands. A green placard at his feet twisted black and orange in flames before Liam leapt into the rubble, reigniting the arson site. He held the burning placard high above his head and threw it toward the building. A dozen police pushed forward. Liam kicked and punched blindly against them.

Orrin struggled against the flow of bodies and flames to get away. Aching and gasping, he turned back around one last time to look. Liam had disappeared under a barrage of boots and batons.

CHAPTER 30

IVY

"Won't they get lost?" Ivy worried her bottom lip between her teeth as she walked.

"Why should they?" Gihn glanced in the direction that Trahg and his dusty haired cousin Turi had disappeared. They were in the branches ahead with Kyah. A half dozen adults trailed on foot, but Shahn and Turi's mother, Floni, were chatting and seemed entirely unconcerned by the missing boys.

"Well," Ivy considered, "they're just so little."

Gihn chuckled. "Compared to you, we all are."

Ivy couldn't help but laugh too. "No, I mean they're so young. They're just children."

Turi was even smaller than Trahg and Ivy guessed he was about three years old. An unsettling memory began to surface and Ivy instantly disengaged her hand from Gihn's, breaking their connection. *We have found the remains of a three-year-old that is half a meter tall,* the Liang Bua excavation director had written. *You could put its leg along an American one-dollar bill.* Ivy suppressed a shudder. The line between life and death was blurring. Fossils had become faces. *There are tens of thousands of years of stratigraphic record in that cave,* she reminded herself. *It isn't him.*

Ivy adored Turi; his mischievous personality far outweighed his size.

She offered the amulet to Gihn again, who took it with a sigh.

"You are keeping knowledge from me Hiranah."

Ivy ignored his accusation and continued her previous question. "Do the children already know the hunting trails? I mean, if they stray they could get lost, or hurt." Ivy recalled the ferocity of the Komodo dragon. A full grown hobbit would constitute an easy meal, let alone a boy half a meter tall.

"They'll stay in the trees. The shirakan can't reach them there," Gihn said. "Besides, they know their way home."

"From anywhere?" asked Ivy. It seemed unlikely for such young children.

"Of course. Does a bird forget its nest?"

Ivy frowned, hesitating. "Well, no, but a bird is different. They *feel* direction." Once again, there was no way of explaining complicated biology to a hominid that wasn't prepared, intellectually or evolutionarily, to understand it.

From her zoology studies, Ivy knew that the instinctual flyway of a bird's navigation was vastly different to a human's capacity to remember.

Although humans still retained elements of the protein cryptochrome, it seemed to be a predominantly vestigial trait. Like the appendix, wisdom teeth and the tailbone, its function was lost, though physical remnants remained. For humans, cryptochrome only lingered to control body clocks and daily rhythms. There were versions of the ancient protein in all branches of life, but for many other mammals, fish, birds and insects, the protein doubled as an internal compass. Cryptochrome was sensitive to the magnetic fields of the Earth. It drove the migration patterns of animals across continents and allowed them to keep their bearing even when no other landmarks were available to guide their way. Somewhere in the branches of evolution, that capability had disappeared from the human line.

"I feel direction," Gihn said simply.

"Humans don't feel it the way other animals do, Gihn." Ivy clarified. "We can't, you or I."

Ivy wondered how she could explain it to him. The concept was complicated. While the Chryptochrome protein still remained in humans, the apparatus needed to detect changes in the molecule had been long lost. People could no longer sense magnetic fields effectively. So they not communicate the information of it to the brain. There was a missing link. Ivy was unsure where humans might even process the data.

All other human senses were catered for by an opening in the bone structure they were housed in - eye sockets for eyes, ear canals for hearing, the jaw for taste, nasal cavity for smell - *but direction?* Magnetic fields were capable of penetrating the human body, leaving no external clue as to where they were once processed. It may have once been in the eyes, the brain, the nerves…

"I am a human and I can feel it," Gihn countered again.

"You mean you have learnt to navigate and find your way. You teach your children to judge distance and see landmarks," Ivy corrected.

"No." Gihn shook his head. "I *feel* it. I *know* where I am, wherever I am. So I know how to get home." He pointed slightly south-east, over his shoulder. "Home cave is this way." He pointed further south, "and The Three Sisters are that way. We face the lakes, with our dusk song each night. That's where you Fell." Gihn turned back to the invisible path they travelled. "But we will find water in this direction, I know it there but I also I feel it." He looked up at Ivy once more. "And tonight after dark" Gihn took a deep breath, nodding skyward, "a lightning storm will break. I can feel that too, here." He touched the skin between his eyes.

Ivy stopped abruptly, stunned by the implications of what he said. The other hobbits continued around them, slowing to look back. Ivy had been stripping fronds of hanging leaflets through her fingers as she walked and was now left with green confetti in her hand and several stunning red seeds with a single black spot on one end. They were vaguely familiar, *like an inverted black widow spider... Life imitating life.* It never failed to impress her when one species evolved to imitate another for its own protection. The hidden dangers of the rainforest suddenly felt close. Ivy quickly brushed the seeds and thoughts of deadly spiders away.

She studied the man next to her, then resumed walking. A hypothesis formed slowly in her mind. Frustratingly, there was no way to test it. Beneath the skin and bone of Gihn's tiny skull, like on any other human, would be his prefrontal cortex. It was the part of the brain responsible for self awareness, higher reasoning skills and intelligence. But in one peculiar way, Ivy knew Gihn's was different to her own. In laboratories around the world, endocasts had been moulded of the inside of fossilised skulls, revealing the shape and size of the Homo floresiensis brain. Compared to Homo sapiens, the prefrontal cortex of a hobbit was proportionately bigger than the rest. It had seemed odd to Ivy, when she read the published findings, considering the remainder of their bodies and brains had otherwise evolved to be so small. *Could that highly developed area account for magnetoception? Can hobbits* feel *the magnetic energy field waves from the earth around them?* If so, what a magnificent evolutionary re-development it was. *Perhaps the cryptochrome mechanism had been recovered as an adaptation to their environment,* Ivy mused. *But why on earth would a human need sensitivity to magnetic fields?*

Phlunk! A little body dropped to the ground in front of her, followed by another. Both boys were panting with exertion. With a much heavier landing, Kyah joined them screeching.

"Shirakan!" yelled Trahg. "Shirakan by the water!" The small boy grabbed Gihn's free hand and began pulling him in the direction the other adults had gone. Ivy followed, quickly gathering up Turi and carrying him on her hip.

Within a few minutes, the forest opened into a small clearing. The other adults were already gathered around the biggest Komodo dragon Ivy had ever seen. She panicked, preparing to hoist Turi back up into the branches. Gihn drew her arm down. "It is already dead, Hiranah."

He was right. The dragon was dead, crushing the long grass beneath its carcass. It was easily three times longer than a hobbit at full height. Its jaw was flopped to the side and a white frothy paste coated the tiled skin around its mouth. Thick red saliva hung in strings on the grass and its glassy eye stared to the sky.

"It is still soft underneath," said Ranu, a young hunter. "We should cut it up and take it home. This is good luck."

"It would be of use," Gihn agreed. Meat had been in short supply since the Swift Death had begun to take their hunters. "Let's carry what we can back home." The hobbits retrieved stone knives from the folds of their belts. An acrid stench hit the air as they slit the dragon from neck to tail, and began slicing and peeling its thick skin back to clean it. Ivy turned away, covering her nose.

Leaving them to their grisly task, she walked over to the hot spring that had been their intended destination. She let Turi down and he ran off to play with Trahg and Kyah again. A rush of water tumbled over rocks from higher up the volcanic ridge, pooling into a geothermically-heated spring. Wisps of steam licked the surface where cold water met hot. Ivy sat on a rock to wait.

"Urgh!" she jumped back up, stumbling backward. The rotting carcass of a rat was lying where she'd inadvertently placed her hand. She sidestepped another body in the long grass, this time some sort of plump bird with a slender, curved beak. *What the hell?* Within a minute, Ivy had uncovered another four animals in various states of decay. She broke off a stick and rolled each one with it, holding her breath.

"Gihn!" The old man looked up and she beckoned him over. Ivy held the amulet against his shoulder, avoiding his bloody hands. "There are more dead animals."

Gihn poked at each of the animals in turn as Ivy uncovered them in the grass.

"We cannot take them, Hiranah. These ones are rotten."

Ivy blanched at his misunderstanding. "No Gihn. I mean you can't eat them, any of them. I think there is something very wrong here." She crouched over the most recently dead animal, some sort of marsupial with a long, curling tail. "Look closer. Every one of them has white paste around its mouth, just like the shirakan. Whatever killed the dragon must have killed these ones too."

Gihn looked sceptical. "They eat different foods Hiranah. This animal eats fruit and that bird there eats river fish. The shirakan only eats meat."

"I know, I know. It doesn't make sense." Ivy shook her head, staring into the steaming water. "Are there often dead animals here?"

Gihn frowned. "I don't know. We are far from Home Cave so I don't come often. Our hunters haven't said so though. But then again, in this part of the forest they have other things to worry about. The karathah, the giant people, come further into our part of the forest now, so our hunters must take care to avoid them."

"The Karathah come here? And your hunters?"

"Sometimes."

Ivy stared again at the water. "Gihn, I'm not entirely sure what happened here," she gestured to the carcasses hidden in the grass, "but I'm asking you to trust me. We need to leave this place, and you can't take the meat of the shirakan home to eat."

"But it will feed so many -" Gihn protested.

"I'm sorry Gihn. You asked for my help and I'm giving it. This means something. I just don't know what."

"You are keeping knowledge from me again Hiranah," he growled.

She looked over to the hobbits, now piling the fresh Komodo meat into separate piles to carry home. "Please trust me."

Gihn met her eyes with a discriminating look. "I do." He bent down to wash his bloody arms in the hot spring before leaving. Ivy pulled him back.

"I'm sorry Gihn. You can't do that either."

"Can I sit with you?" Ivy smiled hesitantly at Xiou, feeling conspicuous. He was sitting with a group of four other hunters, as they expertly snapped stone near the centre of the cave. The news that she had not only prohibited an entire shirakan to be brought home after the butchering had already been done, but also insisted the hunters did not wash or return to the hot spring until she gave permission had been badly received within the cave. But Xiou returned her smile. His face was deeply scarred, horribly disfiguring his youthful features. From a distance, Shahn nodded encouragingly at her, small hands encircling her distended belly.

"I'm glad you joined us Hiranah," Xiou said, holding his hand against the amulet on Ivy's wrist. "We're getting bored of listening to Setian boast of his skill with arrows." Xiou, who was Shahn's mate, good naturedly slapped his friend on the back and was rewarded with a shove back. The bearded man called Setian said something in response and a ripple of laugher broke around the hearth.

Xiou touched the amulet again, inviting Ivy into the conversation. "Setian says I must carry Shahn's baby in my own belly to run as slow and heavy as I do." He laughed at his friend's taunt. "You'll be running from me soon Setian, when I chase the probech in your direction." The five hunters laughed again. A gentle solace dampened their banter though; another death during the night had left them a skilled hunter and friend short. Any one of them might be next.

"We are preparing for a hunt, Hiranah. Probech have been sighted in the lowland forest. We need new weapons and tools for an animal of that size."

"Probech?"

Xiou nodded, sweeping his finger from his nose to the ground. "The giant forest dweller, with spear teeth and an arm for a nose. It's a dangerous hunt." A thrill of excitement coursed through Ivy. *Stegodon.*

Could it be? She wondered. The prehistoric cousin of the elephant and mammoth had once roamed the Asian continents in many forms. Their massive bodies up to eight meters long were equipped with another three meters of ivory tusk to defend their herds. Some of them had four tusks apiece, as straight and deadly as a rack of spears, evolved to impale any predator with an agonising death. The brute strength of a stegodon would have been formidable and from her research, Ivy knew they had thrived in this part of the world for the best part of eleven million years already.

Although she had no desire to see one killed, the opportunity to witness a herd of *should-be-extinct* Stegodon was thrilling. Terrifying, *slightly insane*, but thrilling all the same. The bizarre subspecies of Stegodon that had survived in Flores had been the most extraordinary of all. Ivy squeezed her eyes shut, trying to remember her research notes. *If I'm right with my estimate of* when *I am in time*, she thought, *then they can only be talking about Stegodon florensis insularis. The Dwarf Stegodon.*

Trapped in this bizarre wonderland of isolation, the species had also dwarfed to adapt, reduced to the size of a modern cow.

They became unique, another stroke of nature's genius in the struggle to survive.

"Brilliant," Ivy exhaled, grinning.

"You can help us prepare, Hiranah." Xiou smiled with his lopsided mouth. He picked up a fist-sized chunk of volcanic glass. Black stone glinted red as he studied it by firelight. Then, holding it pressed to the dirt floor, Xiou struck it hard with a smooth hammer stone. A thick flake flicked onto the dirt. Ivy retrieved it while Xiou continued to strike the core. Piece by piece, uniform shards fell away. With each blow, he skilfully reduced it to the triangular preform of a spear point.

The discarded flake glittered in Ivy's fingers. A distinctive swollen bulb surrounded the scar where the impact had forced the flake and core apart. The convex surface sat neatly under her thumb as she held it up. The distal edge glinted, cone shaped and at its finest, only molecules thick. Deadly sharp, it threw light as she twisted the tool slowly before her eyes, mesmerised. When the razer edge bit her finger sending a dribble of dark blood across the glossy surface, Ivy threw her head back and laughed.

Oh, the bloody irony.

For ten years, Ivy had stared down a microscope at stone tools exactly like this one, searching for the tiniest insight into the long-buried lives that created them. Now here she sat, immersed in a culture so elusive it had survived hundreds of thousands of years in isolation and the ancient weapons she knew almost better than her own body were being created and used around her. Crafted by hands *she knew*. Ivy would never see them as mere stone tools again.

With an exalted grin, Ivy gave her attention again to Xiou. He was gathering the pile of thick flakes beside him. He handed them to Setian who began delicately shaping the edges into micro blades.

Xiou reached for a small length of bone that had been ground to a fine point on one end. Clasping a crude spear head in his left hand, he pressed the sharp bone tip into its edge, breaking off a small linear flake. Many times he repeated the delicate work, occasionally abrading the surface with a coarse-grained stone to prepare better platforms from which to press the flakes. Finally, a scattering of shining chips lay in his lap like fish scales. He passed the finished spear head to Ivy.

"It's beautiful," she said.

"It's strong too," he replied. "Take it over to Kora. She'll haft it onto a spear that you can use."

"Me?" Ivy repeated, surprised.

"Of course. We can't have you eaten by a hungry shirakan, can we? You're terrible at climbing trees, you know," Xiou teased.

Sitting opposite him at the hearth, a young woman patted the ground beside her in invitation. Ivy recognised her as the hunter who had offered her hand when Ivy slipped while being led to the cave. Ivy stood and sat cross-legged beside the woman, noting the others sat with their own, shorter legs, not quite crossed. Given the length of their feet, Ivy guessed it would feel awkward to do so. The woman, who she now knew was called Kora, continued her work with Ivy's amulet pressed gently to her thigh to communicate. On her right, Kora's mate, Guntah, was bent low over arrow heads that he was flaking upon a large stone mount.

"This makes a good strong shaft," explained Kora, dragging a length of stripped bamboo across her knees. One end of the shaft had been soaking in water. "I have softened it with water so we can attach the head. She dug a strong fingernail into it to illustrate her point. Her voice was quiet and clear. "We use different types of wood for different seasons, depending on what the earth can provide. This is the rainy season, so plants and animals are thriving in the forest. When the earth is dry, we hunt in the grasslands instead. Water is hidden in roots under the soil and the animals come looking for it. Plants always know how to survive."

With a sharp blade Kora cut a ridge across the top of the soft end of the bamboo.

"Make it deep to hold the point, see?" Kora took the sharp point Xiou had given Ivy and slid its neck into the ridge, pulling it out again briefly to widen her cut. "This will make a good spear when we bind it."

Dipping her hand into a bowl of murky water on the hearth coals, Kora pulled a thin strip of hide from the bowl. With slow deliberation, she wound it tightly around the flanges of the tool taking care not to overlap the leather. Tucking and slicing the spare skin off swiftly with her blade, she passed it to Ivy.

"It will pull tight as the skin dries. It will be strong enough to pierce the hide of a probech, I think."

"It's wonderful," Ivy whispered. She spun the weapon in her hands by the firelight.

"It's yours."

"Thank you." Ivy's gratitude was not just for the spear, but for the acceptance it implied. Ivy moved her fingers slowly along the shaft, testing the unfamiliar weight. The deadly point glittered.

"Would you like to try?" Kora passed Ivy a new length of bamboo. They sat in comfortable silence, listening to the others talk as they worked. Ivy found the technique more difficult than she expected, and her hafting, although Kora was diplomatic about it, left a lot to be desired. On numerous occasions the sharp blade preferred her soft fingers to the bamboo. Ivy handed the bloodied spear back with an apology.

"It takes a lot of practice," Kora said. "Here, try another."

Ivy began again, while Kora corrected the binding on her first attempt with a soft smile.

As the evening wore on, Ivy spent time with each toolmaker, watching them work and occasionally testing her skill with a shower of shards and apologies. When Kyah joined them, and quickly surpassed Ivy's own skill in producing simple stone flakes, she sighed. She was a fast learner, with agile fingers and thick skin that didn't cut so easily. Kyah soon progressed to creating the standard of tools used by early humans. They fell far short of the sophisticated weapons of Homo floresiensis, but still, compared to Ivy's own efforts, they were impressive. Ironically, Ivy recalled that crafting tools from stone was once considered a hallmark difference between apes and early humans. By that definition, Ivy was the least evolved ape in the cave.

Eventually Kyah wandered off to find Trahg and Ivy settled back next to Xiou. She found a palm-sized pebble stone, perfectly rounded by timeless rolling in a riverbed. With a discarded flake, she scratched absently on its smooth surface, listening to them talk.

"We should approach from the direction of the sea," Setian was saying. "The herd has moved toward the rising sun, so we will have more cover from rifts." A few others gathered around the fire to listen.

"Perhaps we should approach from the setting sun instead," Xiou countered. "The rifts are dangerous. They'll slow us down."

Setian scratched his face, considering. "That's true. But if the probech travel too far from the river while we bypass the rifts, we will lose them. Krue should decide."

He called out across the cave, and an older man joined them. Ivy's face grew red as she recognized him. It was the man who had spat at Ivy's feet when the hunter Terap had been killed. The old man seemed of similar age to Gihn. Unlike Gihn's more graceful features, Krue was solidly built, muscular and still strong for his age. His skin was a battlefield of scars and on both hands, he had missing fingers. He stepped past Ivy, ignoring her as the others continued talking.

"If the probech were sighted by the river below the rifts, then they will have to follow the grassland to where the white water falls," Krue said, with gruff authority. His lips and teeth were stained dark red. He spat red saliva onto the ground and Ivy wrinkled her nose. *Betel juice.* "We should approach with the morning sun behind us; it will be easier to travel from that direction. But Karathah hunt the lands past the river now, so we must be careful. They're crossing further into our territory." Krue looked pointedly at Ivy. "If we meet them, there *will* be trouble." He pressed his stained lips tightly together and challenged her with a cold stare. Ivy's mouth dropped open in surprise. Apparently, she was not as welcome as she'd been led to believe. She shrank a little closer to Xiou.

Oblivious to the exchange, the other hunters continued to discuss their plans. Krue spat on the ground again before he responded to them with a sour expression. The others nodded deferentially.

Ivy watched him. She'd never disliked a person so quickly before. He was a morbidly serious man and Ivy gathered he was still well respected for hunting strategy, though his aging body and many disfigurements probably limited an active role. Krue shot another look of disdain at Ivy as the conversation continued around them.

"Hear this, Hiranah," Xiou turned cheerfully to Ivy, interrupting her silent stand-off with Krue. "You will see a probech before the week is out." His enthusiasm was infectious.

"That would be -" Ivy began.

"No!" Krue interjected. His eyes stayed fixed on Ivy. "The karathah can not come with us. She already forced us to leave fresh shirakan meat to waste. It could have fed everybody. She is bad luck." The old man's eyes sought support from those listening beyond the circle. A few of them his cronies grunted in agreement.

Gihn walked over from Shahn's hearth, his hands open in placation. "She is here to help us, Krue. We left that shirakan for our own good."

"So says she." Krue shot Ivy a look of deep distrust. "She has given us no reason the meat could not be used. Where is the proof that it was bad? In the time that karathah has been here, she has done nothing to help. For all we know, she is trying to starve us to death."

Gihn scowled. "Hiranah may be a giant one, but she is here to help us survive the karathah, not kill us as one of them."

Krue's eyes narrowed and his mouth twisted with anger. "We will all regret her, Gihn," he said. "The karathah are nothing but poison to our land. They are hunting our probech too hard, they are stealing our food. There are more of them every day while we slowly die, and now -," Krue glared at Ivy, then spat a mouthful of red juice at her, "Now you have brought one into our home."

Xiou jumped to his feet, furious, but Setian held him back.

Instead, it was Kora who spoke up. Ivy saw a flicker of fear in her eyes as she straightened her shoulders to address Krue. "Stop insulting her! Hiranah fell from the sky to help us!"

"Then we should have left her where she Fell!" Kora shrunk back from his rebuke. "This karathah has done nothing to save us; she is as bad as the rest of them," Krue continued. "It will already be a dangerous hunt with so few hunters; we don't need the burden and bad luck of a woman who contributes nothing!" There was a muted scattering of agreement at his words.

Tears stung Ivy's eyes and she blinked them away furiously. As much as she wanted to defend herself, in all honour, she couldn't. *Krue is right*, she realised. *I have contributed nothing. His family are dying around him and I'm letting it happen.*

Xiou shook off Setian's hands. He spoke with an even tone but hostility suffused his words.

"Hiranah will come to the hunt, or I will not." There was a sharp intake of breath around the hearth. Ivy knew that Xiou was the strongest and most fearless hunter they had. His face wore terrible scars to prove it. Shahn had told her that it was through Xiou's leadership that the younger hunters still managed to bring as much food as they did.

Krue kicked the ground, burning Ivy's eyes with a pall of ash and dust.

"Then we will come back empty handed," he growled. With a final look of resentment, the old man turned and retreated to his own hearth at the back of the cave.

As darkness fell, Ivy sank against the cave wall on her sleeping mat. She watched Xiou and Shahn at the fire, conversing quietly with Shahn's young sister Leihna. Kyah and Trahg had spent the last hour rolling tight raffia balls to each other across the dirt. Now, the tiny boy lay dozing in Kyah's lap as the bonobo gently groomed his hair. Kyah caught Ivy's eye in the flickering firelight.

"Baby- sleep-", Kyah signed.

"It's time for bed," Ivy replied quietly. Kyah relinquished the little boy to his sleeping mat and soothed him as his eyes fluttered. Shahn rubbed her forehead against the bonobo's affectionately as she took over the task of settling him. Kyah didn't even flinch.

"Sleep- good- Ivy", the bonobo signed. Then she picked her way to the mouth of the cave to find her nesting tree for the night. She always nested close by and rose at sunrise to search for food, usually with Trahg and Turi in tow. Ivy had never seen Kyah so calm and self-assured.

After all this time, she's healing.

Gihn had also disappeared into the forest tonight. Although Shahn had tried to ease Ivy's guilt, Ivy knew his faith in her was faltering. *Krue was right. I contribute nothing.* Krue and his followers were turning on her and Ivy didn't blame them one bit. It was the others she quietly blamed, the ones that wanted her here. The ones that called her here in the first place. Deep down, Ivy didn't want to give them what they sought from her. What they had stolen from her to save themselves. *Life.*

An aching loneliness bit her heart.

The smooth river stone was still clasped warm in her hand and she rolled it over. The silhouette of an ivy leaf was now engraved deeply into its surface. The shape hadn't been intentional; it had just seemed to belong there. Ivy had etched it without conscious thought.

She squeezed her eyes shut and let her fingers seek its twin image on her thigh. She could feel it there, beneath the fabric of her jeans. That birthmark that had once made her feel so unique, now made Ivy ache with loss as she desperately wished that the fingertips caressing it were not her own. *Orrin.* Her heart willed him to hear the words. *I miss you. I really do. And I'm so sorry.* She didn't notice the tears that slipped down her face and pooled in the hollow of her throat.

Ivy saw Orrin's face in the darkness of her mind. Once again, she felt the crushing intensity that he had awoken within her. *He saw right through me.* She clung to the memory of him like a living, breathing thing. *I don't want to give you up. Not yet. Where is that moment? The one where I wake up and find this was all a bad dream?* Ivy pushed her forehead down into her knees in silent anguish.

She was paralysed. Never had she wanted more desperately to break away and run, to smash the faith of these people to pieces. *I want to save myself.* The horror of that realisation should have drowned her in guilt but it didn't. *I want to be faster and stronger than them. I want to run away and leave them to die. I'm the very thing they're begging me to save them from.* It was pitiful. *Because I only want to save myself. And I want him back.* Her head dropped back against the wall, but she refused to open her eyes. The anger welling up inside her was so *human.* She pushed it away, but it fought its way back. She was drowning.

A flash of warm hazel eyes dragged her back up and Ivy ground away the tears with her fists. She squeezed the river stone hard.

I'd fight for you, Orrin.
I'd fight for my old life. And a new one, with you.

If I had a choice.

She blinked her eyes open. The cave was still there. The hobbits, with their all vulnerabilities and naive faith were still there. *But I don't have that choice anymore, do I?*

I have an entirely different one. An impossible choice.

I could save them. Of course I could. But I shouldn't.

Because the very traits Ivy had hidden from for so many years, were out there now, waiting for them in the form of the Karathah. Humans were callous. They were selfish. Violent. They stole and then pushed and pushed the weakest to any edge they could find.

And I am human. Ivy couldn't even try to deny the very same urges that fought within her.

But they need me.

Ivy strongly suspected that the fates of these people were no longer moved by natural selection. There were forces at work here, stronger, urgent forces that were stealing their potential to exist.

Human forces.

And if the hobbits were dying by human hand, then perhaps it was only right that a human hand should reach out to save them.

Ivy pulled back the edge of her sleeping mat. The hide and dried grass she slept on had begun to smell familiar. Like a new home.

If I have to stay here, then I'm doing this on my own terms. This is my life now.

She dug into the compacted cave floor with her nails, scraping and dislodging the dirt until the hole was big enough. She pressed her lips to the ivy-engraved river stone.

Even if I can't have you Orrin, perhaps one day, fifty thousand years from now, you might have a part of me.

Ivy covered the stone again with dirt, pushing it hard with the heel of her hand. She flattened the corner of her bed roll back on top of the disturbed earth. It was buried now, just like the life she had lost.

I'm beginning again, and this time, I'm choosing my own fate.

Ivy searched her mind for answers long after sounds of sleep filled the cave.

CHAPTER 31

NEIL

I'm a fucking genius.

With a smug grin, Neil sat pulping the vomit flavoured fruit against a rock.

An idea had struck him like lightning in the dead of night. He'd left immediately, and picked the fruit under-ripe. He had no intention of eating it. When he was finished, Neil placed ten tiny marsupial skulls in a horseshoe row, one beside the other, tipped upside down, like makeshift bowls. It hadn't been easy to catch so many, the little bastards were fast. But his patience had eventually paid off, both for food and for this experiment. He filled each skull-cup to the brim with pulpy fruit then turned to his next task.

Neil grunted as he twisted the copper bracelet over his wrist bones and hand. It had been there a long time. He'd put on weight. Years ago, he'd been offended when Francine had insisted he wear it to ease the arthritic twinges in his joints. It was a sign of weakness. Of age. Not to mention a complete load of crap. *She was so damn gullible.* He almost smiled at the memory, but not quite. She'd always had a weakness for those palm readers that lure tourists in foreign markets. But his then-wife was insistent on the bracelet and in a rare effort to appease her, he'd put it on and left it there. He barely noticed it these days. Now, it might finally be useful. The copper was hard but malleable enough. It took Neil the best part of two hours to chop it into five sections using a roughly sharpened stone, each piece a little more than two centimetres long. Disassembling his watch band was easier. With a bit of force, the zinc alloy broke into heavy links of three a piece, giving him five separate bits. He pocketed the cracked analogue face.

Neil lay the short wedges of copper and zinc in alternate fashion along the connecting edges of the bowls; *zinc, copper, zinc, copper...* until he had a line of ten. Each end of metal arched between two skulls, dipping down into the sour fruit cupped inside. *Ten perfect battery cells, about half a volt each.* Once all ten skulls were connected in a single line, he pulled the USB cable he still carried from his back pocket. One end was jacked for his mobile, the other for a computer. In his frequent travel between offices, this cable was a lifeline for transferring and storing files on the go. It had been Dimitri's idea, and though Neil had not admitted it, it was a good one. He'd been seconds from downloading the data in that physics lab with this cable.

Using his stone blade, Neil sliced the computer jack from the end and stripped the plastic coating from the cable. He separated the long, delicate wires out. He pushed the first wire into one end of his line of skulls, then the other wire into the opposite end. He wiped his hands clean on his trousers and pulled his dead mobile from his pocket.

Neil hesitated. His fingers were shaking. The handset of glass and metal was more than it seemed. It meant *control.* It was a scrap of reality in an unreal world. The prospect of failure seemed crueller than a dead battery was worth. Gritting his teeth, Neil plugged it in. Moments passed. *Nothing.* His heart sank.

Suddenly, the screen lit up. The battery icon switched to charge.

Neil exhaled a breath he didn't realize he'd been holding. His shoulders relaxed and he laughed to himself.

Fucking genius.

With a sigh of relief, he sat back against the tree to wait.

The pale light streaming from his cell phone screen illuminated Neil's haggard face. It was nearly midnight. He stood high on a barren ridge south-west of his river hideout. He'd paced silently through the forest for nearly an hour to get there, with only the waxing crescent moon to light his way.

Neil was filthy but renewed in purpose. His hands held steady. All trace of alcohol was gone from his system. His body was stronger, his thoughts clearer. Neil spun the device in his fingers, contemplating the threat he'd been issued such a short time ago by his colleagues. The CEO had cornered him at a media junket.

"You're walking a fine line, Neil. I'm not going to cover for you again. The women, the booze... the press are all over this event. Go home before you do something stupid."

"Who's complaining Barry?" He'd turned with a leering smile to the blonde trailing him. "This one's not, that's for sure."

"The Board is and I am. Get out of here and sober up. We can't afford another mistake."

Neil had straightened up. "You give me incompetent staff and tell me I make mistakes? That project was a mess from the start; I'm just your bloody scapegoat."

"There'll be an internal review. It was badly managed. You're losing your edge, Neil. You've let yourself go and you're sure as hell not taking the whole department down with you."

The memory jarred. Neil took a deep breath and looked out from the frigid precipice. He was high above sea level. His breath misted as it left him and he gritted his teeth. The company had lost faith in him. They sought to send him quietly into retirement, like an old horse shot behind the shed. He wouldn't let it happen. Another dark cloud resurfaced in his memory.

"Dad, it's me, it's Benjamin." The voice through the telephone receiver was hesitant.

"Benjamin? Yes, what is it?"

"Well, I was just wondering- I haven't seen you in a while and I thought maybe... well there's a Fathers Day lunch at school. Mum says I'll be back home next Wednesday so I can go. Maybe you could come with me?"

Neil could hear the beeping of medical equipment in the background. Another round of chemo.

"It won't take long... it's just lunch." The boy's voice implored softly. "All the other dads will be there."

"I'm sorry Benjamin; I'm travelling interstate at the moment. You'll have to take Stephen." Francine's new husband would no doubt have offered anyway. Neil looked at his watch, aggravated by the guilt. Francine probably put him up to it. She'd made the boy too soft.

"But I was hoping... Okay Dad. I'm sorry I called."

"It's fine Benjamin. But I have to go. Perhaps next time."

"Yes Dad."

The quiet voice faded from his mind.

Benjamin was nearly eleven. Neil still resented the way Francine had indulged the child. Especially now. Life was hard and the sooner the boy understood it, the better he would survive in the world. The stronger he would be. And he would need to be strong.

Neil squeezed his eyes shut and shook the chill from his neck. There was nothing he could do for Benjamin, he knew that. What the child really needed was more time. Time to find a cure for the disease that bound him. Time was something Neil couldn't provide. No father could. Once more, the bitterness of another's disappointment seethed in him.

Neil refused to accept that loss, just as he refused to accept the other. He resented their judgement. The Board of Directors, the whole damn department, his own son.

I can't control time, but I can damn well control this situation. I'm not too old. I'm not losing my edge.

I'll prove them all wrong.

Dark strategy was his ally tonight. He had theories that needed to be tested. This place was far enough away from the cave to hide from those damn abominations that he spent so much of his time watching. He needed space to breathe and fully dissect the ludicrous hypothesis unfolding in his mind. But most importantly, this was as far as he'd needed to hike to get a clear view of the stellar night sky.

In his current abysmal circumstance, the built-in digital compass of his phone was now proving a life-saver. The dense canopy of the forest usually prevented him navigating by star-path; he couldn't get a clear enough view to identify the South Celestial Pole. Tonight would be different. He held the device up to test its accuracy. The true magnetic compass swung a digital pointer to North and Neil looked out across a dark sea of volcanic jungle. His forehead creased anxiously. Although he used it sparingly, the battery was nearly half gone again.

He flicked his finger across the cracked screen searching for the GPS display. A series of twelve empty receiver boxes greeted him once again. He'd hoped that having such a clear view of the night sky might allow him to pick up any remaining GPS satellite transmissions available, however weak they may be. Neil knew that they were up there; thirty-two satellites in medium earth orbit spaced evenly around the globe. At any point in the world, he should have been able to receive four satellites simultaneously, and the earth-bound receiver would compute his exact position. If he could only access the GPS, he could find out where he was and navigate his way out. Once again, however, the receivers remained empty on the screen.

It was clear he was no longer in Melbourne, or Sydney or anywhere else he knew – the jungle told him that much. But where he was, Neil had no clue. He shifted his fingers around the edge of the device, trying not to obscure the antennas he knew were hidden in the circuitry and aesthetics of the phone. *Nothing. Over three thousand artificial satellites are up there, and not a single one functioning. Shit.* It seemed impossible, that this energy mutation could have had such a dramatic effect on every individual orbit. Even geostationary satellites were known to drift when faced with solar wind and the gravitational effect of the sun and moon. Surely one of them, somewhere, was still operational. Neil had seen many of those satellites launched himself, in years gone by. He'd worked on their transmission logs and monitored and relayed their feedback. *Nothing.*

Once more, the ludicrous hypothesis that had sought him out earlier, returned to his mind. *What if the satellites aren't actually there at all? Not just dysfunctional; but not even in the sky? What if they no longer existed?* It was insane. It was the thought of a desperate man. He pushed it aside once again.

He needed another way of finding out where he was. As he searched through the bright icons. A solution came to him quickly. The only non-standard application he had ever downloaded was a star map. All employees in the Division of Astronomy and Space had received it; a lark by the administration team for a department full of astronomers. *Pocket Universe.* He flicked through the introductory notes and settings – his Sydney location had already been input. *But there are no satellites for global positioning - would it even work?*

His cracked lips tightened as he held the star-studded screen to the night sky. He exhaled with relief. The screen swivelled as he turned, needing only the magnetic compass to determine the direction he faced. Obediently, the star map shifted, reflecting back to him what he saw in the sky above him – *or didn't see.*

The bright celestial sky did not match the one stored in his phone's memory files. The screen was off centre, twisted. He raked the sky for a familiar constellation. *Crux.* The Southern Cross sparkled to his west in the middle of the Milky Way. It stood vertical in the black sky, with its four brightest stars depicting the tips of a Latin cross. The fifth faintest member of the cross, epsilon Crucis, sat snugly under the right cross bar of the lower quadrant. Often misleading young astronomers with its dim light and random placement, Neil recognized it instantly as the orange giant it was, nearly one hundred and fifty times more luminous than the sun. *Good, a place-mark.* A strict Christian upbringing had highlighted its importance before Neil's career watching stars had even begun. In biblical days, the Crux constellation was revered in the Near East before finally disappearing over the horizon at the time of the Christian crucifixion in Jerusalem. It was no longer visible in the Northern Hemisphere at latitudes north of twenty-five degrees. This gave him a starting point. *I'm still in the Southern Hemisphere.*

Neil fumbled through the search mechanism of the software. *So where should the Southern Cross actually be positioned?* The constellation Crux appeared on the tiny screen. It lay sideways against the black backdrop littered with name labels. He blinked, stunned. Not only was the cross displaced in the night sky, but it had rotated ninety degrees. He blinked again. *Holy Shit. This can't be. I'm an astronomer for Christ's sake - and this is impossible!* The only explanation for a rotated constellation was that the earth itself had travelled further in its rotation around the sun since he'd left– three months further. He counted on his fingers; he had been here less than a week. Even if he had lain unconscious on the forest floor for another one or two days, Crux should still have held its position. *Three months?*

Again, that ludicrous hypothesis reared its ugly head. So you're not where you should be... and you're not when you should be. Time itself has shifted...

Furiously, Neil punched his fingertips onto the screen. The

exact position of the Southern Cross where and when it *should* have been on March 12th, Sydney Australia – popped up on the screen. Latitude 215 degrees... Longitude 36 degrees. He committed the numbers to memory and picked a new default location in the long list of settings. *Brisbane, Australia– latitude still too far south.* He couldn't go above twenty-five degrees or the Southern Cross wouldn't have been visible to him the way it was. *Below twenty-five degrees...* Neil stared at the volcanic jungle thoughtfully. Hawaii was the only US state below twenty-five degrees' latitude. *It was volcanic, heavily forested.* He selected the location and studied the new map. *Both latitude and longitude are way off now. Something a bit closer to home...Papua New Guinea – still too far North-East. Asia? Jakarta, Indonesia.* Very close. Neil bent to his task, engrossed. He needed to get further east, but there were no other options. *Somewhere between Jakarta and Port Moresby...* he considered the archipelago of volcanic islands crowning the top of Australia. *I'm somewhere in there...*

Hanging above him, the Southern Cross lent weight to his conviction. He was in the wrong place, *obviously*, but at least now he had a ballpark. *The Indonesian Archipelago.* The location seemed to fit. The volcanic rifts, dense jungle, humidity... *but when?*

Time *had* changed. According to the celestial sky above him, that base measure of time and navigation for all humanity, it was June. Three months later than it should be. But was it June this year, or June last year? And if time had travelled instantaneously, as it seemed to have done, perhaps the year he had woken up in was not a year he'd ever been meant to see at all. *And if that was the case... those cave-dwelling monkeys the woman is with - what if they* are *proto-human?* Neil pushed his imagination to its limit. He had trekked for hours yesterday with no sign of civilization. Since he'd arrived, the miniscule freaks had had no contact by researchers or scientists or the outside world. Had he travelled so far back in time that civilization didn't even exist?

The ludicrous hypothesis that had thrown his logic suddenly

did not seem so ludicrous after all. *Time has shifted. I am in the wrong time. I have travelled through time.* There was no other explanation. Short of moving the very stars themselves, there was no way he could be *here, now,* without a time shift. Gulping down the horror of being so inescapably disconnected from the world as he knew it, he sat motionless on the cold rock. For a long time, Neil considered.

Maybe I'm looking at this all wrong. Whether that lab knew what they were doing or not, they created this potential. The energy field that I discovered– I uncovered their research, I tracked them down. Whatever happened in that lab happened for a reason. It happened for me. I did it. I've travelled through time and space and I survived.

Neil dissected his epiphany.

Maybe this primitive death-trap isn't the curse I thought it was. Maybe it's an opportunity. Can I use it? How? Not just to control energy but to control time itself. To control time... the possibilities were endless. The opportunities it offered, infinite. *Benjamin... What the boy needs is time. A chance for me to recognise his condition sooner. To travel forward in time where a cure could be waiting. To return it to him and save his life. My son would have time then. Time to grow, time to live his life. Time to see his father for what he really is. A hero. There's no greater control than to control time itself. But how did it happen?*

In any experiment, there was always a conduit, Neil knew. A reactant. *What am I missing?* He tried to remember. The time shift had happened in that laboratory as soon as the woman had walked in. *The woman... what could she have possibly done to create...?*

In his mind, he saw a flash of black stone against the white skin on her throat, before it pulsed electric blue like a neon light, stunning his eyes.

It was her necklace. That black stone.

The thought solidified his lingering resolution in sweat. The black stone, the one that now dangled from her wrist, had reacted with the lunar energy field. It wasn't the physics lab that was drawing the energy field toward the earth – *it was her*. More specifically, it was her necklace. The lab must have amplified the frequency, distorting and fracturing it somehow. *They had the gear. All those damn machines.*

Neil let out an exalted whoop. *So I'll figure it out, recreate it. Control it. If I did it before I can do it again.*

So his path of action was going to be easy after all. He looked down toward the cave in the dark.

The red-head *was* dispensable – but that stone wasn't.

The stars above Neil glorified his singular new purpose; *Get that stone.*

CHAPTER 32

ORRIN

*O*rrin paced as far from the riot as he could, pushing through people until the night was once again quiet between the tall buildings. Blood streamed from his nose. The woven ivory of his shirt soaked it up with a wipe, leaving his face smeared and bruised. Orrin wandered, dazed. *It's all so wrong.* The city was a stranger. Everywhere he looked, Orrin struggled with the discontinuities of the space around him. Landmarks were the same, but just different enough for uncertainty to crawl under his skin. It was surreal and disorienting. His eyes burned as they sought recognition in the dark streets. Sporadic neon lights illuminated the city's ruined face and Orrin noticed more and more peculiarities. *Are there more electrical cables than usual?*

Two carriage horses clipped him as he turned a corner, and Orrin jumped backward. A load of tourists misbehaved drunkenly in the back and he felt a twinge of sympathy for the beasts pulling them. Blinded by eye covers and assaulted by traffic, they still managed to keep in perfect step. The rich smell of manure fought with gasoline in the streets. Orrin gingerly pushed the swollen bridge of his nose and cursed as pain shot into his forehead.

Liam doesn't know Ivy. It made no sense. *No one knows her.* Again there was nothing but a void where she should have been. His gut wrenched and Orrin felt himself drifting again. Nothing else mattered but this sinking disorientation. It was swallowing him up and dragging him under. He stopped resisting it and vaguely considered the alternative truth. *I am the problem here. I don't even know myself anymore.* Had he crossed some dark, invisible line, sanity on one side and fantasy on the other? Had Ivy been a fantasy? *I can't fix what I don't understand and nothing here makes sense.*

Orrin got swept into a wave of night commuters. A small boy shadowed his mother ahead of him through rush-hour pedestrians. Distant clangs from passing trams broke through the quiet spaces in Orrin's mind as he relentlessly tested his own sanity. *No. I didn't imagine her. Did I? Am I that desperate? That crazy?* He tumbled over her face in his mind and breathed the faint scent of vanilla. His hands trembled. Orrin shoved them into his pockets. His gut told him that Ivy had existed; intelligent and intriguing. She wasn't the sort of woman he'd conjure up for private fantasy, like the magazine blonde he'd crushed on in his teens or fine things gyrating in his head after a few pints.

No, Ivy was real. He'd felt her breath on his face. He'd felt the goose-bumps of her skin under his fingertips. *Hadn't he?* Again the vanilla scent plagued him like a dying man seeking white light. *Ivy Carter, where are you?*

There was a giggle nearby. It was the small boy. Deep in thought, Orrin had stopped walking in the middle of the pavement, splitting the flow of pedestrians behind him. He ducked to the side where an audience had gathered around a street performer. Laughing and clapping, the little lad's attention had been caught by an animal dressed in a gaudy jester's hat and jacket. The boy's mop of ringlets frizzed as he bounced to the music, like the halo borne of a static balloon. The child's mother edged to the outskirts of the crowd, relieved with his distraction as she argued into her mobile.

The jester spun awkwardly for his audience, with bird-like movements and tapping feet. Orrin pushed through the laughing crowd to stand beside the boy. *Jaysus, no.* A slow churning of acid in his stomach rose to his throat. *Please, no. Not this.* It was the same type of creature he had come across in the lab. *A hobbit.* Olive-skinned, tiny, an extraordinary fusion of familiar and bizarre. *A man.* His hair had been crudely chopped under the three-pointed fools' hat he wore to more closely resemble a miniature human. Terror-stricken eyes kept his flat feet moving. A plastic tambourine was clutched in his hand. The ground shifted under Orrin's feet. He swallowed bitter bile and reached for a street lamp to steady himself, squeezing his eyes shut.

"Watch'it! Don't you go puking on my gig!" The bark came from a man who sat beside the jester, crippling a portable chair with overhanging weight. All eyes turned to Orrin. Realising he had inadvertently distracted his audience, the man in the chair dressed his face with a cheery smile.

"What do you think our little monkey-man, folks? Isn't he great?" He surveyed the pedestrians with greedy eyes. "Dance, monkey-man, dance! What'd'ya say folks? Look at him spin! That's got to be worth a dollar or two; can you spare some coins for charity? Ma'am, how about you?"

From his canvas throne, he slid the tin toward the woman with a filthy boot. Orrin clenched his jaw. There was nothing charitable about him.

Only now did Orrin notice the chain that snaked its way from the man to the ankle of the jester. The hobbit had its lips pulled back into a grimace, in pretence of a gummy smile. Orrin felt a surge of disgust as he realized the hobbits' teeth had been removed. The hobbit twirled and hopped, clapping his hands maniacally. His audience cheered in delight. The fat man grinned. Roars of laughter and exclamations pitted the crowd.

"Isn't he cute."

"Look at him jump!"

"It almost looks human!"

Clapping pulled more passers-by into the audience. Gold coins flew into the tin. Orrin stared at the people around him, appalled by their sanction of the spectacle. Only the small mop-haired boy at the front was not laughing now. Orrin guessed he was about five years old. The boy's face was suddenly serious and concerned, his jaw jutting out pensively. His bottom lip quivered and he looked at the crowd, at the fat ringmaster and then back to the tiny jester. The hobbit's shaved body was mottled with bruises under the too-short jacket and pants.

"What a funny little fellow," the fat man was saying, "he can even somersault for the kids!"

The audience laughed. Parents smiled indulgently to their children as the hobbit broke the tedium of their day with a few minutes of entertainment for the price of a gold coin. The ring-master returned to reading his newspaper with a grin. With the exception of Orrin, the crowd's amusement made them oblivious to the little boy's escalating distress.

Poor wee lad. Orrin looked for the child's mother but couldn't see her through the crowd. *This has to stop...* He patted the boy's shoulder in comfort.

"It's not right, is it, mate," Orrin said, quietly. The little boy looked up at him with tears spilling from his eyes.

Abruptly, the dancing hobbit froze and spun to face the child. He stepped closer. The audience exclaimed and shuffled back, bumping into each other as they watched, wide eyed. No one reached out to help the child. Orrin tightened his grip, unsure what to do. The boy sniffed loudly. He pulled away from Orrin, stepping cautiously toward the chained hobbit instead. The crowd drew a collective breath.

Child and hobbit were the same height. But there, the similarities ended. The jester's face suddenly carried the shadow of an old man. All pretence was lost to the dirty pavement. His ridiculous outfit hung on his skeletal frame, all its humour dissolved in an instant. Miserable, tortured eyes spoke to the child. Compassion poured back. Seconds passed. Only seconds, but an eternity to the unlikely pair in the street.

The little boy reached out his hand. The hobbit man took it.

There was a collective draw of breath from the now silent crowd. Time hung suspended as they finally realised the misery behind their entertainment.

What do they see in each other's eyes? Orrin wondered.

Transfixed by their connection, he stepped forward, accidentally kicking the collection tin in a shower of gold and silver.

"Oi, you!" The fat ringmaster looked up. "I thought I told you to get lost!" Heaving to his feet, the man realised all at once that his audience were no longer amused. They all turned to look at him, caught somewhere between hostility and confusion. The tinny music played on, but the tiny dancer was not dancing.

"Dance for the people!" The ringmaster pulled hard on the chain, sending his jester sprawling onto the concrete. He grinned nervously at the crowd with cracked lips, knowing he'd lost them. He angrily tugged again on the chain, sliding the helpless creature along as he scrambled to his feet. "Come on, now, dance!"

"That's enough!" Orrin took a step forward, with flashing eyes and gritted jaw. "Leave the poor thing be, you can't treat it like that." The little boy rushed forward, reaching out to the fallen creature.

"I can do what I damn well want to." The ringmaster spat back.

"You're hurting it -" the boy cried.

"I own it!" the man hissed down at him, then grabbed a registration tag that was hanging on a lanyard around his neck. He waved it at Orrin. "So mind your damn business and bugger off!"

"Finn! Come here this instant, don't touch that animal!" The boy's mother appeared, shoving her mobile into her handbag to grab his hand. "Good god, darling, you don't know where it's been, you could catch something!" She pulled the little boy away through the crowd as he argued and twisted, struggling to see what had happened to his fallen companion. His wails echoed up the street.

"Right, you, I said move it!" The ringmaster glared accusingly at Orrin as if he were responsible for the rapid decay of his spectacle. The crowd around them began to move on. Orrin hesitated, caught between his pity for the creature and a desperate need to escape its reality.

"It just doesn't seem right, having him on a chain like that," Orrin said.

"You going to feed my family are you, dero?" The ringmaster lowered his voice to a spiteful whisper. "You bloody activists, you think you know everything. Here's a dose of reality for you - a bleedin' heart'll get you nowhere in this world. You think I like doing this?" At his feet, the crouched hobbit was now gathering gold and silver and throwing it back into the collection tin. His jester's hat had fallen away. "I can't stand the filthy animals," the fat man said. "I'm barely scraping by, working three jobs myself – you think I chose this life? You think I wanna sit here every night in the cold? *This is my reality, not just the animal's.* Now get the hell off my gig."

The hobbit looked up at Orrin from the pavement. He had the eyes of a man. He was intelligent. He was broken and resigned to his fate. He *knew.* Dumbed with shock and cold sweat, Orrin clenched his fists in his pockets and stumbled away.

Orrin made his way to Flinders Street Station. All about him, commuters wove in and out as they hurried for their homes. He felt like the only person alive, the only person to see the world for what it really was. Or wasn't. *Or perhaps it's them who are alive, and I'm dead.* Perhaps this was what death felt like - isolated, confused and disembodied.

Orrin sunk on the train, lulled into mindless chaos as it began to move. Opposite him, dark hoods and shared earphones cocooned a pair of young lovers from the outside world. The thrum of bass echoed from their direction as they stole kisses. Orrin felt a sudden pang of envy. He'd thought he might have had that again. He'd thought wrong. His whole mind was wrong. Perhaps it had never been right.

The train rattled on, taking its weary passengers with it. Orrin was brought out of his reverie by soft singing. A young man sat opposite with a violin case strapped to his back and folders in his arms. He looked like a typical conservatorium student. His scuffed shoes tapped as he serenaded the nearly empty train car. Orrin tuned in, surprised by his lack of inhibition. 'God' he heard over and again. *God.* As Orrin listened, he was comforted by the deeply religious overtones emanating from the boy. *Just like aul gaff,* he sighed. *It's been too long.* The student smiled encouragingly at Orrin. He began a new song and when he disembarked a few stations later he left a stack of folded pamphlets in his place. Orrin reached over and took one.

Genesis 26: Then God said, "Let us make man in our image, in our likeness, and let them rule over the fish of the sea and the birds of the air, over the livestock, over all the earth, and over all the creatures that move along the ground."

When God created Adam and Eve, they were fully developed human beings, capable of communication, society and development (Genesis 2:19-25; 3:1-20; 4:1-12). The Book of Genesis is clear that Adam and Eve did not evolve from lower life forms. They were perfect humans from the time of their creation, fully formed, intelligent and upright. As humans, God has given us the right and responsibility to rule over animals - "all the creatures that move along the ground."

Some will claim that they are our brothers. Some will claim that they are our equals in the eyes of God.

As Children of God, do not be taken into the arms of Satan's temp-

tation. Repel the forces of evil! Embrace your sovereignty as the true Children of God, who stand alone in His image.

Stand tall in God's light and reject the abominations - they are creatures spawned by the devil in trickery to imitate and mock a righteous God. These creatures embody the work of darkness and evil. They are a test of your faith. They are no brother of Man; they are no part of Almighty God's design.

Bear witness that the Children of Satan shall be punished for their sins against humanity.

Below the diatribe, was a macabre graphic of the same creature that seemed to haunt Orrin everywhere he turned. But this time with wild, barbaric eyes and an aura of evil that sent a shiver down his spine.

CHAPTER 33

IVY

A bowl of food sat uneaten in front of Ivy as she twisted her fingers absently in the short hide skirt she wore. It had been a gift from Shahn. Considering that the only animal on Flores large enough to provide a hide so big was a stegodon, it was an expensive gift. Ivy had no doubt that Shahn had traded some of her own belongings for it. Ivy was grateful. She was glad to be rid of her filthy jeans.

"Do not think on Krue, Hiranah, his bitterness is not your fault," Shahn said, diplomatic as always. "There is no beauty in his world anymore. I pity him, he wasn't always that way."

"He has every right to be bitter," Ivy said. "Krue clearly hates the karathah and I'm guessing with good reason. He sees me as one of them, which is fair enough. I am one."

"You're different."

"No, I'm not." As much as Ivy hated to acknowledge it, the weakness of her own species had tarnished every move she had made so far. She took a deep breath. "What did they do to him?"

Shahn looked away for a long moment.

"Nothing," Shahn said. "It was his mate's daughter, Tikan." A memory came into Ivy's mind, from Shahn, to compliment her words. She saw a girl not much older than Leihna, with dark, bushy hair and a wide smile. "Krue was so proud of Tikan. He taught her to hunt himself. Three seasons ago there was - an accident," Shahn said quietly. "Tikan was hunting alone and didn't return. She was strong and independent so at first, no one worried." A tear slipped down Shahn's face and Ivy quite literally *felt* her grief through their connection. "Her mother Lahstri, our medicine woman, was worried that Tikan may have hunted too far into karathah territory. Perhaps she was right. After searching for two days, Krue found Tikan's body by the Northern River. She'd been killed, and..." Shahn took a deep breath, "brutalised. By a karathah man."

Ivy shook her head, trying to push away her disgust. No matter where she hid from it, the dark side of humanity kept taunting her.

"Krue lost his mind in grief," Shahn said, shivering at the memory. "He ran to the cave of the karathah and tried to attack them. They laughed at him. One man came out and knocked him down. He left Krue unconscious in the forest and took his fingers as punishment. Krue has carried his hatred for them ever since that day."

"I don't blame him."

"Tikan was killed by one bad man," Shahn replied gently. "I can't believe they are all so bad. There is light and shadow in all people, even Krue himself." Shahn looked to the back of the cave, where Ivy knew the dying hunters were being tended to by their loved ones. "His real torment is that the karathah thrive while we are dying. There are so many of them Hiranah, many more than us. Each day more of the forest becomes theirs. Their hunting tracks are growing closer to our cave and the food animals are disappearing." Shahn's fingertips traced her belly and her brow furrowed. "I don't know why our hunters are sick, or why our babies don't survive, but I do know that every part of our family is precious."

Shahn was right of course. This wasn't only about Tikan. There was a bigger game at play. Anger flared in Ivy's chest. If history had taught her anything, it was that Homo sapiens could justify genocide for personal gain. *But what motivation could they possibly have here? This is* prehistory. *These hobbits have nothing of value.* Ivy flattened her palms onto the dirt behind her. *Or do they?*

"A nice morning for you, Hiranah." Xiou's hand encircled the amulet on her wrist. Ivy looked up from the rippling water that had her mesmerized. "I think I found your favourite place." Ivy just smiled. Xiou sat down beside her, his oversized feet falling far short of the river in which Ivy swirled her toes.

She'd never dreamed a place of such intense beauty could exist. Birds spilled from the treetops and hidden creatures rustled among the leaves and volcanic soil. A breeze danced across the river catching rays of sun and throwing them into her eyes. Tiny silver flashes darted below, hitting her toes. Turtles, eels and water snakes lurked in the shadows. The very essence of tranquillity was all around her.

"It is beautiful, isn't it?" He bowed his head briefly to the river. "Water soothes pain in a way that earth can never do."

Ivy looked at him. "I'm not in pain."

"Don't be ashamed, Hiranah," Xiou said kindly. "Your own pain allows you to understand others'. It's your strength." He paused, and then added, "I know you are lonely."

Ivy's eyes burned as they had threatened to all morning. She had dreamt about him again last night.

Orrin.

Every nerve felt scalded by the memory of his face and it only seemed to grow stronger day by day. This morning, even the river couldn't soothe the ache it left in her heart. There was such clarity in those dreams. Where other fragments of her old life were drifting away, Orrin kept Ivy chained to her loss. She smoothed her fringe behind her ear.

I've made my decision. I chose this. Let him go.

"It helps to talk," Xiou said. "At least that's what Shahn keeps telling me." He chuckled.

Ivy smiled reluctantly. She'd forgotten her thoughts weren't private.

"Tell me about him."

"What do you want to know?"

"Whatever there is to say."

So Ivy told him. Over an hour passed as Xiou listened to Ivy relive the fear that she had tried to hide from. The exhilaration of daring to open her heart. The loss that now plagued her dreams.

"I pushed him away," she admitted bluntly. "I've lost people I love before and I couldn't bear the thought of trying to survive it again." Ivy laughed bitterly through tears she hadn't felt fall. "Now he's lost to me anyway."

"So we stole love from you too," said Xiou. "And yet, here you are. Surviving. Perhaps you are stronger than you think." He let gentle rush of water fill the silence. "Don't live in fear, Hiranah. What we fear most can always find us. We can only be prepared to meet it. You must trust yourself to be ready for it."

There it was again. *Trust.*

Xiou gestured to a spill of grass not too far upstream.

"She has a gentle heart, your friend Kyah."

The bonobo sat with Trahg in her lap as she groomed him. Trahg giggled as her fingers tickled the little boy's scalp. He pulled Kyah's hand away restlessly and ran to the base of a nearby tree.

"Up. Fruit." signed Trahg. Ivy shifted a little uncomfortably at the ease with which he'd picked up Kyah's hand symbols.

Kyah scooted to Trahg's side and ushered him into the branches, then followed. A moment later, a shower of leaves and fruit hit the ground. The two friends dropped to their feet and began to knock them apart and scoop out the middle.

"I worry about her," Ivy said. "Kyah should be with her own kind. Even in my world she had other bonobo's to live with in her cage, though here she has more freedom," Ivy admitted. "But she's still isolated, she's…"

"…one of a kind?" Xiou ventured.

"Yes." A warm breeze rustled the grass. Ivy plucked a tiny flower and tossed it into the wind.

"I wouldn't worry, if I were you," Xiou said. "Kyah is loved. She is teaching us her pictures in the dirt, so we can understand her too."

"Mmmm." It was never Ivy's intention to teach the lexigrams and hand signals she and Kyah used together to the hobbits. The blame fell squarely on Kyah. Once Trahg began emulating Kyah's drawings like any child would, the bonobo had taken it upon herself to keep teaching him new ones. The ripple effect was inevitable. Already, many of the adults had shown interest in learning too. Ivy tried to justify it by telling herself that her other interferences would impact their lives much more than knowing a few symbols.

A dangerous path ahead had already begun to form in Ivy's mind. Although she should have felt overwhelmed by the magnitude of her decision to interfere with evolution, she was resolved and calm.

It was only what Ivy had lost to be here that haunted her now.

Orrin.

CHAPTER 34

ORRIN

Small boats bobbed in the inky black water. The glass felt cool under Orrin's palm and forehead as he stared unseeing at the stunning expanse of bay stretched below him.

The crystal in his hand tremored. Orrin downed his fourth scotch, but comfort was elusive. He felt no warm dissolution in his veins, no vague satisfaction or happy numbness of memory and circumstance.

He was still angry. Still confused. Still helpless with the sickening frustration of not being able to understand what he was missing. It plagued every waking moment and broke him from his sleep in terrors. Failure taunted him.

What is the missing piece of this puzzle? He could feel it there, just a finger tip away. *Am I too blind or stupid to see it? Where* is *she? And what is this god-damned hobbit that's everywhere I turn?* Orrin turned and slammed his empty shot glass onto the coffee table.

Collapsing back onto the leather lounge, he closed his eyes and picked the insanity apart piece by piece. Again. He was a logical man. There would be a logical answer.

Ivy was gone, that much he knew. It was like she'd never existed. She left no note, no phone, she was simply... *gone.* There was no record of her at the archaeology lab or in her own department. No office. He'd combed the postgraduate library for her work records, journal submissions, anything. He found nothing, no references to her classes, no thesis. Jayne denied even knowing her. No one seemed to know her. Phil never met her. Dale never met her. Liam, who had studied and rallied alongside Ivy for eight years, didn't remember her - or Orrin himself - and had nearly broken his nose to prove it.

No one saw a chimp. There was no chimp. The chimp lab now housed some pitiful manifestation of man-ape that seemed to be the source of a cultural upheaval the likes of which he'd never seen before. *I'm missing something.* The world around him screamed *different*, like it had been tilted on its axis and everywhere he turned there was *wrong* that left him stumbling.

Orrin refilled his glass, slopping amber liquid on the marble table. His eyes squeezed shut as the bitterness ran down his throat. *Nothing.* He slumped against the couch.

There wasn't a single damned thing that tied Ivy to this earth. If she had existed, there would be something- however small or remote. But there was nothing in her place but a black void. And only he seemed to notice. Mute devastation clawed at him, tempting insanity. Orrin had never questioned himself before, never needed to. Even in his darkest moments, in the broken realisation of divorce, he still knew his own mind. He'd trusted himself. But this, this was different. This obsession for a woman that had never existed, a woman who *couldn't* exist, was all consuming.

I need her.

He hadn't recognised the loneliness within him until it had almost been filled. Now, acknowledged for what it truly was, the black void Ivy had left threatened to drown him. He searched desperately for something to fill the loss. The nothingness that took her space.

Black.

Orrin's vision blurred, eyelids drooping. *Black.*

Black!

He jolted upright. The blood drained from his face. A memory pierced his brain with singular clarity.

Scattered stone tools in small plastic bags.

Jayne backed to a bench, with accusing, frightened eyes.

He'd slammed her desk.

A single stone tool under his hand.

The faint temptation of recognition.

Orrin knew now why it was familiar.

Black, smooth beneath its crust of dirt. Evenly shaped. Unique.

He knew it. He'd seen it before.

It was Ivy's amulet.

PART III
SELECTION

CHAPTER 35

IVY

The soles of Ivy's feet beat hard against the jungle floor as she ran through the tangle of roots, branches and ferns. Kyah shadowed her in the branches above.

Leihna, Shahn's younger sister, and her cousins Rinap and Filhia were like ghosts between the trees. Tinkling laughs filtered back to direct Ivy's course. Ivy guessed the two eldest to be about twelve with Filhia a couple of years behind. Their slender figures had not long come into womanhood but their faces still had the endearing glow of childhood.

They were like faeries in a children's story, wisps that exist in the moment before sleep. Lurking megafauna could easily have made a meal of them, but the girls weren't defenceless. Their arms were muscular and strong and they could retreat to the safety of the branches in a split-second. In addition, each girl carried a stone blade in her belt and the older two, Rinap and Leihna, carried spears.

Filhia crossed Ivy's path with a bright smile then melted back into the undergrowth. Ivy sprinted after her. The warm air filled her lungs with intoxicating freedom. This place was special. Glossy, heart-shaped leaves touched her face as she passed.

Twigged fingers combed her hair. Her toes thrilled in the sinking peat underfoot. Ivy danced through vines and stretched them along her trail.

Ivy realised the irony of her fear on that first night in the forest. Claws nor tusks nor venom held the greatest threat to her life here. Of all the predators in this forest, Homo sapiens were the most deadly. And not all death came at the end of a spear. Ivy stopped abruptly. It had suddenly occurred to her that a spear was just the most obvious way to kill someone. But there were other ways as well.

"Aaargh!" Ivy shrieked as Rinap landed in front of her with a thump. The other girls pounced onto Ivy from the undergrowth laughing. An instant later, Kyah had dropped from above too, hooting and swatting Ivy's hand playfully. Ivy held out her arms but Kyah signed "catch" and jumped back into the branches. Filhia, who had paid the most attention to Kyah's lessons, returned the sign with a giggle and obliged by chasing her upward.

"Where are we Leihna?" Ivy asked, touching the stone to Leighnas hand. She stepped over the buttressed feet of a tualang, stripping a handful of red seeds from a vine. Each seed had a glossy black spot on one end. She rattled them together in her palm. *They'd make a nice necklace all strung together.* Ivy recognized the seed from her ill-fated expedition to the hot spring.

"This is the oleos grove," Leihna said. The thick patch of trees they had stopped within was umbrella'd beneath higher branches creating a second canopy. Mint green leaves grew out of watermelon-coloured buds en masse, with the tips of fully grown leaves boasting a pink crown.

Ivy ran her fingers along a fallen trunk. Insects had mottled the wood with a rusty coating of clay. Misty patches of grey silk hid tiny spider holes. *Of course. Oleos.* The tree had made it onto her phytolith reference chart.

"You use the Oleos fruit for washing?" Ivy asked. "The pulp makes a good soap." Leihna looked surprised.

"That's right," the girl said. "Also torches. We crush the nuts for oil and soak kapok fibres in it to wrap around a palm frond. They burn well."

"Is that what we're here collecting for?" Ivy said.

Leihna grinned. "Not today. We have a surprise for you. You're coming with us to the trade offering. But Phren wants us to gather oleos and durian first."

"A trade offering? You trade with other tribes?" Ivy's smile was huge. The prospect of meeting more *Homo floresiensis* tribes was thrilling, not least because it could resolve some of her unanswered questions.

"We trade every half moon," Leihna explained. "There!" She said pointing above her, "That's the best spot to pick from."

Ivy looked up. The base of each trunk was surrounded by a thorny tangle of vines, feet deep. There seemed no way to reach the clusters of pale green nuts hanging above. Beside her, Rinap stood with her head back surveying the heights. She suddenly seemed absurdly small.

"I'll go," the girl announced casually. Rinap gripped her toes and fingers tightly on the rough bark of an adjacent dalunut palm and shimmied up. With a leap she landed safely on the branch of the oleos tree, pulling sprays of berry nuts off the branches and dropping them down onto Leihna's head with a wicked laugh. Kyah and Filhia clambered across to join her, bombarding Ivy with handfuls of nuts as well.

Hit! Rain! Kyah signed as she screeched, bouncing on the branch above Ivy. Ivy laughed and tossed a handful of them back up, hitting herself again in the face as gravity returned them. Kyah hooted and instigated a cascade of ripped leaves in retaliation.

With a shout, Leihna tossed a raffia bag up to Rinap and Filhia and before long; it was full, then another and then a third.

"We should take some dalunuts too, so Phren can make more tuak," Rinap called down. Leihna agreed and left Ivy's side to scoot up a palm, knocking the hard green cases down with sharp blows from her blade.

"What's tuak?" Ivy asked, after Leihna had returned.

"Drink," Rinap cut in, landing beside them with a bag of oleos nuts. "The elders like it, especially Krue. The last time he drank so much he climbed a tree and fell asleep up there. Xiou had to pull him down."

"He had a sore head too," added Filhia, rolling her eyes as she dropped down beside Ivy.

"He deserved it," Rinap muttered, ignoring a shove from her younger sister.

A prehistoric hangover. Ivy chuckled ruefully, trying to imagine the ill-tempered old man drunk up a tree. *I guess that's another shared trait for humanity.*

"Let's go," Rinap said. "We still need to pick durian before the trade and I want to be home before sunset."

"You just want to see Kari before sleeping!" Filhia teased.

The older girls burst into a fit of giggles.

"Maybe I do," said Rinap, sparkling with mischief. "If he wants to be my mate, shouldn't I make sure he's up to the job?"

"You tease him too much." Filhia frowned. "He'll get trampled by a probech trying to impress you!"

"I don't tease him," Rinap's wide eyes feigned innocence, "I just test him a bit, that's all. Anyway, Kari *should* try to impress me. You just wish *you* had someone to visit before sleeping!"

The youngest girl scowled indignantly. "Perhaps I will soon, you don't know who I'm watching." Rinap and Leihna looked at each other, surprised, then doubled over in laughter.

"Well, now we'll both watch you to find out!" Rinap snorted.

A cloud of self-consciousness darkened little Filhia's face. She took Ivy's hand and tried to pull her along, rolling her eyes.

"Come Hiranah, these two are stupid," Filhia said. "We should leave them behind." Ivy bit back a laugh and nodded gravely to the youngest girl, letting her lead the way.

Rinap was a little firecracker and reminded Ivy in many ways of Jayne. The women of the cave were well aware of Kari's infatuation. When the boy wasn't strutting about hoping to catch Rinap's attention, he was staring moon-eyed from his hearth. He was certainly no match for Rinap's wiles. *Poor boy*, Ivy thought. *I hope he has his wits about him.*

The wretched smell of the spiky green durian fruit was now all too familiar. They collected a half dozen of the larger ones, each over a foot long, while Kyah stuffed her mouth. Leihna showed Ivy how to grate the barbed points on a rock, making them easier to carry.

"I still hate them," Ivy muttered. She breathed through her mouth for as long as she could to escape the stink.

The girls were met halfway by Phren who had come as escort to the trade bearing more gifts. They each carried two woven palm baskets, now heavy with durian and oleos nuts, dalunut, volcanic glass cores and bladders of fermented tuak. Not long after Phren arrived, the girls spotted a beehive. At Rinap's suggestion, they each threw a spear into a knotted tree to determine the loser. With the poorest aim, Ivy had drawn the proverbial short straw.

"Just do it, Hiranah! You're so big that you don't even need to stretch!" Filhia encouraged.

Ivy crouched precariously on a high branch with Rinap on a branch above her so that their faces were at the same height. Ivy held a shell bowl in one hand filled with dung and a flaming torch in the other. Rinap held her hand against The amulet on Ivy's wrist, so she could give instructions.

"We have more than enough to trade already," countered Phren from far below. The old woman shot a warning look up at Rinap. "You girls will carry her home if she falls."

Leihna failed to hide her amusement behind her hands. Rinap was outright laughing.

"Just keep staring at them Hiranah, eventually your face might scare the bees away," Rinap chortled.

Ivy gave her a solid nudge with her elbow. Rinap's endless taunts about Ivy's appearance were a running joke between them. The girl surveyed the cone-shaped beehive dangling above Ivy's head and took a dramatic breath for her audience below.

"Even a baby like Turi could do this. But I suppose if you're scared…"

Ivy shot Rinap a glare.

"Never!"

A swarm of guard bees buzzed around the entrance to the hive, colourful and alert. Inside, the older bees worked, unaware of the threat, but more venomous by far. Below, Leihna and Filhia cheered Ivy on while Phren frowned.

"Be brave, Hiranah!" Filhia called. The littlest girl's positivity at the outcome far surpassed Ivy's own. Rinap leant in close, one hand still stabilizing Ivy's wrist and the other curled around the branch beside her. Her features and voice softened uncharacteristically.

"I won't let you fall," Rinap said, squeezing Ivy's wrist gently.

Ivy smirked. "You'd better not. If you do, I'll tell Kari I heard you singing about him again."

"You would not!" Rinap exclaimed. Ivy winked at her, leaving Rinap frowning in confusion.

"Hurry up!" yelled Leihna from below.

"Alright. Ready. Now!" Ivy lit the bowl of dung into flames then dropped the burning torch down through the branches into Leihna's waiting hands. She sprang up, balancing on her toes. Ivy blew the heavily smoking dung as forcefully as she could into the hive. The guard bees were hoodwinked. The smoke dulled their senses, circumventing the release of pheromone alarm odours to alert their venomous brothers to sting. Instead, the older bees instinctively gorged into the honey, pacified with the sudden urge to fill their stomachs in case a fire ruined their hive and forced them to build another. Squinting through the smoke, Ivy fingered the sticky mass inside. With a grimace she pulled out large combs of dripping honey and dropped them into Rinap's bowl. The stunned bees were brushed off and returned to their hive.

"Ha!" Ivy descended victorious, sticky and smelling thoroughly like dung. She winked again at Rinap and tapped her gently on the nose before touching the amulet to her hand. "And who doubted me then?"

Rinap grinned and pulled Ivy's face down to rub against her own forehead affectionately. "I knew you could do it." She raised her voice, "You're still big and ugly though!" She ducked Ivy's hand and ran ahead, cackling.

The walk was long but passed quickly as the girls chatted. They headed steadily north-east. Ivy glanced at Filhia, who showed no sign that her heavy baskets were a burden. Ivy shifted her own uncomfortably. Rinap caught Ivy's eye with a reassuring smile and disappeared in a protective sweep of the surrounds. If there was an ambush by the karathah, they would be forewarned.

When they arrived at the fringe of a small clearing, Ivy quickly retreated, scanning the hazy undergrowth ahead. The prospect of coming face to face with more hobbits was exciting, but she knew how intimidating her appearance was to them. She'd wait for Phren to make introductions first.

"Where are they?" Ivy asked.

"Gone. They will return at the mid morning sun," Rinap said.

In the centre of the clearing, a wide, flat stone was already piled with woven bags and gourds. The girls milled around the stone while Phren inspected it. *Salt. Shellfish. Fruit. Fish. Bone plates with ornamental grooves.* Ivy had noted that, with the exception of Phren, none of the hobbits wore ornamental jewellery. Comparing the marking on the plate, to those on the beads around Phren's neck, she realised that the jewellery was a gift from the other tribe.

"It is an acceptable trade" Phren announced finally. "Let us see if the others agree." She gestured for Ivy to come forward.

Ivy unloaded her bags onto the stone. The women all retreated to the cover of the forest to wait.

"Why are we hiding?" Ivy asked.

"It's a silent trade," Leihna explained. "We take our goods to the offering stone and leave it for them. If the other tribe have already left theirs and it's fair, then we take it and it's done. But if we think our trade is worth more than theirs, then we leave the stone untouched and they will add a new offering. If they want more from us, we add to ours. And so it goes on until both tribes feel we have equal value. When we are happy with it, we take their offering home, or they take ours."

"So you never see them at all?"

"Well…" Leihna twisted her long toes into the grass. "We don't always leave straight away. Sometimes we stay to watch." Rinap and Filhia listened to the exchange restlessly.

"I don't understand why you don't speak to them. They could help you -" Ivy started. Rinap choked on a scoffing laugh.

"You'll see why, Hiranah. Just wait," she said.

To pass the time, Kyah drew lexigrams in the dirt. The girls copied her. They already recognized at least fifty of the signs Kyah used to communicate. Ivy rearranged her long legs as they began to numb. Ants bit at their toes in the mulch, their food trail disturbed. Minutes passed and the insects eventually dispersed, punctuated and harassed by Kyah's prodding finger.

"They're coming."

Ivy looked up, through the veil of forest in front of her into the clearing.

Homo sapiens. Two young women stepped from the northern tree line. Ivy sucked in a breath and tried to scramble for her spear.

"Karathah!" Ivy hissed. The girls pulled her back to the ground.

"It's alright, Hiranah," Phren hushed. "We're safe. This is women's business; it always has been."

"What?!" *How could such a contradiction exist?* Ivy thought, astonished. *Why trade with the Homo sapiens that multiplied so prolifically, stealing their forest and food? Not only that, but why risk another brush with the violence that had marred their recent history?* "But they're dangerous," Ivy hissed, "and Krue *hates* the karathah!"

"Krue isn't allowed here, he is a man," Rinap said. "Besides, the karathah girls never even see us. It's a *silent* trade." She shook her head, as if stating the obvious. If Rinap shared any of Ivy's concern, she didn't show it.

Ivy was astounded. She looked at the karathah girls again. I haven't seen another human for three weeks. At least, one that reaches past my waist...

Clothes. Although Ivy shouldn't have been surprised, she had grown so accustomed to the near-nakedness of the hobbits, clothes suddenly seemed a novelty. The karathah women's hide wraps were longer than the hobbit girls' and better crafted. Ivy guessed Shahn had used them for inspiration in making Ivy's more modest version of her own utilitarian one. The women themselves were tall and lithe. Their dark brows were painted red and shells tinkled as they moved. *Decoration. Symbolism. The beginnings of art unfurling across the globe.* Ivy fought back the urge to approach them. *Humans.* No, there were other humans here too. But these were *Homo sapiens.* Although these women felt so fundamentally familiar to Ivy, it was actually their kinship to her that was their biggest threat.

"I just don't understand," Ivy whispered. "Is it really necessary to put yourself at risk like this?"

Phren's fingers found the string of beads hanging from her neck and rolled them gently between her fingers. "We women have traded with the karathah women for a very long time. It is only the last few seasons that their hunters are coming into our territory and becoming violent. Something's changed." Phren closed her fist tight around her necklace and looked at Ivy, resolute. "This is a risk, but a necessary one, Hiranah. It's better for us to bring them what they need, than to give them a reason to come looking for it. This way, we keep them away from the oleos grove and Home River. Besides," Phren said, trying to pull her arthritic back straighter and lifting her jaw, "We can't hide from them forever. If we have any hope of survival, the karathah must see us as equals. At least when we trade, we have that."

Ivy frowned and shifted her arm, surreptitiously breaking their thought connection. *Homo sapiens have no equals.*

The karathah women moved confidently around the stone. Neither could be more than eighteen years old. The taller girl with long black hair ornamented by strings of turquoise feathers began gathering the bags, apparently deeming the trade acceptable. Once done, they disappeared back into the trees.

"Let's leave," Phren said. Rinap, Filhia and Leihna skipped to the stone and began to fill bags.

Ivy followed the girls into the open glade, carrying Kyah on her hip with her spear in her free hand. Kyah's long arms twisted affectionately around Ivy's neck.

A terrified scream shattered the forest. Then a second wail that continued over the first, sending birds screeching in fright.

Ivy spun around, her heart racing as she sought the danger. She hugged Kyah close to her body as Rinap appeared beside her with a spear held high. She pointed.

The two karathah women were crouched, frozen, in the shadows. Their mouths gaped in horror. It broke Ivy's heart when she realised they were staring directly at *her*. The screams began anew. Ivy stumbled back in shock. *They're terrified of me. What have I done?*

The youngest karathah woman scrambled to her feet and tore

away into the tree cover, leaving the other to fend for herself. For the briefest moment, the taller girl hesitated. She was alone. The azure feathers in her hair floated against her lips as she stared from Ivy across to Filhia. Even across the distance between them, Ivy saw concern and fear for the littlest hobbit girl in her eyes. But when she turned back to Ivy, the woman's face blanched. She took in the bonobo's body connected to Ivy's hip then wailed a string of babbled words and began scrambling backwards through the ferns.

"No! Please!" Ivy cried, running toward her. But the hand Ivy raised still held her spear and the woman with blue feathers shuddered even more violently at the sight of her. She screeched again, struggling for her footing as Ivy tossed her own spear to the ground, still running.

Petrified at the sudden turn of events, Kyah exposed her teeth in a grimace of fear and arced violently backward in Ivy's arms trying to escape. They arched together, imbalanced, as Ivy tried to support her weight, like a twisted, two-headed beast.

The sight was too much. The karathah woman launched up from the ground with heaving breaths, tripping and flailing in her desperation to escape. There was a wisp of blue feathers. The girl was gone.

CHAPTER 36

ORRIN

*O*rrin pushed through the glass doors of the Social Sciences building. The memory of Ivy's amulet, dirty and cast aside in a specimen bag, brought a feeling of lead to his stomach. But he was sure it was hers. So if *it* existed, so did she. And he had a plan.

He rounded the corner past the small university museum, sidestepping a display stand of tribal masks. He was hammering on the door of the Archaeology Residue Laboratory within a minute. Orrin paused and took a deep breath, remembering his last confrontation with Jayne. *Pull yourself together. You need that amulet.* The security keypad on the door ensured he would never get it without her help.

"Hang on," a voice called. A stool scraped across the linoleum. The door opened revealing Jayne's sunny face. When she saw Orrin, her smile dropped instantly.

"I don't have time for you," Jayne said, pushing the door closed again. Orrin shoved his foot in the crack, jarring it open. She looked at him angrily.

"Please Jayne, wait -" Orrin pleaded, "I'm really sorry about the other day. It wasn't like me at all - I swear I'm actually a socially acceptable person. Or at least I used to be." He smiled as sincerely as he could. "I just want to talk for a minute. I need your help... your professional *opinion* actually. You can leave the door open - and I'll go as soon as you ask me to, I swear. Please?"

Jayne looked at Orrin doubtfully, eyeing the busy corridor. She sighed.

"Okay, I suppose if there are witnesses to your insanity this time," she said. "Although I've already told you I don't know Ivy or any chimp, so I don't know what help I can give you." She retreated to her bench and sat down. Leaving the lab door wide open, Orrin dragged a chair opposite her and took a deep breath.

"Right. Here's the thing. What I'm going to tell you will sound nuts."

"You don't say."

"No, I mean, I honestly thought I *was* a header until last night. But you can prove me sane."

Jayne raised an eyebrow. "Unlikely. But go on," she said.

"Okay, it's like this," Orrin said. "The woman I'm looking for, Ivy Carter, she used to work in this lab. Up until last week, I swear she used to work right here, on these stone tools from Flores, with you." He noted Jayne's pursed lips and tight eyes. "I know, I know, you're the only one working on these tools – please just hear me out." He took a deep breath. "I don't know what went wrong, but she's gone now. It's like she never existed. She worked here for eight years and there's no sign of her anywhere. I've been through every journal article, every dissertation, every reference to work she mentioned. She even told me about you Jayne, she told me about your supervisor, Professor Ellermy."

"Ellery," Jayne corrected, looking impatient.

"Sure, Ellery, sorry." Orrin rubbed his eyes under the black framed glasses, not sure this was going as well as he'd hoped. His bruised nose ached and he knew he looked a mess. "Just hear me out, there's more. Ivy was an animal rights activist. There was a chimp, no; I mean a *bonobo*, which she sort-of looked after from the behavioural sciences lab. Anyway I went there, hoping I might find her and the bonobo was gone too. They're both gone." An edge of pity entered Jayne's eyes. *Shite.*

Orrin braced himself to divulge the final thing he felt sure would snap her remaining shred of respect for him.

"The thing is, the bonobos weren't just gone. They were *replaced.* There was this hobbit creature there, a tiny wee animal, like people, only with a round face and long arms…"

To his surprise, Jayne cut him off. "*Homo floresiensis.* I've seen them. I don't know about any bonobos, but the hobbits were brought in a year ago for behavioural research. Liam told me they were here, he knew my research would involve analysing their subsistence patterns and thought I might be interested in seeing them."

Orrin's relief was palpable. "Jaysus! You saw them? You know they're here?"

"How could I not know they're here?" Jayne said. "They're a little hard to miss. Liam's been using them as a platform for his animal rights campaigning. He thinks they should be allowed basic human rights - that they should be exempt from experimentation and exploitation. There are a lot of environmentalists pushing for preservation of their natural habitat too, although it's well and truly too little, too late for that."

"But – how do you know Liam?" Orrin asked. "I assumed Ivy introduced the two of you."

"I know a lot of people," she said, bristling. "As it happens we met at a faculty event. For a while we - hang on, how is this even relevant?"

"I guess it's not," sighed Orrin. "Just a coincidence. Ivy introduced me to Liam. I really don't know him, but I think I should tell you – I saw him yesterday at a rally in the city, and he looked ill set." Orrin hesitated, not sure whether to continue.

"Yeah, so?"

"I left him at it; but the whole scene was diabolical. Liam got totally out of hand. I think… actually I'm pretty sure he got arrested. He set the place on fire and got violent with the guards. Then the bastard nearly broke my nose." Orrin gingerly pushed the bridge of his nose. It was still swollen.

Jayne eyed Orrin's nose critically. "Maybe you deserved it."

"Fair play, though I don't think so."

Jayne's indifference abruptly dropped. "Wait – he got arrested?" Lines of worry pinched her forehead. "That's not good. Actually, that's *really* bad. Not for Liam, he can handle himself okay. But for those hobbits in the lab…" For a long pause she considered, seeming to forget Orrin was there. Finally, she looked up. "Not your problem anyway, I'll deal with it myself." Impatience crept back in. "What is it I'm meant to be helping you with?"

"The hobbits actually, the ones in the lab," he said. "Where did they come from?"

"Transferred from a breeding facility I'd say," said Jayne. "Before that, maybe the black market. Young females are usually in high demand."

"No - no I don't mean those ones specifically." Orrin could see he had no choice but to reveal his apparent insanity again. "I mean, where did they come from *at all*? This species didn't exist a week ago Jayne. Except as fossils."

"Of course they existed. You're a pretty lame scientist if you haven't heard of our closest evolutionary relative."

"Apparently so. What can you tell me about them?"

Jayne rolled her eyes. "Seriously?"

At Orrin's nod, she leant back in her chair, arms crossed. "Okay, well, they evolved in Flores, obviously. Then spread to the rest of the archipelago. They were discovered by Portuguese explorers. Their prehistory is fairly intertwined with ours in South East Asia. It's complicated. Needless to say, in the last few hundred years they've become as exploited as every other 'natural resource' on the planet."

"You mean the pharmaceutical research that Liam's fighting?"

"That's part of it," Jayne said, relaxing a bit. "They're perfect test dummies for human research. NASA even sent them to space in the first test launches in the early 1950's. The most desperate issue is habitat though; hobbits are uniquely adapted to Indonesia but their forests are all but destroyed now. The concentration of rare earth metals in that area is unprecedented. It's been strip-mined for the last fifty years. The industry is booming. Once the metal is stripped, the Palm Oil plantations go up in their place. It's double consumerism. Even if the captive hobbits were to be rehabilitated and protected, there's nowhere left for them to go. They'll be extinct in the wild within a few years."

"Jaysus," Orrin muttered. "So, why do you bother studying them at all?"

"The same reason we study past civilizations of our own species of course. And why we study indigenous populations, colonial settlements and other primates we're genetically close to," Jayne said. "We learn more about ourselves in the process; what makes us human, what defines our humanity. We study the past to shed light on our future."

"It doesn't sound like there *is* much of a future for these hobbits," Orrin countered.

"Well there should be," Jayne said. "They're an amazing species. People don't realize how close to human they really are. Not just their DNA I mean, but their way of life."

"But they look so primitive and well, *manky*," said Orrin. "I think the one in the biology lab would have belted me given half the chance. She has an eye like a stinkin' eel."

"What the hell does that mean?"

"I mean she was watching me all the time," Orrin said. "And

whispering, really nasty. I've no idea what she was saying but if looks could kill, I'd be six feet under."

Jayne rolled her eyes. "They have their own language, but it's almost impossible to interpret because they're so guarded with their communication. They don't trust us, with good reason. We kill them." Jayne looked thoughtful for a moment, and then continued with surprising reverence. "The thing is, *Homo floresiensis* are still very much a mystery. It fascinates me."

"How so?" Orrin asked.

"Well, up until about fifty thousand years ago, hobbits had stone tools and subsistence patterns analogous to early human hunter-gatherers," Jayne said. "They probably had family groups and care systems to match, of course, but archeologically speaking, it's all quite primitive. Then suddenly, *bam!* Out of nowhere, they developed culture, art and symbolism. Maybe it was already there but they hadn't found a way to express it. But I think something happened at the time, to trigger a transformative change in their culture."

"What might have happened?" Orrin leant forward, intrigued.

"No idea," Jayne said. But something. No one knows why their culture evolved so suddenly. But it did. That's the mystery, I suppose."

"How can you tell something changed?"

"Art." Jayne leant forward conspiratorially. "Prehistoric cave art is my real passion. Trust me, these hobbits had no art, absolutely nothing and then *wham!* There it was, fifty thousand years ago, complete with beautiful expression and form. With modern humans, you see a progression of change over time, you know? Art develops in it's complexity. But with hobbits, there's nothing, then suddenly everything. That's one of the reasons I think they need to be saved. To figure out why."

"And these stone tools you're working on, they're part of this research?" Orrin asked, skilfully re-directing the conversation.

"Sure, that's what I do."

Orrin studied Jayne's face. She seemed less hostile. He took a deep breath.

"Well, this woman I know – *knew* – she wore an amulet around her neck on a silver chain," he begun. "It was a black stone shaped like a large teardrop. It was… unusual. I'd never seen anything like it. It wasn't fancy, but it just sort of, held your eye somehow. It had her initials engraved on the front 'I.C.' and on the back it had weird puncture marks, just five random dots."

"Okay. I don't see what this has to do with me though. I told you I've never seen her or the stone."

"I think you have, Jayne."

"Are you serious? *This again?*" Jayne's patience slipped quickly back to irritation. "You think I'm lying?"

"I don't think you're lying, just that perhaps you didn't recognize it at the time. There's no reason why you should." Orrin's heart hammered as he hedged around the reason for his visit. *If she refuses...* "Jayne, could I see those tools you're working on? The ones you had on the bench when I came in the other day?"

His request seemed to take her by surprise.

"I guess." Jayne hesitated before pulling a labelled box from the cupboard under her bench. "But only because I'm morbidly curious." She spread the specimen bags on the bench between them. Quickly Orrin sifted through them, his heart pounding. His fingers fumbled over the stone shapes. *What if he'd been wrong?* He gently turned the last stone tool over in his fingers and exhaled.

"This is it," he said.

"This is what?"

"This is Ivy's amulet."

Jayne scoffed. "No it's not - that's a stone tool from the Liang Bua excavation site in Flores. I've done DNA testing and radiocarbon dating on it. It's fifty thousand years old."

"It can't be."

"Well, it is. Hey, don't do that! *Stop!* You don't even have gloves on!" Jayne launched off her bench stool but it was too late. Orrin twisted away, slipping the stone from its plastic cover. Its surface was dull and layered with dust, with the exception of a small spot on one end where Jayne had taken her sample for testing. With feverish intensity, he ignored Jayne's loud protests and rubbed his thumb against its smooth black surfaces wiping it clean.

"My God! You stupid, bloody idiot! You've just contaminated a fifty-thousand-year old artefact!" Jayne's eyes flashed ferociously. "Get the hell out of my lab! I'm calling security!"

Orrin held the stone up to her. "Look, Jayne! Just look at it! It's Ivy's amulet – look at the markings, the initials, they're all there!" He held the black stone in front of her face. Sure enough, cursive lines swept the dark surface. *I.C.* He spun it around. "Five random dots puncturing the black surface. The initials I.C. on the front" He poked the hard dirt through the top hole. "A hole, Jayne – for a chain. A silver chain." He pulled the broken chain from his pocket with his spare hand and held it up. "This is Ivy's; I know it is. I've seen her wearing this amulet, so she must exist!" *Brilliant!* The week of insanity Orrin had endured dissolved around him. He was right. *Ivy was real. She* had *existed.* The satisfaction Orrin had sought so desperately finally blanketed him, warm and forgiving.

But his internal revelry was short lived.

Jayne's expression passed from anger to confusion and back again. She grabbed the stone from his fingers and retreated behind her bench.

"I don't know why these markings are here," Jayne growled. "I haven't even had a chance to do any microscopy on it and now you've totally screwed my chances. What I do know, is that this stone tool was dated at fifty thousand years old. It was found in the same stratigraphic layer as all of these others. So it's not your friend's damn amulet." Despite the conviction in her words, Jayne's voice tremored.

"But the markings!" Orrin argued. "They can't be fifty thousand years old – they're in English! And engraved! No stone tool could be that precise with calligraphy. There's no *way* this is a real artefact."

She hesitated, scowling. "Well, I obviously can't explain it. *Yet.* But I do know that you've totally stuffed my chances of doing any further testing on it, you damn idiot. It's time for you to leave, Orrin. *Now.*"

"Testing," Orrin exclaimed. "Yes! What about the DNA testing you already did? Ivy wore this so her DNA should still be on it - skin cells or something?"

"I don't have the results yet," Jayne fumed. "But regardless, there would be very slim chance of getting a positive cell extraction with that much dirt covering it. If it was blood it might be different… *what am I saying? Get out!*" With the amulet scrunched in her fist, she backed Orrin towards the door. Her face was blotchy and red.

"But what if it *is* hers, Jayne?" Orrin said. "What if she's over there now, at the excavation site and she dropped it?"

"A site contaminant?" Jayne froze in place, clearly frustrated with the possibility. "I guess it could be, but the dates were very clear. This wasn't found on the surface Orrin; it was dug from a pit over a meter underground, photographed, mapped and labelled. Archaeologists don't just accidentally drop artefacts into pits and contaminate their sites - they're not as inconsiderate or stupid as you are. Now you said you'd leave when I asked you to, so I'm asking you now. *Leave.*"

"Fair play, I did say that." Orrin held up his hands in surrender. "I'm sorry I ruined your work, but I had to know for sure. That thing *is* Ivy's. I don't know how, but I swear to Jaysus, Mary, Joseph and all the Holy Martyrs that I'll figure it out!"

Jayne's face showed no sign of sympathy as she backed him into the corridor.

"Goodbye Orrin. Feel free *not* to visit again."

"Sure, sure. I'm dead sorry for disturbing you, really I am."

Orrin placed one hand back on the door. "Jayne? Just one last thing - seeing as you can't use it anyway now, could I borrow that stone? I could run my own tests…"

The door slammed in his face.

Orrin pulled into the busy car park. Above him, the golden wings of the mythical Garuda spread wide across the flag in the midday sun, its chest adorned with the shield of the Pancasila. The red and white checkerboard shield glinted proudly in the sunlight, boasting the five principles of Indonesia's national philosophy. *One and only one God, just and civilized humanity, unity, democracy and social justice.* Gripped in its talons, a large scroll underscored its holistic message 'Bhinneka Tunggal Ika'. *Unity in Diversity.* The motto had become an essential doctrine in the spirit of religious tolerance that had been passed through the ages by the 14th century poet sage of the Javanese Majapahit Empire, Empu Tantulat. Nowadays, the many islands and faiths of the Indonesian Archipelago flourished under its wings.

The Melbourne-based consulate looked out of place on the hectic motorway, as if it had been placed there long ago and then forgotten. Surrounded by sparkling corporate offices, the consulate was a whitewashed heritage, its small rendered face peering from behind thick bushes. Beyond the busy motorway, a channelled river glittered towards the city suburbs. Strangely, at least two dozen people were gathered on the lawn in front of the building.

With a deep breath, Orrin crossed the grass of the Consulate General for the Republic of Indonesia. He stopped halfway, slowed by a throng of reporters and camera equipment. He gaped.

In the centre of the lawn, two Indonesian men were chained

to a palm tree with their heads bowed in what Orrin could only imagine was exhaustion. A dozen sympathizers and medics stood by watching but making no move to unchain them. Cameramen scuffled for the best view as their reporters spoke gravely down the lens. Orrin pushed his way closer to the spectacle, intent on hearing what one woman was saying.

"...marks the fourth day of the hunger strike by radical activists Budi Natalegawa and Darma Kusumaatmadja. In an effort to bring international attention to the environmental devastation faced by Indonesia and Malaysia as a result of strip mining and mass palm oil plantations, these two men have chained themselves outside the Indonesian Consulate." The reporter thrust her microphone toward the closest protestor. "Mr Natalegawa, what message do you want the government to take from this action?"

The man looked up at her, with dark circles under his eyes. He sat next to the second protestor with his back to the palm and multiple chains linking their waists to the tree. He replied slowly, but with grim determination.

"Seventy-three villagers were killed last week in the forest fires that are sweeping across Indonesia and Malaysia. Thousands more are endangered every day." He lifted his chin defiantly. "I am lucky, I was safe here, but my brother and his family - they had no choice." Tears shone in the man's eyes. "The government blames the weather, says it is 'unseasonably hot' from the problem with the sky, but that's not true. The heat only makes existing fires worse. The fires spark from the burn cycles of the plantations." He pointed a shaking finger at the camera lens as an older woman placed a cup of water on the grass next to him. "The companies know it and the government knows it and none of them will do a single thing about it!"

The second activist put a hand on his comrades' shoulder. He gestured for the microphone. "Our countries supply ninety percent of global palm oil. A decade ago, the government thought it was an opportunity for local economies who were desperate to exchange land for money, but it's a *curse!* We have droughts because our old-growth forest is no longer there to bring rain. We are left with nothing but blood money and tears."

The camera shifted back to the reporter. "This comes at a time when environmental concerns plague our leaders and magnetospheric decay hits an all time high. Another unsuccessful research probe has marred NASA's latest attempt to identify the cause of our rapidly declining magnetosphere," the reporter said gravely into her microphone. "Billions of international research dollars have intensified the program in recent years. However, the destructive radiation itself has proven to be paradoxical for the satellite-derived data required for research."

The reporter shifted slightly to ensure the men behind her could be seen. "The exponential decay we've experienced over the last one hundred years continues to point to a human origin, however no direct cause has been found. Sea levels continue to rise with polar caps melting up to 20% per year as they suffer the worst of the sun's increased radiation. Areas of highest altitude across the mountainous Asian belt have already experienced carcinogenic levels of exposure. International aid agencies are flocking to remote communities in the Himalaya and Karaoram ranges, to assist with solar education and relocation support." She turned to look dramatically at the men chained behind her. "It seems however, that there may not be enough humanitarian aid to cover the costs."

Orrin felt nauseous. He turned slowly and pushed away from the crowd.

It has to be a mistake. But he knew it wasn't. His own data confirmed the devastating decay of the magnetosphere. Radiation and melting ice caps were inevitable. Droughts and fires as well. *But why now, when it wasn't before?* Human origin, she'd said. *But what did we do?*

The red and white flag fluttered above him at the entrance.

Two armed guards checked him by the door. The idea that Ivy might be working independently on the archaeological site in Flores was really pushing it. Still, he had to hope, even if it was faintest of glimmers.

The softly spoken woman at the desk listened patiently to his plea. *My friend is missing. I'm sure she was in Indonesia recently; if I could just confirm her VISA application is on file... to be sure I'm looking for her in the right place...*

"Are you the next of kin?"

"No - sort of. Yes– yes, I am. I'm the only one who seems to care, if that counts. I'm not sure about her immediate family, or where her parents even are." As the questions came, Orrin realized how little he really knew of Ivy's life.

"The Australian police handle these matters, sir; if your friend is missing you should file a report with them," the woman said.

Please.

Despite the spectacle outside, the office was near empty and the administration clerk finally gave in.

"Ivy Carter? I see no tourist visa on record for anyone with that name. If your friend travelled through an international airport, she would have arrived at Soekarno Hatta airport in Jakarta, or alternatively at Ngurah Rai airport in Bali. I see nothing here suggesting a person by her name was travelling to either." She studied her database. "No tourist card, no visa or passport checks."

"She was studying," Orrin offered, "on an archaeological dig."

"A research student? Well, there's a separate process for work and research travel. Your friend would have submitted a formal letter and quite a comprehensive research proposal to obtain access on a limited stay visa. One moment please, sir." The keyboard clicked like a metronome. "I'm sorry, nothing again." Her dark eyes showed genuine concern. "Perhaps your friend did not reach Indonesia at all? You really should file a police report. They can perform a more thorough search."

Orrin rubbed his fingertips under his glasses. *Another wall.*

"The thing is ma'am, I *know* Ivy was there," Orrin pleaded. "She must have been. She was working on the island of Flores, in a cave. Liang Bua cave."

"Flores?" she said, frowning. "Well, that complicates things a little. Flores has heavy mining infrastructure, so most visitors arrive via sea." Her words softened as she took in Orrin's crumbling composure. "Hypothetically though, assuming your friend *did* have a visa…" she stressed her words to make it clear she was overstepping her role. "There are only two airstrips and two seaports she could have arrived at providing visa facilities, one on each end of the island, East Nusa Tengarra and West Nusa Tengarra."

"How would I know if she arrived?"

The woman's eyes were thoughtful as she ran her fingertips across the coral coloured scarf that kept her hair and neck hidden from view. She lowered her voice to barely above a whisper. "Well, I suppose I could make some calls. Strictly off the record, of course."

One by one, she rang the air strips and ports of Maumere and Labuan Bajo, and after a brief pause searching through records, each returned the same response. *There is no visitor in Flores by that name.*

Softly hanging up the phone, she offered Orrin a sympathetic smile. "I am very sorry sir; I can't help you anymore. If you put in an official report, they may be able to request a search of the island." She hesitated, clearly uncomfortable. "But – well, I do feel obligated to tell you sir, Flores is one of the most remote and uninhabitable areas of the archipelago. Past mining has been extensive and its volcanic activity has been… severe. The island is considered very dangerous, especially to a person unequipped for such a place. If your friend really has gone missing there… if she is *lost…*"

Please, God, don't say it. "I understand. Thank you, you've been

– very helpful. I appreciate your time." With a sinking heart Orrin turned to leave. *Defeat tugged at his heart. Ivy never went to Flores. So how did the amulet get there?*

The guards closed the door behind him. Orrin skirted the edge of the lawn with his eyes to the ground, unable to shoulder the burden of grief in the chained men's eyes again.

As he sank into his car seat, his mobile rang.

"Dale?"

"Yeah, it's me," came the reply.

"Any use?" Orrin asked, hopefully.

"Sorry man, they've never heard of her either."

"Right."

There was an awkward silence. "Um, Orrin…?"

"Yeah?"

"It's just – I'm worried about you."

Orrin gritted his jaw. *Then believe me.* While Dale shot sideways glances at him all day in the lab, Phil was being downright condescending.

"Well don't, I'm just *grand*," Orrin snapped. "Or at least, I'm about to be." The amulet was a clue. It was proof that Ivy had existed. Orrin knew he was sane after all. Frustrated, angry, obsessed perhaps – but still sane. "I saw Ivy's lab partner this morning, the one I told you about."

"She remembers Ivy now?" Dale sounded relieved.

"Not quite." *Silence.* "But she has Ivy's amulet," Orrin added. "The one she wore on the silver chain I found in the lab. It's hers, unequivocally. It has the same engravings, her initials, everything."

"So why does she have-" Dale began.

"That's the part I'm trying to figure out. Jayne got it from the dig site in Flores. That's why I needed you to check it out, just in case she was over there now. I thought maybe, if she was working on site and she dropped it…" His voice trailed off.

"I gave the excavation team her name, just like you asked,

Orrin. They've never heard of her before, the dig supervisor said she wasn't working with them, never has." Dale sounded reluctant to continue.

"Right." *Right.* Orrin pushed away the defeat.

"Did you try the consulate?" asked Dale.

"Yeah."

"And?"

Orrin dropped his head, pushing the heel of his hand into his forehead. "There are other ways to get into Flores. Maybe she was working independently."

"But she'd need - "

"She was there!" Orrin said. *"In Flores, at Liang Bua cave. I'm sure of it!"*

Dale sighed. "Okay. Let me know if there is anything else I can do."

"I'll see you later," said Orrin. As an afterthought, he added, "Thanks Dale."

"Yeah."

CHAPTER 37

NEIL

Neil carefully triangulated river stones around the edge of the hole. He laid a thick piece of bark across the opening, resting on the stones. The windows underneath suggested there was just enough room for an unsuspecting creature searching for a place to hide. *A rat could be tasty.* The inside walls of the hole sloped backwards, preventing his prey from escape. Leaving the trap, he checked another he'd dug yesterday. It was filled with the cold sleeping body of a python. Neil cursed and left it. His gut churned in memory. *No more snakes.* The other two traps were still empty so he returned to his newest to wait.

As luck would have it, he didn't have to wait long. A hand-sized forest shrew with her caravan of young trailing mouth-to-tail scurried under the hollow. *Gotcha.* Neil lifted the bark ceiling, his sharpened stick poised. To his surprise, he was too late.

The mother shrew already lay immobilised and twitching. Neil snapped his hand away from the trap. Moving from victim to victim, a downy back spider caught each of her young in turn, filling them with venom. Before Neil could utter the expletive on his lips, they were all dead.

His stomach rumbled. Neil sat back on his haunches in the

dim light, considering. For once his thwarted meal did not upset him.

A non-descript spider lurking in the wet leaves; a natural neurotoxin... one spider bite is all it would take. I don't need her dead specifically, just incapacitated. Unconscious for long enough to grab that stone amulet and get away unseen...and unfollowed. It's not murder. It's not. For a long time, he sat, all thoughts of hunger forgotten. Neil spun his lighter slowly. If I don't do it, I'll die out here. Benjamin will die. The stone is wasted on her, instead of using it; she's sitting around drawing in the dirt. God, the things I could do with that stone. It's self-preservation, really. It's not murder. Besides, I won't be sticking around to watch. Maybe she'll survive. She's bigger than a shrew.

I really need that stone. Survival of the fittest.

Neil's plan formed meticulously, played out in his head like film noir. He couldn't approach the redhead directly; her personal guard of well-armed monkeys saw to that. Resentfully, he had accepted his limitations. *'He who knows when he can fight and when he cannot, will be victorious,'* Neil reminded himself. He was outnumbered one hundred to one, out weaponed by far - he wouldn't stand a chance. He needed to get her on her own. Get her while she was vulnerable, without the protection of those damned abominations that watched her every move. *Just one bite. That's all it'll take.*

He tasted the potentiality of his success. *I'll study the energy field, control it, and manipulate it. Create enough energy to feed an entire city. The future of industry at my feet. Unlimited resources. Politicians. Utilities. The energy crisis averted. Through me.*

His musing brought forth his son. For once, he didn't push the thought away. Benjamin was half there, weak, closer to death. Neil's resentment grew. *And time ... time itself in my hands. There's a bigger picture here. I can do it alone if I have to, I'll hide the amulet - they don't need to know how I'm controlling the energy fields. They'll thank me for saving the masses from their miserable plight. What greater reward is there, than the gratitude of an entire civilisation? A* hard smile crept slowly to Neil's lips. *Many rewards, no doubt. So I let one woman die, an accident really - this is a damned jungle after all. And what difference does one death make to a world of immeasurable benefits? Sacrifice one to save many. Sacrifice her to save myself...*

Long and hard he schemed, as the spider wove her coffins.

As the dawn sun broke the canopy, Neil was waiting. Not stretched in his usual discomfort in the spiky hollow, but hidden, with his back pressed to a tree on the far side of the river. *Their side.* Minutes felt like hours. *She was late.* He knew he didn't have much time. If the redhead took too long bathing they would come looking for her; the pregnant one, the old man or the scarred hunter. A biting chill quickened his senses and he wondered if he had chosen the one morning she was not going to show. *Rustle. Snap.* Neil quietly exhaled, releasing the tension from his lungs. *It's not murder.*

The redhead stepped out of the trees and crossed the narrow river bank. The rocky ledge she always swam from curved the river at its closest point to the trees, an advantage he planned to make good use of. Hidden only meters away, he watched her through foliage, cradling the hollowed dalunut shell in his hands. *It's self-preservation.*

The redhead dropped a handful of fruit onto the grass. She lay a soapy bone plate on the flattest rock and stretched her arms towards the sky, breathing deeply. Her body was pale and lithe and he realised he would actually miss watching her. *Pity it came to this.* Neil tried to calm the rush of adrenaline that gripped him as the woman shook her red hair out of a long plait and dropped her hide skirt and stained singlet onto the grass. She stepped into the water, shivering and sinking low. She pulled her underwear off and washed it, leaving it on the stone to dry, rubbing the remainder of the soapy pulp across her body and into her hair. *A bloody waste really.* Languidly, she pushed off from the bank, red ribbons of hair trailing on the water's surface.

Neil sprung to his feet. Making sure she was still swimming toward the opposite bank, he ducked the few paces left toward her clothes. *Immeasurable benefits,* he recited. *Sacrifice one to save many.* With steady hands Neil pulled a large wad of compacted grass from the opening of the Dalunut. He pulled the hide skirt towards him, tipping the imprisoned spider onto its folds. With quick fingers, he trapped it again under layers of fabric. Her fingers would find it first. He backed to the safety of shadows.

The minutes ticked by. Neil held his jaw in his hand, breathing deeply. A steely determination crept into his heart and radiated, outwards through his veins. It was almost *too* simple. Once he had the stone he could walk away, no one would follow; no one even knew he was there. He fingered the shape of the sharpened stone blade in his pocket. *Just in case it takes too long.*

Kill her to save myself... Neil almost relaxed now as she spun in the water, swimming back toward the bank. She pulled on her underwear, squeezing water from her now dark hair. Her face lit up as she stepped out of the water. Her porcelain skin was covered in goose-flesh and her eyes looked unnaturally green.

"Hello there," she said, taking a step toward her clothes. She crouched, reaching out her hand. "I was hoping you'd be here."

Neil's breath shuddered at the sound of her voice, so close and clear. He stiffened his neck against the rising urge to come forward. *I'm not a coward. It's her or me.* He sank into the shadow, resentful of the feeling. *No one has to know.*

Pick up the clothes. He willed for the end of it. The part where he could walk away and prove them wrong.

Instead she picked up a small round of fruit, rolling it across the grass. An oversized rat appeared from its hollow and darted across the grass to her. It took the fruit, nibbling. She rolled it another one, closer to her. Then another. *Pick up the god damned clothes.* Instead, again she offered more fruit, this time from her outstretched hand. The vermin crept forward inch by inch and devoured each morsel it was offered until there were none left. She petted its fur.

"Sorry little one, all gone," she said. "I'll bring more tomorrow."

No. You won't.

Still crouching on the grass, the redhead's fingertips sought her clothes. She pushed her hand under, scooping the fabric up to her chest, making to stand. Neil caught his breath as a black shadow passed beneath her fingers. Like lightning the rat pounced forward. The woman fell sprawling back onto the grass.

"What the-?" the redhead laughed.

The rat snatched the spider in nimble fingers, turning and crunching it between oversized hypsodont teeth, its venom given no chance to save it. Predator turned prey.

Fuck! Steel cold anger pricked at the pores in Neil's skin. He pushed his jaws together, grinding his fury into silence. The redhead kept laughing, oblivious to her narrow escape.

"Still hungry, hey?" she said aloud. "Sorry sweetie, I didn't mean to steal your breakfast." She pulled herself up from the grass, leaving the rat to finish its meal. Wrapping her hide skirt around her waist and pulling the singlet over her head, she bent one last time to smooth its fur. "Till tomorrow, little one. You be good." The redhead stepped lightly back into the forest and disappeared, very much alive.

Seething, Neil stepped out onto the grass.

"You stupid little *bastard.*" His sharpened stick pierced the marsupial's neck. It hung twitching from the shaft as Neil held it up to his face. "You just cost me a great deal, rat." Neil's voice was barely controlled. "You stupid, fucking ugly little bastard. You know what you are now, huh? What you just made yourself? *Dinner.*"

Leaves rustled behind him and Neil spun around. *Fuck!* His

knees buckled to the ground. The chimp was behind him. Watching.

Its thin lips were pulled tight and it stared, unflinching, straight into Neil's eyes. His scalp crawled in fear. The animal was bigger than he'd expected. It looked strong. Its body was tense with arms and legs coiled like a spring ready to be released. Neil scrambled back, stumbling and falling against the tree.

The beast didn't move. It just stared menacingly, standing on two legs. It slowly opened its mouth drawing pale lips across its teeth. *It's threatening me.* Time slowed and Neil's instincts pounded through him. *It's just an animal. Fight it. Kill it now.* He squeezed the rat tight, slowly pulling the stick from its corpse. The chimpanzee lifted its chin. Its dark eyes bore into Neil's own and he suddenly realised his entire morning's actions had been witnessed by the animal.

No! It's just a fucking monkey. It doesn't know anything. Neil choked on his own lie. The intelligence in its eyes was more frightening than its bestiality. The animal was suddenly not looking at him, but more… into him. *Almost like it knows... What I tried to do, how I failed. That I'll try again... I have to.*

Neil's heart thundered in his ribcage. The rat was clenched against his shirt and a trickle of blood found its way down the valleys of his hand. *It knows.*

Deliberately, the chimpanzee turned its back to him. With one swift move, it was gone.

CHAPTER 38

IVY

In the dead of night, Ivy woke in a cold sweat. Muffled cries and whispers echoed through the cave and a strange low hum seemed to hang in the air. Ivy sat up and her eyes adjusted to the faint glow of coals flickering as figures moved in front of hearth fire. The cries became louder for a moment and then softened again under whispers. A disturbed child was hushed back to sleep nearby. Ivy pulled herself up from the sleeping mat and felt her way gingerly along the cave wall.

"Shahn… Shahn." Her whisper came louder than she intended in the dark. Xiou's face appeared in front of her and Ivy crouched down with her amulet wrist extended. In the coal-light, Xiou's scars looked frightening. If she hadn't known the gentle heart that beat beneath them, she might have run.

"Something's wrong," Ivy said. It wasn't a question.

Xiou looked hesitantly in the direction of the disturbance. "Shimma is giving birth," he said.

Ivy's throat seemed to close over. Births were dangerous, for the hobbits - now more than ever. Her senses heightened against the pitch dark and Ivy realized the atmosphere was thick with collective anxiety. The shadow grip of the Slow Death was threatening them tonight. Miscarriages, stillborns and complications of childbirth were all too familiar - the hobbits' future was being stolen with their most vulnerable.

"Where's Shahn?" Ivy asked.

"Helping Lahstri prepare the medicines," Xiou replied. "The birth is not going well."

Please, no. Not Shimma too. In her quiet way, Shimma had been one of the first to make Ivy feel welcome. She was all soft smiles and tinkling laughter and had taken it upon herself to gather the additional food that Kyah preferred to eat, along with her own family's requirements each day. By that gesture, more than any other, Ivy counted her as a close friend. *Please let them both survive,* she found herself praying.

Groans on the opposite side of the cave grew louder again and the low hum rose in intensity. Ivy squeezed her eyes shut, listening. *They're voices.* Each had a slightly different pitch, and unlike their dusk song, each voice sounded distinctly male. Each man of the tribe seemed to be at his own hearth, keeping vigil by glowing coals with a soft, low monotone.

"They're singing to *aneirlah,* the life energy," Xiou explained, "to call the child out safely and give strength to Shimma while she labours. It's all we can offer." Xiou's brow was deeply ridged and Ivy knew he was dreading Shahn's impending birth as well.

"Shahn will be fine, Xiou. And Shimma too," Ivy said. She gently pressed her forehead to his in the dark. "They're strong women."

Xiou exhaled. "They are, you're right," he said. "But somehow I don't think either of us will sleep any more tonight. Shahn needs more water from the river; let's go together."

Ivy nodded gratefully, glad for the distraction. She looked tentatively at Trahg still sleeping near her feet.

"He'll be fine," Xiou said. "Leihna will comfort him if he wakes."

Ivy looked toward Leihna's sleeping mat and was surprised to find her sitting wide awake with a grim smile that ghosted in the dark. The girl was no stranger to death. Nestled in her arms was a sleeping toddler, curled into a snug ball of hide covers. Ivy guessed the boy must be Dalu, Shimma's first born. Ivy smiled back, but it didn't reach her eyes. *Please let them survive.*

Ivy picked her way to the front of the cave, where Xiou lit a torch. They descended into the crisp night air.

The night was alive with rustling marsupials and chirping insects. The waxing quarter moon broke weakly through the topmost layer of foliage, drawing more darkness underneath. Giant tree ferns dominated the path. Green branches were mirrored underneath by fallen dried brown ones, still attached to black trunks. They stood in sharp relief in the fiery torchlight, one inverted triangle on another's point, with a flowing gown of sharp leaves below to balance the soft spray above.

The breeze carried a trace of citrus scent. Ivy took a deep breath, stilling her nerves. *Please let them survive.*

She stepped into the shallows of the river, filling one of the large bladders Xiou had brought with him. Her toes curled around smooth pebbles as water swirled at her calves. Shadows touched her ankles and fallen leaves twirled on the black surface, catching on needles dripping from overhead branches as they spun downstream. The night forest was beautiful.

Please let them survive. Ivy continued her mantra as they returned to the cave.

Dousing the torch, Ivy followed Xiou. Shimma was circled by women at her hearth. She rested her hands on her engorged belly, lost in concentration and pain. An older woman moved around her, anticipating each shift of weight. It was Shimma's mother Bosxoi, a smaller than usual hobbit with peppered grey hair and a soft body. Her face was a web of worry as she held hides warmed with hot stones to Shimma's lower back and whispered soothing words under her breath. The pregnant woman moved constantly; rocking, bending and squatting with eyes squeezed shut.

In the darkness, Shimma's mate Raspik watched with concerned eyes. At Xiou's approach, Raspik took the water bladder. A deep bowl sat beside the fire in a hollow, supported by a ring of small rocks. The bowl was made from a circular piece of hide, stiff and moulded through repeated use. The rim was supported by a pliable willow switch and hemmed with a threaded strip to keep it together. Raspik poured water into the bowl and picked up three rocks from the ashes with a bone trowel. Gently shaking the ash away, he dropped them into the pot with a hiss. Within a few minutes the water was boiling. Raspik knelt by his mate, whispering words of encouragement. Shimma acknowledged him for a moment with a weak smile, and then winced again lost in her contraction. Her agony was mirrored in Raspik's eyes; of no help to his mate, he would fret until it was done.

"Come Raspik, have a drink." Xiou led Raspik away and Ivy turned to follow. Shahn caught her wrist.

"Stay Hiranah. It's a woman's duty to support a sister during childbirth."

Lahstri, kneeling by the fire beneath a sheen of sweat, eyed Ivy anxiously. "No Shahn, the karathah is bad luck."

Ivy's heart dropped. As useless as she felt, she was petrified for Shimma and her unborn baby. She wanted to help.

As Ivy turned away, Shimma, who had fallen back to rest between contractions, noticed her. She let out a weak, shaky breath. "Stay, Hiranah. You can stay -" Another contraction began and Shimma once again turned inward.

"The baby was not due for another half-moon," Shahn said, lowering her voice. "It hasn't turned within her belly. Lahstri needs to help her shift it or neither will survive. So you can help me instead. Shimma needs relief from the pain."

Lahstri spoke again, soft but stern. "Shahn, I've told you before, Krue doesn't want - "

"But Shimma does!" Shahn hissed. "Krue is not our medicine woman - you are Lahstri! Must you always do as your mate says?"

With a scowl Lahstri turned her eyes to her own dark hearth. Ivy guessed Krue would keep away tonight. Birth was the domain of women, and Lahstri had assisted with many.

Ivy held out her wrist, offering Lahstri the amulet. With a hesitant glance into the dark cave, Lahstri placed a single finger on the stone. It was more than Ivy had expected.

"I know what they did to your daughter," Ivy said. She saw the shadow of grief across the woman's face. "And I saw the arrows in Terap and Kiran. I understand why Krue hates me." Ivy crouched low, meeting the medicine woman's eyes. "When he looks at me, he sees them. He sees a murderer. But that's not what I am. When I'm here, in this cave, I'm like you. My family was *lost,* just like Tikan. My friends are *lost*. I've lost my own life as a karathah." She took a deep breath. "This is my family too now, Lahstri. I want to help them. They're all I have left."

Lahstri considered her intently. Then she turned to Shahn, giving a slight nod. "Keep her out of sight."

Lahstri's skill as a midwife was clear even to Ivy's untrained eye, as she massaged and shifted Shimma's belly with quiet encouragement. She soaked a small hide cloth in warmed water and gently rolled it across Shimma's shoulders and lower back.

The night crept by too slowly. Ivy helped Shahn prepare herbal analgesics. Progress was slow and Ivy caught frequent anxious glances between Shahn and Lahstri. Shimma was exhausted. She shook uncontrollably as she urged her body to cooperate. Ivy was critically aware of the low hum that grew in intensity as the labour progressed, leaving everybody's nerves frayed.

As the first ray of sun burst through the cave opening,

Shimma bore down for the last time. Harmonic notes were left hanging in empty air as each voice, low and hoarse from hours of vigil, finally fell silent.

Please let them survive.

A weak newborn cry broke the silence.

"Api," Shimma breathed, "Baby Api is here."

Ivy met Xiou's eyes across the cave and they shared a smile. Immense relief washed over all the women as Shimma leaned back against the pile of hide covers behind her, panting with pride. She pulled her newborn up to her face, gently rubbing its greyish forehead against her own and nuzzling into its neck with her warm breath. Then she guided the baby to her breast.

"A healthy boy," said Shahn to Ivy. "When he has fed, we'll clean him so they can rest together."

While the baby fed, Lahstri continued to deliver the placenta. As the source of new life, it was honoured and ritually cleansed and wrapped for burial. When Api had settled, Lastri cradled the newborn as Shahn handed Shimma a sharp blade; the sanction to cut the umbilical cord separating herself from her baby was hers alone. With a quick flick it was done.

Ivy hung back, entirely overwhelmed. From the way Shimma had called to her baby during labour to the way she now held him against her heart, Ivy knew they were already connected by so much more than blood. For the first time in over three years, both mother and baby had survived the ordeal that had stolen so many before. One tiny victory against the Slow Death.

Shimma noticed Ivy watching from the hearth, and beckoned.

"Hold my baby for me, Hiranah. I need to clean myself," she said.

"I was so worried for you," Ivy whispered as she knelt down, "for both of you." Shimma gently placed the sleeping newborn in Ivy's hands. The baby seemed too tiny and fragile to touch. Ivy looked over to Shahn for help, but found her busying herself with a smile.

"I was worried too," said Shimma, shifting under Lahstri's instruction, "but I think perhaps you are good luck after all, Hiranah. What do you think Lahstri?"

The medicine woman frowned; fully aware she was now in full view of her mate. "I think you need to rest."

Shahn finally joined Ivy and together they rinsed Api with warm water and the cleansing juice of a tamarind fruit that Ivy had prepared under her instruction. Shahn dressed his umbilical wound with an embrocation of turmeric root and mashed leaves. Soot was rubbed into the mixture to dry it out. Finally, a betel leaf was placed as dressing and a thin strip of hide was wrapped around his tiny waist.

The baby's face was unlike anything Ivy had ever seen before. The water had woken him and he seemed alert, more than Ivy felt he should rightfully be. His tiny lips searched and puckered soundlessly. He had a small flat nose, strong brows and deep brown eyes.

Api lacked the chin and high forehead that Ivy was used to seeing on human babies. Instead of being bald, elongated and smooth, his head was round and already covered in a thick layer of glossy black hair. Like other ape juveniles, the infant was still recognizably more 'human-like' than its grown parents. But his size was the most obvious difference between him and his baby sapien counterparts. His tiny body, perfectly formed, was entirely smaller than Ivy's forearm. She held onto him, transfixed by the way his little chest rhythmically rose and fell.

The fingers on his hands were tiny and perfect. Ten fingers, ten toes.

Just like human.

CHAPTER 39

ORRIN

"Orrin, are you still here?"

"Yeah."

For three days, the idea of going home had seemed too unappealing. Plagued with nightmares, each worse than the last, meant that Orrin slept as little as possible, instead holed up in his laboratory office. He wondered how many times he would lose her in his dreams before he finally cracked for good. His thoughts rarely left the amulet dug from that pit. *Fifty thousand years... How the hell did it get there?* He slid his glasses on and straightened up.

Dale appeared in the doorway. His nose wrinkled reflexively as he held out a coffee and sandwich bag. "Brought you breakfast."

"Thanks man," said Orrin, inviting him in. "I'm completely knackered."

"Any luck?"

"Kind of. Actually, I could use your opinion here."

"Really?" Dale's smile was nervous as he looked around for a chair. The office floor was littered with encyclopaedias, journal articles and food wrappings. An ancient, cracked oscilloscope beside the desk was piled high with dirty shirts, coins and scribbled papers.

Orrin looked abashed. "Let's use the lab instead. It's time for a history lesson for both of us."

"History?"

"About these so-called 'hobbits'. I want to find out why the bollocks I've never heard of them when it seems the rest of the world has."

Dale looked thoughtful. "I might be able to help you out there actually. Of everything Phil says, that's the thing that annoys me the most." Orrin raised an eyebrow but Dale stammered on, "I mean, not just because he's right, but I mean, because *he shouldn't be.*"

Orrin nodded, encouraging Dale to continue.

"Okay," Dale said, "I'm no expert on evolution but I did grow up with biologists as parents and like I said at the time, I'd never heard of hobbits either." He pulled a dog-eared piece of paper from his pocket. "I ripped this page from one of my dad's textbooks. It's a phylogenetic tree."

Orrin studied the image. Spread before him, the evolutionary relationships of hominids splintered from the earliest known branch of *Sahelanthropus tchadensis* roaming West Africa nearly seven million years ago, into an elaborate genetic tree of descendants, with modern *Homo sapiens sapiens* at its most recent tip. Between the two names, a myriad of early human ancestors dotted the tree's branches, marking their place in the evolutionary prehistory of humankind.

Dale pointed to a name, parallel with modern humans at the top of the tree. "Look, this tree shows Homo floresiensis as *extant* – in other words, it's recorded as a current, living species in the present day. So, not *extinct*. I don't know about you, but I don't think it should be there - whatever Phil thinks." Dale's tone was uncharacteristically abrasive. "I mean it wasn't there before."

"So where the hell did they come from, and why are we the

only ones who think these *hobbits* shouldn't be here?" Orrin asked.

"And another thing," Dale said, "this magnetospheric decay, it's *really* bad. I know I don't have to tell you that, of course I don't," Dale reddened, "but it would take years of disintegration for the Earth to respond the way it has - all these environmental problems - but a few weeks ago it was fine, right? Well, not fine - we anticipated trouble, but I thought we had time to figure it out -"

"Dale," Orrin interrupted, "I get it. *I know.* The whole world is screwed and no one seems to realise it shouldn't be." He squeezed his eyes shut, willing the earth to shift on its axis and throw normalcy back over his head.

"And about this 'Ivy' woman," Dale continued and Orrin's eyes narrowed, "I don't know if this helps but I looked further into that archaeological site you said she was working on."

"Liang Bua Cave?"

"Yeah. There's some stuff there that just doesn't add up." Dale said. "Firstly, did you know that the government is suing a huge multi-national corporation for environmental negligence right now? They're claiming that a mining company is wholly responsible for the Great Barrier Reef dying. All the coral is bleached by chemical run-off and half of the fish are already gone."

"You mean *gone*, gone?"

"I mean extinct. Entire species have been wiped out from chemicals leached into the Celebes Sea flowing down to the Coral Sea on the East coast of Queensland. "

"Shite."

"That's what I thought," Dale said. "Well anyway, when I spoke to the dig supervisor in Flores they were adamant that Ivy wouldn't have been needed. He said it was what they call a 'salvage dig'. Apparently it's a bit like a grab and run for archaeological sites that are about to be bulldozed."

"Bulldozed for what?" Orrin asked.

"That's just it," Dale said. "It's the same company that's being sued. IPM - International Pulp and Mining. It's a conglomerate that's already strip-mined most of Indonesia, including Flores. There are massive deposits of some rare earth metal underground, so they've been systematically ripping it out for the last fifty years and backfilling the land with Palm Oil Plantations when they're done. It's a financial double dip for them."

"Palm Oil Plantations?" Orrin exclaimed. "That's what the rallies were about before Ivy disappeared."

Dale shrugged. "I just don't understand how things got so bad so fast. Floods and droughts. There are more news reports about melting ice caps and biodiversity loss than I've ever seen in my life. It terrifies me."

"You and me both, man." Orrin felt the rush of adrenaline. *It's real.* "I keep finding holes everywhere," he said. "No, not holes - more like, *aberrations* to the way it's meant to be. Little changes."

"There's another thing Orrin." Dale shuffled in his chair. "I guess it's - kind of personal."

For the first time, Orrin noticed the pale pallor of Dale's skin, the red-rimmed, tired eyes and frown creases. He seemed raw, his normally nervous energy at breaking point.

"Shite, I'm sorry, man," Orrin said. "I've been putting so much pressure on you." Orrin dropped his elbows to his knees and shoved his thumbs under his glasses. The instant pain was a relief, distracting him from the frustration that cut the very hollow of his bones. *Dale's losing it too now. This is all my fault.*

"No, it's not you," Dale said. "It's... it's my whole life, there's something just not right. I can't put my finger on it, but there are *aberrations*, like you said - little things that seem like nothing on their own, but they're adding up." Dale's lack of confidence seemed to have decayed even further.

Although he knew he shouldn't, Orrin felt a surge of satisfaction. *Dale felt it too.*

He clasped Dale's shoulder. "You're not losing your mind, lad.

I'm seeing the same things but I just can't work out why. Clearly you and I have something in common because no one else is affected. But all we physically share is this lab."

"And Phil uses the lab as much as we do, but seems entirely at home with his reality," Dale sighed.

"His reality?" Orrin considered. "Yeah, when you put it like that, it makes sense. It's *our* reality that's changed. The world for us is different – the politics, the environment, the people. I *know* Ivy existed before, but now, well, she just doesn't. The only thing that's left of her is that amulet and that excavation pit says it's a fifty-thousand-year old artefact."

"You're sure it's hers?" Dale asked.

"Positive," Orrin said. "Ivy was wearing it the last day I saw her. The day she disappeared." Orrin pulled the silver chain from his pocket remembering.

"The day she disappeared?" Dale repeated. His face drained of colour. "We were in the lab together that day! Phil didn't arrive until the afternoon. Remember?"

"Of course!" exclaimed Orrin. "He walked in just after Ivy disappeared." *The animalistic scream.*

Dale jumped up, shot across the room and disappeared into Orrin's laboratory office. He returned a few moments later carrying an encyclopaedia ensigned with the letter 'H'. "This is yours, right? It's been in your office since we moved here."

"Sure," Orrin said.

Dale flicked through the pages, finally resting it open under the heading 'Hominid Evolution'. His fingers trailed the page until he found what he was looking for. "A phylogenetic tree."

"Another one?"

Dale exhaled, as if he'd been holding his breath for days. "A different one. The *right* one." He handed the book to Orrin.

There in black and white, the same illustration that Dale had brought in now clearly depicted Homo floresiensis as *extinct*, its genetic timeline ending fifty thousand years before present. Only

Homo sapiens sapien carried on, the sole survivor of the hominid family to modern times.

"Jesus, Mary and Joseph," Orrin whispered. His fingers shook as he traced the lines on the page.

"What does it mean?" Dale asked. He pulled the dog-eared paper from his pocket and unfolded it, laying the images side by side. "Which one is right?"

"They're both right," Orrin said, slowly. "But, I think… I think this one is right for us." He let the pages leaf through his fingers. *Maybe she didn't run away. Maybe she just… left. Fifty thousand years… how in the hell…?*

Minutes ticked by as Orrin stared at the papers without seeing them. Instead, another image formed in his mind, of an impossibility that tossed everything he understood to be real aside and replaced it with a new kind of logic. *An impossible logic.*

Finally, he took a deep breath and met Dale's eyes.

"Something has shifted," Orrin said. "I know this sounds mental, but hear me out. Something has changed *in our past* and so the future has changed too. Fifty thousand years worth."

Dale's shoulders stiffened. His eyes were wide and his breathing almost stilled. "What do you mean, *something has changed in our past?*"

Orrin took a deep breath, steeling himself from his own thoughts as they tumbled out. "Something critical has interrupted our evolutionary timeline," he said. "You saw the phylogenetic trees, something to do with these 'hobbits' has changed - and that change kept them alive instead of letting them become extinct. The whole world is different in millions of tiny ways but because human evolution skewed so long ago, no one alive would remember it. Everybody's lives have just developed the way they should, in this alternate reality. But for some reason, we were protected, you and I."

"But why should we be? Why wouldn't we change like everybody else?"

Orrin looked around. The white walls shone with monitors. Racks of equipment were gleaming and buzzing. Huge screens still displayed their attempts to decode the bizarre readings recorded after Ivy and the bonobo had left. Electromagnetic fields whipping and waning, the temperature and humidity of the room had soared, the extreme wavelength fluctuations and light intensity gone haywire. All systems had been affected in some way, all had been recalibrated and now they were trying to re-connect the dots. The giant monitors illuminated their failure so far.

"Because we were in the lab." The answer came clear and simple and Orrin was surprised at the certainty in his own voice.

"When?"

"When the system shut down. You and I were in the office when we heard them scream. When we heard Ivy and Kyah – *disappear.*"

"So what? I mean the office is right in the lab – shouldn't we have been the first to change our reality?"

Orrin sat quietly for a minute, contemplating.

"This whole lab is a giant faraday cage," he said. "They installed mesh on the inside walls when I moved in - it was a condition of the OH&S requirements of our experimentation."

"Why did the data change then?" challenged Dale. "Our computers are in this lab too."

"But all our *data* is virtually hosted on servers outside the lab," Orrin said. "These are just server terminals - the rest of the world changed so our data did too."

He glanced at his office door. An old radioactive sign still hung above the architrave, the lighting bulb long since broken. *A shield.* "The lead lining in the walls of the office must have protected us - it stopped us being taken with Ivy and Kyah," Orrin said, more certain now than before. "The office used to be a testing laboratory. Just because they refurbished it, doesn't necessarily mean it no longer has the original paint or protective elements … when we were in there, we were safe - like a time capsule or a vault."

"So the office protected us?"

Orrin looked up, suddenly grateful for Dale's complicity. He'd expected more condemnation of his sanity.

"I think so. It didn't protect them though– in the lab." The animalistic scream echoed through his mind. "We did this, Dale. We've changed history - no, *prehistory*. Ivy and Kyah are lost because I couldn't let her go home that day, because I insisted she come here, to this." Orrin looked around the room. His head swum. *I did this. I lost her forever.*

"So where is she?"

Orrin pulled the chain from his pocket and rolled it gently through his fingers. That one, he knew.

"Flores, Liang Bua Cave. Fifty thousand years ago." *I moved time.*

The words echoed off the walls and both men sat silent, processing the enormity of their mistake and the potential of their discovery.

Finally, Dale stood up. "So, we need to fix it, right? We need to change it back. If we get them back, we can go back to the way things were?"

"Get them back?" Orrin murmured.

"What choice do we have?" Dale replied. "We have to figure out what went wrong and get them back. We can't leave the world like this. The magnetosphere is barely holding. It can't last. We have to undo whatever we did. If we did it once, we can do it again, right? Only the opposite." Orrin studied Dale. The student's pallor had lifted and a dim light burned within his eyes. "You have a plan, right, Orrin? Just- just tell me what to do."

Orrin's heart sped up. He curled his fingertips into his sweaty palms. A plan. *Fix it. Fix it and get her back.*

"Yes!" Orrin said, jumping to his feet as well. "You're damn right, we'll fix it! God only knows how, but we'll figure it out." He took a deep breath and it felt like the first. "We'll need Phil to analyse those environmental variables again. And you start with the electromagnetic equipment. I'll search for anything we've missed." Adrenaline coursed through Orrin's veins and his nerves felt on fire. *I'm going to move time. Again.*

Half an hour later, Phil breezed in. Dropping his bag and phone onto his desk, he sat down and then launched his roller chair to the monitors where Orrin and Dale sat hunched.

"Wow dude, you stink. Did you sleep here again?"

Orrin grinned. He could always count on Phil for the truth. "Thanks and yeah." Deep breath. "And we need to talk."

The talk didn't go well.

"You're losing it man. No, you've *lost* it!" Phil yelled. "Whatever trip you're on, I'm not joining you." He looked resentfully at Dale. "It's one thing to suck up, but buying into this crap isn't doing anyone any favours. Especially him."

Dale's face reddened. "I'm not buying into it, Phil. I'm living it," he said. "Orrin's right, our experiment has stuffed everything up and we've got to fix it."

"You honestly think you're that effing important, that you've single-handedly screwed up the entire world? Come on, man." Phil eyed them scornfully.

"I'm not saying we've single-handedly screwed the world Phil, I'm saying that by sending Ivy back in time we've interfered with something we shouldn't have," challenged Orrin. "We've changed the way things should be for the worse. Much worse."

"Who says it's worse?" Phil yelled. "From where I'm standing the world is doing just fine, thanks. Who the hell are you to play God?"

Orrin leant forward. He picked up a week's collection of newspapers and threw them at Phil.

"Pick one, pick any one, and tell me it's not bad!" Orrin yelled. "The magnetosphere is decaying! I don't know how it's related to what we did, but I do know it's not bloody right! Thirty species extinct a day! Forest fires out of control! Droughts, floods, tsunamis - people are dying, Phil! Explosive population outbreaks of vector-borne viruses that are spreading with the heat. And these damned 'hobbits' - they shouldn't even be here! People seem torn between loving and hating the things. The very definition of humanity is under fire and rioters around the world are threatening civil war over it. Jaysus Phil! How can you say that's 'just fine'?"

"It's not like this happened overnight Orrin," Phil spat back. "It's the way the world's been going. Sure, it's getting worse, but people are still living and enjoying their lives."

"*Some* people Phil. Not everyone is going to get that opportunity," Orrin said accusingly.

"And since when are you the bloody social justice committee, O? You've accepted it all up until now," Phil yelled back.

Orrin threw his hands in the air. "I never even knew about it until now, you gobshite! That's what I'm saying!"

"So you keep saying." Phil crossed his arms tight against his chest.

Orrin took a deep breath. He tried a different tack. "Look, you witnessed the aftermath of Ivy's disappearance. Every single variable we'd set had changed and the readings were off the charts. The tesla coil was spewing electricity all over the place. We check that equipment every day and there wasn't a single anomalous reading until then. It was all set up, ready to go and then *bam*! Totally screwed." Orrin's fingertips pushed behind his glasses. "Please, Phil," he pleaded. "Help us. Search again, analyse the data one more time, check your code. *You* wrote these programs – this is *your* code, man. You know this shite couldn't happen by itself."

"So maybe you two did it," Phil jeered. "I came in after the fact, didn't I? Who's to say you didn't screw the systems before I got here?"

"And why the bollocks would I do that?" Orrin exploded, his face turning red. "You think I enjoy ruining my own life? Yours? Dale's and the whole bloody world?"

"Hell, I don't know," Phil said. His normally blithe features were unrelenting. "You seem capable of anything lately Orrin, you've bloody flipped."

"That's because of this, Phil!" Orrin yelled. "Look, I know this all sounds mental, but somehow the faraday cage of the lab and the lead walls in the office kept us safe from the repercussions of this time shift. Anything in my office, including Dale and I, remained unchanged – objective observers, if you will – to whatever happened to the rest of the world. Look at this - phylogenetic trees from before *and* after the shift." He thrust the papers at Phil's face. "These hominids are meant to be dead Phil. *Extinct.* Not a damn cuisine that's causing a social apocalypse!"

Phil pushed Orrin's arm away. "Sorry man, but it sounds to me like the ginger ditched you and you can't handle it. *She dumped you. Get over it.*"

"You can talk, you bloody gobshite, throwing shapes around campus without a damned care in the world!" yelled Orrin. "This situation is desperate Phil, and you're not even listening to me! Grow the fuck up!"

Phil's fist slammed the table between them. "You're losing your bloody mind, Orrin," he growled, his voice low and dangerous. "*You can't control time.* You did not send a woman and her pet monkey into the Stone Age. And you're not roping me into your lunacy." Phil turned away, his hands up in surrender. "You know what, I'm gone."

"Fine!" Orrin shouted at his back.

The door slammed shut and Orrin's fist smashed the table where Phil's had just been. Cursing he turned around, kicking a roller chair across the room. *Bastard!* Orrin pinched the bridge of his nose, hearing his own teeth grind in the deafening silence.

"We needed him, Orrin," said Dale, quietly.

With feverish intensity, Orrin and Dale poured over data for seventy-two hours straight. In the back of his mind, Phil's words echoed. *You're not roping me into your lunacy...*

"Dale?" Orrin said. It was nearing lunch time again.

There was no reply. He turned to find Dale fast asleep with his head on the keyboard. Quietly Orrin slipped into his office. He needed to make a call. The mobile number he had stored in his phone recited an unavailable message. *Come on.* Orrin quickly tapped on his keyboard and dialled the listed administration number of his friend's employer instead.

"CSIRO enquiries, how can I direct your call?" answered a receptionist.

"Hi, I'm looking for Dimitri Angelis please? In the Division for Astronomy and Space."

"Please hold for one moment."

It had been a year since they'd caught up over a pint; reminiscing about their post grad shenanigans together. Orrin hoped above all else, that Dimi still worked at the CSIRO in this reality, as he had in the last. The soft on-hold music pacified his frustration. *You're not roping me into your lunacy ...* lunacy? Perhaps he had been looking at this whole thing wrong.

Of course, he hadn't for a moment considered that Phil was actually right. *Not this time.* But the word lunacy evoked a second meaning that resonated in him more than was customary. *Lunar...* Perhaps the premise that he'd caused the time shift single-handedly was wrong. Perhaps there were external forces operating… forces he'd had no knowledge of at the time. In that respect, Dimi might prove to be invaluable.

"I'm sorry sir, but Mr Angelis is out of the office this month on a research project. Would you like me to leave a message?" the receptionist said.

A month. "Is there no other contact number for him?" Orrin asked.

"I believe not sir, apparently he's at one of our deep space telescopes but the details are confidential. He can't be contacted by phone. If you like I can give you his email address?"

"Thanks."

Orrin scribbled the address onto his whiteboard then tapped out an email.

Urgent – Dimi, please contact me. I'm desperate man, I need your help – Orrin

Orrin stepped back into his lab and was surprised to find Jayne waiting for him, a grim look on her face.

CHAPTER 40

IVY

"I need to go back to the waterhole."

Gihn looked up. He took the bowl of warm water Ivy had brought from Shahn's hearth and passed it on to Lahstri. The medicine woman took it without a word and continued her ministrations on the two dying hunters in the back of the cave. Since Truen had passed away, they had lost another two men to the Swift Death. Thankfully, no more had fallen ill since. Ivy thought she knew why.

Gihn raised an eyebrow, waiting for an explanation.

"I can't tell you why," Ivy continued. "I will, but I need to… check something first."

"Secrets, Hiranah. You are holding back knowledge again."

Ivy sighed. "Not for long. Something is very wrong there but I need to see for myself. I don't even know what I'm looking for yet." That wasn't entirely true but until Ivy could define the danger without causing more panic, she'd decided it was best to handle the situation alone. Three deaths within a week had already shattered the tribe with fresh grief.

"I'll ask Xiou and Setian to take you tomorrow then, perhaps Kora and Kari as well - "

"No, just me and one guide," Ivy interrupted. "And it has to be today," she glanced at the two men at her feet. "Too many have died already from this."

Gihn frowned. "Setian can take you then. Xiou is out hunting." Ivy nodded. She liked Setian. The hunter was quiet and good natured. His mate Kora had also become a close friend.

Within minutes, Ivy had tied a water bladder to her hide skirt and wrapped some travelling food for them both. It would take perhaps three hours to get there and back, depending on what she found. She met Setian at the cave entrance.

"Are you ready to go then, Hiranah?" Setian smiled.

"No, she is not." A gruff voice interrupted. Krue pushed his way between them. "I don't like this. What is she hiding?"

"I'm hiding nothing Krue," Ivy said, resentfully. "And I don't need your approval to go out."

"Well… you do need my approval to take Setian. I have work for him here." Krue looked around, as if trying to think up a task. Setian intervened diplomatically.

"I can assist you with plans for the probech hunt as soon as I return, Krue," Setian said. "We have plenty of time yet."

Krue looked livid. "You turn my best hunters against me, woman?" He turned to Gihn, who had followed Ivy, anticipating trouble. "The karathah wants to go alone on our hunt trail and won't even tell us why?" He looked at Ivy with as much disdain as he could manage. "Why we should trust her? She's done nothing but draw lines in the dirt and you fools cheer for it! She is one of *them*." Krue spat in the dirt at her feet.

"Stop doing that!" Ivy yelled. "I'm not a karathah, not anymore!" Her face was red with humiliation. Ivy wanted to believe her own denial. There was a reason Krue hated Homo sapiens and she couldn't forget what that reason was. *Murder.* The very thing Ivy suspected of them again. The karathah had drawn and twisted the pain within this man into a bitter point and now he stabbed her with it. She *was* a karathah. Deep in her gut, Ivy knew that her suspicions of what was to come justified his hate even more than he knew. It wasn't the first time she was ashamed of her own species.

"Ha! Of course you are," said Krue. "You take from us and give nothing in return. Now you ask us to trust you on a hunt trail so close to their territory? You want to meet with them there! You'll betray us and lead Setian into danger." Krue's eyes steeled with hate, and Ivy sensed the loss that was locked underneath. She took a deep breath, stifling her anger. Ivy understood the misplaced accusations of grief, but it was getting harder to bear.

"I am not meeting the karathah, Krue," she said through gritted teeth. "And no harm will come to Setian for taking me there."

"You are right that no harm will come to him." Krue lifted his chin stubbornly and stepped closer to Ivy, entirely unintimidated by her height. "Because he will not go. It is me who will take you. And if the karathah are there to meet you, woman, I will kill you myself."

The trek passed in silence. Krue walked ahead, refusing to acknowledge Ivy but for the occasional icy glare behind him. Although it was much less pleasant than the friendly banter she might have exchanged with Setian, Ivy was not entirely upset. It gave her time to think.

Ironically, it was Krue's own hostility toward her that sparked her realization. *Karathah are nothing but poison to our land,* Krue had once said. And he was right.

The waterhole was poisoned. That fact was critically obvious, as much as it pained her to realise it. Ivy had discussed the symptoms of the Swift Death with Gihn on numerous occasions. It couldn't be contagious or those tending the sick would have contracted it too. The victims shared no peculiarity of diet or living conditions. It favoured men and women of previously good health, but no children or elders. Hunters were clearly the target and the only consistent links between them were the trails they took before falling ill. The ones dying were the strongest hunters, and as such, regularly ventured the furthest. The hot spring was apparently on the boundary of their territory with the karathah and a favourite place to refresh during a hunt, to wash the blood and dirt from their bodies, *or to take a drink.*

Why the karathah would deliberately poison a known water source for the hobbits was still unclear, but Ivy had no doubt a justification had been fitted to the crime. It had been done before. The heinous act of poisoning the most necessary of human requirements, *water,* was historically renowned in her own country. Humanity had no limits to its malediction. In Australia, it had been for colonial possession of land.

Is that what they want? Land? The hobbits used so few resources as it was, but what else was worth killing them for? They had only their cave, their hunting territory and the trade goods. It didn't seem enough. *But then, no justification is ever enough.*

They were nearly at the hot spring when Krue turned. His face slipped from suspicion to irritation in an instant and Ivy followed his line of sight. From where they had just walked, Kyah appeared in the lowest branches. Trahg and his tiny dusty-haired cousin Turi were clinging to the long hair on her back. They were all smiles.

"Hiranah! We followed you!" Trahg looked inordinately pleased with himself as he tumbled off and grabbed her hand. "Kyah missed you so we came too."

Ivy scooped the five-year-old into her arms. "Trahg! It's dangerous to be out here alone! What if a shirakan tried to eat you for dinner? Or if you became lost? You know better than this. And dragging Turi along too -" Trahg rolled his eyes and wiggled out of her grip, keeping his hand wrapped around the amulet on Ivy's wrist. "I never get lost and anyway, it was Turi's idea." Ivy raised her eyebrow at the smallest boy, who only buried his face into Kyah's back with a shy smile.

"I see you found a new way to travel," Ivy noted. Kyah didn't seem to mind the burden. On the contrary, she looked perfectly serene.

"Turi got tired," Trahg said, shrugging.

"It is a stupid way to travel Trahg," Krue growled. "It is too far for children to be alone and the karathah are nearby. They would kill you faster than the shirakan. I will make sure you are both punished by your mothers when we return." Despite Krue's harsh words, Ivy saw an undercurrent of worry in his eyes.

"I'm sorry Tua," Trahg said, with a quivering lip. Although Ivy was familiar with the more respectful title given to elders, she didn't often hear it.

"Stay close and keep quiet," he grumbled and turned away to continue walking.

Trahg looked to Ivy with a frown. "I thought you came with Setian," he whispered loudly, "he's much nicer." Ahead of them, Krue huffed.

Ivy smirked and resumed walking, one hand wrapped tightly around Trahg's tiny fingers and the other hand loosely around Kyah's elongated ones. Turi stayed clinging to the bonobo's back, watching the goings on imperiously.

Ivy stopped dead. "Krue, wait!"

The old man turned back, clearly annoyed by a second delay. "What now?"

"This," Ivy whispered. Where she had stopped, a mass of creeping vines suffocated the undergrowth and spiralled up the trunks of ancient trees. Hidden in the long leaves and confetti of leaflets that the vine produced, were bright red flowers. The flowers should have sparked the panic that now rose in her chest. But no, they looked as innocuous as any other in the greenery. It wasn't the flowers, nor the leaves that Ivy had examined under a microscope in her laboratory not more than a month ago and then forgotten. It was this. *Cherry red seeds.* A single black spot glossing one end of the hard shell. They hung in profusion from the underside of dry, splitting pods and it suddenly occurred to Ivy why these seeds would indeed *not* make a nice necklace. She knew this plant. It topped her botanical reference chart of phytoliths in the residue lab. Ivy had identified plants of importance to native Indonesians for food, medicine or utility in anticipation of the stone tools she was expecting from Flores. Each crystalline phytolith was unique to a species level and could be identified even thousands of years after the organic body surrounding it in life had decayed to nothing. Every plant on that chart was important. But this one topped them all – and for a very good reason.

This was the Rosary Pea. Exotic. Beautiful. *Fatal.*

As the pieces fell into place, each one felt like a glass shard to Ivy's heart. This was no ordinary plant. Abrin, the poison within its gilded skin, was seventy-five times more potent than its mephitic cousins. As little as three micrograms of the substance could kill a human adult, less than the amount contained in a single seed. To remove the toxin from its hard case was to risk death itself. In her modern world, Ivy learned there had been fatalities caused by simply pricking a finger while drilling a tiny hole to bead the pretty things for jewellery. To ingest the toxin of the Rosary Pea seed was to trigger a debilitating breakdown of every cell in a person's body, as each cell was stripped in turn of its cardinal ability for protein synthesis. The bloody vomiting and diarrhoea, seizures, hallucinations and fluid within the victims' lungs would begin after only a day. Within a week, the liver, kidneys and spleen would shut down. There was no antidote and no way back from the pain. A victim could only hope for death.

A Swift Death.

Ivy gingerly touched the glossy seeds hanging from their broken pod. The cherry red and black markings no longer seemed beautiful. She recognised their true intention - in nature, they symbolised a warning. Ivy couldn't hold back the shiver that traced her spine. *Like an inverted black widow spider.* Yes, nature did have a way of imitating life - and death. There was no relief in the validation of Ivy's suspicion, in fact, she would desperately rather have proven herself wrong. *But it all fits. Abrin dissolves in water. It remains stable through heat and time. Even diluted it was more than enough to murder.* It was the perfect weapon to kill someone at arm's length.

Urgency stung her into action.

"Trahg and Turi, hide! Stay here with Kyah until I return. Do *not* follow me." The waterhole was close. Ivy needed evidence. Only then would she tell Krue and the remainder of the tribe that they had so much more to fear than the loss of their hunting trails by the karathah. They would now fear genocide.

She needed evidence. Only then would they truly believe her. Ivy raced ahead in the direction they had been travelling and with a snarl of annoyance, Krue followed.

Ivy burst through the trees into the clearing. Low movement by the hot spring startled her and Ivy tripped, landing heavily on her knees in the grass. A Komodo? She scrambled up again, wide-eyed and panting, realising her carelessness. She braced for an attack. She met the eyes of a man. *A karathah man.* He had jumped to his feet at her sudden appearance, scattering a handful of red seeds to the muddy bank, and now he stood tall and rigid with a look of horror frozen on his face. Ivy recoiled at the sudden strangeness again at seeing another person as tall as herself. Weeks of towering over the hobbits had reconditioned her to a new normality and she stared at the man, unable to pull her eyes away. His skin was dark and smooth and his eyes bright. His face was chiselled, with high cheekbones and cropped thick, wiry hair. Long strings of red beads hung from his hair. Ivy realised, with a sickening jolt, that the beads were all too familiar. *Rosary Pea Seeds.* Dozens of them, threaded tightly and falling to his shoulders in a bunch.

As the man drew his eyes from Ivy's pale feet up to her blazing red hair, he recoiled. Instinctively, Ivy tightened her fist around the spear. The man's eyes flicked back to his own spear against the tree behind him.

Ivy's muscles contracted, ready to defend herself. The man copied. He growled, menacing and deep in his throat like an animal.

With a shout, Krue charged out from the trees behind Ivy. He was yelling, furious at having been left behind. Krue followed her line of sight to the karathah man beside the waterhole.

The two hunters, so unequally sized, locked eyes and Ivy watched, horrified as the karathah's pupils narrowed and his lip curled into a sneer. Then he dragged his scrutiny back over Ivy's body as if surveying her in a new light. She spun to face Krue, who had pulled up short beside her. *Dear God, no.* Krue's round eyes burned with pure hatred.

"Tikan." The name fell from his lips like a prayer. "Mira hea, Tikan."

Ivy didn't need a translation. The pain was carved into his face. *My child - Tikan.* The ghostly fingers of his ruined hand gripped the spear shaft as he tore his fury from the man's eyes up to meet Ivy's. There was no fear, none at all. Only accusation. Betrayal. He spat at her feet.

"No, Krue!" He moved fast, launching forward and hurling his spear toward the man beside the waterhole. The Homo sapien was faster. He sprang aside, anticipating the spear which landed with a *thunk* into the tree trunk behind. He dropped to the grass, grabbed something, then hurtled himself toward the hobbit. Ivy leapt between them as the karathah man bore down. With gritted jaw and a snarl his intent switched to Ivy as he raised a thin bladed knife high above his head.

With an ear-splitting screech, Kyah barrelled by Ivy's side to aid her defence. Ivy screamed, both for Krue in his blind rage and Kyah in her blind protection as she struggled to reach the man's knife. Kyah leapt toward the karathah hunter, knocking Krue off his path with such force that he fell, snapping his head onto a rock at the edge of the waterhole. He lay still.

Ivy felt the full force of the karathah's weight as he knocked her down. Her own spear fell out of reach. The man spat words into her face as she struggled to push him away. He grabbed Ivy's throat with one hand and brought his knife down hard with the other. Ivy grabbed his wrist with both hands. He stabbed at the air in front of her chest forcing the knife down. Ivy struggled to push it back, reeling. Her lungs felt as if they would burst. Suddenly the added weight of Kyah was on them. The bonobo threw her fists against the man's back, pummelling him. White blurred the edges of Ivy's vision. In desperation, she brought her knee up hard between the man's legs. His limbs crunched inward, giving her a split second of relief. She heaved air into her lungs, choking on it as it came. Ivy pushed the man aside, blindly punching and kicking him off. He screamed in pain as Kyah's sharp canine's found the wrist that held his knife. The blade fell to the ground. Ivy snapped her elbow to his nose, hearing a sickening crack as his septum split. She pulled herself shaking to her feet. The man was struggling to knock Kyah away.

"Kyah - No!" Still screeching in fear and possessing far beyond the strength Ivy had herself, the bonobo responded. She retreated a few steps away with an open mouthed grin of fear. Ivy grabbed her spear from the grass. A glint of stone at her feet revealed the hunter's knife. She threw herself onto it as the man reached out. She flattened his hand underfoot and picked up the knife. With a weapon in each hand, Ivy aimed both at his exposed neck. She carefully flicked the spear through the curtain of red beads in his hair.

"I know what you've done," Ivy said.

She knew he couldn't understand her, but still, Ivy felt compelled to make him bear the accusation. There was no doubt in her mind this man had poisoned the hot spring. The seeds he had dropped were the same as the empty husks he wore shamelessly threaded through his hair. *Fatal.* He was responsible for the deaths of at least twenty hobbits, and, with a sickening twist of her gut, perhaps Krue indirectly as well, who still lay unmoving by the rocks. The hobbit's reaction had been instant; he had recognised this man. With the beaded hair and arrogant sneer he wore, Ivy wasn't surprised. She would never forget his face either. Ivy guessed that Krue's missing fingers and murdered daughter were somehow linked to the karathah that now lay sprawled before her.

"You killed them. Why? What's worth killing for?"

The man snarled in response, his eyes darting away, assessing his options. He was clearly outnumbered and had lost his knife. Ivy saw his spear, twice the length of her own, still leaning against a tree near the water's edge. She had caught him off guard and knew she wouldn't be so lucky again.

"Go!" She prodded her spear against the man's bare neck and he scrambled to his feet. "Leave!" Recognising the escape she was offering, the hunter gave Ivy and Kyah a final look of cold calculation. Almost against his own will, he turned and ran. He was gone within seconds. Kyah shrieked after him into the forest, then turned and raced back the way they had come. Ivy guessed the bonobo wanted to check that Trahg and Turi were still safe, wherever she had left them. Ivy rushed over to Krue.

The hobbit was breathing but unconscious. A dark bruise was swelling on the side of his head.

"You're going to have a terrible headache old man," she said. Ivy rearranged his limbs so that he was curled on his side and then walked over to collect the karathah's spear. It was slender and ornately decorated with a delicate stone tip. The hobbit-made spear she carried herself was crude in comparison.

Holding a spear in each hand - one hobbit made, strong and utilitarian; and the other sapien made, beautiful and fast - Ivy had never felt more conflicted. One species was killing the other.

Systematically. Deliberately. Violently.

Even without the aid of poison, Homo sapiens would come to triumph through their own ingenuity. They were an adaptive species, prolific and clever. Unstoppable. The hobbits could change, but had done so only when they had finally recognised their handicap. They chose change because they were desperate to survive. It should be too little, too late.

But now Ivy was giving them something which was not rightfully theirs. The adaptive knowledge of another species of hominid.

The very ones that were killing them.

On the ground was a wooden bowl, again, intricately carved. It was over half full of the Rosary Pea seeds. Beside the bowl was an awl. It was made from bone, finely ground to a needle point. It was sharp and strong enough to pierce the black, glossy shells. Ivy guessed that he simply threw the punctured seeds directly into the water, letting the poison leach out. A quick look confirmed her theory. A handful of seed husks had already been washed into the pool crevice by the movement of water. Ivy stripped several large leaves from a nearby tree and wrapped the bowl, awl and some of the whole seeds tightly within it. She wound the package tightly with dry grass. She now had evidence.

Kyah returned. Turi and Trahg were again travelling on her back. Ivy took Trahg's tiny hand with the amulet between them.

"What happened to Krue?" Trahg's bottom lip trembled. Clinging in front of him, Turi watched with eyes like saucers.

"Kyah accidentally knocked him over and he hit his head," Ivy said. Trahg stiffened slightly on his bonobo perch.

"She's never hurt anyone before," Trahg said.

"She didn't mean to hurt him," Ivy assured the boy. "She was trying to help him. There was a karathah hunter here - a bad man. He's been turning the water bad and making our hunters sick. That's why they are dying."

"And Kyah killed the karathah to save Krue?" The boy looked curiously around the waterhole clearing for a body. Death had never been hidden from him before.

"We didn't kill him, we chased him away."

"You should have killed him. Krue would have killed him," said Trahg.

"Yes well, Krue was hurt and I, well, I decided not to."

"But why?" Trahg said stubbornly. "The karathah are stealing our land. I heard Gihn say so. And you said he killed our hunters." Trahg puffed out his little chest proudly. "I would kill him back."

"Then you would die, Trahg," Ivy said, sighing. "The karathah are much too big for you. And you too Turi," Ivy added to the littlest boy who was nodding emphatically to Trahg's declaration.

Was it that simple? *I would kill him back.* An eye for an eye. Could this struggle for survival only end with warfare? Ivy shuddered at the memory of the man with his hands around her throat. The Rosary Pea braids had hit her face as she struggled. The poison in them was indestructible. Like him. Like the species he belonged to. *I fought him with my bare hands.* The memory brought bile to Ivy's throat and she turned away from Trahg and closed her eyes tight against the rising nausea. Now that she was safe and she had the evidence of his attempted genocide, her nerve failed her. Ivy's hands began to shake. *Could I have killed him? Would I have been justified if I did? He tried to kill me. Yes. My life is worth fighting for.* Ivy took a deep breath, calming her nerves. *He was killing them. They deserve to live too.* She had never felt so dislocated from her own species. *No, not all of them. It's just one man.*

Ivy surrounded herself in thoughts of a different man, in a different place, and a different time.

Eventually, her breathing evened out and she gathered her

resolve. Ivy tied the two spears to her back using a spare strip of hide from Krue's utility belt. Krue stirred slightly when Ivy moved him, but remained unconscious.

"We have a problem," Ivy said to the waiting boys. Trahg had climbed off Kyah and taken her hand. "Krue was my guide, so we're just going to have to wait for him to wake up."

"You're lucky we came then; I can show you the way!" Trahg announced.

"No, it's too far, you'll get us lost." The little boy looked offended.

"No, *you'll* get us lost," he pouted. "I know where my home is. I can *feel* it." Without a moment's hesitation, he turned on his heel and strode back into the trees. Kyah looked sideways at Ivy, and then followed Trahg, still carrying Turi on her back.

"Fine." With a resigned sigh, Ivy placed the wrapped bowl gently on Krue's belly and then picked up his lax body in her arms. He was no bigger than a five-year-old child, but had the dense muscles and bones you would expect of an active man. Still, he weighed about the same as Kyah, whom Ivy was used to carrying.

Ivy mulled over Trahg's words as she walked. *I know where my home is. I can feel it.* The tantalising analogy of a homing pigeon came back to her mind.

Trahg was right. Although it took longer with Ivy's burden of Krue, the child led them directly back to Liang Bua cave. Krue had regained consciousness halfway but was weak, so Ivy continued to carry him. Ivy imagined his headache was agony, so made no attempt at conversation. As they ascended the hill to the cave entrance, a crowd gathered. Ivy lowered Krue to his feet. Hands shot out to support him as he swayed unsteadily and exclamations of concern and questions began. Ivy looked down to see Gihn and Xiou pushing their way through. Shahn swept Trahg into an embrace as Turi climbed from Kyah's back into his mother's arms.

"You naughty children! You didn't even tell me where you went, Turi. I thought a Shirakan had eaten you!" Floni scolded. "What happened?"

"I can answer that," someone said. Ivy turned, surprised to hear Krue's voice for the first time since the attack. The old man shot her an accusatory look and then spoke clear and loud across the cave. "Your *Hiranah* went to meet with the karathah." Exclamations of shock pitted the tribe. "The hunter who murdered Tikan was waiting and when I tried to kill him, she and her animal," he pointed a finger stub to Kyah, "attacked me!" He drew a deep breath and turned to face Gihn directly. "I warned you and you didn't listen. You will regret everything. This woman - this *karathah* - has betrayed us all."

CHAPTER 41

ORRIN

"*I* hope you don't mind I came by."

"No! I'm so relieved." Orrin took in the woman's stiff posture, the crease between her eyes and heavy frown. "At least I think I am," he faltered.

Jayne glanced at Dale, snoring softly, slumped over his desk. She raised an eyebrow.

"My lab assistant Dale," Orrin said. "Three days straight trying to figure this thing out. He had to crash sometime."

Jayne scrutinised Orrin's appearance and opened her mouth to comment, but apparently changed her mind. Instead she looked intently about the room, her gaze lingering on the buzzing equipment before finally resting again on Orrin's face. She stood, taking two steps forward and met Orrin in the middle of the room. Holding her hand out, she dropped a black stone into his palm.

"It's yours," she said. "To borrow, mind you. I'll need it back when you're done. It's still an important artefact."

Ivy's amulet felt warm in Orrin's hand. Astonished, Orrin turned the stone over. *I.C.* His heart skipped a beat.

"Why did you change your mind?"

"It's a long story. Let's just say I have an ulterior motive," Jayne said.

This time it was Orrin who raised an eyebrow. "Ulterior motive?"

"Like I said, long story." She glanced to the door. "Look Orrin, I'm not saying I believe you, all I'm saying is that things are bad. If your insane story turns out to be true, it might be better for everyone." Jayne's frown was set and she was clearly going to offer no further explanation.

"Fair play," Orrin said. "What about the amulet though? Like you said, it's an important artefact. Not that I want you to change your mind of course."

Jayne looked agitated. "I'm finished with it – for now. I got the DNA results back. Nothing conclusive, any residues have decayed. The dating is definitive at fifty thousand years though so it's not a site contaminant. Anyway, I can't test it again; it's been contaminated by your DNA now so you may as well use it for your experiments." Orrin had the decency to look ashamed.

"Thanks Jayne, I really appreciate it."

"You'd better. I'm risking my job by giving it to you, not to mention my research." From her jeans pocket Jayne pulled a small plastic artefact bag. She weighed it in her hand momentarily, chewing her bottom lip. With a deep breath she handed it to Orrin. It was another stone tool. "It's this one that's got me stumped. Take a look at it - *through* the bag, do *not* take it out." Curious, Orrin held the bag up to the light.

"What is that scratched on the surface?" The florescent roof lights glistened off the plastic as he turned it. The stone was almost perfectly round and flat on one side.

"It's a river stone, rolled underwater to become smooth - you can tell by the rounded edges. It was found in the same stratigraphic layer as the other one, about a meter away against the interior cave wall. It's not utilitarian; see - it has no sharp edges, no hafting point. There's nothing else like it. It seems entirely non-functional. My guess would be that it's ornamental."

"Okay?"

"Not okay. This stratigraphic layer is found right on cultural transition mark," Jayne said.

"Cultural -"

"Anything found below this layer, in other words, anything we've dated to earlier than fifty thousand years, shows absolutely no inclusion of art or culture. It's all entirely functional. Tools were made to be used and then thrown away or lost. Above this stratigraphic layer though, on our side of the last fifty thousand years, the hobbits in that cave suddenly experienced an explosion of culture - ornamentation on artefacts, symbolic drawings, and cave paintings." At Orrin's perplexed look she explained. "It's not normal, Orrin. Usually there's a transitional period, a few thousand years at least where the old way of life bleeds into the new. With these hobbits though, it's like, *bam*, art appears. Right there, at fifty thousand years ago, and this little guy," she flicked the bag Orrin was holding, "is the earliest one we've found."

Orrin studied the engraved image on the river stone. His mouth went dry and he swallowed hard. "Jaysus, Mary and Joseph - it has five points Jayne. Look at that shape - it's an ivy leaf."

"Yeah, maybe," Jayne said, scratching her fingers through her honey-coloured hair. "It shouldn't be there Orrin. I googled it. Ivy plants are native to the Atlantic Islands, Europe, North-western Africa and Central Southern Asia but only as far as Japan. Fifty thousand years ago, this leaf would never have been seen in Indonesia, much less on a remote island like Flores."

"It's identical to the birthmark on Ivy's thigh," Orrin said.

Jayne spluttered in surprise, and then looked mildly amused. "Well, I'll have to take your word for that." Her voice dropped again, almost to a whisper and she met his eyes cautiously. "The thing is though; I found blood residues on the surface of this one.

That's highly unusual in itself, considering this isn't a tool – it wasn't used for hunting or chopping or scraping, in fact, it wasn't used for anything at all as far as I can tell. But still, there was blood. Red blood cells, dried, mostly degraded. But there were enough. So I did DNA analysis on this one too."

Orrin inhaled sharply. "And?"

"And I found genetic markers for European DNA. *Modern European DNA*. That means that the blood belonged to a modern Caucasian person of European descent; not an archaic Homo sapien and certainly not one of Indonesian origin."

"Ivy's blood?" He cradled the smooth river stone in his fingertips, memorising the shape of the ivy leaf etched on its face. *She made this, I'm sure of it.* The thought that he held a fifty-thousand-year old stone artefact smeared with Ivy's blood terrified him. Perspiration pricked on Orrin's neck and he dropped into a chair.

"I'm not saying it's *Ivy's* blood," Jayne said. "I mean, that's mental. She'd have to have been there- she had to have been there fifty thousand years ago for that to be true. I just can't- I'm just saying it's *something*. Something that really shouldn't be there. I thought you'd want to know." Even so, she looked apologetic. "I'm going to test it again." Jayne held out her hand and reluctantly Orrin handed her the small bag. She turned to leave but stopped at the door, facing him again. Her frown was set hard.

"There's one more thing," Jayne said.

"Yeah?"

"I don't know anything about this woman Ivy and I don't know if you're right, and if she was there," Jayne looked down at the specimen bag in her hands, "or whether she left these – *clues* for someone to find. I don't even know what you did to make this happen- but I'm pretty sure you did something- just- whatever it is, for the sake of those hobbits, I hope you can fix it."

By five in the afternoon, Orrin's vision was blurring with exhaustion. He left the lab and walked towards the refectory, hoping to grab a coffee from the cart vendor before they packed up. The dusk sun fell behind the mostly empty car park ahead. A man in a business suit approached him from a gleaming parked car. He walked briskly but his face was weary.

"Excuse me?" The man called out.

Orrin stopped and waited for the man to reach him. When he did, Orrin glanced at the heavy clipboard in his arm, noting a government seal on its cover. *Animal Research Regulation Department.*

"Do you think you could point me in the direction of the Anatomical Sciences Building, please?" the man asked.

"Anatomy?" Orrin inclined his head, trying to remember where in the sprawling university it was. He vaguely recalled a new wing on the eastern side of campus.

Just as Orrin was about to admit his unfamiliarity with the campus, a plain white van pulled into the loading zone close by. An overalled man jumped out, pulling the back doors wide open and jumping inside. The man beside Orrin sighed and muttered something under his breath.

"You alright, man?" Orrin asked quietly. Although he was a complete stranger, Orrin felt a strange affinity for him. Perhaps it was the dogged look that reminded Orrin of his own exhausted frustration.

The man looked back at him, surprised. He took in Orrin's genuine smile and returned it. "You know those days when you just don't want to come to work?" he said. "This is one of them."

Orrin nodded in sympathy. "I hear you loud and clear." He offered his hand. "Orrin James, physics department."

"Alex Kraymer." *Alex Kraymer.* The name sounded familiar but

Orrin couldn't place it. At least, not until Alex had ushered over the overalled man who was now rolling a large metal crate toward them on a trolley. The crate had a complicated number lock on its door and a widely meshed opening at the top.

"Delivery from DHS?" Alex asked the courier.

"Yeah, for the Anatomy Department. Someone named Greyson's meant to sign for it."

"Tyrone Greyson. Yeah, I'm heading over there now. You can bring the hobbit along." *Hobbit?* Immediately, the familiarity of the suited man's name became apparent. It had been in the newspaper article that Phil had so carelessly tossed onto the table, headlining the civil riots that had brought pharmaceutical giant Cosmitech to ashes. This man had been the government spokesperson that had investigated their malpractice. And right now, Mr Alex Kraymer was looking at Orrin expectantly.

"Right, of course!" Orrin gushed. "Sure, sure, the Anatomy Department. Actually, I was just heading that way myself. Why don't we walk together?" The lie came too easily. After Orrin's endless path of obstacles, this man felt like a prize.

"So," Orrin tried to look nonchalant, as he eyed the cage, leading the men by the longest route he could think of toward the Eastern wing, "Another hobbit, hey?"

"That's right," Alex replied politely.

"They're quite the topic of conversation lately, aren't they? After that holy show in the city." For all his attempts to seem casual, Orrin couldn't mask his nervous habit of pushing his fingers into the bridge under his glasses as he glanced back to the steel cage. He shoved his hands in his pockets.

"Famous for all the wrong reasons," Alex sighed. "Cosmitech was a bad case and believe me, that's saying something."

Orrin couldn't help himself. "Why hobbits though? I mean, why didn't they use chimps or rats?" Alex glanced at Orrin as they walked. He seemed hesitant to answer, searching Orrin's face for some sort of judgment on the matter. Orrin reassured him with a shrug of his shoulders and tried to look disinterested.

"Honestly, I don't know the first damn thing about them, I'm just genuinely curious as to why they're causing such an uproar," he lied.

Alex nodded and visibly relaxed. "Other animals do get used of course," he said. "Plenty of them. There are too many lab rats out there to count. They breed fast, share basic anatomy with us and they're easy to contain. Other primates, yeah, lots of them in research labs too." Alex's eyes searched the sky as he walked. "Maybe in the vicinity of 130,000 worldwide. Chimps, bonobos, gorillas and orangs included. But hobbits, well, if you can get a hobbit for your research, you're getting the cream of the crop. There are maybe 40,000 of them in labs already, used for everything from neurosurgical trials to cosmetic surgery techniques. Lots of deep brain tissue research on live hobbits is being done using micro-electrode stimulation under the cranial plate - you can't do that sort of thing on humans obviously. Ugly stuff. It's kept out of the pubic eye for a reason." Alex looked grim.

"Not lately, though." Orrin pushed, remembering the graphic placards of the Cosmitech riot.

"No, not lately," Alex agreed. "The thing is, hobbits share 99.5% of our DNA, so for human medical trials, they're perfect – you get the human component without the ethical barriers."

"Do they get results?"

"Sometimes. In 1955 almost one hundred thousand of them were killed to create the vaccine for polio. Virtually eradicated the virus by 1965 and we still use that same vaccine today. Big sacrifice, big reward for humanity."

"Sure, but which version of humanity?" Orrin couldn't help but note.

Alex took a deep sigh. "It's the age old argument, isn't it? Whether advances in the human condition brought about by hobbit experimentation are undertaken at the expense of human character. Do unto others..."

They continued walking for a few minutes in silence as they each considered those words. Orrin followed the line of buildings, hoping he was still on the right track. The courier pushed the cage behind them as they walked, content to keep to himself.

Finally, Alex spoke again. "I don't like what I do, you know. I enable pain and death everyday. But if I didn't do it, imagine how much worse their lives might be. The animals in labs get the raw end of the deal, but at least I can make sure they get food and water, vet care and pain relief while they're being used. I make the corps accountable. You don't want to know some of the cases I've had to deal with, mate. It'd make your stomach turn. It's a hard line to walk, but I feel like I'm making a difference."

Orrin nodded. "What are the chances it'll change for them?" he asked.

Alex considered that for a moment. "Pretty slim I'd say. I mean, there's been a push for legislation to extend basic human rights to them for some time. They'd have the right to live, the protection of individual liberty and the prohibition of torture. Same as us. To extend our rights to non-human primates would ensure invasive research practices are more regulated. Some practices could be outlawed."

"So why not do it then?" Orrin asked.

Alex shrugged. "Well, the argument goes back and forth in parliament, never any closer to a resolution," he said. "Giving them human rights would likely affect human welfare, as in *sapien* welfare. Obviously, the benefits to human medical research could be severely stunted as potential new discoveries are shunned in favour of civil rights for hobbits. Does the greater good to human society outweigh the cost of hobbit lives in laboratories?"

"Surely they'll need a lab alternative at some point though? Computer simulations, tissue culture, that sort of thing," Orrin argued. "In my reality, I mean, um, from what I understand, most apes are on the brink of extinction anyway aren't they?"

"Absolutely. But that weighs against them just as strongly. Most politicians advocate that the remainder of apes including hobbits, should be used for human medical advancement while they're still a viable resource."

"A viable resource, hey?" Orrin shook his head. That term had once been used on him. *So clinical.* He inclined his head toward the steel cage rolling behind them down the path. "So what's happening to this *viable resource* then?"

Alex flicked through his folder of paperwork. "It's publicly accessible information so I guess I can tell you. Twelve-year-old male. Bred in captivity - looks like this one's a brain study. Greyson has an extensive research grant and runs a pretty strict lab. Apparently we never have any problems with his treatment methods. Aside from the obvious of course - his resources need to be euthanized for the protocol to work. He's got a bunch of PhD's in there analysing the magnetite in their frontal lobe, trying to figure out how it all works."

Orrin stopped walking. "Why on earth do they have magnetite in their brains?"

Alex looked up at him, more surprised than before. "I'd have thought you'd already know, being a physicist and all." He frowned at Orrin's blank look. "Magnetism. For their navigation, of course. They have homing capabilities like a pigeon, an amazing directional sense. Not to mention the high amount of cryptochrome proteins in their eyes and sinus bones – they've got magnetoception all sewn up. It's some sort of synchronistic development from evolving in South East Asia. All that metal that's getting ripped out of the continental shelf; we only found it because of the hobbits. Colonials discovered them and their hardwired connection to the deposits underground, then mined the bejeezus out of it. If it weren't for those hobbits, half of the planet would be missing its electricity right now."

Orrin was stunned. *Hard-wired connection to the metal deposits under South East Asia.* He felt like his mind exploded and had no idea what to do with the new information. There was something so tantalizing about the idea that an animal, human, whatever is was - had evolved such an intimate connection with metal. And not just any metal, but *magnetite,* the elusive crystals thought to give animals the ability to sense the polarity of the Earth's magnetic field. And the Earth's magnetic field, now *that* was something Orrin could get excited about.

Miraculously, they had paused in front of a sign welcoming visitors to the Department of Anatomical Sciences. The cage behind them jolted on its trolley and a quiet whine came from inside.

"The tranquilizer's wearing off," the courier offered.

Orrin stepped closer to the cage and saw that the ends of five small fingers had curled through the wide mesh opening on the top, gripping the crossed wires. Again, a soft whine came from the black hole inside the cage and Orrin could just make out the shine of eyes looking up from the dark. *Twelve years old.* Orrin felt sick. He turned to Alex who was eyeing the building laboratory directory.

"Will he feel it?"

Alex's grim expression returned and his shoulders sagged under the weight of responsibility once more. "Absolutely." He shook Orrin's hand and laid the other on the top of the cage. "But I'll do what I can for him. I always do."

The physics lab was empty when Orrin returned. He was relieved. Dale's confidence in their ability to recreate the energy shifts seemed desperately hinged on Orrin's own. Those times that Orrin inevitably felt he'd hit another wall, Dale floundered and it took all of Orrin's remaining energy to drag him back up to keep working. Exhausted and sick of being under an emotional microscope, Orrin collapsed into his office chair.

There was no doubt in Orrin's mind that Ivy was the catalyst for some monumental shift in human evolution. *Homo floresiensis. Hobbit.* The very name itself was absurd, but the reality of their impact was devastating. Their existence had brought environmental ruin into the twenty-first century and social chaos onto the streets. For all that he'd tried not to think of it, the blood on that river stone came back to plague him. *What did they do to you?* Orrin shuddered at a new vision that swum behind his burning eyes. Ivy bound and helpless, a sacrificial blade bearing swiftly upon her throat in primitive appeasement to some archaic idol. *Jaysus, no. She would fight. Wouldn't she?*

That shield she cloaked herself with had deflected Orrin's prying questions so skilfully he'd almost missed her talent for it. She had let him stumble around her instead, hidden and safe in her own mind, always the objective observer.

No, not always.

Her blanket of self-protection couldn't hide the rebellion in her eyes during that rally.

A shield it was, but shields could be cast off. There was fire inside of her.

And Orrin knew. *She would fight.*

He considered going home for the night, but not seriously enough. *What's the point?* Here he could work. At home he would be plagued with nightmares, failing again and again. He needed something to distract him while he worked. Orrin looked around. Fallen from the side of his desk onto an old oscilloscope, Orrin noticed his headphones. *Music.* It was as good a distraction as any.

Orrin pulled his phone from his pocket and thumbed through his playlist. *<Untitled>*. He sucked in a breath and felt the chill that raced his spine. He'd forgotten.

*

Ivy had pushed her fringe behind her ear and he'd watched, wishing he had the nerve to reach out and do it for her. The cello case was balanced on her foot, almost standing as tall as she.

He'd looked around the room curiously. "No audience?"

"Just me. It's a good place to practice," Ivy had shrugged, blushing. "The acoustics are great and there's an audio recording facility set up for tutorial sessions. Students use it so they can slacken off in class and download the lectures later." Typical. Orrin laughed as she continued. "When it's empty, I record my cello practice so I can play it back at home. It helps me pick up mistakes."

"I bet there aren't any. Mistakes, I mean."

*

And he had done it. On a whim later that night, he'd logged into the tutorial room audio files and downloaded the track before it was deleted. *Le Cygne - The Carnival of the Animals.* And it was beautiful. Orrin didn't know much about music; he'd never played an instrument. But he'd listened to Ivy's cello sing against its bow and was sure he was hearing perfection. He'd played it a few times over, then gone to bed and forgotten it. Until now.

As he touched the play button on his phone, he almost thought it wouldn't work. That this one final thing, undisputed evidence that he had known her and touched her, would disappear as well. But *no.* The recording began. Strings humming softly under a bow. A few notes and plucks to tune.

Then Ivy. That haunting melody that took him right back to her kitchen as if it were yesterday, where she had closed her eyes as she played, lost in the music. Her fingers had danced on the neck of it and Orrin was transfixed, holding his coffee as it went cold, unable to look away. He'd never understood music before. He'd enjoyed it, appreciated the artistry, of course. But finally,

Orrin suddenly understood it. Ivy's soul and fire were resonating within the cello's song. *The Carnival of the Animals.* Her passion and purpose. *The Animals.*

It had survived. Of course it had, his phone had been with him, in his pocket. It had been protected, as he had himself. And he had never been more grateful for small mercies. More than the river stone or amulet, this was truly Ivy.

Orrin listened to the track on repeat for an hour. Unlocking his desk drawer, his hand closed over her amulet. Removed from its archaeological wrappings, it should have been stone cold against the locked metal drawer, but instead it radiated heat like warm skin. He couldn't put it down again.

The sky grew dark unnoticed. Trapped in his tiny office, Orrin sank back into his work, looking for that elusive link that might explain how the bizarre measurements his laboratory had undergone could unravel Ivy's disappearance.

A shrill ring tone jolted his attention from the computer screen. It was past midnight. *Dimitri Angelis.* He thumbed the receiver in relief.

"Dimi?"

CHAPTER 42

IVY

*I*t was all Ivy could do to hold herself back. She clenched her jaw as Krue regaled the entire tribe with a tale of her duplicity, revelling in the shocked whispers and panic he provoked. As much as she itched to grab Krue and shake the truth out of him it would only have served to validate his lies. Gihn held the amulet tightly against her wrist, acting as translator.

"How dare you!" Ivy finally said, towering over him. "I saved your life! That karathah hunter would have killed you without a second thought if I hadn't got between you. I nearly died to save you and you're still questioning my loyalty?" She was livid. "I've already lost everything for this tribe. It was *you* that brought *me* here, Krue. *Your* people! You stole me by calling me here and now you thank me with horrid accusations! Perhaps I *should* join the karathah; at least they might appreciate me!" The minute the words left her lips, Ivy regretted it. A collective gasp echoed through the crowd and for a moment, Ivy imagined many were seeing her as she really was; an outsider and Homo sapien, and not the saviour they'd received her as. No doubt some of them, like Krue, saw only a threat in her presence, but for the most part, the tribe had accepted and perhaps even loved her. She scowled at Krue who looked spitefully gratified at her outburst. Ivy took a calming breath. She addressed the group at large.

"I went to hot springs to find proof of what is causing the Swift Death. And I did find it. The karathah hunter that we found there has been poisoning the water. He has been deliberately killing your hunters with this plant." Ivy held down the bowl of Rosary Pea seeds that the man had left by the waterhole. The tribe members shuffled forward, each taking a look at the seeds.

"Spider seeds," Lahstri said. "The juice inside does kill." Krue shot her an angry look, but she lifted her chin slightly. "I should have recognised the symptoms in our hunters."

"I figured out that the only thing the sick hunters had in common was that they all travelled furthest from the cave on the hunting trails. It's not a place you would often go, Lahstri," Ivy said kindly to the medicine woman. "These plants don't grow near the water source, but I saw them in the Oleos Grove, and then again on our journey to the hot springs where I recognised them." Ivy said. "You would not have expected them to be collected and drilled open then emptied into the spring," Ivy said. "This is not your fault."

"Still," Lahstri looked downcast. "If I had suspected it earlier -"

"You may have put yourself in danger by going there." The tiny old woman was no match for a karathah hunter if he happened on her at the hot spring. "It was the same hunter that killed Tikan, Lahstri," Ivy said gently. "Kyah and I fought him and chased him away, but he left his belongings behind. I brought them to you to prove what he did." She shot an angry look to Krue. "The most important thing is this; the Swift Death is over as long as the hunters keep away from that waterhole."

A hush fell across the crowd as they processed Ivy's words. Seconds later, she heard a wail from somewhere within the group. Like a shock wave, the pent up grief and anger rippled through the tribe.

"They were murdered by the karathah," someone shouted.

"They suffered!" Called someone else. "A pitiful death. Such pain!"

"It was murder! Just like Tikan!"

They turned to each other in consolation. Juna and a handful of others with dead mates let silent tears fall at the injustice. But many raised their fists in the air, clamouring and shouting for retribution. There was now a face to blame. A very specific face.

"Please! Listen to me." Ivy said over the din. "We must be very, very careful. This karathah hunter will not give up; I saw the determination in his eyes. I don't know why he's doing this to you but now that he's seen me, I think he'll only try harder." Ivy had no doubt that the girls from the trade offering had alerted their tribe. Now the red-beaded hunter would confirm it. If anything, her presence may have put the hobbits in more immediate danger than they were already in. "His intentions were clear. This man wants me dead just as much as he wants to kill all of you." She choked back her own fear.

For what seemed the hundredth time since she arrived, Ivy ached to go home. She wanted to brush aside the faded lemon curtains from her kitchen to see Tom down below with his rake. Or lose herself in the comfort of her books and skulls and papers. Ivy's fingertips ached to feel the softly vibrating strings of her cello and smell the faint musk of resin on her bow. *And Orrin.* A touch that was so far out of reach, it no longer existed. She pushed the ache down and pulled herself up tall.

"But how can we stop him?" called Floni, still hugging Turi close to her chest. "The karathah are too big to fight."

Ivy knew she was right. Homo sapiens were a formidable enemy to have. The odds were not only in their favour, but in the future, they had already won.

The eyes of the tribe all turned to her, waiting for a reply. Ivy summoned every ounce of conviction she had left.

"Krue was right about one thing," she said, "you are not too small to fight back. And I will fight with you."

Ivy had fed the surviving poisoned hunter charcoal from the hearth, in the hope it would absorb the toxins within his digestive tract, but he was too far gone. His wasted body was removed before sunrise and the tribe grieved anew.

Later, Ivy joined a group of women foraging, leaving Kyah to teach symbols to the children at the cave. The women held digging sticks and carried long hide bags draped across their backs. Bending to dig a turmeric root, Shahn groaned loudly, holding her distended belly. Ivy, not far behind, dashed over.

"Is something wrong?"

"No, sweet one." Shahn smiled up at Ivy, a little breathless. "The baby moves, that's all. She is close to joining us and tells me so more frequently." Shahn pulled Ivy's hand gently onto her pregnant belly. It felt as hard as a rock but after a few moments, softened.

"She?" Ivy asked. "Do you think you're carrying a girl?"

Shahn smiled. "A mother always knows."

"Well, I don't want you to hurt yourself or her. I'll do this," Ivy said. The tiny mother reluctantly lowered herself onto the grass. A handful of women gathered around her.

"Do you need to return home?" Lahstri knelt down, her hands spread across Shahn's middle. With skilled fingers, she assessed the unborn baby's movements, then answered her own question. "No. The false contractions have begun though. It won't be long now, perhaps by the next full moon."

Ivy glanced at the sky. A waxing moon was creeping up. *Just over another month then.* Although she had no way to test it yet, Ivy suspected that Homo floresiensis may differ from her own species of human in yet another way. Using Rinap and Leihna as a reference, Ivy guessed that young hobbit women reached sexual maturity by about twelve years old. Whether the gestational period of hobbit babies was similarly shortened was an idea that intrigued Ivy. A common ancestor to both humans and hobbit may have carried their babies for as little as eight months and despite other factors being involved, the general tendency was for smaller mammals to have shortened periods of gestation. If it was true, the marginal time advantage that gave the hobbits in creating each new generation might one day prove invaluable. Ivy made a mental note to add the hypothesis to her field journal and keep track of the next pregnancy. *Not that anyone will ever read it of course, but still.* The battered journal had become the only bridge between her old life and new. She wrote in it religiously, dreading the day she would inevitably run out of pencils.

The other women began discussing the upcoming labour. With the mortality rate extreme and their family declining so rapidly, they rushed to ease Shahn's worries.

"It will be a strong child, you will see," one woman reassured her.

"Another gift like Trahg," added Floni.

"We'll celebrate for many moons to come," Kora patted Shahn's arm.

Ivy wandered away with Shahn's digging stick. A few metres ahead, a woman was standing alone, with only her head and shoulders above the long grass. She was staring at the gathered women with a look of utter wretchedness on her face.

Ivy knew that look. She had once worn it herself, before she learnt to mask her heartache for the sake of other's comfort. The woman's face wore a shroud of grief.

"That's Emiri." Ivy looked down to find Leihna standing beside her.

"Is she alright? Should I say something?"

"She wouldn't answer you if you did." Leihna adjusted a heavy bag of tubers on her shoulder. Her digging stick hung from her wrist by a string of woven bamboo. "She doesn't talk anymore."

"She looks so sad," Ivy said. "I've never even noticed her before."

"I don't think she wants to be noticed."

Ivy felt a familiar twist of concern. "Was it the karathah?"

"No," Leihna answered. "Emiri has grieved for a very long time. Her mate, Budi, was the first to die of the Swift Death, so I suppose the karathah are to blame for that. He suffered badly. But she was already silent. Emiri has lost five children, all born too soon or died not long after birth. She's been broken by sadness." Leihna turned to look up at Ivy and suddenly seemed much older than her twelve years. "It's the Slow Death, Hiranah. It is worse than the Swift Death because it strikes us at our heart - our family. Without our family, we're nothing."

Ivy took a deep breath. "There must be something I can do to help her?"

"No," Leihna said. "It's especially difficult for her now with Api just born and my sister not far due. She enjoys watching the children play though, I've seen her. At times we think perhaps she's coming back to us. But then, after dusk song every night, Emiri walks through the forest calling for them." Leihna stopped abruptly and looked up. Her eyes brimmed with tears. "It's the only sound she makes."

Ivy bent down and hugged the girl. She rubbed their foreheads together gently.

"I'm going to change the way things are, Leihna," Ivy promised. "It might be too late for Emiri, but it's not for you."

By now the group of women had begun to move on. Ahead, the forest closed in and sheltered the river from view. Phren ushered Emiri amongst them, so Ivy and Leihna followed behind.

Leihna took her hand. "There are berries growing in this thicket, I'll show you where. Yesterday Filhia ate so many she was sick."

A shrill bird call broke the breeze. Leihna yanked Ivy's arm down roughly.

"Lie flat, Hiranah! Quick! There are karathah ahead!"

Ivy collapsed to her stomach, pressing her cheek to the ground in the long grass. Her heart was hammering.

"How do you know?" Ivy asked.

"That call was Rinap, scouting ahead. She must have seen them."

A different bird call sounded, but this time Ivy recognized Rinap's tone underneath it.

"There are lots of them," Leihna breathed. "More than us."

"But what about Shahn! Where is she?" Ivy strained to see through the grass, but saw no sign of the women she had been walking with until a moment ago.

"Shahn knows what to do. Stay here while I find the others." Leihna jumped into a crouch and took off like lightning, disappearing into the sea of grass.

Slow minutes passed. Ivy's face prickled with dirty sweat. Ants began to trail up her arms and legs, biting as they went. She flicked them off, barely daring to breathe. *Shahn's pregnant belly,* Ivy worried, *she can't run as fast as the others, or hide as seamlessly, either. Leihna's been gone too long. Something must be wrong.* Making up her mind, Ivy inched forward on her elbows, taking care not to let her bright red hair break the surface of grass. Crawling in the direction that Shahn had been standing, the shadow of the forest grew cooler and heavier. A rush of water told Ivy she was close to the river. Raucous voices bounced off the water's surface. Raking the undergrowth with her eyes, Ivy crept toward the voices, hugging the darkest patches of cover, then sat back, crouching against the side of a buttressed tree. The long grass had thinned. She was barely hidden.

Then she saw them.

A group of sapien women stood, ankle deep in water, chatting and swaying drift nets through the shallows. They were slender and graceful, with thick black plaits hanging down their backs. A handful of small children played on the opposite shore, giggling and splashing in the shallows. Further upstream, three men stood intently still, knee deep in the water with long fishing spears frozen just above the surface.

Ivy's breath hitched. She thrust her back hard against the tree behind her, willing it to swallow her into safety.

It was Him. The toxic red seeds hung in clumps from his hair, tapping his shoulders as he turned his head incrementally, angling the spear. *Murderer.* Ivy's hands shook as adrenaline hit her veins. For the briefest moments, the scene before her had seemed so harmless. The children's joy was infectious and the good natured chattering of their mothers was serene. But this man, Ivy knew, was anything but safe. *Snap!* He lunged his spear down, dragging up an impaled, writhing fish. He grinned at one of his comrades, then pulled it from the shaft, and tossed it into a basket on the river's edge.

Ivy's heart thundered as she cursed her stupidity. *My spear is at the cave. I don't even have a blade...* Ivy swallowed drily, preparing to back away. There was no way she'd survive if he caught her here. *God knows how I managed it the first time.*

As Ivy slipped backward, someone brushed by.

"Emiri!" Ivy whispered as loud as she dared. The woman didn't respond. Instead she stood staring at the karathah, her body barely concealed by the undergrowth. Emiri's pupils were dilated. She cocked her head to the side. A faint smile haunted her lips. Ivy stretched toward her as far as she dared. Her fingers grazed the woman's wrist. Emiri stepped forward, directly toward the riverbank.

"Please, no! Come back." Ivy begged in a whisper. "Emiri!" Ivy couldn't follow her. Where the hobbit was small and naturally concealed by dark skin and soft movements, Ivy was too big, too white and too clumsy. When her second whispered plea was ignored, Ivy followed the woman's line of sight. Instantly, her gut twisted in fear and a fresh break of sweat drenched her face. *No please! No, no, no!*

A Homo sapien baby was asleep at the forest edge in a basket made of woven grass. It looked no more than six months old and was curled peacefully in the shade while its mother netted fish. No one was paying it any attention. They had no reason to fear for it with the hunters nearby.

Emiri stepped clear out of the forest cover. She walked across to the baby. Her face was suddenly radiant, lit up like a candle from inside. Pure maternal love poured from her into the sleeping form as she picked it up. The child was markedly different to the tiny woman holding it. It had a stub of a chin and a wide forehead and was almost as big as three-year-old Turi. But Emiri clearly saw no difference that mattered. She turned away, oblivious to the danger the baby held as Ivy watched, petrified from the long grass. Emiri walked slowly back to the trees, cooing softly as she cradled it in her arms. For the briefest of moments, the broken woman was whole.

I have to stop her. As Ivy stepped forward, she caught a glimpse of one of the karathah women turning. A shrill scream shattered the tranquility. Emiri looked up, as if seeing Ivy for the first time. But there was no fear within her eyes. Instead, Emiri looked down again at her own arms, pulled the baby tightly to her chest and, with a glint of resolve, began to run.

Straight toward Ivy. With the sapiens close behind.

Ivy turned and raced through the trees behind Emiri. Shouts rose behind them. Ivy stumbled. She threw a look over her shoulder. The red beaded hunter was gaining ground; the two fishermen and two women at his heels. The baby's mother was pleading through tears as she tore ahead, fuelled by a desperate surge of adrenaline. Jostled from its slumber, the baby woke and began to cry. Emiri hugged it tight. It cried harder.

The broken woman looked down at it. She slowed. The unseeing glaze began to shadow her eyes once more. Ivy watched, nauseated as the tiny mother turned away, letting the shroud of grief fall back over her. *She knows.*

Emiri collapsed to the ground, curling over the baby's wailing body protectively. With eyes for no one but the child, Emiri stayed there, waiting for her pursuers to catch up. *It wasn't hers.*

"No!" Ivy spun back. A strong arm grabbed her wrist, then another. She was dragged away by Rinap and Xiou. They led her like an arrow through the grass, until Xiou pushed Ivy hard and yelled an instruction to Rinap who took over the lead. Xiou disappeared into the shadows back toward the karathah. Ivy tried to tear her arm free but Rinap was relentless, towing Ivy in her wake. She didn't stop until the cave was in sight.

Ivy shuddered. Kyah's warm hand touched on her shoulder. No one spoke. Firelight flickered across the open pages of her journal. Ivy inscribed memories to the paper that she wished she could expunge from her mind. The page was wet with tears and the graphite smudged under her fist. In the cave around her, Ivy's new family grieved once more.

The karathah couldn't see what was right in front of them. Emiri's pain, her loss, her desperation. The way she cradled the baby. The way she worshipped it. They didn't see a woman at all, much less a mother. In their fear and anger, they saw only an animal stealing their child. So they killed her, like an animal.

"What will you do with her body?" Ivy asked.

Gihn looked up, his frown deepening. "What do you mean? There is nothing we can do."

They were crouched over Emiri's ruined body, laid out under the stars at the entrance to the cave. The woman's long hair had been cruelly hacked off by her murderers, although to what end, Ivy couldn't fathom. When Xiou had returned to protect Emiri, the best he could do, was carry her body home in his arms. It was a pitiful sight. Ivy's tears had fallen as thick and fast as anyone else's.

"In the time I've been with you, five people have died of the Swift Death and another at the hands of the karathah. Now Emiri as well. Where do you take them?" Ivy asked. She recalled the archaeological evidence presented by researchers fifty thousand years ahead of her. Liang Bua cave had offered no clear indication of deliberate burial of the hobbits fossilised within it. But that wasn't to say the concept was entirely out of the question.

Ivy knew well that a minute percentage of bones ever survived the fossilisation process to become representatives of their species within the archaeological record. Bones were more likely to be scavenged by wild animals or washed away by rain. The conditions must be *just so* to allow fossilisation; early post mortem processes, such as mode of death, rapid burial, the depositional environment of sand, mud or water and its consequent attack of bioerosion all played a part. The chance of a particular skeleton undergoing the combination of factors to ensure survival over thousands, or perhaps millions, of years relatively unscathed, was minimal. The evidence for deliberate burial in Liang Bua cave may simply have been destroyed over deep time.

"I'll take her body to the forest or to the high caves, like the others." Gihn sighed. "The animals will consume her, the birds or shirakan. That way the land will be nourished by the life she lost. We are part of nature, it's best if we return to it."

So, no burial then. "I'd like to help you," Ivy said.

There was no small degree of guilt behind her offer. Emiri had clearly been unwell, and for a split second, Ivy had been in a position to help her. Ivy's mind had been too slow to realise the grieving woman's intentions by the river, and her muscles too terrified by the inevitable consequence of acting once she knew. *I could have saved her.*

The following morning at sunrise, Ivy helped Gihn wash Emiri's body by the river. With Shahn's assistance, Ivy had prepared the turmeric root they had collected, in the way she knew traditional Indonesian tribes had done for centuries. Homo sapien tribes of course, but for once Ivy had no remorse at stealing the custom. Sapiens had taken her life; they should give something back. It wasn't much to give. Ivy had ground the turmeric roots and soaked their course filaments in a bowl by the hearth. The burnt orange dye bled into the watery mix, which she collected in a Dalunut mould and set in the fire. After it was baked into a coloured cake, Ivy wrapped it in banana leaves to set and then grated it to a fine powder on a course rock. She rubbed the turmeric powder into Emiri's clean face, hands and the souls of her feet.

"She looks beautiful," Shahn said. The pregnant woman had barely spoken since it happened. Her usually tranquil smile had been replaced with deep creases of worry. Her mate was the fastest and best hunter but Shahn feared it was only time that kept him safe. When Xiou had finally returned with Emiri's body, Ivy saw the battle of devastation versus relief conflict Shahn's features. The woman was exhausted and Ivy knew that could not bode well for the baby she carried.

"We will take her to high caves," Gihn said.

Ivy lifted Emiri in her arms and began the familiar trek along the base of the valley to the place where they would begin to climb. As difficult as it was, Ivy pushed herself, grateful for the burning muscles, sweat and pain she was able to give. Xiou had offered to carry Emiri of course, and Ivy knew he was far stronger despite his small size, but Ivy *needed* to do this.

At the top of the mountain, small caves dotted the terrain, worn away by the travels of shifting water over millennia. Ivy placed Emiri's body in one such cave, no bigger than a bed. She hesitated, watching the birds overhead begin their downward spiral, then, with a swift decision, she reached into the shallow cave and ran her spear across the underside of its dirt ceiling. In a fine shower of earth, Emiri's body was covered. It was buried.

"You be careful little ones, don't get under Gihn's feet today." Shahn sat on the cave floor with a pile of shredded bamboo lengths across her legs. She carefully knotted and wove them into watertight bowls while she rested her aching back and cumbersome belly.

"I'll watch them." Ivy reassured her with a smile. She followed Kyah, Trahg and Turi down the lip of the cave.

"So what is this mystery you want to show me?" She caught up with Gihn, eyeing the hide bag he carried.

"You'll see," he said. Gihn brushed his hand against hers affectionately and continued walking. He hummed under his breath as he went, looking a little smug.

Half way up the barren ridge was a small limestone shelter surrounded by rosewood. This, apparently, was their destination. Kyah drew the symbol 'chase' onto the dirt floor as soon as Ivy looked settled and the boys and bonobo disappeared, giggling into the surrounding branches.

The charred remains of a hearth sat under the overhanging rock and Gihn set about gathering kindling. He pulled a small marsupial skull from his waist pouch and dropped a glowing coal onto the dry grass. He blew it gently. Within minutes, flames were licking at the wood he piled on top. Gihn retrieved a bladder of animal fat from his bag and let it melt on the coals.

The old man smiled conspiratorially. He lay a bone plate on the ground in front of him, then pulled a hide pouch from his bag. It was a roughly cut circle that had been pulled together by a drawstring of fibrous bamboo.

"It was you who gave me the idea, Hiranah," he said.

Ivy felt a sickening lump form in her throat as he tipped the contents of the pouch onto the plate. *Ochre. Damn it.* Gihn had already crushed the rock into a fine golden-brown powder. Now he poured a small amount of liquid fat into it.

One by one, he pulled four more pouches from his bag onto bone plates, each a different shade of ochre, sienna or umber. Each crumbling stone had been washed, dried and burnt or heated to produce their vivid colours and now Gihn mixed fat into the side of each dish. Golden-yellow, reddish-brown, warm brown, dark brown and flame red.

"When you rubbed Emiri's skin with turmeric powder, it was beautiful. Everybody thought so," Gihn said.

Ivy knew Krue and his allies had not been remotely impressed, but decided to let Gihn's compliment stand. Krue had caused her enough grief this week.

"But once her body has been taken by animals, there is nothing left of her. Nothing to say she was here. We have memories, of course, but I thought, if there was a picture, like the ones you use with Kyah, that reminds us of our loved ones, then after they are dead they could still remain."

Oh no. Ivy's stomach was lead. Gihn's actions were leading him to a revelation she had never meant to inspire. With each word, her guilt multiplied and the potential repercussions of it needled at her conscience.

Gihn raised an eyebrow at Ivy's shift in mood, but otherwise didn't acknowledge it. He had grown used to her secrets and Ivy knew his own conscience kept him from invading her privacy any further than necessary. Gihn continued mixing the ochre and fat into a thin paint.

"When we coloured Emiri's hands with turmeric, it was as if she was part of the earth again," he said. "So I wondered what might happen if we painted her hand onto the earth itself. The print might stay there after her body was gone. She could have been remembered by it. So I've been trying, these past few days, to bind coloured clay to the rock the way you bound it to Emiri. I tried first with water, but it washed away in the rain. Then with animal blood, but it too washed away. But now this," Gihn looked triumphant, splaying his hand against the bone plate and holding it up for Ivy to see, stained golden brown and dripping, "This fat keeps the colour in place. If we leave our print with this, we will always be remembered when we die." Ivy pulled the amulet away from him, breaking their connection.

And there it was. *Art.* That incredible shift in culture, that brought symbolism and story together to leave a permanent mark on the world. His species would never be the same. With art came self-expression, imagination and the representation of abstract thoughts. Where their primitive tools were now utilitarian and entirely functional, they would gradually morph into objects of beauty and ornamentation as well. Function and form would be twisted in the endless dance of subjective expression. Ivy had brought Art into their lives.

She had wanted to save the tribe. But she'd never meant to influence their *culture* in such a profound way. It was a golden rule of ethnography broken – Ivy had biased their behaviour with her own. And so much more than she had ever intended.

But I was always going to change them. Just being here has changed them already. Homo floresiensis are meant to become extinct and if the Swift Death was a contributing factor, then I've already changed the course of evolution. That last thought sent chills up her spine.

But were sapien hands the only ones to blame for their extinction? Ivy had her suspicions that the roots of the so-called 'Slow Death' ran far deeper than a poisoned waterhole. *And if I do what they're asking of me - if I help them to understand, adapt,* survive *- then painting and symbols are nothing compared to the impact this* *will have.* And deep down, Ivy knew she had already begun down that path.

"It seems only fair," Gihn rejoined their connection, oblivious to Ivy's internal dilemma, "that your hand be the first to mark this wall, Hiranah. After all, you are part of our family now -"

"No! I can't do that-" Ivy pulled her hand away, her heart racing. It was one thing to change prehistory, but another entirely to leave the archaeological equivalent of a hallmark card on a rock saying *'I was here!'*

She gave a nervous laugh and shook her head. "Thank you but that's not a good idea, Gihn."

The old man frowned. "And why not?"

Ivy gently dropped his hand, stung by an errant thought. *But then again... If I did it, my hand print would survive a lot longer than I ever will here. It will remain in time. Become a part of the future world. Orrin's world. What if he found it? What if he could date it...*"

Ivy held up her hand in the sunlight, wriggling her fingers. She grinned. "No, you're right, of course. I worry too much. It would be an honour to be first on your wall."

"Part of our family, then." Gihn smiled and smeared a dollop of pigment across her open hand. Ushering Ivy forward, he smoothed her hand onto the stone, leaving a golden imprint. He then added his own hand print alongside in ochre red.

"I know it can not fill your loss Hiranah, but you and Kyah are both loved here. This is your home now," he said, earnestly, "and you can consider us all your family. Remember that, you must stay here with us. You belong here. Please, you have to stay."

Ivy raised an eyebrow. "Where could I go anyway? I can't go home."

"No you can't," he said again. "Because this is your home now." Gihn lifted his chin and broke the connection, then turned away, busying himself with the paint. Ivy watched him, her eyes narrowed. She cleared her throat, plastered a smile on her face and took his hand.

"Gihn?" Ivy said, looking thoughtful. "What were the stars like the night I fell from the sky? Can you draw them for me, here on the wall?"

"Why?" Gihn shuffled uncomfortably and looked down at the children playing. Ivy was surprised. Although he often questioned her secrets, Gihn had never once questioned her motives.

"I suppose I just want to remember it. That night changed my life. I know you track the stars, you do it every night. Surely you remember?" Ivy gave her most disarming smile. It was a half truth.

She couldn't simply write a love letter on the wall. Twenty first century English script in a prehistoric Indonesian cave painting would spark scientific anarchy when it was discovered. Ivy bit back a laugh, imagining the fallout. No, if she was going to leave Orrin a message, it should be written in the stars.

"Besides," Ivy added, reconnecting with him, "that night is part of the story of the Life Stone too now, isn't it? The story of your family. I mean *our* family. So you should record it, like the handprints. For future children."

Gihn nodded slowly, seemingly appeased by her response. "You are right; we should all remember it." Appraising the wind-smoothed wall carefully, he dipped his finger into the paint and drew five dots on a clear wall.

"Do you know these stars?" he asked.

"Of course. That's the Southern Cross," said Ivy.

"Southern Cross? Perhaps, to your people. To us, these stars are shaped like the kites of the karathah fishing rafts. We call them karathin." Again he dipped his fingers in the thick yellow dye. "Tonight the moon will be here," he drew a waxing crescent moon near the constellation. "When the moon was full – here -", he traced a perfect golden circle with his index finger, "this is when you fell from the sky at the Falling Place."

"I don't understand," Ivy lied. *Had it only been three weeks?*

Gihn completed the drawing, adding an arc of lunar positions around the constellation at seemingly random angles. "The stars shift with the moon. Every season is different, even every night they sit differently in the sky. Can you not see it?" He frowned, surveying his calendar.

Perfect. "Oh yes, I see what you mean," Ivy smiled. "So this is the where the stars sat on the night I Fell?"

"Yes," Gihn said, stepping back to look at the constellation map. "You are right, Hiranah, we should remember this night."

"Thank you Gihn." *For you, Orrin. The stars.*

They sat under the shade of the Rosewood trees nearby and talked. Gihn was infuriatingly naïve. He was determined to save his tribe from the karathah and the slow death. In his eyes, Ivy's triumph in solving the mystery of the Swift Death only cemented his determination and belief in her.

Gihn assumed the earth his species would survive into, would be as natural as the one he now occupied. Ivy knew better. Modern humans had all but lost their connection to land and those indigenous cultures that still honoured it were often bull-dozed from their sacred sites and gifted shopping centres and concrete in return.

Instead of tainting Gihn's hope further, Ivy simply listened, asking questions occasionally and remembering as much as she could to record in her journal back at the cave. Behind them, the Southern Cross shone in yellow ochre on the rock wall, and Kyah, Trahg and Turi laughed and rolled about in the leaves all afternoon.

No one noticed when Trahg dipped his own little finger into the remaining pigments as any child would, who could not resist. And when they left as the sun set, no one noticed the yellow woman with flaming red hair left painted on the limestone. Nor the dark haired creature and small boy drawn beside her, holding hands.

CHAPTER 43

NEIL

The chimpanzee shuffled loudly above him. Neil held his breath as it passed. It was almost too easy. For the last two days the chimp had foraged ever closer to his hide-out. Today it was alone, lacking its usual entourage of man-ape children, but Neil cared little of its reason for solitude. All he cared was that the chimp was alone. The animal was a clear threat. It was time to be rid of it.

Neil had spent the night with a sharp chunk of flint in his fist, stripping and shaping a switch. His own blood stained the shaft of the spear that he now had to show for his efforts, along with the cuts and bruises that were etched into his palms and fingers. Still, the spear offered Neil a degree of protection, and what better initiation for it, than to kill the only thing here that knew he existed. *One less obstacle.*

Seemingly oblivious to his presence, the chimpanzee skirted low branches, further and further into the forest. Neil was unfamiliar with the dark trees it led him through, but wasn't concerned. He ran his fingers over the curve of his mobile tucked away in his pocket. It was almost always switched off to conserve battery power, but in the unlikely event he needed it, the compass would point him back to the river.

Neil let out a soft grunt, ducking under a branch and pushing through a thorny tangle of vines. Ahead, the chimp kept moving. *Take your time.* Neil held back as far as he dared, wanting to get enough distance between himself and the cavemen to ensure he wouldn't be seen or heard when he rammed his spear into the chimp's soft belly. Its constant presence goaded him.

The deliberate threat as it stood over him by the river's edge still cut into Neil's memory. He was loathe to admit what he knew now was an undeniable truth. *It didn't just see me. It* saw *me. My desperation. My intentions. My fear.* Ever since, it had followed in the redhead's shadow as a silent sentinel, waiting for him to act again, no doubt. *But I won't be so careless again. This time, fear for yourself, chimp.* Neil wiped a trail of sweat down his trouser leg and re-gripped his spear.

An advantage wasn't given, it was created. That first defeat had been hard, but it had been an opportunity to learn. *There's more at play here than a fucking game of* Survivor. There were lives at stake. His own life, obviously. And Benjamin's life. *I can give him time. I'll do it all again, start over again. I'll give him my time. This time.* There would be no more tubes and chemo if he could get that amulet. The boy had put on a brave face but Neil was next to useless against death's shadow. It was kinder to keep his son at arms' length and save him from the disappointment that came from seeing a parent's inevitable fall from hero to human. *Kinder to whom?* Neil thought, in a rare moment of self-truth. *To me? To the boy?* His stomach twisted with guilt. *Benjamin needs a hero, a real one. No more pain. A chance to live.*

And soon, I could be that hero.

Neil was no fool. There was life to be had. For Benjamin, but also for himself. There would be opportunities going begging in a world that would devour an energy source he could provide. The world was hungry for resources. Hungry for knowledge that he could steal from its own future and carry back, by bending *time* itself.

And no damned monkey is going to take that opportunity away.

Neil crept forward. *Far enough.* The chimp seemed to be slowing, waiting for something. Neil moved slowly, closing the distance between them. It was so close now. The chimp's head swivelled and he saw its eyelids narrow. It ducked beyond the shadow of trees and momentarily disappeared from view. Readying his spear, Neil broke through the forest edge after it, a smirk on his face.

He stared, blinking dumbly into the sunlight, swivelling his head in search of the chimp.

"Where are you, you little bastard?" he said, turning slowly. "You can't hide forever." Neil heard a slight movement above him. Concealed on a low branch amongst dark foliage, the chimpanzee stared down. Its eyes bore into his own, fully aware of his presence. It pulled its lips back, baring teeth. Then slowly, deliberately, it pointed over Neil's shoulder.

He spun around.

A trap!

Only seconds had passed with Neil standing exposed and distracted in the forest glade. But as the shouts went up and sharp spears surrounded his chest, Neil glimpsed his deceiver one last time before it disappeared silently back into shadow. *You clever bastard.*

Spears jabbed into his belly and arms, forcing Neil to his knees. Tiny rivulets of blood broke from his white skin. His captors shouted at each other over his head, clearly incensed by his sudden appearance from the undergrowth. Sweat stung his eyes. His long-neglected heart pumped furiously. Truth be told, this was what Neil expected to find in this archipelago jungle, whenever in prehistory he'd fallen. Hunters - tall, dark-skinned and possessing all the reasoning skills of a modern human.

One man stepped forward, red beads swaying from his cropped hair. His face was young but he had the indefinable carriage of a leader. The red-beaded hunter grimaced at Neil's white skin, and then boldly leant forward. Where the other hunters were clearly nervous, this one showed no fear at his white face. With a flint blade tight in his fist, the hunter pushed his own hand through Neil's greying hair. As Neil tried to twist away, the man scraped his exposed neck with the knife in warning. He grabbed Neil roughly by the jaw and studied him carefully. The others argued over his head, spears poised.

Neil sensed the beaded hunter assessing him. The man pulled Neil's spear from his hand and surveyed it with critical eyes. He ran his fingers over the point, clearly unimpressed. He tossed it into the undergrowth. He picked at Neil's shirt collar and ran his fingers across his trousered leg, scowling. He plucked at the shirt buttons with his fingernail and scuffed his bare toes into Neil's shoe. Then he simply stood, considering, while the others argued around him. After a few minutes, the red-beaded hunter turned to the others. He said something, gesturing toward the North.

A rabble of objections broke out. Some spat at Neil, furious with whatever had been suggested. The closest man, older and heavily muscled, pulled a sharp flint blade from a band at his waist. In one swift move, the knife was pushed to Neil's bare throat. Neil felt a trickle of warm blood and squeezed his eyes shut. He braced himself for the inevitable.

It never came.

Through squinting eyes, Neil saw the man struck hard across the jaw. The older man stumbled back, dropping his blade in surprise. A snarl of warning came from the red-beaded hunter. All around him, the others' eyes were wide with shock. But no one stepped forward to defy again. In protest, the defeated hunter pulled something from his waistband. It was a plait of long matted hair, dark and coarse. *A woman's hair?* He indicated the direction from which Neil had come. He grabbed at the long spear of a comrade as he spat his argument back to the red-beaded leader.

Neil watched the plait of hair swing back and forth in the other man's hand. It was unlike the hair on these men. Their hair was black and glossy in the sunlight. The severed cord of hair swinging was different, thicker with hints of rusty brown. It was dirty and caked with blood at one end where it had been bunched unevenly.

In a moment of clarity, the realisation hit him. *The ape-men.*

These hunters didn't want a hostage. They were as unwitting in the chimp's plot as he had been himself. These men were out today to hunt. To kill.

This hair was hers. The dead one. Neil's stomach turned a little at the thought. He'd watched two days ago as the sun came up in his usual spot. But instead of her morning swim, the redhead had brought the old man with her and washed the dead female's body by the river. When they were done, she carried it back up to the cave. Neil had noticed the body's crudely cropped hair – an anomaly in the cave dwellers. He'd assumed it was some sort of a ritual and left it at that. Despite that, it was clear that her wounds were severe, and now, it was obvious. *This lot killed her. And now they're spoiling for a fight.* He wondered what she could have possibly done to provoke a death so barbaric.

Neil watched the men around him argue, their tempers heightened by the promise of violence and his own unwelcome disruption to their plans. They didn't know what to do with him. Most seemed scared by his appearance. Others looked suspicious and angry and no doubt would slit his throat without a moment's hesitation if given the chance. Some again, like the older, muscled hunter, looked increasingly intent on finishing him, if only to continue to their goal. They wanted the ape-men dead. Neil steadied his breathing as another spear was pushed dangerously close to his ribcage. He felt fabric gather on its tip as his chest rose and fell. He could die here and now.

Or he could fight. On strength or skill, he would lose. But perhaps, a different kind of fighting was required here. He closed his eyes for a moment, shutting them all out. An advantage wasn't given, it was created. *And where there was violence, there was potential...*

The red-beaded hunter won his argument. For almost two hours, Neil was pushed and dragged through dense forest. The hunters took him North, bound at the wrists. He watched the trail closely, memorising what he could. A half dozen spears jabbed his skin to keep him moving and when he stumbled and fell, he was kicked to his feet again. Neil considered his options. He didn't know where he was being taken or how long he had left before they reached their destination. Once there, he had no doubt that his life would once again be contested. Neil glanced surreptitiously to the red-beaded man who scowled at him. Once again, Neil felt he was being evaluated. There was only one thing for it. Neil glared back with a silent message. *Do your worst.* The hunter grunted, surprised. He turned away with a thoughtful look, continuing his lead. *This one is different,* Neil realised. For whatever reason, he had kept Neil alive. To remain that way, was clearly goal number one.

They were hunting the ape-men when they found me, so they're angry with them. And if that hair is any indication, the animals will come off worse in a fight. Neil saw the ape-men in his mind's eye, dead or scattered, leaving the redhead alone. Vulnerable. With the black stone tied to her wrist. The ape-men were already on the wrong side of a losing battle. Against these humans, they didn't stand a chance. *There's no blood on my hands this way either, because they're already marked.*

Instead of fighting for his own life, Neil could make the

humans believe they had to fight for theirs. *Goal number two. Use these humans to get the stone.*

There was potential here. Neil scowled at the broad shoulders of the hunter in front of him. The bright red beads snapped against the man's neck as he moved. *So, the enemy of my enemy...*

The remainder of the journey was swift. Dark strategy again became his ally.

For the remainder of that day and through the night, Neil sat in the dirt and waited while his fate was argued. During the night he was freezing and had stared longingly at the flickering camp-fires occupied by his captors. By the following midday, oppressive humidity and unrelenting sun had turned his skin red. There was no chance of escape. To dissuade him from trying, two hunters stood spear-ready by his side at all times. Of those that took turns guarding him, none had seemed too pleased. They too shared his discomfort of the elements while waiting, their moods fouling as the weather took it's toll.

After an initial unwelcome by the human tribe, a number of elders had retreated to the cool recess of their limestone cave. Neil assumed his own life was the topic of discussion. While Neil waited, he learned, never letting an event, however trivial, pass unnoticed. There were approximately eighty men that came and went at various times of the day. Mostly they sat in small groups on the far side of the camp, drinking and talking, or sleeping under bamboo shades. Neil had counted another sixty or so women, going about their daily chores with children at their heels, avoiding his eyes and skirting his virtual prison with a wide berth. The only exception was a young woman with blue feathers in her hair. Upon the direction of the red-beaded hunter she had delivered water to Neil several times in a cured bladder, and then scurried away, leaving the faint scent of salt and herbs behind. The red beaded hunter sat nearby, watching Neil closely as he hafted a quiver of wood with his knife. It was clear he was irritated at his exclusion from the council.

No time like the present, Neil thought. He wiped his face with his filthy tie and knotted it around his forehead to slow the stream of sweat that stung his eyes. Neil pulled his mobile from his pocket and flicked it on, holding it toward the watching hunter. Immediately, the red-beaded man approached. He muttered a command to the two guards and they left.

Neil spun the phone slowly in his fingers. The hunter watched him suspiciously, kneeling, with a long bladed knife casually resting against his knee. The implication was clear. One wrong move and Neil's temporary reprieve would be gone. The hunter grimaced and shifted his chin toward the device.

The enemy of my enemy... With quick flicks, Neil opened the last photo in his gallery. It was a clear shot of some of the little beasts by the river, taken from his brambled hollow. With a look of deliberate collusion, he turned the screen face to the kneeling hunter. His reaction was just as Neil had anticipated. Yelling and stumbling backward, leaping to his feet, grabbing his knife. Its stone blade came to rest inches from the screen, the photograph still glaring like a miniature prison for the creatures displayed within it. He shouted again, looking fiercely between Neil and the device.

Neil knew what he did was risky. But it was a calculated risk. With no comparable concept, the very idea of capturing the image of a person onto a surface was heinous. Blasphemous even. Surely it would be taken as clear evidence of evil, this act of capturing a soul. Neil hoped so. To steal a soul represented power, evil or not, and only a god would be capable of such an act. Neil knew nothing of ancient religions, but assumed primitive cultures venerated some kind of deity, perhaps more than one. It didn't matter to him which ones. Surely they feared their god, or feared the wrath of bringing evil spirits into their village through disobedience or disrespect. Neil figured there could be only two alternate repercussions for his attempt at feigned supremacy - he would be murdered or he would be idolised. He desperately hoped for the latter. If Neil was a god, he couldn't be punished. In fact, he would have to be obeyed.

Quickly, Neil flicked to a second photo, not wanting to lose his audience. The man growled at the reflected image. Relentlessly, Neil forced more photographs on the hunters' eyes. His detailed chronicle of the daily lives of the ape-men illustrated his obsession. With each photograph, the hunter grew less fearful and more critical, until his face betrayed open curiosity.

Finally, Neil tapped hard on the knife still clutched in the hunter's fist. With deliberate provocation, he tapped on the image of the pregnant ape-woman remaining on the screen. He drew his own hand across his throat.

Kill it.

Again Neil pointed to the knife, and again, another photo.

Kill it.

The imitation left no doubt as to his intention. *I want them dead too.*

The red-beaded hunter nodded, eyeing the mobile device. Neil sensed his distrust of it. *But he doesn't need to trust the machine,* thought Neil. *He needs to trust me.*

Neil decided it was time to establish the only two spoken words he felt he needed. After a few minutes of miscommunication, the first word was this man's name - *Charat.*

Then the photographs prompted the second name. *Ebu Gogo.* The little man-ape creatures.

The mood between the two men shifted imperceptibly. A glimmer of understanding passed between them. Neil had clawed his first inch of respect.

As night descended, the humid air turned cold, and chilled the sweat clinging to Neil's skin. Trailing from the cave in small groups, men and women crowded around him. The faces of the council flickered behind the firelight. Each one was heavily adorned in shells and carved bone with ochre patterned across their skin. They held no weapons, which only served to symbolise their power. At their slightest indication, any number of hunters would spring forth to protect them.

Neil was not used to feeling intimidated. He pushed his tense shoulders straight and lifted his chin against their authority. He refused to let his own fear reach his eyes. Neil imagined that to the Ebu Gogo, these humans must be terrifying. They stood twice as high, broad shouldered and strong. Humans outshone them with sophistication and culture. They must have religion and tradition and the inevitability of dominance over their natural world. The Ebu Gogo were nothing in comparison. They simply couldn't compete and for a split second, Neil almost felt sorry for them. Almost. *It's them or me*, he reminded himself. *If I don't get that stone, I'll die here.*

The entire tribe had turned out for the spectacle, eager to hear his fate. Behind him in the darkness, the guards shifted closer. Charat addressed the council while Neil stood, awaiting his part. Finally, the hunter turned and signalled him to come forward. His audience was waiting.

Neil strengthened his resolve, internalising his commitment to follow the Art of War. *Let your plans be dark and as impenetrable as night, and when you move, fall like a thunderbolt.*

Neil garnished his face with his typical intimidating glare, daring his audience to doubt him. Anything less and he would give himself away. Neil walked deliberately to the council of elders and held his mobile to their faces. When he was sure the majority could see, he opened the first photograph. The image elicited a reward of fearful shouts. Neil waited for all council members to see it and then flicked slowly through his selection of photographs. The luminescent screen face was all the more fantastic against the dark night.

His images seemed grotesque and otherworldly, like souls trapped and frozen in time. The crowd pushed forward to get a closer view. An old woman wailed and fell away shaking and a rabble of feverish chanting broke out across the group. A number of young men yelled to Charat. Neil recognised some of them as belonging to the hunting party who had captured him. Although he didn't understand their words, Neil guessed by their expressions they were seeking direction. Charat answered his men with a violent shout and nod. It did not escape Neil's notice that the man enjoyed his own power.

Fear isn't enough here. I need to be a god. I need awe.

Neil felt in his pocket for his talisman. He spun it mechanically in his fingers and felt a rare shot of gratitude to his ex-wife for the gift. The polished silver lighter briefly reflected the firelight as he brought it up to his face. He turned to Charat, who was now coolly regarding the frantic crowd. They had an accord. *Power for power.*

With a hard nod, Charat turned his back to Neil and roared at the gathered tribe. With disquiet they complied. Charat was now their connection to the soul-stealing stranger and that fear lent him a new authority. In his hands Charat held an unlit torch of bamboo. Its fibrous knob had been soaked in flammable oils, ready to ignite. Charat turned to Neil expectantly, a knowing glint in his eye.

Between his palms, Neil flicked the lighter and a flame appeared. Gasps escaped the crowd. Neil held the flame high above his head. He knew what they would see. He was like a spectre in the dark night, with his white skin, strange hides and a superhuman ability to capture souls and freeze them in time. And now this. He created fire, from nowhere, and held it in his bare hands. The fear of such magic held no bounds. With a flourish, Neil set Charat's torch alight with a violent *whoosh*. The crowd gasped. Inwardly, Neil was elated at his own performance. *Surely, I am a God.*

But he had one more trick. This one he had kept to himself. Neil extinguished the lighter and pulled out his phone once more in flourished silence. The possibility of a stone-age conspiracy had grown like a dark humour within him.

It is time to give these people something to really fear.

A new photo.

The redhead.

With a flash he held up his device to Charat. There was a flash of recognition across the hunter's face. Then Charat cried out with such rage that Neil was taken aback. He punched the air, yelling at the others and sounding... *vindicated?* The crowd pushed forward to see. They looked angry. But not surprised. *They already know she's there.*

Neil had chosen this photo specifically. He anticipated what the humans would see in it. The redhead stood tall and pale above at least two dozen Ebu Gogo. Her hair was the colour of fire and her skin was pale like death. Bright green eyes looked down on the ape-men around her as she clutched a black hairy beast, misshapen and bent on her hip like a child. An animal that didn't fit into their knowledge of the natural world. The scene was disorienting in its deviance. A tall spear, one of their own Neil now realised, was clasped in her fist and the creatures were rallied around her with primitive weapons.

Neil knew his captors would understand *that* at least; the threat she held and the power she had, as she stood dominant amongst the Ebu Gogo.

Neil caught Charat's eye with an unspoken agreement. The hunter raised his fist to the air, punching violently to the dark sky. The red beads shook and rattled as he shouted, filling the crowd with fear. He turned to Neil, and lowered his body to the ground in mock deference. *Power for power.*

Neil raised his fist. He heard his voice break as he screamed above the confusion. *Ebu Gogo must be killed!* The authority in his voice was undeniable. A wave of fear rippled through his audience. They fell at his feet.

Now I am a God.

CHAPTER 44

ORRIN

"Yeah it's me Orrin, it's Dimi." The phone crackled, threatening to drop out. "Hello? Are you there?"

"I'm here Dimi, and I'm desperate glad to hear you, man. Where are you?"

"I'm in a sheep paddock on the side of a highway. I've been at the Parkes Observatory for weeks. Sorry for the midnight call; it's been hard to get away. I had to drive a few clicks from the dish to use my mobile – the signal screws with our readings." Dimitri's voice was strained. "So what's happening, O? What's so urgent?"

"Oh Christ," Orrin laughed with relief that bordered on the maniacal. "Where the hell do I begin?"

As he relayed the events of the past two weeks, Orrin found himself rushing through details, for the sheer release of confiding in an old friend. To his credit Dimitri did not interrupt, but rather grew quieter as Orrin spoke. When he finally finished, Orrin waited apprehensively for his reaction.

"Well, you can't say you lead a boring life, O." The attempt at humour only barely concealed Dimi's concern.

"I wish I did."

"And you're sure she's gone, this woman? You're absolutely sure this isn't some kind of joke or misunderstanding."

"I've been to hell and back, Dimi. I did this to her. Believe it or not, the world is totally screwed on account of my mistake. I don't need you to believe me," exhausted, Orrin pushed his fingers into the ridges of his eyes, "but I do need you to help me. Please, man."

"How?"

Orrin took a deep breath. He was crossing a line. "Information. Data. Astronomical survey results from the last, say, three weeks. Unpublished. Anything that looks anomalous or out of the ordinary and anything that impacted on the earth's magnetic fields or might have caused my lab to go haywire. Lunar, deep space, solar flares… whatever you've got."

Silence. "You're asking a lot, O. Some of the projects we're running are classified."

"I know."

Dimi's sigh crackled down the phone line.

"I wouldn't put this on you if I had a choice," Orrin begged. "But I'm running out of options here. I'm desperate, man."

"Yeah, I know, Orrin. I know. Look, I think I already have what you need."

"Serious? What have you found out there?"

"I can't go into it now. I'll need time to get my data together and it's not going to be easy. But if you're at Melbourne Uni then this information makes more sense to me than you realise. We've been at the Dish for the past month tracking some seriously massive electro-magnetic radiation over you. The fields were declining with the waning moon but they're picking up again now. I've also got hotspots of reversed polarity cropping up in weird co-ordinates across the earth. I'm still trying to find a common link, the places and environments seem entirely discordant to one other. But these hotspots are phasing in and out with the lunar interference as well. The strongest pulse seems to be heading your way from the Clavious Crater. The magnetosphere is already our priority, and now this. We think it might be linked somehow. It's got the powers-that-be scrambling; if we get a magnetic energy surge from this thing – well you know what that could do."

"Jaysus, man. Why the hell are they keeping it quiet?"

"My boss. The Director of Astronomy and Space is seeing dollar signs. She wants to understand its potential before she gets the media involved. Misunderstood, this flux is potentially devastating, but if we can manipulate and control it – well, she thinks there's something in that for her. Only a handful of us know about it at all. She has friends in high places, particularly government officials. If she says jump, we jump, if she says figure it out and keep our mouths shut, then…" Dimi sighed.

"She's a damned header!" Orrin growled. "People need to know what's going on! Who is this woman?"

"Her name is Cassandra. Cassandra Chevalier. Or to us lowly engineers, 'Director'," said Dimi. "We were friends once actually. She started not long after me in Digital Systems, but she's shot through the ranks like a rocket. She's sharp as a knife edge and a downright bitch most of the time. But I have to give it to her; she knows what she's doing. She filters the raw data by sight. And she's shrewd. She can read me like a book. That's why I'll need time to get the information to you. She's overseeing this project personally and nothing gets by her."

"Do you think you can do it? Transfer that level of data under her nose?"

"I don't know," Dimi said. "She does trust me, I've worked with her the longest. I'm not promising anything. But I'll try."

"I understand. You know where to find me. And thanks man - for believing me," Orrin said.

"I'm not saying I do believe you O, at least, I need time to figure out what I believe. But I'll help you." Dimi hesitated. "There seems to be a lot at stake here for a lot of important people. I'm just sorry you're involved in all this." There was an edge to his voice Orrin couldn't quite place. He shook it off as concern.

"Yeah me too. Believe me Dimi, I *am* sorry."

"Yeah," said Dimi. He was quiet for a moment. "No, no. You shouldn't be sorry. Not really. Not if it's true."

"What do you mean?"

"I mean, you *found* her, man. And then you went and screwed it up, but before that, you found *her*. The one you've been looking for. I'm happy for you, O."

"Thanks. I really did find her, didn't I?"

"Huh," said Dimi. "I'm actually kind of jealous."

"Of this bloody mess?"

"'Course."

Orrin smiled sadly. He pictured his best friend pulling his shoulders back, staring at the empty paddocks.

"Don't give up," Orrin said. "He's out there, somewhere, waiting for you to come along and sweep him off his feet."

"Never been good at that part," sighed Dimi. "I'd better go; I'm bloody freezing out here. I'll be in touch. Be careful, O. Seriously."

"You too, man."

As the disconnection tone beeped in his ear, Orrin sat back in his chair, flipping his mobile shut. Finally exhausted beyond the ability to dream, he walked slowly from his lab and made his way through the empty car park. It was nearly one in the morning and the night felt full of ghosts. Dimi's words drizzled through his mind. *There seems to be a lot at stake for a lot of important people. I'm just sorry you're involved in all this.'* It was growing apparent that the situation was even more dire than Orrin had realised. And he wasn't the only one who knew about it. Why had Dimi been sorry he was involved? What would the 'powers-that-be' do, if they knew Orrin had caused it? The relief he felt at knowing Dimi was on his side, was offset by the apprehension of what it might cost his best friend. With a heavy head, he drove home.

It was past noon when Phil Chan appeared in the laboratory doorway, coffee in hand. He leant against the wooden frame, his eyes narrowing. Dale had stepped out for lunch and Orrin sat alone contemplating an oversized whiteboard of scribbled data.

"I'm not saying I believe you Orrin."

"Of course you don't."

"But I'm saying I'll see this thing through," Phil said. "Whatever's going on here, I want to find out the truth. If it turns out you've screwed up my systems yourself– well, let's just say you'll be looking for a new lab assistant."

"Fair play. Should I ask why you changed your mind?"

"Don't push it." And with that, Phil planted himself before the whiteboard and joined Orrin's silent analysis.

When Dale returned from lunch to find Phil back, his ever-present storm cloud seemed to lift somewhat, despite the fact that Phil's return seemed more to prove their collective insanity than otherwise. Still unimpressed by Dale's pandering, Phil regarded the younger student with cool indifference and Orrin with little more. True to his word though, he poured diligently over his code, recreating the statistical analyses that had been lost or changed. A growing list of environmental variables appeared on screens above them. The resultant mess of their last experiment was compared to their original parameters. Slowly a pattern emerged and the three men sat well past midnight comparing the old against new. The following morning found them again in front of the whiteboard, but this time contemplating their new data with less weary eyes.

"The variables were incrementally rising from a week before

it happened, we just didn't realise." Orrin couldn't believe he'd missed the pattern. So distracted was he with his theories, he'd paid no attention to the changing conditions in his lab. "Something set off the crash though, there must have been a catalyst."

Phil scrutinised the whiteboard. "If the magnetospheric fluctuations were gradually increasing in your version of earth, as you insist, and ours have degraded exponentially in comparison, then something must have happened to throw the fields."

Dale leant forward. He'd been silent most of the day.

"The same thing that threw us into this field collapse?" Dale said. "That degradation is the greatest environmental variable we've got. It seems too coincidental. There must be a link - something that connects the two events."

Phil looked from Orrin to Dale. Between them a bag of doughnuts sat uneaten. "Yeah well, until we know what caused this, we won't be able to replicate it."

"Yeah, I know," Orrin said. "But we're a lot closer than we were. We know what went wrong now; we just need to know how to recreate it. If we can recreate those other variables, then maybe we can get her back."

Phil rolled his eyes but this time it was a little less convincing.

"Any news from your friend at CSIRO?" asked Dale.

"No, but don't worry, he'll come through," Orrin replied. "Dimi's one of my oldest friends."

"Are you sure you can trust him?" Phil asked, looking dubious.

"Sure," Orrin replied and shook off the chill it brought him. He had no choice.

There was a sharp knock at the door and Jayne pushed through without waiting for a response. Dale and Phil straightened in their chairs, surprised. With an anxious scan of the men, Jayne's eyes settled on Orrin.

"I need you to see something. Come with me."

Orrin jumped to his feet. "What's wrong?"

Jayne twisted her hands together. She looked close to panic.

"My ulterior motive. You wanted my help; this is why I'm giving it. Just come and see for yourself."

Orrin immediately followed the blonde woman from the room. Behind him, Dale and Phil fell into step as well, intrigued. After perfunctory introductions, Jayne ignored the other men and led Orrin silently through the streaming daylight, hugging pathways and shortcuts before finally arriving at the Biology Building. Orrin noticed Phil walk taller than usual, a purposeful stride keeping him to Jayne's right, always in her clear view. Dale fell behind a step. They took a few short-cuts through the maze of laboratories. Orrin easily guessed where they were headed. As they arrived at the steel door of Behavioural Research Laboratory 6, the stink of formaldehyde and chemicals saturated his nostrils.

The lab door was wide open and an unmarked van was parked metres away in the narrow laneway. Throwing Orrin a critical glance, Jayne stepped through the open door and led the way through dim light towards the rear enclosure. The inner mesh door was also unlocked and open, leaving only a row of steel bars separating the false habitat from the viewing area.

Two men in beige overalls bent over equipment at the far end of the viewing area, a large rifle propped between them. A uniformed security officer straightened up from where he had been lounging against the wire wall. He cleared his throat pointedly.

A man with a thin, sallow face looked up, scowling. "What the hell are you doing here again, Williams? I told you to keep out of this area. As of yesterday this room is restricted to authorised personnel only and I don't care who you slept with to get a key."

Jayne stiffened with anger. "You can't do this Professor Nerov! Liam Kent is the only person authorised to transfer these animals. Without his permission…"

"No permission required," Nerov growled. "Your boyfriend

went and got himself locked up. I don't like his chances of getting his job back either."

"He's not my –"

"It doesn't matter, he's not here!" Nerov shouted. He turned his back on them and took a deep breath, calming himself before he continued. "This authority comes from the Head of Department. As far as they're concerned, these animals have become a liability. Perhaps Mr Kent's time would have been better spent looking after his resources, rather than setting fire to pharmaceutical buildings."

There was a crash of noise in the front laboratory and a man came running into the viewing area. He skidded as he slowed, pushing Phil and Dale aside. There was a flash of recognition in his eyes as he stepped in front of Orrin to face Nerov.

"They're not resources! They're here for behavioural studies and because I had no other alternative in trying to keep them from the likes of you!" Liam yelled.

Nerov gritted his jaw and shot a look to the security guard, who was now standing tall with one hand on his holstered gun. "How nice to see you again, Mr Kent."

"Wish I could say the same." Liam was incensed. His mop of curls was dull and messy and his eyes were shadowed with dark rings. He was filthy and wearing the same clothes Orrin had seen him in at the rally a week ago. The telltale stains of blood and ash were on his jeans and sleeves. Orrin guessed he'd just made bail.

"Thank God you made it," Jayne muttered. Liam shot her a grateful look and turned back to Nerov.

"So what's this? The minute I turn my back you slither in?" Liam spat.

Nerov met his cold anger head on. "You did this Kent! I warned you they were after your little tribe down here. How many times did I warn you? I tried to protect them. But you pushed it too far and now they're lab fodder."

"No! I fought against this for months! I protected them!" Liam's face was red and his voice broke over the words.

"You failed them!" Nerov spat back.

The accusation hit Liam like a physical blow. He stumbled back. Behind him, Jayne let out a soft cry. Orrin's heart was pumping furiously and his mind raced. Dale and Phil edged around him. Dale's mouth had fallen open in horror.

"You have to do something," Dale whispered to Orrin.

Beside him, Phil quietly scoffed. "Do what Dale? Let them go in the park? They're wild animals."

Liam seemed to recover enough to harden his voice again. He stepped toward Nerov, who was still holding his tranquiliser gun with tense hands. "You can't take them Nerov, I'm here now, and they're under my direction."

Nerov's anger lessened slightly at Liam's bluff. "You don't even have a job here anymore, do you? You have no authority. What the hell are you thinking, Kent? You think I *want* to do this?"

Orrin could see Liam's chest rising and falling more heavily now. He looked close to collapse. "Say they're sick," Liam implored. "They don't want defective test subjects. It'll give them false data."

"You know I can't do that." Nerov's face was hard again. He looked detached from his task, working to keep the emotions around him in a place out of reach.

Orrin willed his legs to step forward, not entirely sure of what he was doing. He just needed to do *something.* "You can't take them! I need them in my lab. Um – physics," Orrin stuttered. "Um, research, on electromagnetic fields. I need test subjects -" Even though he had no intention of doing it now, Orrin felt instant shame as he remembered his eagerness to use Kyah for that very same purpose.

Nerov rolled his eyes and gritted his jaw. "Nice try. You think it really works that way? Put in a formal resource request and throw your money around. I'll bring some down to you in about *two years.*" He gestured to the security officer to hold them at bay. The overalled assistant shuffled behind him, unclear whether to intervene. Nerov waved him away and turned back to Orrin. "I have a job to do here. These resources have been allocated to the uni medical lab and from there they'll be on-sold as contracts require them." Nerov straightened up, his slender tranquilizer gun poised between the wire bars.

"But you can't separate them, they're a family," Jayne cried. "There are young ones in there – children – infants!" Jayne was close to tears.

"Get a grip Miss Williams or I'll get security to throw your little rally out by force." Nerov stared her down. "I have *no* choice in this whatsoever and neither do you. They are university property, and they're animals. Not people. *Animals.* They'll live with it. Or not. I did what I could *for as long as I could* to keep this from happening. It's on your head now, Kent." Nerov aimed his trigger into the shadows.

Appalled, Orrin followed the gun's trajectory. Huddled in the corner, a group of eight *Homo floresiensis* stood naked and exposed. The aesthetic rocks and branches had been removed from the enclosure leaving it bare. Tiny against the wire mesh, the smallest were gathered to the back, fear and confusion clear on their near human faces. Two adolescent males stood snarling at the front of the little group, their eyes snapping back and forth between the overalled men and the onlookers. Their hands were empty. In front of the group standing alone and defiant, Orrin recognised the tiny woman he had encountered on his first visit. Her dark matted hair clung to her forehead with sweat and she looked all the wilder for it. She glared at the gun with piercing, dark eyes and then followed it upward to meet the shooter's face. Clinging behind her shoulders, her baby whimpered. The mother twisted her too-long arms up, slowly pulling the infant down and pushed it to the ground behind her legs. Swiftly, it was pulled behind the group, protected by bodies. The woman's round eyes never left the face of the gunman.

Tensed and ready to fight, she stepped forward with deliberate antagonism and spat towards the gun. Her voice broke the silence in a low whisper of sounds, suffused with hatred.

"We're going to play this game again are we, old girl?" Nerov sighed.

Mute with repulsion, Orrin realised there were at least two less hobbits in the enclosure than there had been previously. From the corner of his eye, there was sudden movement.

Liam sprang forward, pushing Nerov with force against the steel bars and sending the man and his tranquiliser gun clattering to the ground. Liam lurched for the gun which had fallen half into the cage, tilting dangerously onto its loaded trigger. Orrin and Jayne both rushed forward to grab it. Liam was closer.

"No, you damn well don't!" The security officer leapt forward and grabbed Liam by the neck of his shirt, hauling him backwards. Liam kicked hard into the guard's stomach, and then scrambled to his feet. The guard doubled over, heaving in air, as he staggered toward Liam. His fist hit Liam's jaw head on. Liam's head snapped back and he fell at Dale's feet, hitting the concrete with a sickening thud. Dale dropped to his knees at once, eyes wide. Liam groaned. He grabbed a fistful of Dale's shirt to try to pull himself up, but failed, collapsing back to the floor.

"What the hell do you think you're doing?!" Nerov stepped forward and snatched the loaded gun from Orrin's hands. He leered over Liam, his face blotchy and red. "You think this is going to help them? Christ, Kent, you're out on bail! I should haul your arse away right now and throw an assault charge onto your time!"

Liam's skin had turned a nasty shade of grey and his breath was fast and shallow. "They deserve better than this, Nerov. And you know it."

Nerov's scowl sank a little and the grit of his jaw softened reluctantly. He turned to the security guard, who was standing behind him looking thunderous. "Just restrain him until I leave." The guard pulled Liam to his feet a little more roughly than he needed to. He snapped a set of handcuffs onto Liam's wrist, pulling the other arm behind his back and joining them together.

The sallow professor turned back to the hobbits. The mother was still in front, her long arms out either side pushing the others back. Nerov sighed and set his face with a steely resignation. He aimed the gun at the woman's naked middle as she leapt toward him. The shot was almost silent. A furious cry strangled in her throat and she fell to the concrete floor mid-stride, her body pathetically small. The tranquiliser dart punctured her chest with a tiny hissing sound. She gasped as she fell, the dart working quickly on her impoverished muscles. Behind her, the two adolescent males lunged forward to break her fall. Before they could reach her, they fell at the mercy of the gun and crashed to the floor, twitching in unconsciousness.

"Jesus Christ, man! You can't just -" Orrin pushed forward toward Nerov, but the cock of a gun's hammer caught him short.

"Damn right he can," the security guard said.

Liam was trembling with fury, his eyes shut tight.

Nerov looked back to the cage. "Sorry boys, you're up today. They're after some healthy males." He followed the steel bars back to where Dale and Phil were still standing near the entrance to the viewing room and unlocked the cage door. Nerov stepped over the female's unconscious body. Against the back wall, the remaining collection of young ones whimpered and sank to the floor.

His assistant followed Nerov into the cage. Deftly, the professor plucked the darts from his victims.

"Will they be a problem?" The other man nodded at the remaining hobbits before lifting one of the drugged males easily.

"The juveniles? No. They're easy to control when they're scared." Nerov gathered the other male and led the way back through the cage door. He kicked the door closed behind him and returned to where two transport carriers were sitting. The men lay the unconscious males at their feet and began preparing their trolley and paperwork. Jayne stifled a sob.

Phil stepped closer to her, looking appalled by the entire situation.

"I know it sucks, but you realise these are just animals right? This stuff has been happening all over the world for hundreds of years. You're putting human emotions on these things, you're *anthropomorphising* them and that's why you're upset. Don't do it to yourself. They don't think like us. They're not *intelligent* like us. They're not *human*."

Jayne looked to the *Homo floresiensis* female still unconscious on the floor then regarded him coolly, wiping her eyes. "And what exactly is 'human'? Enlighten me."

"Well," Phil shrugged. "Humans are smarter. We've got bigger brains."

"A Neanderthal had a bigger brain than you, *Phil*, and to be honest I don't doubt it was more intelligent too."

Phil rolled his eyes, unperturbed by her insult. "Fine. We're more intelligent than hobbits. We have weapons and make tools to create things we need or want. Think about it, a human can create something from nothing – we can turn an abstract thought into a physical creation – an artwork, a piece of music, an invention. Even a city."

Liam looked up angrily and took a deep breath. "Phil, is it? You seem to suffer from what I like to call 'The Human God Complex'. Yes, we humans do have greater control over our environment than other animals. We've developed more complex connections within our brains and higher intelligence is attributed to that. We *are* smarter." He took a step toward Phil, but the security guard stopped him, pulling him back by his handcuffs. Nerov looked over from his ministrations and shook his head as Liam continued. "I'm not denying human intelligence," Liam said, "I'm denying our understanding of its complexity – for ourselves, other hominids and animals in general. Think about this, mate - *what is intelligence* and *how do you quantify it?* And are we talking about academic intelligence? Emotional intelligence? Social intelligence? If there are cultural differences, or even species differences," - he nodded toward the cowering group of hominids - "How do you measure intelligence if it's a different kind of intelligence to what you're used to? How do you even begin to understand it?"

Phil looked between Liam and Jayne, scowling. "So, test them, then. Isn't that what you do here? Teach them something and make them read," he said.

"I see. So if the hobbits learnt words in your language, *then* you would find this -" Liam nodded to where Nerov and his assistant were lowering the males into travel crates - "less acceptable? The concept of measuring a higher intelligence in some humans over others is entirely subjective. Those sorts of tests are only appropriate to people measured within a shared cultural background and education standards. These *people* have their own culture. And they have every evolutionary right to do so."

Jayne turned back to Phil. Her eyes were like ice. "Can't you see past yourself?"

"Throughout history," Liam interjected, "Perceived 'higher intelligence' has led to unspeakable atrocities against other humans, not to mention, against other species. It's a superiority complex that justifies slavery, sexism and the Holocaust."

Jayne scowled. "You can't measure intelligence if you don't understand the way another creature thinks," she said.

Phil stepped forward angrily. "*You* don't know how they think Jayne, any more than you know how a cow or a cat or a goldfish thinks! You're pushing your feelings onto animals that aren't like us! They're born with innate behaviours. They do what they need to do to survive, to eat and to reproduce – that's life! Do you think a tiger gives a second thought to its prey? Chimpanzees have been known to rape and cannibalise their own young. Polar bears will play with a dying seal relentlessly before they eat it. Where's *their* empathy?"

"So essentially you're saying that *some* other animals have no concern for the welfare of other species or even some of their own?" Jayne raised her eyebrows. "Sounds familiar - sounds pretty *human* to me. In fact, that sounds practically *universal*. I can tell you've never had a pet dog and I pity you for it. Anyone who has would tell you they feel emotion."

Liam cut in, this time more quietly. "That's what I do here, Phil. I mean what I *did*." He corrected himself, shooting a glance at Nerov who was loading the transport carriers onto a cart. "It's been proven that animals can form incredibly close bonds. They can recognise and discriminate between hundreds of individuals. They have friends. Family. Loyalties. *Love*. Denying them the possibility of having emotion simply provides justification for committing violence and atrocities against them. It makes our lives easier. How do you know that other animals, including these," he nodded at the body lying on the cage floor, "don't feel pain, loss, fear and love?"

"How do you know that they *do*?" Phil argued.

Liam stood quietly for a moment, his shoulders sagging beneath his filthy clothes. "One of the greatest scientists I know once said, that if you don't understand other primates from a human emotional viewpoint, then you can't understand them at all. There are countless examples of animals sacrificing them- selves or their safety for other creatures; including humans. They show true friendship, regardless of species; they show concern and love for one another and grief when they experience loss or death. What's more definitive of the kind of humanity we aspire to, than being so *humane?*"

Phil shook his head. "Fine, so they show glimpses of what we consider to be humane. But these hobbit creatures here are clearly not human. We don't mate with them; so they're an entirely different species. Sorry, but I'm not buying your one-family love-in."

Jayne grit her teeth. "Maybe they aren't human, but even so, we still share 99% of our DNA with them."

"Sure, and we also share 60% of our DNA with a banana."

Liam growled and flexed his wrists against the handcuffs behind him. Nerov walked over and pulled on the cage door, checking it was securely locked. The unconscious female was still sprawled on the ground by the steel bars and the juveniles remaining were huddled together, terrified to come closer to the men to be near her. From the middle of the group, the baby that Orrin had seen her try to protect, whined quietly and broke out of the group. The others hissed, clearly conflicted as it crawled toward its mother on shaky hands and knees. It couldn't have been more than a few months old, far younger than a human baby could posses such advanced gross motor skills.

"You don't get it do you?" The sight of the baby's single-minded need to be near its mother, seemed to give Liam renewed courage. "I'm not saying they *are* human Phil; I'm saying your definitions of humanity are unresolved. The way you define what makes us human is entirely subjective. The majority of defining characteristics that you've attributed to humanity – strength, skill, intelligence, the ability to feel love, fear and grief, the ability to create and use tools, language and communication, the ability to understand abstract concepts and experience spirituality in some form, having a complex social or kinship system – none of these abilities are unique to humans!" Liam was jolted back by his handcuffs as Nerov and his assistant began pushing the trolley toward the wire exit. Loaded on top, the two cages sat side by side, an unconscious body in each one. As they left, pitiful crying came from the huddled juveniles.

Liam shuddered violently, trying to break free from the guard. He faced Nerov. "Look at them! That's a god-damn baby,

Nerov! How can you be so callous? You used to have a heart! What the hell happened to you?"

Nerov stopped, staring him down with cold eyes. "That's your problem right there, Kent! It's not a *baby*. It's an animal. Genetically - socially - physically - they're not like us. *They're not human.*" Nerov's chest stiffened and Orrin knew Liam had hit a nerve. "You want to know what happened to me, Kent? I grew up. I live in the real world now. The real world where I have my own god-damn babies and mouths to feed. This is a job. This is reality, Kent. Grow the hell up."

Orrin glanced at the female's body in the cage. The baby was now sitting in the cocoon of space where her legs curled up to her belly. It pulled itself forward across her chest, trying to rub its face against her forehead. She didn't respond. Nerov's assistant drew the professor's attention.

"What about that female there, sir? I think you might have hit a lung with that dart."

Nerov turned and surveyed the body still lying in the cage. He narrowed his eyes at Liam then continued walking. "Leave her. Maybe she'll be a little more cooperative next time."

"You bastard!" Liam spat at him, his face twisted and angry. He launched himself forward, pulling the security guard behind him. All three men fell sprawling to the concrete, sending the trolley and assistant into the cage bars with a crash.

Nerov scrambled to his feet, wiping his hands on his overalls. "That's it!" He and the security guard wrenched Liam roughly from the ground. "Charge him! Make sure he never sets foot in this lab again!"

The men pushed past Orrin, Dale, Phil and Jayne, dragging Liam with them back through the laboratory to the waiting van as he yelled obscenities at them. The assistant and his trolley quickly followed.

After a few moments, they heard the engine start and the van drive away. Jayne turned to Orrin. Her face was drowning in tears.

"Do you still think that you did this Orrin? You honestly think you created this reality?" Her voice was hard.

"Yes." Orrin wished more than ever that he could deny it.

"Good."

"Good?" Orrin was stunned. "I'm admitting to inadvertently causing species genocide and you think it's *good*?"

"Of course *it's* not good. I mean good that you think you did it," Jayne said. "If you did it, then maybe it can be undone. If there is an alternative to this existence, then I'll do whatever you need to help bring it back. You said I was here, alive in the last one. So I'll be here again. Hopefully though, these poor wretches won't." She pulled a set of keys from her pocket and unlocked the open cage door. Gently, Jayne arranged the unconscious woman's limbs into a more comfortable position, leaving the baby clinging to her while she slept. Stepping back into the viewing area, she locked the enclosure door behind her. "Honestly, I have *no idea* what I'm doing. And now that Liam's gone... even if he hadn't been arrested again, he's lost his job here. I'm an archaeologist for god's sake. And a student at that. I don't know how to deal with this."

Phil stepped forward, looking honestly confused. "I just don't get it, Jayne. You've always lived this life. This is *your* reality. Why change it now? Why help Orrin? Do you actually believe this crap about sending a woman to the Stone Age and messing with evolution?"

Jayne looked tired. "You're helping him too, Phil. And yeah, I'd rather believe his *crap*, than believe that this is all the integrity and compassion we have left in the world." She turned away, and then turned back to face him again. "And it's not *the* Stone Age for the record, it's *a* Stone Age. There have been many, depending on which culture and region you're referring to. Go buy an encyclopaedia, you moron, you might learn something." She turned to

Orrin. "I'm going to the vet department. I know someone there that might help her." She glanced at the female on the floor. She was beginning to stir feebly as the drugs wore off. "You know where to find me."

Orrin tried to smile, but couldn't. "Yeah, I do."

CHAPTER 45

NEIL

*N*eil *was* a God.

It was a good plan and if Neil was honest with himself, he was surprised it had worked. Maintaining the illusion was proving difficult of course, but intimidation went a long way in keeping spears at bay. There was nothing familiar nor comforting about Neil for these people, so he played on that fear as much as he could. From his white skin to his magic fire keeper, from his bizarre clothes to the souls trapped in his pocket, Neil was everything they never wanted in their lives. To amplify his effect, Neil took to silently staring at anyone who challenged his gaze while flipping his mobile slowly in his fingertips. The implied threat of having their soul torn from their body and encased in the glass device seemed to be effective enough a warning. Families were shifted to provide him room in the limestone cave, and they hurried away with their belongings, eager to be out of his sight. All eyes were averted, except those of the youngest children that were wide with fright and awe at the whisperings of their parents.

This morning, the young woman with the blue feathers in her hair waited nervously at the perimeter of his hearth. She had brought a breakfast of fruits and smoked molluscs on a polished shell dish and Neil ate slowly, content to analyse the comings and goings of the tribe. In this world where his wits and keen observation were his only defence, he used them voraciously. They had already rewarded him with more information than he expected. This young woman for example, seemed as frightened of Charat as she was of Neil himself. The hunter preyed on her specifically, making sure it was she who brought Neil's food and drinks and emptied his toilet bowl each morning. Charat kept her close, and Neil could see why. The woman was alluring. She was strikingly pretty with pert breasts and long legs. The hide skirt she wore did nothing to stay Neil's imagination. Strangely though, as closely as Charat watched her, he was rarely kind to her. Apparently the red-beaded hunter was enjoying his newfound authority in more ways than one. The prospect of control over women, or at least this one, seemed to be as high on his agenda as killing the ape-men. Neil pushed the empty plate away and the young woman took it, tripping as she scurried away from him. He pretended not to notice.

It seemed the elders had designated Charat to be Neil's point of contact. This was probably due to their unwillingness to be near him as much as Neil's own request. He had refused to communicate with anyone else. Neil needed to survive and Charat clearly craved power. There was an interdependency at play.

There was no overlap of language between them, so strategy was infuriatingly slow. Neil had no idea how the redhead had navigated the lack of communication. Of all the time he watched her, until now, he'd clearly underestimated the impact of the language barrier. She had seemed content to talk as if they understood her when clearly they hadn't. She'd accepted their dirty hands on her arm and their foreheads pressed to hers constantly. God knows how or why she put up with it. A weak mind, Neil supposed, and weak sympathies. It was difficult, trying to communicate with Charat, but he at least showed more intelligence than the redhead's menagerie. The hunter had a sharp mind. They shared the same intent, and that was enough for now.

Neil looked around the cave, noting its smaller size to the one of the Ebu Gogo he had spied on. There were more people crammed into it too; indeed, it was almost suffocating with humanity. The walls boasted dark brown and red paintings of human and animalistic shapes. Macabre stalactites dripped from the ceiling like teeth. Stalagmites clawed upward to meet their counterparts, occasionally joining and dividing the cave in hazardous columns of limestone. Shades of moss covered the walls of the cave and a damp smell clung to the air. There was also a more pungent, sinister odour this morning.

Neil eyed the freshly cracked limestone that wounded the far ceiling of the cave. Shattered rocks were strewn on the floor underneath the break. A loud drip of water fell incessantly onto the rocks from the fissure. It washed away stains of blood.

Not only was the cave too small for the burgeoning community within its walls, it was unstable. A heavy crumble of rock had fallen again during the night, leaving a messy reminder of the cave's unsuitability, along with a cracked skull. The unfortunate man who had been sleeping underneath it was now dead.

Apparently, this pleased Charat no end. The hunter strode imperiously to Neil and pointed to his mobile. Neil turned it on, flicking through the image gallery until he came to the redhead. Charat had held up his hand. *Stop.* He'd gestured between the dead man and the redhead, then to the dark cavern of Liang Bua cave behind her. It quickly became clear to Neil why the man was so willing to cooperate with him. His agenda was real estate. He wanted the spacious limestone cave by the river for his own people. Its resources and position were far superior to their own.

Neil suspected that Charat had been working to this goal for some time. Judging by the hunter's apparent frustration, the elders had been overly tolerant of the Ebu Gogo, and hesitant to disturb the status quo. But that was changing. Somehow, the Ebu Gogo had defiled a long-held peace. Neil suspected the murdered female had provoked the undercurrent of resentment. Now, the little ape-men had brought the red-head into their fold as well, bringing malcontent to a head. The Ebu Gogo had suddenly become a threat.

Not long after the dead man was carried outside, Charat had motioned Neil to his feet and flexed his jaw as he led him outside. A funeral pyre had been build a short way aside the mouth of the cave. Charat swept his arm across the grieving inhabitants of the cave. He pushed Neil forward in front of them. As flames ritualistically devoured the dead man's flesh, Neil seized the opportunity he'd been handed and lived up to his end of the bargain.

"Ebu Gogo!" He held the photograph of the redhead and the Ebu Gogo before their grief stricken faces. "They bring evil spirits! They destroy your home!" Beside him, Charat bellowed what Neil assumed was his own version of the words. The morning's death took on a whole new meaning. An accident of nature had become an act of evil spirits. Retribution was required.

Neil shook his fist, then pulled Charat's knife from the other man's belt. He turned to the entrance of the cave. With quick carvings in the rock, Neil shaped a large teardrop. He smeared scalding ash across its middle from the pyre, colouring it black. He yanked a shelled necklace off a nearby woman and held it up for all to see by its leather straps. Neil had already made it clear to Charat that the amulet was the only bounty he required. Charat also knew whose neck must be broken to acquire it. He seemed only too pleased to accommodate Neil's request. Now, Neil counted on Charat to translate his desire in a way humans would respond to. By inciting war.

"The Ebu Gogo are bringing death upon you!" He shouted. "They cast evil spirits to ruin your cave! The white woman is evil!"

Although he knew they didn't understand his words, it didn't matter. Actions spoke louder.

Neil dangled the necklace over the shape he'd drawn on the rock. The polished mollusc shell fit over the etched amulet. *Stab!* The sharp flint of Charat's knife shattered the shell as he thrust it in. It stayed there, embedded in the crumbling limestone.

"We must steal the woman's power! Kill the Ebu Gogo that protect her! Save yourselves!" The veins were straining in Charat's neck as he yelled his version in turn. Neil had no doubt of their persuasion as war cries erupted around the funeral pyre. The foul smell of burning flesh finally overpowered the adrenaline coursing through his veins. The body was engulfed in flames. Neil swallowed back vomit, determined not to show any sign of weakness. He spat at the etching on the wall, then turned away in mock fury and strode beyond the tree line, out of sight. As soon as he was alone, Neil heaved and emptied his stomach into the bushes. *They're going to kill her for me. They're going to kill her. I'm a murderer.*

This was not the normal price of ambition. He had never asked for any of this mess. But what of survival? *Her life is the price of my survival, isn't it? I deserve to survive. Benjamin deserves to survive. Oh God, what would he think of me for this? Would I still be a hero in his eyes?* Neil resolved never to tell him.

He collapsed back against a tree. As he sat, willing his heart to slow, Neil became aware of Charat's presence once again. Although Neil was free to wander, Charat was never far behind. A God he may be to the others, but to Charat, Neil was a contrivance that he could not afford to lose. By the look on his face as he sat beside him, the hunter was pleased with their performance. His jaw jutted proudly and his eyes spoke of success. Neil took a deep breath.

He dug his fingers into the weedy ground, feeling for stones to use as markers. After a minute, Neil ripped the mosses away between them and smoothed out the ground. He tossed a collection of small and larger rocks onto the soil. They had played this game before, and Charat now understood the symbolism Neil used for strategy. Neil gathered the smaller rocks under the hollow of his palm.

"Ebu Gogo," he said, gesturing at the rocks. Charat nodded, popping a dried betel nut into his mouth from a pouch and beginning to chew. Most of the tribe chewed constantly. The dark red juice stained teeth, lips and tongue and often dribbled from the corner of their mouths in macabre bright red before the inevitable spit onto the ground. Charat did just that, as Neil arranged the larger stones around the front and sides of the smaller collection under Neil's curled palm. One by one the attacking force was shifted toward the metaphorical cave. "Charat - Charat's men." *Yes.* The red-beaded hunter nodded with a gleam in his eye. Confident he was being understood, Neil played out his strategy, and the Ebu Gogo pawns were swiftly fallen.

Let the games begin.

A megalith of slated stone shadowed the tribe gathered beneath it. The sun was split blood-orange against its back as evening fell. Two great skulls rested on either side of the stone, one pointed to the rising sun and the other to bid it farewell. The skulls were long and flat, with great orbs where eyes should be, and each held a burning wick of fire instead. Flames licked through the lattice of cavities and the jaws of short, serrated teeth that had been propped open for effect. Neil guessed they were reptiles, not as long as an alligator, but much larger than a snake. He couldn't help but be grateful he was no longer sleeping in the under-growth while creatures like these were around. The megalith itself was imposing, haphazardly designed with jutting edges and carvings in the rock. It was positioned a short walk toward the north of the cave mouth, so Neil hadn't seen it when he'd been brought as prisoner from the South. Offerings of animal flesh, shells and flowers were scattered at its base, no doubt as appeasement to some ancestral spirit or deity. *I wonder if they'll build me a stone pile when I'm gone too?* he wondered.

An elder stepped forward. The tribe fell silent. With the quiet, came anticipation. After a few minutes, foreboding leached through the crowd to claw at Neil's gut. *What are they waiting for?* He felt Charat press close beside him, spear in hand, and Neil swallowed hard. *Have I played the wrong card?* When the hunter had disappeared earlier to discuss Neil's plan with the elders, Neil never questioned his loyalties. But the man was more assured lately, in position and demeanour. Only Charat knew of Neil's false immortality. The others believed it; they believed Neil was a god. *Has he changed his mind already? Given up our alliance for some other promise of power?* Charat knew he could damage Neil as much with his words as his spear. *Either way, I'm dead.*

From somewhere in the centre of the group, a terrible wail broke the night, sending a surge of adrenaline through Neil's veins. His knees jerked, preparing to run. But the scream was purely ceremonial it seemed, for a moment later a handful of other voices followed, including Charat. He held the long braid of ape-woman hair above his head and thundered above the rest with a lament for the man killed by the crumbling cave. It was a promise for retribution against those they blamed. Neil suppressed a shudder and swallowed hard. He summoned his own voice to aid Charat's. The man beside him swelled with vindication.

The elder standing before the megalith pushed his chin upward with an air of authority and began tossing handfuls of the dead man's crushed skull onto the offering place. The remnants of his cremated body had been buried, and now they called for his spirit to join the ancestors. Neil startled as a cacophony of bats suddenly took flight, screaming overhead in a great black cloud. A few faces away, the woman with the blue feathers caught his reaction and looked surprised. She quickly turned away. *Get a grip. Nothing scares a God.* Neil quickly settled an intimidating scowl onto his face instead.

A second wail sounded. This time, a boy was brought forward. He was trembling and looked no more than twelve. *Like Benjamin.* The child stood resolutely before the elder, but his eyes were shut tight. *Slice.* His skin was split in three shallow markings across the crown of his left shoulder. His back and chest turned bright red as he faced his tribe. An older woman wept with concern while the remainder cheered at his bravery. The boy faltered, knowing the other shoulder was due too. His eyes watered with the pain and his bottom lip quivered. The elder looked to Charat for approval and the hunt-leader nodded grimly. *Slice. Slice. Slice.* It was done. Apparently, this child was now a hunter and would be allowed to partake in the ceremony, in honour of their upcoming ambush against the Ebu Gogo.

Neil stepped further back from the cheering spectators, uneasy. In his pocket, he found the silver lighter and felt the cursive engraving with his fingers. *He's just a kid too. Just a boy.* Neil willed himself to continue his pretence. *It's my only way out of this psychotic hell-hole. This is my only way to get home.*

Taking a deep breath, Neil pushed forward until he was standing beneath the stone. He signalled imperiously to the new hunt leader. "Charat! Begin!"

Charat took up the command and the tribe circled out, widening the fighting space around the megalith. Fire sticks swirled as the hunters leapt forward, eager to be the last one standing. One by one, the contestants tested their strength against one another. Each man wore a wooden mask and dodged and hit with blazing flames and fists. They were impressive, not least of all Charat, who brought his fist so hard to the side of one man's head, he was dragged away unconscious. No other man could beat him. Charat roared with victory. The hunter shot a gloating look to the blue-feathered woman and she shrank back.

A new test of skill began. This time the hunters leapt and ducked, brandishing carved whips with painful accuracy against their opponent's body. Neil watched mesmerised. *At least I picked the winning team.* The thin, trailing leather flew gracefully through the air, leaving a lacework of bloody cuts in its wake. After what seemed like forever, the exhausted victor was celebrated and a feast began.

Not a single twig cracked underfoot as they made their way along the river. Dawn was not long due. There were only six hunters, Neil had insisted on that. A bloodbath wasn't necessary; this was simply an… *eradication of pests.* Six men would be enough to get the job done, including the youngest recruit, who looked more terrified than useful. Neil had insisted on the fastest runners. The ambush would be swift and then the perpetrators gone in the blink of an eye. Charat had wanted more of course, the man craved warfare like a drug. But Neil won. After all, he was a God.

Insects chirruped and shuffled over decaying leaves in the dark. Far above, bats clamoured in the trees searching for fruit. Neil hurried to keep up. In his mind, memories replayed like a film. The CEO's accusations mocked him over the hazy tinkling of champagne glasses. *You're losing your edge, Neil. You've let yourself go and you're sure as hell not taking us all down with you.* Neil lifted his chin indignantly. He scowled into the darkness as he paced silently behind the others. He ducked under an over-hanging branch and swept vines from his path with a strong arm. *Losing it my arse....*

To strike just once and succeed was Neil's preference, of

course. He knew his Art of War rules well. *'If he is taking his ease, give him no rest'*. During Neil's career, the wisdom of ancient military general Sun Tzu had been invaluable in conquering wars of business and politics. Real warfare, its intended purpose, seemed to give the words more weight. It was no longer just a power game; it was a game of death. Neil wouldn't be instrumental in the attack though; he only came to see it done. He had come to claim the amulet from her body.

Charat appeared beside him in the dark and held up his torch. The whites of his eyes were ghostly. Conscious of their audience, Neil pulled the cigarette lighter from his pocket and with a flourish, lit the end of the torch. As it burst into flames, the hunter's face appeared in sharp relief against the darkness, then disappeared again as he turned the flame to his comrades. They each met the torch with their own. Within seconds, a half dozen faces shone with grim readiness, each one illuminated by two blazing torches.

The strategy was to drive them out and kill as many as possible in the process. Neil knew that the redhead slept toward the rear left wall, trapped by numerous hearths and obstacles, not least of which was her own conscience. Neil had watched her well enough to guess she'd be the last one out and therefore the first to die. The Ebu Gogo were defenceless. The river was too far and any that weren't killed tonight would surely leave the cave forever. *Charat can have his prime real estate. I get my amulet.* The plan was flawless.

Each hunter crept to the top of the steep entrance. They threw their torches hard and fast into the wide mouth of the cave, then dashed back into the darkness. With each torch, a thinned bladder of oil was also aimed at its landing place. The bladders burst, exploding into flames. It had been pre-decided that sleeping mats of dried grass, oiled hide covers and bamboo spears would be the first targets. Neil quelled his guilt at aiming for a sleeping bed. Not a bed, a nest really. They're just animals, after all. He'd hunted before. Ducks, foxes, kangaroos. *This is no different.*

The screams came sooner than Neil had expected.

The cries were desperate. Chilling. *Not human.* He thought he heard a child wailing. *No, not human.* Then suddenly, the pre-dawn was alive with smoke that fingered its way toward the front of the cave and rose up into the air. With a flash of inspiration, the final hunter broke his oil across the tendrilled vines that grew along the lip of the entrance, igniting them in a strip of fire. There was no way out.

Neil shuddered, safe in his hiding place. Charat's hunters had been swallowed by the black night and were on their way home as they had been instructed. Neil didn't want any of them killed tonight, especially the boy. It was unnecessary. Neil felt a warm breath on his neck and spun around. Charat had stayed to watch too. The flickering of distant flames caught the hunter's face. He was smiling in the dark.

The screams grew louder. So far, not a single one had found his way out.

Silhouettes raced within the dark cave. Bright red fire licked at their backs. Neil heard the sharp sizzle of thrown water and a gap appeared in the flames. The Ebu Gogo spilled out of the cave mouth, tumbling and sliding down the green descent. Some were pushed. Others threw themselves down the hillside. They cried out as they fell, but Neil knew such injuries would be minor. *Disappointing.* There were less escaping than Neil had expected and he wondered how many more were caught in the back of the cave. There was no sign of the redhead.

The burning strip roared and snaked its way back along the entrance, cutting their escape route again. A small group threw themselves forward and beat the flames with mats, forcing it back from one edge. A line of them formed through the gap, like a trail of ants from the cave to the forest. They threw small objects from one to the next. Neil was almost impressed at their strength. Those closest to the flames stumbled and fell. The smoke was choking them. Still they arose again and again, tossing their valuables along the line and coughing the black air that billowed around them. Neil strained to see what could be so worth saving. One of the objects moved. A tiny arm flailed, grasping for stability.

Neil averted his gaze, sickened. *I need it though. I need that amulet.* He raked his hands through his hair. *For the good of many....* Neil pulled his lighter from his pocket, forcing the whorls of his thumb into the engraving on the back. *For Benjamin.* HE squeezed his eyes shut. But he couldn't block out the screams. Strangled cries battered the forest. He opened his eyes to find Charat watching him with a look of dark humour. The hunter raised an eyebrow at Neil's weakness. *He's right. What did I expect? This was the plan all along.* Charat was the last person that Neil could trust with his own weakness. The man was ambitious and Neil was only an ally while he had something to offer. Neil pulled himself straight and cleared his throat. Charat narrowed his eyes, unconvinced, but turned back to the spectacle.

Still no sign of the redhead. Maybe she's already dead. Neil's eyes were watering and his throat was parched. He couldn't help but choke on the putrid air.

With a spray of sparks, the hillside caught light. The fire ripped downhill from the mouth of the cave, chasing the fleeing Ebu Gogo into the forest. *Too many got out, god damn it.*

Neil and Charat were well hidden. In the chaos, they wouldn't be seen. The break of fire that had been beaten down was quickly reclaiming its territory. Behind the flaming entrance, shadows shifted and fell. It seemed that all those who could escape already had, and those who remained would die. Terrified screams echoed from the cave mouth from those trapped on the other side. *She's as good as gone.*

In a blur of motion, a tall figure ran from the mouth of the cave. She was bent and Neil realised that two Ebu Gogo were clutching at her back and chest. She raced through the licking flames and dumped her cargo on the unclaimed stretch of the hillside, then fell forward with wracking breaths. More screams assaulted the night followed by deafening thuds as ancient stalactites desiccated and broke from the ceiling. Chunks of limestone spilled over the fiery cave mouth and pummelled the undergrowth as they crashed into darkness. Without hesitation, the woman sprinted back to the cave, leaping over the trail of flames so close to closing the entrance once more. Inside, the great cave yawned orange and red like the gates of hell itself.

Once more, the woman appeared behind the line of fire, a struggling body in her arms and another clinging to her back. She raced through the gap, the flames licking her waist. No doubt the Ebu Gogo would have been consumed by flames of the same height. The one on her back fell away as she lay the other down. A handful of others grabbed at the second one, but it was clawing its way back toward the cave, refusing to be led to safety. The redhead screamed and pushed it hard into the arms of the others. It collapsed on the ground in a fit of emotion. Neil's heart missed a beat. *She's outside the cave. She's safe when I need her dead. I need her dead!* His moment of weakness was all but forgotten. His chest rose with fury and he stepped forward. *I'll kill her myself!* Neil was blind to anything but his desperation. Blind even to the danger of appearing exposed and outnumbered to his now very alert enemy. A swift arm caught him across the chest. Charat grunted and nodded toward the hillside.

The redhead was facing the inferno once more, stock still. Suddenly, she ran, her feet barely skimming the burning earth. She leapt high into the flames. The undergrowth was burning ever closer to their hide out. Neil was forced backward from the billowing smoke. He smothered his face with his shirt, overwhelmed by the radiant heat. Charat pulled insistently at his arm.

He seemed confident that their mission was complete. They would come later to claim their reward.

"Not yet!" Neil tore away, turning back to the cave. Charat may have his reward – the Ebu Gogo had lost their home. Many would be dead. But Neil needed assurance of his own reward. He wanted to know the woman was dead too. That the amulet would be his when he returned in daylight.

Neil willed her dead, his eyes squeezed shut.

I need that amulet.

Benjamin.

Control.

Home.

The words became a chant. Neil smeared the perspiration from his face and stared again desperately into the smoke. *Please just die!* He almost hated himself for saying it. But he could taste the acrid victory in his mouth. *Control.* He could smell his triumphant return to the modern world in the carbon monoxide that filled his lungs. *Home.*

"No!"

Out of the depths of hell, she raced one last time, breaking over the fiery serpent that now guarded it fully. Wails of desperate relief greeted the woman as she delivered her final treasure to the one collapsed on the ground. The shrill cry of a newborn pierced the air as the dawn sun finally cracked brilliant gold against the midnight blue horizon.

Charat's rough hands grabbed his shirt. As Neil felt himself pulled away, a single, desolate thought broke him.

I failed.

CHAPTER 46

ORRIN

"The electromagnetic fields are increasing daily. Dimi was right." Orrin poured over the data he had risked his friendship for. True to his word, Dimitri had uploaded the encrypted folder of data to an untraceable international server, and Orrin now sat analysing each file in turn.

Dale peered intently over his shoulder. "Geez, it's so obvious now, I can't understand why we didn't see this before."

"Because we didn't know what we were looking for," Orrin replied. "Look here, when I track the electromagnetic fluctuation from the Clavious Crater onto a lunar calendar, the energy spike clearly peaked at the last full moon. That date corresponds exactly with the date that Ivy disappeared. There are fifteen similar hotspots of increased activity across the globe but it peaked most strongly at these two sites. Almost off the scale. Here, at Melbourne University and also at these geographical coordinates. Dale, find out where this is; 8° 37' 12.4572" South, 121° 4' 1.7004" East."

Darting to his computer, Dale plugged the coordinates into his Global Positioning Software. "Okay, there's no landmark specified, but you're looking north, north-west of the village of Ruteng in Flores, Indonesia."

Orrin let his trapped breath escape all at once. "Liang Bua Cave, precisely. And the date of the full moon corresponds exactly with the energy surge and the peak coming from the Clavious crater." Orrin smiled despite the implications of what he said. For the first time since Ivy had disappeared, he felt vindicated. "We're finding the logic beneath the chaos - it's finally happening."

Dale smiled hesitantly.

Orrin addressed Phil, who watched them critically from behind his own computer monitor. "Okay, so if the environmental variables were rising in accordance with the waxing moon and then peaked with the full moon, we should be seeing them decrease with the waning moon accordingly."

"That's exactly what we're seeing, or at least what we *were* seeing for the past two weeks." Phil said. He flicked the stream of data onto the large display screen above his desk. "The variables are still changing, apparently now rising again with the waxing new moon. I predict that by the coming full moon, they'll be at the same levels as they were with that energy peak."

Dale spoke softly. "So in just over a week the full moon will be back, of course, and it looks like the electromagnetic fluctuations will peak again to correspond with them. But we still don't know what caused the actual time shift. If it was only the trifecta of these three energy fields, Liang Bua, the Clavious Crater and the university, then you and I should have been taken too, shouldn't we? We were both in the lab before it happened, and all of these variables co-existed at the time. Nothing happened to us. So why her?"

Orrin rubbed his eyes, dislodging his black-framed reading glasses. "That's the missing piece of the puzzle. The catalyst, so to speak. Something set off the crash, but I'll damned if I can figure out what it is."

Turning from his screen, Phil's eyebrow rose. "Not that I'm saying this will work, but for the sake of continuing my personal entertainment here, I'll get the systems back exactly as they were for the last full moon. But whatever this supposed catalyst is," Phil slapped his hand on the edge of his desk, "you've got one week to isolate it. Good luck with that." The screen went blank as he switched off his monitor.

"Aah, Phil, your eternal optimism delights me," Orrin grinned. "At least we know the pattern now. I'll find the catalyst; I won't sleep until I do. It's probably staring me right in the face."

Phil got up, stretching, and folded his laptop. "Then I feel sorry for it, dude. Your face needs some serious beauty sleep." He walked to the door. "I'm going home; I've had enough of this damn cello on repeat."

"Is that right?" said Orrin. With the progress they'd made, Phil's mocking couldn't dent his good mood. But perhaps he *had* played Ivy's *Le Cygne* one too many times. Since he'd rediscovered the recording, Orrin had found his efforts more focused and determined while listening to her. The music was like a connection between them across time, perhaps the only one that he would ever have. Still, he flicked to his classical playlist instead and laughed in the face of Phil's groan. "What's up, Chan? Too much culture for you?" Orrin teased.

"Too much age for me, old man."

"Then you're forgetting your bread and butter," Orrin grinned. "Music *is* physics. The mathematical equations that govern the vibrations on those cello strings are the same ones that underpin our universe - simple harmonic motions. Do you need a refresher, lad?"

Phil snorted in laughter. "O, I can officially say you're a man in love." He shook his head with a smile. "Thanks for the insight, but I'll leave you with your rocks," he nodded at Ivy's amulet, sitting on the desk next to Orrin, "and your music. I need some zzz's. I'll be back later."

Phil turned away but was stopped short. Jayne scowled and stepped out of his way.

"Phil," she greeted coldly.

"Jayne," Phil replied smoothly and strutted from the room.

"I've got something for you." Jayne walked directly to Orrin and handed him two large sheets of paper. On each was a coloured photocopy. The shapes were faded and mottled, barely discernable and Orrin rotated them, trying to find the correct way to view them.

"What are they?" Orrin asked.

"Cave paintings." Jayne nodded toward the table and sat herself down, placing the photographs between them. "Most of my undergraduate research focused on prehistoric cave paintings. I transferred to residue analysis because the opportunity came up with Professor Ellery. But these," she sucked in her breath, clearly enthralled, "these are what it's all about."

"Okay." As uninspiring as the paintings seemed, Orrin waited for an explanation.

"I've been looking into the archaeological research done for *Homo floresiensis* in its native environment," Jayne continued. "There isn't a lot of information to be honest, and what little there is hasn't been widely promoted. Perhaps scientists are trying to keep their humanity as unrecognisable as possible?" Jayne frowned. "Anyway, I happened across these cave paintings in an old journal. They were attributed to prehistoric sapiens, but I think they've got it wrong. Let's start with this one; I think you'll recognise the shape."

Orrin studied the large image Jayne had pushed toward him. Pale smudges seemed randomly placed on a grey rock wall. Orrin guessed the paint was originally golden in colour, but now only hints remained, the majority faded to almost white.

"Sorry, I don't see it. What am I looking at?"

Jayne grabbed a pen and began tracing over the image. The five smudges were suddenly familiar.

"It's the Southern Cross." Orrin exclaimed. "You think the hobbits did this painting? How old is it?"

"About fifty thousand years," said Jayne. "The same radio carbon date as the amulet and river stone. But there's more." With the tip of the pen, she isolated five more marks, further from the constellation on the rock and so faint, they were easily overlooked. Two complete filled circles with the shell of an empty circle between them and two vertical semi-circles, opposing each other in direction and spaced evenly between the others. The entire group arced around Alpha Centuri and its four stars.

"Shite! Hold on a minute." Orrin dashed over to his computer. "Stellar mapping software - I use it for astronomical surveys," he explained. He input the dates of the energy transference and the black monitor littered with stars. "Look, Jayne. This is the last full moon. See the position of the Southern Cross in relation to the moon…. Now follow the moon to its half crescent waning position… new moon… waxing crescent…Oh my god, it's perfectly aligned."

Jayne watched the screen, her mouth agape. "I thought it was a reference to their position in Flores - a stellar map, but it's –"

"A calendar!" Orrin finished for her. "A fifty-thousand-year old calendar. This map gives the relative positions of the full moon and Southern Cross the night Ivy was taken – and look," he pointed to the final darkened orb, "the next full moon! The full moon that we will see in one week, right here, when the energy fields will peak again." Orrin walked back to the photographs on the table, astonished. "They predicted when the time shift was going to occur. Or recorded it after it happened."

"There's more." Jayne pulled a second photograph from under the first and laid it on top. Again the faded ochre smudges made little sense to Orrin, although this time he could discern that multiple colours had been used. "This was from the same shelter," Jayne said, "further west and quite low to the ground. It's a little harder to make out." Once again she used the black pen to highlight what Orrin couldn't see. Quickly the shapes became obvious, and once complete, Orrin was mute with the implications.

It was a simple composition, almost juvenile. A black creature with a single arched line representing the body, long arms and a heart shaped face. The animal was joined at one hand to a smaller figure, on a simple crossed body in dark umber. Beside them both, a white figure, tall and simply shaped with a hint of face. Now faded almost to nothing, bright red ochre had once crowned its head.

Orrin stared. He couldn't breathe.

"It's her," he said.

"What does it mean?" Jayne whispered.

"I don't know."

This time, the knowledge that he was right, truly right, left Orrin in a cold sweat. Ivy had touched this place, fifty thousand years ago, with them.

And Kyah. The black shape with rounded shoulders and a hunched back, curling under its rump. The black lines were understated, but somehow brought the cold stone to life. Most strange perhaps, was the hint of its hand connection to the diminutive third figure. Was it deliberate? Was the other figure one of them? A *Homo floresiensis*?

But she, Ivy, stole back his attention. Orrin closed his eyes and flaming red ochre, as it once was, burned beneath his eyelids, haunting him. Orrin saw her there, in those weathered rubs of paint on rock.

The flyaway red hair, the pale face. The emerald eyes that hid from him and scorched him all at once.

These paintings told a story. Orrin traced the faded constellation with his fingertips, memorising it.

"I'm sorry, Orrin," Jayne said quietly. "I suppose it's only useful if you can figure it out."

Orrin looked up at her. He'd forgotten she was there. He felt lost. "I'll figure it out," he said.

Jayne shuffled uncomfortably. "I have stuff to do, um, phytoliths need classifying…" Jayne walked to the door leaving the photographs on the table. She hesitated. "I wish I could help more," she said.

"You're helping more than you know," Orrin smiled.

Jayne sighed and turned to leave.

"I can help, not that anyone cares." Dale's voice rose, uncharacteristically bitter. Jayne spun back, surprised. It was clear that in her enthusiasm to show Orrin the photographs, she hadn't even noticed him. Dale curled his shoulders behind the computer monitor, looking resentful and strangely young.

"Oh, Dave, I'm so sorry!" Jayne said.

"Dale."

"Of course." Jayne looked abashed. "*Dale.*"

"How?" Orrin asked, frowning.

"Well, it seemed fairly clear you didn't need my input," Dale said, resentfully, "so while you were talking, I decided to look more into the fifteen geographical hotspots that peaked with the energy mutations."

"And?" Orrin pressed. His annoyance at Dale's immaturity itched but he ignored it for the promise of new information.

"And I found a common link between the hotspots," Dale said, refusing to meet their eyes. "They all have constant low frequency electromagnetic fields and each one is emitting photons in random phase, peaking at the energy surge. Including the Liang Bua Cave, which was the strongest by far. They're all natural fields, with a geological commonality."

"Which is?" Orrin pushed.

Dale hesitated, scowling, and then said, "They're all archaeological sites."

"Seriously?" Jayne exclaimed. She moved close behind Dale, looking intently at his screen. "Where?"

"All over," Dale said. He shifted nervously in his chair. "Badanj Cave in Bosnia, the Mayan site of Acacaxtla in Mexico, Biache-Saint-Vaast – a proto-Neanderthal site in France… there are others in North Africa, China, Tanzania…"

"Jaysus, Mary and Joseph." Orrin strode across the room and scanned the map on Dale's monitor. *Well I'll be damned.* Each set of co-ordinates had a matching archaeological site associated with it.

"What about this one?" Orrin asked, pointing at the screen.

"I'm not sure," Dale said. "That's the Atlantic Ocean. There can't be any sites out there." He looked agitated at the discrepancy. "It's probably a fault in the data record."

"Dimi doesn't make mistakes," Orrin said.

Dale's face hardened but Jayne looked thoughtful.

"A major archaeological site… underwater… perhaps-Atlantis?" she offered.

"That's just a myth," Dale said.

"So says you," Jayne said. She pointed to the screen. "Look at the position, West of the Straight of Gibraltar. Isn't that where Plato suggested? In any case, I don't know of any other site it could be."

"Right," Dale scoffed, avoiding Orrin's glare. "So by default it must be a lost empire built by the God of the Sea, who rode six winged horses?" His mouth was set in a hard line. "It's an anomaly in the data record."

Jayne straightened up. "You never know. Maybe we have the exact co-ordinates for The Lost City right here. You'll be famous, Dale." She smiled at him, and Dale, clearly confused at whether he was being made fun of, hunched further into his keyboard, eyes down and straight-faced.

Jayne's smile faltered and Orrin scowled at the younger man's rudeness.

"Let me walk you out," Orrin said.

Outside the building, a small gathering of students were making their way toward the Eastern end of campus. They held placards and waved flags emblazoned with the words 'Stand with CHRIST'.

"They're picketing outside the Anatomy Building," said Jayne, noting Orrin's interest. "I passed a group earlier and they gave me a flyer. Apparently the media finally got wind of hobbit euthanasia on campus, so now the C.H.R.I.S.T. group is all over it." She shuffled in her bag, pulling out a piece of paper. "Here, keep it. I've got to get back to the lab." Jayne flicked her hand in a gesture of farewell and walked away, leaving Orrin holding the pamphlet.

It was titled with the acronym C.H.R.I.S.T. and underscored by its meaning - *Christian coalition for Human Rights In Soul Truth*. An image of a hobbit watermarked the background, haloed by an ethereal crown. Underneath, it read:

In the eyes of God, humanity is defined only by the gift of an Immortal soul within the body. Our hobbit brothers were also made in God's image and are self-aware. They possess his spirit and therefore have a soul.

'You shall not murder,' Exodus 20.13
End the genocide of God's humanity.
Walk with C.H.R.I.S.T.

It seemed yet another definition of humanity had now arisen from the rubble of cultural apocalypse. Orrin frowned, turning back to the physics building as his mobile phone rang. He pressed the receiver.

"Dimi?"

"Orrin!" Dimi said, urgently. "You need to stop whatever you're doing and delete those files."

"What do you mean? Why? You just sent them to -"

"Listen, I don't have time to explain. Just do it. Delete them."

"No!" Orrin said.

"Yes! Pretend you never spoke to me," Dimi pushed. "I've got to cut this thing loose, O. I can't be involved with you. It's too big for either of us."

"What do you mean cut it loose? You know I can't do that Dimi! This whole damn world is banjaxed on account of me. I did this, I have to fix it!" Orrin's hand was shaking.

"You can't fix it, O!" Dimi growled, a desperate edge to his voice. "All you're going to do is land yourself in some serious shit. I shouldn't have sent the files to you. This energy surge is not just another investigation anymore."

"Why? Is it the Director? Cassandra whoever?"

"She's more influential than I thought." Dimi's breath shuddered down the line. "I underestimated her. It seems she has some personal stake in uncovering this energy surge - I think she wants to control it herself. She's pulling in favours everywhere to track down who's responsible. The military is getting involved; NASA has been tracking all our data. I think she knows I copied those files. If she traces them to you, I don't know what could happen. Get out while you still can. Destroy the files, pretend you've got nothing to do with this."

"But we need this data -"

"Just let it go, man," Dimi pleaded.

"I can't! I can't let her go!" Orrin cried. The phone was shaking in his hand.

"You have to. This isn't a choice anymore, O."

"It's always a choice!" Orrin said. "What the hell, Dimi? You're braver than this! I know you! This isn't right. What the hell has this woman got over you? What's she done?"

Silence

"Dimi?"

"I can't guarantee that I know you anymore Orrin," Dimi said quietly. "I've warned you and I'm sorry. You're on your own now."

The line went dead.

CHAPTER 47

IVY

The air was acrid and stale. Ivy's eyes pricked as she entered the cave. Quiet tears fell onto the ashen ground. Kyah had seen the fire first, safe in her tree nest by the cave entrance. Her shrieks had found Ivy in the dark, and as the first flames exploded by the central hearth, Ivy was already on her feet. They were lucky. Minutes of sleep could have cost countless more lives.

If Kyah hadn't been there... watching... Ivy shuddered at the thought.

Gihn, Shahn and the others were slowly filtering into the cave. They looked wretched. Ivy's belongings were all destroyed with the exception of her journal and a single pencil folded into it. She'd fallen asleep writing by firelight and had shoved it down her shirt as she raced through the burning cave at Kyah's alarm, her protective instincts in full flight. Kyah was the first she sought out, screaming for the bonobo to retreat to the forest. Kyah didn't, of course. At least not until Shahn, who happened to be lying awake and restless due to her aching belly, grabbed Trahg from his bedroll and practically threw the child from the cave mouth and into the bonobo's strong arms. Kyah disappeared with him into the darkness immediately.

They had lost seven. Seven members of their beloved family were dead. In a tribe of less than one hundred, already mourning the Swift Death, it was nothing short of devastating. Ivy stifled a sob.

Shimma had lost both her devoted mate, Raspik, and her elderly mother, Bosxoi, to the flames. Raspik had pushed Shimma aside from the crumbling stalactites, only to be crushed in her place. Ivy had tried to help him, but he was dead before the flames swept through. She left him where he fell. Bosxoi had become lost in the thick smoke, clutching newborn Api to her breast after her daughter had fallen in the dark and been carried outside. Bosxoi was small, even for a hobbit, and her aging body had failed her. Her lungs were too weak to withstand the suffocating air and although Ivy had found her in the end, she was already gone. Ivy had rescued the newborn from Bosxoi's arms and left her body for the flames, delivering Api to his hysterical mother in her place.

The cave that had been warm and vibrant with life was now cold and desolate. Remnants of their home-life littered the floor. Cracked stone tools and bits and pieces of cooking bowls were scattered around the central hearth.

Another man had died, called Hushik. Although he was old, his fishing and regular catch of turtles and river snakes were a staple food for the cave, especially when larger game hunts were unsuccessful. Hushik had rarely talked to Ivy and seemed to follow Krue's distrust of her. Still, he was family and his death was as much a loss to her as the others. Another elder, Garun, his daughter Kinut and her mate Ranu, whose hearth was at the very back wall of the cave, all died too. In the chaos and terror of the flames, no one had realized they were missing. Now they would be missed forever.

Ivy looked around for Kyah, and saw that she was sitting by

the cave entrance, comforting Trahg in her lap. The bonobo's long fingers gently groomed him as he cried silently, clinging to her belly. The final fatality of the fire broke Ivy's heart. She slid to the floor where only a scrap of burnt hide remained of her sleeping mat.

Turi, the glowing and perfect dusty haired little boy that was cousin to Trahg, was dead. Since Ivy had arrived, he had been rarely a step behind Trahg's shadow and more often than not, on Kyah's back as well. Ivy stared into her empty hands, tears now falling unheeded. They'd searched for him. Ivy had screamed for him amongst the flames, but hadn't noticed him curled, hiding from the barrage of feet. The smoke had been too much, and Ivy had found him too late. He was barely past toddler-hood. There was no sense to his loss. No justification. For the past two days, Ivy had fought her heart through fury and despair and back again so many times she was almost too exhausted to move. Turi's mother, Floni, was an empty shell. There was nothing left in her but grief. She had already lost her mate to the Swift Death, and now her only child, her sun and life and breath, had been stolen from her too.

Ivy shuddered out a cry. She had a single possession left in the world – her battered journal and the flint-sharpened pencil that lived in it. She opened the book across her lap and gently flipped through the pages. Thousands of words stared back at her. There were busy years written in this journal, and sad years, hopeful years and happy years. The loss of her first love, then her mother, were buried in words as well. The slow estrangement of her father followed. Loneliness underscored it all.

She'd thought she was numb to it, all of that loss, but she'd been living a lie. Because now, in these last few days, it had come rushing back. The pain she had tried to protect herself from for so long, had found her yet again. The terrible ache left by Turi's death was the most desperate she'd ever felt. *I could have saved him. I should have saved them all.*

Orrin's note fluttered out and landed on her dirty toes. She picked it up.

7pm - 25 Beach Street, Port Melbourne. And those three words. *Please trust me.*

Ivy ran her finger over the little O at the end of the note. Her eyes were red-rimmed but now dry. Her expression was bitter. *Another loss for the pages.* She dropped her head back against the cave wall and closed her eyes. If she tried hard enough, she could still see him there. His teasing eyes and those dark curls that had made butterflies in her stomach. The way he pushed his finger and thumb under his reading glasses when he was nervous. The false bravado. Ivy understood now. Orrin had been just as vulnerable as she; he was just better at hiding it.

It stung - the futility of pushing him away for the sake of never losing him. She'd lost him anyway. *Now I'd trade a million lost days for a single day together.* Another day with Orrin, or another chance to see Turi riding imperiously on Kyah's back and giggling in a swirl of fallen leaves.

They were under her skin now, all of them. And Ivy knew they always would be.

The bodies of those who died had been left exposed upon the limestone cliffs where she and Gihn had left Emiri.

All except for Turi. Ivy had been the one to suggest he be buried. Against the back wall of the massive cave, where no one would rebuild the hearth belonging to Garun and his family, the hobbits had their first true burial. It was an epiphany of symbolic meaning. Instead of being left to the elements and predators of the cliffs, Turi would always be protected. They left his tiny ochre handprint on the rock wall above his grave. Although Ivy played no small part in the ritual, this time, she felt no remorse for her actions. She had given Floni a new way to express the grief and love that was drowning her. Cultural-interference be damned.

The hobbit tribe had slept in the forest the following night, too afraid to return to the cave. But winter wasn't far away. The night air was cold. Light clouds of ash had begun drifting across the sky leaving a dusty film on the ground. Somewhere on the island, a volcano was stirring.

And then, there was the threat of more karathah attacks. Ivy had expected them to return, but so far, they hadn't. *Planning their next attack, no doubt.* By the nature of the ambush, Ivy had no doubt that they had intended more fatalities. If it weren't for Kyah, they would have had them.

The tribe needed protection. They needed their home.

Ivy finally convinced them to return to the cave. She volunteered to sit up all night guarding the entrance. Xiou beckoned her to the remnants of the central hearth where the others were already gathered.

"Why did they do this to us?" asked Kipi, the dead fisherman's youngest daughter. The question had been asked many times since the attack. "They already punished Emiri for taking their baby, why set fire to our cave as well?"

"It must be retribution, pure and simple," an old woman said. "They continue to punish us for Emiri's mistake."

Krue shook his head. "You are all fools if you can't see this for what it is. They did it because of her, your *Hiranah*." The venom in his voice was matched in his eyes. "The karathah know she is here. If she doesn't conspire with them, then her presence here must inflame their hate for us! The woman is bringing death upon us faster and faster."

Ivy drew herself tall, towering over Krue. She was sick and tired of his accusations.

"I saved your life at the waterhole!" she said. "Do you think that karathah hunter would have been content to cut off a few more of your fingers? You are nothing to him Krue! Just a pest he is trying to get rid of. I stopped the Swift Death and I've done everything I can to prove my loyalty to you all!"

"But even if they do know Hiranah is here," Kipi said, "what difference does it make to them? She means them no harm."

Ivy wasn't sure if that sentiment was entirely true. Not directly perhaps, but if the Flores hobbits survived, sapien lives would be affected, for better or worse.

Ivy sighed. "I'm different, Kipi. They fear me." Racial intolerance, or in this case, *species intolerance*, was a benchmark for most Homo sapiens. And deny it though she might, Ivy was still more a part of that family tree, than this one.

"So because you're different, they will kill us all?" Kipi's voice was shaking.

"This isn't just my fault," Ivy shot a scathing look to Krue, despite her own misgivings. "They were killing your people before I came. Poisoning the waterhole for months, I've just – given them a reason to try harder I think. You're different too." The grief in Ivy's chest was solidifying into fury. "They're threatened by you, and I think, perhaps, there's something else as well. Getting rid of you isn't that easy, but they keep trying. They must want something that you have."

Shahn looked up, confused. "We have nothing they need."

Standing beside his mate, Xiou looked less sceptical. "Of course we do, Shahn. We have this cave. We have the oleos grove and the tourak trees and everything else we trade with them. We have the digging pit for the best weapon stones. Hiranah is right; there are plenty of reasons to kill us."

At Xiou's words, Krue looked at Ivy, narrowing his eyes slightly. He nodded his head slowly in consideration and Ivy felt a small rush of victory.

"Xiou is right," Ivy said. "They have plenty of reasons to tear your tribe apart. The karathah fear what they don't know and they want what is yours. They're not going to stop trying."

Ivy looked away, past the cave entrance and over the forest ceiling below. Her bare toes scuffed the ash underfoot and she scraped the loose red curls away from her face in disgust. She felt ugly. *Of course they want to kill me. They fear me. Fear always begets murder.*

The ignorance behind their motive infuriated Ivy almost more than the attack on her own life. She felt different. Isolated again. *Maybe I'm not human after all.* At the memory of Turi's ashen little body, a tremor of anger shattered her introspection to bits. *So we fight.* She turned back to the group.

"The karathah will kill you if you let them," Ivy said, earnestly. "Eventually, they'll dominate every part of this earth. I'm sorry but I've seen it. I've lived it." There was a muttering of fear and shock. Krue though, looked at her in silent appraisal, and for the first time, she thought she saw a glint of respect in his eye. A few voices rose above the others in concern.

"Surely they aren't all bad?" someone asked.

"Of course not," Ivy replied. "But this isn't just going to be a fight against the minority that want you dead, like that hunter with the red beads in his hair. The real fight is against the others, the good people that choose to do nothing against it. So, it is up to *you* to ensure your own survival."

"But how can we survive their strength?" Kipi asked.

"We can't win," said another.

Ivy knew in her heart, that if it came to combat, they stood no chance. They were devastatingly outnumbered. She held her arm up to quiet them.

"There are better ways to fight the karathah than with spears and arrows," she said. "I refuse to let them pick you off one by one."

Ivy's heart was racing. Another flame prickled under her skin now. The one that carried her own fear, as hot and strong as any of those plotting her death. *I don't want to die. I refuse to let the karathah take me too.*

"Hiranah," Gihn interjected with quiet authority. "Perhaps, this is a discussion for another time." He addressed the group. "We have no food left and winter is close. Our supplies are burnt to nothing. We need to forage for plants to cook. And we'll need meat and new weapons to hunt for it."

Xiou stepped forward. "There are some old spears that were not burnt," he said. "Most have cracked points from the heat though. They will need reworking." A handful of young men standing nearby volunteered and Setian began to issue instructions to them.

"Kora," Xiou continued, "You and Guntah should make new shafts. We need as many as possible." The woman and her mate nodded.

"We'll need a lot of food to replace our winter stores as well as feed ourselves," Kora said. "When will we leave?"

"Within two days," said Xiou. "Krue and I have already discussed it. We will hunt the probech."

Stegodon. A strange sense of foreboding filled Ivy's heart.

Hot, rhythmic drumming pushed the hunters from the cave. The mood was tense. There were three less hunters since the fire, and those leaving were terrified for the safety of those staying behind.

Ten had volunteered to guard the cave; older hunters whose agility was leaving them. Still, their new responsibility was perhaps more dangerous than going and none liked the necessary separation. Families rubbed brows lovingly in farewell. The hunters turned away from the wide eyes of their children and anxious frowns of those left behind.

"Look after each other," Ivy said to Kyah and Trahg. The bonobo had followed the hunters down to the river with Trahg clinging on to her back. Ivy knelt down and pulled them both into a tight hug, then pulled back to look Kyah in the eye. "Stay safe, Ky. I need you safe. Always."

The bonobo gently dropped Trahg to his feet and took Ivy's hand. *Love.*

"I love you too, honey," Ivy whispered.

Kyah hooted softly and drew her fingers gently down Ivy's face, collecting her tears. *No. Cry.*

Ivy laughed, sniffing. "And when did you become the grown up here?" She kissed Kyah's face and rubbed her brow against Trahg's.

"I'll keep her safe," the little boy said stoically.

"I know you will," Ivy smiled. With a deep breath, she turned and followed the hunters across the river terrace until the jungle closed in and silence took them.

Forty men and women camouflaged like spectres of children in shadow. They were playing a deadly game. The hunters carried spears and arrows, bludgeoning clubs and stone knives. *To be so tiny but so capable...* Ivy shivered in the warm air.

Today they hunted probech, the tusked giants of the forest. Stegodons were massive in their strength and fierce in their defence. Gihn had told her that often, less hands returned home than had left. The waiting family had cause to worry.

Ivy noticed the intensity of the hobbits as they moved together through the trees. They were silent, like a multi-shafted arrow with a single point. How they communicated while travelling, she couldn't exactly tell. Perhaps it was only a glance from one to another and like a flock of birds; they shifted weightlessly, changing direction.

They were athletic and relentless in their trek but they didn't run. Ivy thought she knew why. Over long distances, *Homo floresiensis* were built for endurance and stability but not speed. Their feet were a bizarre combination of ancient and modern traits. Their navicular bone, the one that formed the arch in a sapien foot, was primitive and depressed in the hobbits, giving them a flat-footed stance. A shorter big toe and comparatively long forefoot compared to the ankle bones were reminiscent of chimpanzees and other great apes. To compensate, their running gait was slightly different to Ivy's own, longer but with less spring and efficiency to it and only good for short distances.

Ivy paced herself to keep up, feeling her abdominal muscles tense and flex, her breath deep. She was barefoot, with a new spear in hand, watching for the fleeting smiles of Leihna, Rinap or little Filhia to correct her path. Her journal and pencil were tied into a fold of her skirt. They ascended a steep mountain range at a fast climb, disappeared into its lush valley and followed a river that cut it neatly in half.

After two hours they stopped. The sun hadn't reached its peak but sweltering heat rose like waves from the dry grass underfoot. Krue was crouching near the tree line, conversing with Xiou, Setian and five others. Hunters re-materialised from the trees and Ivy slumped into the grass, catching her breath. Filhia's petite fingers clasped her amulet.

"You're doing well Hiranah; it's not an easy pass through those mountains."

"I'm trying," Ivy replied. In fact, she'd never looked so healthy. Her light freckles added a touch of bronze to the pink glowing skin shining with sweat. "Are we nearly there?"

"The probech are just up-river from here, Krue was following their trail."

"Hiranah!" Xiou interrupted, beckoning them to where he stood, "Come rub this on your skin." At Xiou's feet lay the largest pile of dung Ivy had ever seen. It was olive green and spotted with half-digested grass, and was the foulest smelling concoction she'd had the displeasure of breathing.

"You're not serious?"

"Of course," said Xiou, "We have to disguise our scent so we don't scare them off. The cows are very protective of their calves and will be quick to charge. We need to get as close as we can before we take one down."

Ivy crouched down. She looked doubtfully at the giant splatter.

"Actually, I'm not getting that close to them anyway, I'll be in the tree line with Filhia and the younger girls waiting." Although Krue had begrudgingly allowed her to come, Ivy had been designated to carry butchering tools and hides to wrap meat in for their return journey. She would be far from the action. Kora had given Ivy the new spear only as a precaution.

Xiou grinned. "It doesn't matter where you are. Their eyes may be bad, but the probech would smell you a forest away." Ivy grimaced as his finger deposited a chunk across her cheek. "Besides, it looks good on you!" He laughed and turned back to Setian and Krue.

Filhia had already begun covering herself, her little nose wrinkled. Ivy dug her fingers into the mess, holding her breath. She gingerly wiped it along her pale arms and legs, careful to avoid the journal tucked by her hip. Ivy imagined how ridiculous she must look with green stripes of stegodon dung adorning her white skin. She tried to clean her face of it, but only added to the mess and wiped her face on her singlet instead. By the time she finished, Ivy wore more of it than anyone. They were joined by Rinap and Leihna, who laughed at Ivy's appalled face. Ivy turned her face into the wind hopefully, but couldn't escape her own smell.

The brown grass waved the hobbits through the river terrace leaving thin trails that closed behind each step, leaving forty broken spaces moving in a tendrilled sea. Ivy ducked down, crawling to afford the same level of cover. Only a faint rustle of grass or twig crack gave them away. The hobbits stalked their prey, bare feet to hard earth and warm blood saturated with adrenaline. As each minute passed, Ivy's chest grew tighter as the tension in the air around her increased.

Rinap's face was unnaturally tense; a far cry from the impish grin and carefree spirit she usually wore. This was her first hunt, along with Leihna, her soon-to-be-mate Kari and two other boys. Rinap nudged Ivy forward, her fingers to her lips. She nodded to the sky, inviting Ivy to silently raise her head. Ivy gasped at what she saw, earning herself a hard poke in the ribs as reproach.

Three stegodon stood on the opposite shore of the riverbank. Two bachelors were acting as sentry, alert and restless, listening to the hot wind with keen ears. Unable to find a source to the noise that had disrupted them, they resumed feeding. One was at the water's edge, flicking his trunk in the cool water. The other shuffled nearby, grass to his underbelly, shredding slashes from the ground with his curled trunk and probing fingers.

But the older male they guarded was the one who drew Ivy's eyes. He was magnificent.

Ivory tusks dragged his massive skull toward the ground. The left tusk was long and proud and the right was worn and torn from a half century of digging and stripping bark. They erupted together from deep within his skull, dead straight and conjoined from his top lip. Ivy guessed that they must have been over one and a half meters long and flared apart at the ends. His forehead was high, parted with two bulbous domes and a distinctive nasal bridge unlike any modern elephant.

At over two meters long and another one and a half high, Ivy knew this was the dwarfed ancestor of those that swam to Flores over 880,000 years before. The dwarf stegodon and their hobbit counterparts were the only large bodied mammals to make it across the dangerous watery divide to find their island paradise. They shared a fated bond, Ivy thought ironically; the hunter and hunted. Two intelligent species that had evolved together in isolation, and now both shared a future of genetic extinction at the hands of Homo sapiens. *But not if I can help it.* Ivy squeezed Rinap's hand tightly in her own.

Six hundred kilograms of flesh and muscle swayed with agitation as the old bull looked up again. The agile fingers on his trunk dripped as he brought it from his mouth to the hot air, holding it high to taste the delicate balance of the breeze. He seemed to detect a new smell, but so faint and diffused that it cast no suggestion to friend or foe. He looked experienced and confident, his solidity and weaponry well used to defend. Newcomers would pose little threat to him. His trunk fell, grasping a fist of grass and delivering it to his plates of ridged molars. Draping his trunk over his tusks for convenience, he resumed chewing.

The hunters were dwarfed by their prey. At best, Ivy's companions would have reached a few inches above its underbelly. Sporting inbuilt spears, a tough hide and massive gait, the stegodon seemed in every way untouchable to them.

Although there was a river between them, Ivy's skin suddenly felt too white, her body too tall, her hair too bright. She sunk low into the grass, spreading it silently with her hands to catch glimpses through the veil. Again Rinap's reassuring touch found her.

"We won't hunt these males; they're too big for us. Krue is following the spoor of the matriarch herd downriver instead. Follow me and keep quiet – if the males hear or smell us, they'll warn the others and charge."

They continued through the long grass. Midday became a furnace and rivulets of sweat ran into her eyes. Ivy blinked as she moved awkwardly on crouched, aching knees to keep her bright red hair well below the grass ceiling. Not for the first time, she wished she'd been born with an inconspicuous shade of brown. Her journal softly bumped against her thigh as she moved. This time Rinap stayed by her side, standing tall but still sheltered by the long grass. They drew back from the river until the relentless sun was broken by the shade of dalunut palms. Another twenty minutes of trekking and their quarry was finally revealed.

The female herd was bigger than expected. Nine adult stegodon waded through the gently cascading water. Some enjoyed a bath in its deep centre, shooting trunkfuls of water across their backs to relieve the sweltering heat. On the riverbank, coarsely haired ears flapped rhythmically, cooling the blood circulating in the rich network of blood vessels under their thin skin. Six juveniles completed the family. One female and one male were almost fully grown and two infants and two calves were splashing in the shallows.

One newborn calf was shadowed under a forest of browny-gold legs, constantly caressed by the trunks of its allomothers. Sisters, mothers, daughters and aunts made up the group of attentive babysitters, and all were dedicated to protecting it. Still exhausted from a twenty-two-month pregnancy, the new calf's mother relied on her sisters to watch over the calf while she fed. Extra strength was needed to nurse her seventy-kilogram newborn and to regain that which she had lost in its carriage.

The nursing mother stood alone on the far side of the river, vulnerable in her isolation. Her attention was consumed as she lifted her trunk high among leaves, tasting the air. With a rumbling groan, her front legs left the ground and landed squarely on a thick tree, splaying with the pressure. The tree was ancient, colossal and strong, but it bowed under her weight. Loud cracks echoed across the valley. She curled her long trunk around the high branch and shook it. A cascade of green fruit hit the ground. The tree straightened as she left it, landing back on her giant cushioned feet with an almighty thud that shook the earth.

Delicately, the stegodon mother smelt the fallen fruit with her trunk, then rolled one into position and crushed it open with her foot. She brought it to her mouth, then reached for another with her trunk as she chewed. Natural selection had provided her with an instrument so incredible, she could use it to tear a branch off a tree or pick up a single blade of grass. Ivy had never felt so humbled.

Rinap's signal drew her attention to the near adult bull at the fringe of the herd. He was so close that Ivy could see his dark lashes framing a treacle-coloured eye. His skin was caked in yellow mud as protection from the harsh sun. He was smaller than the adult females, but Ivy imagined he would grow to tower over them. He probably already spent weeks away on his own and Ivy guessed that within a few years, his independence would lead him to a solitary life, or to fight for dominance in a bachelor herd until he'd lived a half century and was deemed fit to mate.

Standing alone on a rocky steppe, the grandmother matriarch missed nothing. She would be the oldest female and therefore the one to lead the herd hundreds of miles each year through their seasonal feeding grounds. Her experienced eye kept them from danger and the others followed her lead unquestioningly. If such a thing was possible, and Ivy believed it was, the matriarch looked proud of her family.

For the longest moment, all notion of why she was there was lost to Ivy as she crouched, transfixed by the scene before her. She felt alone, watching the stegodon family play and safeguard one another. Ivy knew it may never be hers again, this incredible opportunity that shouldn't have been hers at all. She committed each detail bright and sharp into her memory; the parallel ivory tusks, silty golden mud caked across their broad backs, lashings of grass ripped easily from the hard ground and the gentle, reassuring touch of an aunt to newborn. Ivy longed to pull out her journal right there to keep the memory from fading.

Rinap's fingers closed around her own. Ivy's joy collapsed. *We are here to hunt,* she remembered. *One of these animals is about to die.*

"Xiou is ready. Filhia's waiting for you."

With a sinking feeling, Ivy made her way to the trees. It was no longer her own safety she was concerned about. The stegodon family were devoted to one another and about to lose a member. The matriarch would defend their attack. Ivy suppressed her instinct to protect the animals' lives and forced the faces of the hunters into her mind instead. Xiou, Kora, Guntah, Setian, Krue, Leihna, Rinap, Kari - and all of the others. This was their livelihood. It was necessary and to be fair, the size and strength of the stegodon far surpassed the hunters. It could easily be her own family that lost a member today and suffered for it.

On the sloped forest edge, Filhia found her. Of the forty hobbits that came, eight stayed in the trees. They were there to assist, to butcher, to carry. Some, like Filhia, were too young or unskilled to hunt and others were experts only in butchering or had injuries from the fire that rendered them less agile but still strong. Ivy watched as the dark spaces below wove through the grass in a wide arc. Beside her, Filhia's eyes were straining to follow her older sister's shadow. With both parents killed by the Swift Death, the girls were inseparable.

Ivy watched as the arc closed in precisely, like a shower of arrows. In the centre, the young bull startled from his cud, sensing danger. The vibration of thirty pairs of tiny feet came to him through the soles of his own, as a myriad of nerve receptors shot the low frequency message to his brain.

Rearing back on two legs, his groan escalated to a bellow, splitting the tranquillity of the scene as a jigsaw of hunters suddenly materialised around him. Instantly, trumpeting and bellows filled the air. It was a stampede. With a rush of air, the young stegodon crashed to earth and charged, scattering hunters like mice. The matriarch screamed in fury and stamped her feet sending vibrations far into the hard earth. She rushed in from her outpost.

Water thrashed underfoot. Confusion reigned as the herd sought an escape through the sudden minefield of spears. Calves were swept up in a rush of trunks and thundering feet. With weak newborn eyes, the little one fell, lost in the long grass. Within an instant she was surrounded by a barrage of trunks rolling and lifting her to unsteady feet. With a roar like thunder the mother stegodon reached her, eyes rolling with rage. She led her baby in the direction of the retreating herd. The calves were pushed away from the danger by young adults, while the matriarch and her eldest daughters fanned out, fiercely protecting their precious ones.

Still separated, the young bull roared and fought, holding the hunters at bay. Spears slashed from all sides to weaken and tire him. The mothers rushed to his defence, crushing the long grass and its hidden attackers underfoot. Tusks ripped at the hunters. The hobbits returned lightning jabs of razor-sharp stone.

Bodies flew. The hunters ducked and weaved beneath tusks, caught in a deadly game of dare beneath feet bigger than their own skull. But it was the bull they sought; they had no interest in killing the others.

Ivy's heart was pounding. She had lost sight of Rinap and Leihna in the chaos. *Are they hurt?* The prospect of such fragile girls being tossed or skewered by a tusk chilled her blood.

Beside Ivy, Filhia's face was frozen in panic. Her lips were pinched and her brow so deeply furrowed it cut into ridges. Sweat collected on her lip and her fist was clenched almost white around Ivy's fingers. Ivy squeezed Filhia's hand. It was cold and clammy, despite the heat.

Quickly, the hunters realigned themselves. With a half dozen focused on keeping each of the tyrannical females at bay, the strongest men gathered at the head of the young bull, who now now foaming at the mouth with anger and exhaustion. In one swift move, Ivy saw Krue, Setian and Xiou leap into his path. Xiou's spear broke clean through the centre of his forehead directly below his treacle eyes. At the same moment, Krue thrust his spear into the soft knobbed bone of the stegodon's temple. Setian had sprung high. Clinging to its back, the hunter expertly speared the tender flesh under the bull's shoulder blade with enough force to pierce his heart. With a final bellow, the bull crashed to the ground, dead.

It was done.

The matriarch eyeballed the assassins with rage, burning their faces to her interminable memory. With a summoning call, she and her daughters backed away, faced with the definitive loss of their charge. With resounding roars of fury, they backed along the river brandishing tusks in sweeping warning, then turned and ran into the forest.

The hunters gathered around the slain bull. There were bruises and gashes, scrapes and a concussion, but miraculously all had survived the stegodons' defence. Filhia fell into the arms of her older sister, overcome with relief. Rinap patted her quietly, wanting to reassure her without seeming a child herself. Kari's face was almost as relieved when he saw Rinap unscathed. Apparently he had swept her away from the deadly tusks numerous times, to which she had responded with even more determination to prove her skills. Ivy couldn't help but be proud of the girl's audacity. Leihna had been knocked to the ground early on and now sat concussed and silent in the grass. Ivy comforted her in place of Shahn, who had stayed at the cave, too heavily pregnant to travel.

There was no celebration, nor fanfare. This victory was only a victory of strength, not justice nor worth. The adolescent bull had stood his ground, protected his family and fought bravely. As much a child of nature as the hunters themselves, the hobbits took no gratification in his death, but instead offered humility and thanks to him for the gift of his life. He would feed their family. He deserved to be honoured.

Krue stood at the animal's head and closed his hands over its glassy eyes. Through Leihna, Ivy heard his practiced words.

"We honour you, brother probech, for your courage and sacrifice. We thank your family for the gift of your life. They will mourn and remember you, so we offer them this; we will bring your life back to the forest through our own bodies and you will walk again through our footsteps. We are now a part of each other."

Quiet at first, their voices rose from scorching grass. A single note, held long and low like thunder on the horizon, then another to match its strength, and another on top, rich in it's timbre. Beside Ivy, Leihna raised her face to the sky and offered her song in a young woman's clear, sweet voice.

The Dusk Song.

Forty voices rose and fell together, vibrant but soft in their release. From the slain bull's side, the long grass swept the harmonic offering across the river valley and up into the burning sky, forming a strange bridge between heaven and earth that seemed almost tangible enough to cross.

There was no religion or God designed to receive the offering. Regardless, the reverence the hunters held for their prey was sacred and palpable.

All at once, the voices broke together. The midday valley fell silent. With a single move, Krue's hand was high in the air; blade poised, and then plunged deep across the animal's throat. Warm blood hit his face in streaks of scarlet.

A furious shout echoed across the valley. The silence shattered.

Krue pulled back his blade, looking up, searching for the source of it.

Ivy's pupils narrowed, straining to see beyond her grass veil. All around her, hunters leapt to their feet.

Ivy's blood ran cold.

Belting towards them from across the river, were men. Furious, indomitable, massive men.

The karathah.

CHAPTER 48

ORRIN

*I*t was past midnight and Orrin sat alone in his small office. Food wrappers and empty coffee cups cluttered his desk and worry lines felt permanently etched on his forehead. Ivy's cello recording played softly on repeat through his speakers. Orrin wasn't really listening anymore; he already had every note and run committed to memory.

It had been two days since Dimi had called.

I can't guarantee that I know you anymore Orrin. I've warned you. You're on your own now.

Dimi wasn't the sort to over-react. His cool head had countered Orrin's quick temper on more than one occasion in younger days. But now he'd abandoned their friendship in an instant. Orrin's gut twisted and he buried his face in his hands.

Once more, he picked up his phone and dialled Dimi's number. Once more, it rang out.

Shite. He tossed the phone onto the table. The dull thud as it hit the desk broke the silence of the building and Orrin shivered despite himself. His palms were sweaty and he suddenly felt desperate to speed up time, to get Ivy back before another obstacle presented itself. If only he knew how. He wondered what the Director had threatened Dimi with, to make him react so severely?

I got him into this mess. The guilt of that thought was buried a hundred fold by the creeping doubt he had been trying to ignore. Could he trust Dimi not to betray his secret? Dimi knew everything - the laboratory experiments, the energy surge, the transformation of the earth into a new ugly one where hobbits were facing experimentation and torture and environmental genocide and solar storms increasingly threatened human life. And at the heart of the mess, somehow, were Orrin and Ivy.

Most devastatingly, he'd told Dimi about Ivy. How he'd lost her. How he was responsible for getting her back. How, perhaps, was *in love* with her. And still, his supposed best friend had deserted him.

He opened his desk drawer and picked up the amulet. The surface was smooth now. It's layers of dirt had been rubbed away during the many times he had sat holding it over the past few days, feeling its strange warmth and imploring it to give up the answer to this infuriating puzzle. Orrin traced his fingertips across the surface.

He turned it over. The five circular indentations still marked the back. *What do they mean?* He wondered. *Who put them there?* Orrin held it up to the light.

Well I'll be damned. The five points of the Southern Cross, just like the cave painting. How on earth did I miss that?

Orrin leapt from his chair, grabbing his jacket, and rushed out of the empty building. He skirted the paths and security cameras, hugging the dark places. Orrin hid as a lone security guard doing his rounds passed by with a torch then slipped into the leafy garden surrounding the biology building. The manicured gardens gave way to native bush, thick and deliberately unkempt. Thin leafy branches whipped his face as he negotiated his way further in, hopeful, but unsure of where exactly he would end up. *He smacked into a wire wall.* Orrin reached up high. He began to hoist himself up the tall fence he found in his way.

"Ouch!" He jerked his hand back. Blood dripped down the inside of his wrist. He wiped it on his jeans. *Damn it.* He hadn't expected the barbed wire. Pulling off his jacket to mute the barbs, Orrin gripped the top wire securely with both hands. He drew breath through gritted teeth and scrambled over the top. His shirt and jeans caught and ripped as he fell heavily on the other side, covered in scratches.

There was a loud hiss in the dark. It pricked the hair on the back of his neck.

Orrin turned, finding himself against yet another wire wall. This one however, was the perimeter of a giant cage. A dim globe hung from the wire roof, which was open to the elements. Further back, a covered awning connected the cage to an inside observation room. Only a couple of meters away, on the inside of the cage, four pairs of dark eyes watched his every move.

"I don't want to hurt you," he said aloud quietly. "Just talk, do you understand?" Orrin held his palms up in what he hoped was a gesture of surrender. "I won't hurt you. I promise I won't."

Orrin noticed the cage was now entirely empty but for the hobbit woman, her infant and two children, perhaps three or four years old. They were pitiful in their terror of him as they hid behind their mother. The hatred in the hobbit woman's eyes was gone. Now, there was only true fear and grief.

"Where are the others?" Orrin whispered.

The tiny woman hugged her baby tighter. It was clear she'd lost the battle to save her family many times now. A purple bruise ballooned her left cheekbone and cuts and grazes laced her skin. She frowned at Orrin then turned and pushed her infant into the arms of the eldest remaining child, who seemed little more than a baby herself.

The hobbit woman stepped forward on shaking legs. She staggered but righted herself, clearly determined to see the threat gone. Her breathing was laboured and a wheezing hiss coated her breath. Bones projected unnaturally from her tiny frame. Her matted black hair hung miserably over thin shoulders.

"Ash gitraahn shiwah!" she hissed, clutching the wire wall between them. The malice had returned, but there was no strength to her threat.

"No, I'm not leaving yet," Orrin said. "But I promise I won't hurt you."

Orrin sank to his knees. Less than a meter of dirt separated him from the animal. *No - human. This is a human,* he realised, unexpectedly. He suddenly felt compelled to reach out and touch her.

Orrin pushed aside the thought and instead pulled the amulet from his pocket and held it up to the light.

"I need help, love. There are markings on this. See, here - stars." Orrin pointed to the amulet and up to the night sky. "Stars. Five stars. What do they mean?" He frowned. "What do they mean, these stars?"

The woman squinted at the stone in Orrin's hand, trying to make it out in the dim light. Her eyes grew wide. She looked panicked, flicking between the stone and his face.

He lowered his voice. "Please. *The stars.* There are markings on this stone. It's the Southern Cross, look!" Fumbling in the dark, he found five jagged rocks, each the size of a fist. He shoved them one by one into the lattice of wire, creating a vertical rocky constellation between them.

"*Hiranah,*" she whispered.

"What?"

"*Hiranah.*"

"Hiranah?" Orrin repeated. "Is that was this is called? These stars?"

The woman closed her eyes, deliberating. With slow careful movements, she pointed back to the rocky constellation and then found its counterpart in the sky, barely visible through the clouds. She gestured back to the amulet. *"Hiranah."*

The woman crouched down. She swept the dirt floor with her fingers collecting a twig and poked it through the wire lattice. Her bony wrist and arm easily followed. She began to draw a shape in the dirt at Orrin's knees. Five points coming together. Connecting the dots.

An ivy leaf.

"Hiranah." She whispered again. Her arm swept once more from the constellation, to the amulet and down to her dirt symbol. *"Hiranah."*

She smiled sadly, then turned and limped back to her children.

"She's some kind of Goddess," Orrin declared.

"Who is?"

"Ivy."

"Yeah right man, you wish."

"No listen Phil, I'm serious. I've been looking into this 'Hiranah' symbol that the hobbit woman showed me. It was an Ivy leaf, clear as day. I think they're all interconnected; the symbol, the constellation and the amulet. I think, they are all *Ivy*."

"Okay, I'm game." Phil leaned back in his chair, crossing his arms with a derisive look. "Humour me."

Orrin ignored the sarcasm. "I've been doing some research on the *Homo floresiensis* species. There isn't much to go by, well, there's actually a lot of anatomy and subsistence research available. But not much culturally."

"That's probably because they have no culture, dude." Phil rolled his eyes.

"Actually they do, you smart article. It's just not widely recognised. Listen to this," Orrin adjusted his glasses and read from the computer screen.

"Early behavioural research on the *Homo floresiensis* species was undertaken by Chantelle Miruve, a PhD from Oxford University during the years 1967-1978. Dr Miruve was the fourth and final researcher sent into the field under the umbrella of famous palaeoanthropologist Louis Leakey to study primates in their natural environments. This research stemmed from his attempts to determine the potential similarities between non-human primates and early human behaviour.

'Leakey's Angels', as they became known, consisted of Jane Goodall, Dian Fossey, Birute Galdikas and Chantelle Miruve. These women respectively studied the chimpanzees of Tanzania, mountain gorillas in Rwanda, orangutans of Borneo and the Homo floresiensis 'hobbit' species in Flores, Indonesia.

Initially, Miruve made minimal headway with the species; however, she was eventually able to gain their trust enough to begin ethnographic research as well as behavioural observation. Her work suggests the hobbits have a complex oral history. The species is primarily a nature-worship society incorporating a deity (taken to be a goddess-like figure) called Hiranah. The name is a reference to the sunset and is symbolised by a crude five pointed shape, believed to be a star. This symbol has since been found represented at numerous limestone caves in Flores by archaeologists.

Dr Miruve's sympathies for the species against deforestation concerns and hunting of the hominid for the bush-meat trade, led to frequent conflict with local hunters. Dr Miruve was found murdered in her camp in 1987. No charges were ever laid."

Phil let out a soft whistle. "Murdered?"

"That's what it says" said Orrin, "It seems the debate over hobbit rights began a long time ago, but apparently Dr Miruve's voice was silenced pretty swiftly." Orrin adjusted his glasses as he considered the prisoners, for that is clearly what they were, in the Behavioural Research lab. "At least now there seems to be some backlash to their treatment. It's a shame it's taken this long."

"I don't think life's going to improve for them in a hurry, poor little buggers," Phil said.

Orrin raised an eyebrow. "I didn't think you gave a shite what happened to them."

"Maybe I don't. Dunno." Phil shuffled uncomfortably. "I heard a black-market haul was uncovered yesterday though. It was bad news. Exotic animals, hundreds of them. Mainly young ones being sent as pets from South East Asia to the Middle East. They're considered a status symbol you know, there's big money involved."

"What happened?"

If Phil looked uncomfortable before, now he looked down-right disturbed. He took a deep breath and let his eyes wander around the room as he spoke.

"The shipping containers were pulled off route and confiscated but almost all the animals were already dead. Clouded leopards, heaps of exotic birds, monkeys and hobbits. Lots of them. They didn't have enough food or water to make the distance. Or enough air. Some suffocated, most starved."

The blood drained from Orrin's face. "They did that to the young ones? All those animals? To children?"

Phil finally met Orrin's eyes. His distaste was clear in the set of his mouth. "It's pretty standard apparently. Babies make the best pets."

Orrin screwed his eyes shut at the memory of the injured hobbit mother fighting for her children against the tranquiliser darts. How soon would she lose her last battle? Were her last three children destined to become pets on the black market? Consumer novelties for the rich? The thought was sickening.

"It's been happening for years O," Phil sighed. "There's nothing you can do about it." He looked thoughtful. "So you're saying this 'Hiranah' deity that Miruve uncovered is actually Ivy?"

"I'm saying it has *got* to be Ivy," said Orrin. "Look at the ethnographic evidence. The word *Hiranah* actually means sunset – a pretty distinctive shade of red and also the exact colour of Ivy's hair."

Phil grinned. "You like gingers, hey?" He waggled his eyebrows suggestively.

"Shut your gob and focus Phil," rebuffed Orrin, without malice. "So, the symbol representing this deity is a five pointed shape, I bet it's not a star - it's an ivy leaf." He strode over to the pin board and pulled Jayne's cave painting down. "What is this, if not a clear indication of Ivy living with these people? Red hair, white skin, even Kyah is documented in prehistory."

"But why consider her a deity, even if she was there?" said Phil. "She's human, not a god. She has no special powers." Although Phil countered Orrin's argument, his face showed no disrespect.

Orrin considered for a moment. "Well, I'm sure this Dr Miruve recorded it as objectively as she could. But there are language barriers, obviously, and she didn't have all of the information, did she? How could she have known Ivy wasn't a deity, but was actually just a normal woman – in the wrong place and the wrong time? There is no precedent for something like this. Maybe her observations were correct, but her interpretation was wrong."

"Fair enough." Phil conceded. "As far as the logic goes, I suppose I can accept that. Assuming it all happened of course. And we'll have confirmation of that little stretch of insanity in just under a week."

"Yes, we will." Orrin sighed, sitting back at his desk.

Phil sat forward, pulling a newspaper out from under his half-eaten cafeteria lunch. He folded it back onto itself and expertly ran his fingers down the page.

"Crap," he said, scowling.

"What now?" Orrin didn't look up.

"Stock prices have dropped again. MMR, and consequently most of my inheritance, is going down the drain."

"MMR? Never heard of it," said Orrin. Although, in light of the fact he didn't belong to this version of reality, Orrin wasn't really surprised.

"A mining conglomerate," Phil said. "Most of the rare earth metals being pulled out of South East Asia are mined by MMR Holdings. Including Flores, actually. That's where they started, just a local Chinese operation back then until geologists recognized the link between the hobbits' brains and what was underground. They moved the operation into Indonesia and it's been nothing but champaigne and caviar since then." At Orrin's bewildered expression, Phil added, "Family connections - my grandparents were ground-floor investors."

"And here I was thinking you aspired to the noble mediocrity of an academic salary," Orrin said.

"Hell no, I'm planning to live off my charm and good looks," Phil shot back. "But I did hope my trust fund would still be around when they wear out."

"My heart is bleeding for you. So why did the shares drop?" asked Orrin.

Phil looked disgruntled. "Now it's clear you've been AWOL from reality or you wouldn't be asking. The shares are nearly worthless because we're running out of deposits to mine. There's been a shit-fight over the last tracts of land and MMR lost the job to someone else. Basically, what minimal rare earth deposits are left are worth billions and the rest of the land is worthless. It's been strip mined to buggery and replanted with Palm Oil plantations. Hence, the share prices and my future livelihood, as it were, are going rapidly down the toilet."

"My condolences, boyo. For what it's worth, so's the rest of the damned planet," said Orrin.

"Touche." Phil continued his half-eaten lunch while Orrin considered their conversation. If such massive amounts of rare earth metals had been removed from South East Asia, surely there would be serious environmental ramifications. And what of Flores? The evolutionary adaptation of magnetite in the hobbit brain suggested that their homeland was a sinkhole of valuable metals as well. If those deposits were gone now, strip mined away, as Phil had said, how had that affected the magnetic fields surrounding the area? Or the hobbits themselves for that matter?

There were too many unanswered questions. Orrin rubbed his chin, feeling entirely out of his depth. It was intriguing though and he determined to find out more. After a short while, he looked at his watch.

"You'd better leg it," Orrin said. "My lecture notes are on the desk by the door."

Phil scowled towards the door and the stack of papers he'd been trying to ignore. "How long are we going to keep this up Orrin? I'm not qualified or experienced enough to be teaching these classes for you. Third year quantum physics? I didn't even specialise in that area." He looked genuinely intimidated.

"You're doing grand, Phil, I trust you implicitly with this."

"It's not about trust!" Phil argued. "If the Chancellor found out you've been skipping lectures and sending me to teach instead…"

"Well what else can I do?" Orrin thumped his hand flat on the desk in front of him. He turned away. "I need every scrap of time I can get. I don't have time to teach! I can't just turn up to the Chancellor's office and tell her I sent a woman into the Stone Age! She'd have me committed or fire me on the spot. Either way, I'd be out of the lab and I need to be here to make this right. I can't say I need sick leave, because I'm here everyday, and every night for that matter." Orrin scraped his fingers through his scalp. "My only choice is to bunk off so I can keep figuring this out and get Ivy back. I'm running out of time, man."

Phil scowled. "There are hundreds of students getting an

unqualified substitute everyday. Something's gonna give, you know I can't keep this up."

"Please Phil. I *need* you to do this for me," Orrin begged.

"You're going to get found out and we'll both be in major shit," Phil said. "My future career prospects may not be as important to you as your love life, but they damn well are to me!"

"It's only another week. It has to be you. You're the only one I trust to cover me."

"Well, maybe you're too damn trusting," Phil scowled. "Maybe I don't want to jeopardise my career for you."

Orrin's shoulders sagged. "You're entirely right. *I'm sorry.* But I need you to do this for me. I owe you big time."

"You're damn right you do." Phil picked up the stack of papers and data drive waiting on the desk by the door. "Just don't be surprised when this all comes crashing down on you, man. Because it will." He left.

Orrin's eyes stung. He walked back to his monitor and sat down. For a long time, he stared at the open document without really seeing it.

"I could give those lectures for you." Dale's timid voice sounded hopeful. "I aced Quantum Physics last year."

Orrin looked up, surprised. Once again, he'd been so involved in his discussion that he'd forgotten Dale was in the room.

"I know you aced it, I was your lecturer." Orrin smiled apologetically. "The truth is though, I need someone to get up there and convince those kids that he's meant to be there. They'd eat you alive."

Dale's face fell but Orrin pushed on, feeling obliged to justify his choice.

"I just can't risk any questions. Phil's nothing if not confident, and he knows just enough to get the job done. If any of the students reported this to the Chancellor, well, I'd be looking for a new job and as for Ivy…" It was too horrific to consider.

"Yeah, I know." Dale disappeared behind the monitor. "I'll just keep running these simulations then?"

"Thanks Dale, I appreciate it."

Dale returned silently to work. A minute later his mobile phone startled them both. It was the first time Orrin had ever heard it ring. Dale pulled it from his backpack with a frown.

"Yes, this is Dale Brennan." His cheeks reddened. With a nervous glance to Orrin, he left the room to take the call.

CHAPTER 49

IVY

Twenty men broke the river's edge spraying clouds of white water in their wake. They were tall and intimidating and for a moment Ivy almost forgot she was one of them; their equal in size, if not strength. High cheekbones framed their glinting eyes and wiry, rippling muscles shifted beneath their skin. The men shouted, waving spears and sharp blades as they ran. They were furious.

Behind them, six sapien women laden with baskets, stumbled on the wet rocks with their heavy loads. They were wide-eyed and clearly terrified.

Ivy ducked lower, pulling Leihna to the ground beside her. She brushed the grassy veil aside, barely breathing as the karathah hunters shadowed her family.

It was him. The red-beaded man. He had led the charge and now stepped forward, towering over Krue with clenched fists. The old man was still kneeling by the stegodon's head. Blood was splattered across his stony expression. Ivy could feel Leihna trembling under her arm. Ivy's hand went reflexively to her own throat. This man had already tried to kill her twice. She was angry. At herself for hiding, and at him for his persecution.

Ivy struggled to stop herself from leaping to her feet. In the deepest pit of her gut, she wanted this red-beaded man dead. Every lost face was etched in her memory now; every poisoned hunter that had bled from the inside out. Every burnt and suffocated victim of his arson. *The boy, Terap. The grieving mother, Emiri. The defiled daughter, Tikan. And dear little Turi.* This man was ultimately responsible for all of them. *I hate him.*

The red-beaded hunter was shouting. His shoulders were tense and his arm thrust upward sharply as he yelled. But as she watched him, Ivy realized his eyes had no fire inside. They were cold. Calculating. For all the violent emotion he inferred, the man was perfectly calm inside. *He's not really angry*, Ivy realized in shock. Even still, his fists punched the air. The other karathah responded in furious shouts, following his lead.

Ivy looked over to the karathah women. They were carrying butchering equipment like Filhia and herself.

"They must have come to hunt," Ivy whispered to Leihna, who was breathing hard beside her. "And we've scared the other stegodon away." Ivy guessed that the herd would be far gone now, critically aware of the lurking danger. The element of surprise had been ruined; the stegodon would be wary for weeks to come. The karathah would have to track much further, and fight harder to bring one down. "There's no better justification for a fight."

Leihna suddenly looked much younger than her twelve years. The bravery she had shown only minutes before in face of a stegodon had dissolved in light of an adversary so much more deadly.

"This isn't their territory, we have always hunted here," Leihna said, clasping Ivy's wrist, pressing the warm amulet into her skin. Ivy smoothed the frightened girl's hair away from her face, trying to seem braver than she felt.

"Well it seems they consider it their territory now."

Leihna blinked back tears. "Am I going to die?"

A rush of fear and adrenaline hit Ivy's heart. She squeezed her eyes shut.

"No, you're not," Ivy said through gritted teeth. She looked back at Leihna. "I won't let them touch you."

Leihna nodded and resolutely smeared away the tears that had escaped.

Ivy strained to see through the swaying grass again. Injured pride was drawn on the faces of the youngest karathah hunters. It was clear that they didn't want to return home empty-handed. Red beads rattled as their hunt leader shouted something to his comrades. Sweat flicked from his skin. His men rallied with affirmation, spitting and cursing at the hobbits. Ivy's hand moved reflexively back to her throat.

The hobbits, despite their size, were built with a brute strength far superior to a human man. The sapiens were bigger, faster and more agile but here on the riverbank, they were outnumbered two-to-one. Ivy wondered if the odds might be evenly matched.

The karathah pushed forward, shouting, but the red beaded hunter held his hand up. They stopped. The leader's eyes flashed at Krue, teasingly. Krue stood up, slowly and defiantly. His knuckles were white around his butchering blade. Pure loathing was set into his face. Once again, Krue was faced with his daughter's murderer. The old man seemed barely contained in his own skin. He was defiant and proud in the face of his enemy, and more than willing to fight.

Suddenly changing tack, the red-beaded man threw his head and shoulders back. He let out a derisive, cruel laugh that belted across the grasslands. After a moment, his hunters followed suit. The red-beaded hunter gestured to the size of his adversary with clear contempt then bent forward with glittering eyes and kicked Krue roughly away from the stegodon carcass.

Krue crashed onto his back to a chorus of mean-spirited laughter. Scrambling to his feet, Krue faced his attacker squarely, teeth bare with silent ferocity. His shoulders were high and pulled forward.

Ivy's heart swelled at the sight of him. As miserable and distrusting as he had been to her, Krue was brave. But the futility of his courage doused her Ivy like a bucket of cold water. Even at full height, the top of Krue's head barely reached the other man's rib cage.

A handful of karathah men stepped forward with butchering blades.

A dozen hobbits pushed forward with their spears, ready to defend. Kari and Kiran, the two boys that had been attacked with arrows while trapping birds with Terap, stood bravely among them.

"We will fight!" Krue's warcry echoed in her head through Leihna's thoughts.

"No!" Xiou's plea from beside Krue was hoarse with emotion. "They will kill us all!"

Ivy knew Xiou's appeal was not cowardice. She could feel Leihna's heart drumming against her arm. If the girl died, it would break her sister Shahn's heart, and that in turn would break his.

"They have taken enough from us!" Krue yelled back. "This probech is ours, this territory is ours! We *will* defend it!" He threw himself at the red-beaded hunter, thrusting the stone blade he held towards the man's thigh. But not fast enough. The man snarled and swung his arm around, revealing a thick wooden club he'd had hidden behind his back. Ivy heard a sickening crack as it collided with Krue's shoulder. He fell to the hard earth, crying out. The karathah hunters laughed and whooped. Xiou rushed forward to Krue's defence.

"Xiou! No!" Ivy scrambled to her feet, desperate to spare him. Before a second passed, she knew it was a mistake. The shouts of the karathah choked into dead silence. Their bravado fell away, replaced with utter terror. One woman fell to the ground, spilling her basket. Others wailed, frozen between action and fear.

Ivy knew what they saw. Every part of her screamed alien - from her bright emerald eyes to her blazing red hair and deathly pale skin. She was gruesome in their eyes; far from the dark, lithe beauty of their own women.

The red-beaded hunter slowly inclined his head, making eye contact with a young boy half-hidden behind the group. He looked barely twelve. The man muttered something to the boy. The boy turned, bolting back toward the river crossing alone.

Then, Ivy found herself looking directly into the hunter's eyes for the second time in as many weeks. The corners of his mouth curled into a grin. His eyes locked onto the amulet dangling from her wrist and without looking away, his war cry hit the air.

The karathah rushed forward with strangled shouts.

"Run! To the forest! Go!" Ivy dragged Leihna to her feet and pushed her away as the girl willingly lost herself in the grass ocean out of sight.

The red-beaded hunter leapt toward Ivy.

She tightened the hold on her spear and bolted. A deep rumbling shook the earth and a sharp blow caught her back. Ivy landed with a thump on the ground.

The red-beaded man landed on her and spun her onto her back. The blade of his knife broke the skin on Ivy's chest. She hissed in pain. Ivy brought her elbow hard into his jaw, kicking wildly. She swung her legs and knocked him off her hips then rolled over, scrambling to get away. A strong hand caught her bare ankle and the man threw himself forward, covering her entirely with his body. His fingers groped roughly against her skin and for a split-second her thoughts petrified at the prospect that he might rape her. She slammed her forehead forward into his and his face swam before her eyes. The man growled in pain and anger, then reached sideways grabbing Ivy's wrist, wrenching it toward himself and meeting it with the knife. *He wants my amulet.* His face was twisted as he struggled against her, trying to sever the connection between Ivy's amulet and her wrist. *Why?* The leather knot began to fray as a slice hit its mark.

Ivy fought back like a lion. She smashed her forehead down as hard as she could again, this time into the man's throat, then again. She heaved her shoulder bone forward, pushing him back and punched his still broken nose with the heel of her hand. She was rewarded with a spray of blood to her face. She slammed her knee up hard into his abdomen and the man crumpled on top of her, winded. Ivy pushed his chest off her own and scrambled to kick away the dead weight of his curled legs. She threw herself onto her belly, dragging her knees through the grass.

A searing pain tore through her thigh.

Ivy spun back around. Her hide skirt was ripped down one side. The red-beaded hunter was attached to her naked leg with a cruel leer on his face. The stone blade was fisted in his hand, its razor's edge knapped for the inch-thick hide of a stegodon. He'd sliced through her thigh like a hot knife through butter. Blood streamed from the deep cut. Her ivy leaf birthmark drowned in red. White flecks began dancing across her vision.

With a rush of fury and adrenaline, Ivy kicked the gloating man's face as hard as she could. She staggered to her feet. His club had fallen to the grass beside him and they both lurched toward it at once. Ivy grabbed it first, heaving back and smacking it into his ribs with a sickening crack.

Ivy threw the club across the field as she ran away, limping as fast as she could go. All around her were screams of agony and vengeance.

For the first time, the hobbits were fighting back.

Ivy saw flashes of dark skin within the grass and lithe, sinewy hunters towering above them. Krue was not far from her, with five huge men bearing down on him. His knife flicked lightning-fast from his fingers. One karathah fell. Krue spun around, catching Ivy's eye for the tiniest moment before hurling his spear into another man's gut. He shouted to her over his shoulder as she ducked past. She had no translation, but his meaning was clear. *Fight! Fight, Hiranah!* Grabbing the dead man's club from his hand, Krue turned to face the remaining three.

"Krue!" Ivy screamed. The three hunters imploded their strength onto the old hobbit in unison. He crumpled to the ground. Ivy turned away, mute with horror.

Fight. Find the girls. Pain is nothing. Ivy pushed down the bile rising in her throat and blocked out any other thought. She took off again, chancing a glance behind her as she ran. There was no sign of the red-beaded man. Her feet caught a lump in the long grass and Ivy smashed face first onto the ground. With heaving breaths, she struggled back to her feet.

It was Rinap. Her dark eyes were huge with pain. She was shining with sweat as she twisted in jerky movements. With a muted cry, Rinap yanked an arrow from her own arm. She got to her feet, panting.

"To the forest, Rinap! Run!" Ivy screamed, trying to pull her away from the chaos. But Rinap had her eyes set on something else. She wrenched away from Ivy's grip and ran in the opposite direction. Finally, Ivy saw what Rinap had already known - a sapien hunter was dragging a small body in the direction of the river. Ivy's feet were moving before her mind caught up. Filhia kicked and screamed as her captor yanked her through the grass. Even with a punctured arm, Rinap's eyes were only for her little sister.

"No!" Ivy's long strides passed Rinap's vehement speed, all pain in her leg forgotten. From the other direction came two more would-be saviours, but not those Ivy anticipated.

The young karathah women from the trade offering ran as fast as Ivy. They screamed hysterically through their tears. The older girl was fastest, with strings of turquoise feathers whipping her face and dark hair that flew out behind her. They caught up, grabbing at Filhia and trying to pull her away from the karathah hunter. Their voices grew hoarse as they pleaded and clawed at the man's arms.

As the feathered woman caught his wrist, the hunter spun back, cursing at their insistence. Ivy had no idea why they were trying to save Filhia from a man they clearly knew, but had no time to consider it. The turquoise feathers took flight as he knocked her away and she fell sprawling to the ground. The other woman stepped back, cringing.

With lightning speed, Rinap drew back her spear and rammed it toward him. She missed, scraping his ribs. He shouted and threw Filhia to the ground, leaving her gasping for air. Pulling a club from the back of his waist belt, the hunter swung wildly at Rinap. He found his mark. Ivy heard a snap and Rinap's feet left the ground.

She was dead before she landed.

"No! No! No!" Ivy leapt at the man, tears blinding her and hatred spilling from her mouth. He aimed a kick to Ivy's punctured thigh and it exploded in pain. She fell backwards, screaming.

The hunter grabbed Filhia by her hair again and dragged her over the river edge.

Ivy pulled herself up, curling her fingers around Rinap's spear, fallen to the grass beside her. There was suddenly no thought, no time, no hesitation. Ivy's arm and everything around her slowed as she drew her fist back with all the force she could muster. Then the moment broke.

Ivy rammed the spear through his chest.

Shock muted her senses. *Take them home. They need to go home.* Ivy acted on reflex, heaving Rinap's broken body over her shoulder. Filhia lay by the river, unconscious but breathing. The woman with the turquoise feathers picked the little girl up. With quick, soft movements, she lay Filhia across Ivy's arms. Their eyes met, grief-stricken. There was no fear in the eyes of the woman with the turquoise feathers now, but desperate, inconsolable apology. She stepped to the side of Ivy, cradling Rinap's face between her hands for a brief moment, and then with tears spilling down her face, the woman with turquoise feathers pushed Ivy away. *Run.*

Ivy ran.

She ran as fast as she could manage, desperate to flee with her beloved sisters, not allowing her mind to venture any further than escape. All around her, bodies were falling and fighting. Shouts and screams battled each other in a confusion of noise beyond the thrumming of her mind.

Stumbling over hidden bodies in the grass.

Ivy balanced Rinap between her neck and shoulder as she ran with Filhia draped across her arms. She was nearly at the tree line when it happened. She *felt* it first; a rumbling in the earth beneath her bare feet, followed by ear-splitting bellows that tore the air apart.

From the forest to the fray charged the three male stegodon they had passed upriver. They were massive and rippling with the power of instinctive defence. Their sensitive feet and trunks had received the desperate call of the matriarch's thumping feet, sent through the earth's sub-sonic waves. They had come to the aid of the female herd as fast as they could.

Too late, they found - the smell of blood and predators now suffocated the air. The three bachelors barrelled through the fighters, spilling men and reigning chaos. Trumpeting drowned out the screams as long, sharp tusks smashed and skewered indiscriminately. With the natural camouflage afforded them by natural selection, the hobbits that were still alive collectively sank into the long grass and disappeared.

Scrambling up the desolate ridges.

The next two hours passed as a dream. A nightmare hazed by shock and punctuated by pain until only a dull ache in her heart and thigh remained. From somewhere, Kari appeared, pulling Rinap's limp body from Ivy's shoulder and bearing it himself. Ivy kept tiny Filhia, clutching the girl's unconscious form to her own chest, unable to give her up. The girl's shallow breath became Ivy's rhythm - walking, stumbling, walking, stumbling. Stubbornly she kept on, growing weaker as the blood drained from her thigh, leaving one leg scarlet and the other as white as a ghost. *They needed me. They still need me.*

Descending into the hallowed darkness of the rainforest.

Deep inside Ivy's thigh, bacteria from the stone knife festered. The edges of the cut lay open and raw, an infection just beginning. Blood loss weakened and dulled her senses. Her body fought back too hard, inflaming her blood and impairing its flow. Sepsis began. *No. Can't fall. Have to fight.*

Following the serpent river, her leg washing clean in its depths.

Ivy followed the hunters as they carried the injured and those dead that they had been able to recover in their escape. Only twenty-five of the hunting party remained. Eight of the bodies had been left behind. *Not humanity. Not humane. Too cruel.* The world tilted dangerously, and Ivy stumbled.

Climbing the lonely hillside.

Despite her desperate condition, Ivy would not ease her burden, nor give in to the void that threatened to break her. *For her. Just one more step. For her.*

Her breath and heartbeat came faster. Chills whispered over her skin. The words Ivy sought in her head wouldn't come. It was confusing, all of this walking. Someone held her up. She heard his voice, not in the thudding of white noise outside her ears, but inside. *Orrin?* She stumbled again and her vision swam. *Orrin? I couldn't save them.* In the distance, she heard a woman speak. *Home? Is this my home?* His voice faded inside her head. *Not my home. He's my home....*

Entering the damp, hidden cave.

The band of hunters laid their fallen loved ones by the central hearth. Downcast eyes betrayed the loss when others did not return to be counted among the mourners. The wailing began.

Rinap lay dead, tiny and perfect in her new womanhood. Ivy watched through bleary eyes as Kari fell across her body with heaving sobs. He had left that morning as a young man on his first hunt, full of pride. That afternoon, he had borne Rinap's body stoically and led what was left of them safely home. But now, Kari was a boy again, shattered into a million pieces of darkness in his mind. He held her and stared, seeing nothing but his broken love.

The silence in Ivy's head cocooned her from the chaos outside. A figure, blurry and small appeared in front of her. Ivy recognized the face. *Phren.* She delivered Filhia's sleeping body into the old woman's arms. Like a baby. *I'm so sorry. I failed.*

The fever and loss of blood finally took her. Ivy collapsed. The dull clamour faded from around her as Kyah's soft hand appeared from nowhere to gently stroke her hair from her forehead. Everything went black.

Nobody noticed that her hide skirt was in tatters.

That her journal was missing.

And so, in a cold cave, fifty thousand years before her time, Ivy lay dying.

CHAPTER 50

ORRIN

"Can't keep away from me hey, Jayne?" Phil stretched back in his chair with his arms behind his head.

Jayne rolled her eyes and bypassed his desk.

"Sure Phil, clearly you're my highest priority in life."

She stopped in front of Orrin, who was waiting with a tired smile.

"It's another cave painting," she said.

Orrin studied the coloured printout she had brought as Jayne dropped her keys and bag onto his desk. Unlike the previous paintings, the images on this one were easy to make out.

"Handprints?"

"Yup. It doesn't look much out of context, but these hobbit prints are one of the few artworks from Flores attributed to the correct human species. Because of the size of the hands, of course."

"Hi, Jayne." Dale looked up from his screen, straightening his shoulders.

"Hey, Dale." Jayne nodded briefly, flicking her eyes to him but clearly disinterested in pleasantries.

"How old?" Orrin adjusted the black frames of his glasses.

"About the same – fifty thousand years. Give or take a few. This one's important, too."

Phil wandered to Orrin's desk and raised an eyebrow. "Okay, I'm listening."

"Brilliant." Jayne turned her back on him as she continued. "Anyway, there's an anomaly here. I didn't notice it at first, I doubt anyone ever has. Look really closely, can you see it?"

Although unsure what he was looking for, Orrin studied the photograph. The mottled grey wall of a limestone shelter had been almost entirely covered with painted hand prints. There were hundreds of them overlaid, representing innumerable generations of shared tradition. Shades from dark brown through to red, orange and yellow created a slightly chaotic feel. All of the handprints were faded to dull echoes of their former glory. The effect was pretty but melancholy, like the remnants of childhood once grown.

"I see it," Phil said.

Orrin looked up surprised. "Really?" He looked again. "What am I not seeing here?"

Phil pointed to the top left corner of the image, looking smug.

"This handprint is bigger than the rest. It's human."

"Sapien," Jayne corrected.

"Whatever," Phil said.

Orrin looked more closely. Phil was right. A single large handprint was barely visible under layers of smaller ones. They were all so faint that some were barely there at all.

"Holy Jesus." Orrin traced his fingertips over the image. This was Ivy's handprint, he was certain. He suddenly felt her presence on the mottled stone so vividly that his skin tingled against the paper. *Her hand was right here.* He swallowed the lump in his throat, remembering her touch.

"Would you like a moment alone with the photo, Orrin?"

Orrin scowled at Phil's grin as he pulled his hand away,

clearing his throat and muttering "gobshite" under his breath. Jayne's mouth twisted in amusement.

Phil turned to Jayne. "Seriously, you think this was actually Ivy? There were humans on Flores at the same time as these hobbits. Who's to say this isn't one of them?"

"Hobbits *are* humans, Phil and I'll tell you why it has to be Ivy," said Jayne. "Because for the last - gee, let me think – *fifty-five thousand years*, sapiens have treated hobbits as second class citizens. We've enslaved them, culled them, used them for whatever sacrifice or experiment was in vogue at the time and most unpleasantly, *eaten them*. So, you tell me, do you think it's likely they invited one of their friendly neighbours over as a permanent house guest?"

"I guess not, when you put it that way," said Phil.

"Thank you." Jayne allowed herself a smile. "So it could only be someone they trusted implicitly. Now, traditionally, indigenous hand paintings usually represent a family group or tribe. This collection represents kin – so if this really is Ivy's print," she looked to Orrin, "then she was accepted as family. That's quite an honour. I've never seen anything like this before."

There were a few moments of silence as they considered the implications. If Ivy *was* family at a time of cultural upheaval for the hobbit species, she could certainly have influenced their actions, for better or worse. And if those actions were relived in oral history throughout generations of storytelling, it was no wonder that the Hiranah reference had been mistaken for a deity by ethnographers.

Humans often had a way of embedding influential people and their stories into history, or pre-history as it were, and elevating them to divine status. It was human nature to seek comfort in something bigger than mere mortality. And so Ivy had become, in effect, a false God.

"If anyone could have been accepted by them, it would be her," said Orrin. "I remember what she was like with Kyah. Ivy saw past the differences between them; Kyah wasn't a chimp, I mean *bonobo* to her, she was more like a friend. I've never really thought about it before, but, I don't think Ivy would define family the same way we would. I think Kyah *was* her family, and so, maybe these hobbits were too."

Jayne looked at Orrin with more than a hint of sympathy. She took a deep breath and let her eyes rove the room. She seemed to be steeling her resolve. Orrin watched her, with rising concern.

"There's something else, isn't there?"

Jayne hesitated. "I'm afraid it's not the best news."

Orrin leant forward in his chair. *How much more can I take?* He drew his hand over his mouth and looked up at Jayne, waiting for her to continue.

She pushed the photograph to him again, pointing. "Okay. Look closely, here. One of the fingers on Ivy's handprint has been removed. The ochre has been smudged, almost rubbed away entirely."

"From rain or wind or something? So what?" Orrin said.

"No, no, you don't understand. The rest of the hand is consistently coloured. Weather would have affected the whole print. This finger, the index finger, must have been rubbed off intentionally, with some sort of oil. The rest of the handprints on here were overlaid later. The finger came off first, deliberately."

"What does that mean?" Orrin slid his hand up to his eyes, pushing his glasses away and rubbing the ache that was forming underneath.

"This missing finger," said Jayne, lowering her voice as if it might make what she had to say easier to hear, "It signifies death. There are conflicting theories on how it applies to the *Homo floresiensis* species, but essentially, in many indigenous cultures, a finger is removed from the handprint when a family member dies prematurely. It's a reference to the loss of someone who was dearly loved when a family is grieving. It also represents a supplication to any evil spirits that might be responsible for the death;

a request, if you will, to leave the dwelling of the family." Jayne looked to Phil and he reflexively stepped closer.

"I can't say for sure what it means," Jayne continued, "But the missing finger *is* important. Either someone in Ivy's hobbit family died, or -" she hesitated, biting her lip.

"Or what?" The lump in Orrin's throat wouldn't let him continue.

"Or, Ivy herself died, and her hobbit family removed her finger print as a sign of their own loss."

"No. Not acceptable. You're wrong."

"I'm sorry Orrin, but it actually could be," Jayne said. "At some point, soon after this cave painting was done, Ivy may have been killed."

"No, lay off with it. This is shite! It's not possible," Orrin said again, through gritted teeth. If his resolve failed now, Ivy had no chance of ever returning. He had to believe there was hope. "You have to be wrong about this. If she died there, at any time in the past, that means I failed! I didn't bring her home. No! No! No! She's been gone a month, that's all. Just one month. I need more time! I'll bring her home, I swear it."

Jayne swallowed, looking down. "Alright then. We'll work with option one." The pity in her eyes was too much. Orrin pushed himself out of his chair and tacked the image to the growing collection of clues on the laboratory wall. He took a deep breath to regain his composure.

"Thanks Jayne. I appreciate your help, I really do. I just can't afford to think like that."

Jayne picked up her bag and walked to the door.

"I'll keep looking okay? It's not over yet," she said, turning away.

"Miss me," called Phil after her.

"Bye Phil." And she was gone.

Dale returned his attention to the computer and clicked hard on the keyboard, with a scowl on his face.

Orrin shook his head and downed three pain-killers from a nearly empty packet on his desk. After a gulp of water, he set Ivy's cello recording into the music dock on repeat and got back to work.

"Heads up." Phil rounded the doorway shooting a dark look at Orrin, and then turned with feigned innocence. A woman stepped past him, striding toward the server rack where Orrin stood.

"Chancellor." Orrin took a deep breath.

"What the hell is going on here, Doctor James?" Her voice was subdued, but all the more dangerous for it. "I had dismissed rumours that you've been failing in your duties for the past three weeks - assuming that my newest member of staff, who came so highly recommended and honoured - would not let our department down in such a way. Yet here you are, able-bodied and available, lounging in your office whilst sending an unqualified *student* to do your work. You'd better have a damn good explanation for me."

Orrin looked to Phil for silent clarification. *What did you tell her?* Phil scowled at the polished floor, shaking his head and avoiding Orrin's eyes.

Shite. Orrin stepped forward. His disarming smile fell far short of its goal in view of his dishevelled appearance.

"I apologise, Chancellor. Clearly I've let you down. I didn't intend to, of course. There have been some, *complications...* with my work, that's all. I've been a bit tied up."

Orrin considered the woman before him. His only previous experience of Reshma Thandi involved the fastidious series of interviews he had undertaken to secure his position at the university four months prior. At the time, he had quite liked her refined and understated manner. Her unusual accent suggested an international career in academia, a subtle blend of American, Indian and Australian pronunciation. She had an intuitive understanding of knowing when to apply the pomp and circumstance, and when to cut the crap. Clearly, she had deemed the current situation one of the latter.

"Complications of what nature, Doctor James?" Her tone was cold.

"Ah, well, various complications I'm afraid. Complicated… complications." Orrin's fingers found the week-old stubble on his chin. *Bollocks.* He smoothed his crinkled shirt down and shifted away from the servers, highly conscious of the illuminated plasma screen behind him.

This woman was no bureaucrat. She was a physicist, first and foremost. Given the opportunity, she would recognise the inherent potential in the energy fluctuations he had created. Magnetospheric disintegration was at an all time high and any research that could provide an alternative energy source if grids were wiped out was a gold mine.

Orrin had no doubt that the university would demand full control over his attempts to recreate the energy fields, or worse, they could bring external authorities into the fray. Dozens of pencil pushers suffocating his lab was the last thing he needed right now.

And Ivy wasn't the only concern. If he publicised his belief that he was solely responsible for a prehistoric time shift, Orrin was guaranteed to earn himself either a Nobel Prize or a golden handshake to the nuthouse. He couldn't risk either.

"I'm waiting, Doctor James."

"I'm afraid I can't explain it, Chancellor."

Her neat eyebrows rose in disbelief and Chancellor Thandi swivelled to face Phil. He straightened up.

"Mister Chan would you like to offer an explanation?" she said.

"Um, I suppose not," Phil muttered. *"At this stage. I'm sorry, Chancellor."*

She turned back, her lips pursed. From behind her, Phil glared accusingly at Orrin.

"Doctor James," she began, "I am not entirely without compassion. If there is some personal issue that you are experiencing, then I would strongly consider a leave of absence." The Chancellor glanced toward Phil and lowered her voice even further. "Mister Chan here may be well-versed with your teaching methods, but this is a prestigious institution. I absolutely cannot abide our undergraduates being taught Quantum Physics by an unqualified student only a few years their senior."

"Of course not Chancellor, I understand entirely. There were factors… outside my control."

"Let me make this abundantly clear, Doctor James," the Chancellor turned to face Phil, "and Mister Chan I am addressing you too. This university will *not* accept staff that are consistently unable to meet their commitments. Nor will we abide unqualified students instructing our classes." Phil's face was bright red. "Consider this a warning. Both of your positions on staff are now probationary. If this happens again, I will have absolutely no hesitation in revoking your employment. Am I understood?"

"Trust me, Chancellor. It won't happen again," Phil said, weighing as much resentment into his voice as he could.

"Of course, I understand entirely," added Orrin.

As the Chancellor moved her eyes from Orrin, to the laboratory equipment, they narrowed in suspicion. He shifted uncomfortably under her scrutiny and moved forward in an effort to shepherd her out of the door.

"I'm sorry to take up your time, Chancellor, I assure you, I will attend to all of my classes myself."

Reshma Thandi stopped at the door and turned back to face the room. An uncomfortable silence pressed on them all as she flicked her eyes in turn over Orrin, Phil and then Dale, who sat wide eyed behind his monitor. She glanced at each of the white-boards, the still-broken tesla coil, the plasma screens and finally, the myriad of papers that Orrin had pinned to the wall. Finally, she spoke.

"Doctor James. Let me be frank. I hired you because you're one of the best. The work you're doing to isolate the cause of our magnetospheric degradation is of upmost importance to this department. We've provided you with the resources and budget you require without question and trust me when I say, that is not our standard practice." Chancellor Thandi gestured toward Phil, fidgeting by the door, and Dale, who shrank back under her gaze. "Nor is allowing such swift transfer and employment status for your research students. Perhaps I've been a little generous in your case regarding the autonomy of your work. That being so, I think it's best if the board keeps a closer eye on your progress."

"I really don't think that's necessary -" Orrin began.

"Well, I do. I expect a full report of your current research status on my desk in two days." She turned to leave, but stopped. She turned back to face him again.

"I feel I should also inform you that I've been contacted recently by the Director of the CSIRO Division of Astronomy and Space," she said. "Multiple times, in fact. They're investigating suspicious electromagnetic activity detected within this locality. It seems NASA is involved, along with the Ministry of Energy and Resources. Now, I assume that as one of our senior researchers, you would not hesitate to disclose any details of your research that would affect this school's safety or reputation?"

Orrin's back stiffened and he swallowed audibly. *NASA is involved?* Of course they were. It was only a matter of time before the CSIRO traced the origins of the fluctuations to the university. He'd done it himself, with the help of Dimi's stolen data, but he'd already known what he was looking for. *How far behind me are they? Did Dimi lead them here?* Orrin had the distinct feeling in his gut, that things were about to get a lot worse.

"Sure, I mean, of course, Chancellor, I um, assure you I'm *not* involved," said Orrin. He was all too familiar with the look of deep scepticism he received back.

The Chancellor nodded slowly, poised to turn.

"One more thing, Doctor James."

"Yes, Chancellor?"

"Do something about your appearance. This is not a frat house."

Chancellor Reshma Thandi turned and walked away. Orrin closed the door behind her, confining himself to the tirade Phil would undoubtedly release.

Orrin was home before midnight for the first time in two weeks and the mess around him reflected his neglect. He was resolute to clean himself up after the Chancellor's mandate. That job was vital. Without access to his lab, he was screwed. After a hot shower and shave, he scanned the internet for scraps of logic linking hobbits to the environmental devastation of his new reality. Nothing made sense.

Orrin lifted his socked feet off the coffee table and set his open laptop in their place. He grabbed his empty scotch glass and stood up.

He froze, spellbound, between his lounge and the glass windows overlooking Port Phillip Bay.

"Holy Mother…" he breathed. Orrin stumbled forward, dropping the glass to the floor, no longer seeing the room around him. He pressed his hands against the cool glass.

Beautiful. Magnificent. Glorious. None of the words that raced through his head even came close to the vision before his eyes.

The night sky was glowing. Vast curtains of neon green light filled the skyline, curling and folding in thick striations across the horizon. Above this layer, vibrant patches of pink, pure red, yellow and electric blue chased the night sky upwards. Where the colours met, violet and orange and white twisted the hues together like hazy ribbons.

Aurora Australis. I shouldn't be seeing this. I'm too close to the equator. Holy show, what have we done?

It must be the storms. The stunning display of charged light could only be caused by the geomagnetic storms that were threatening the earth more each day. The magnetosphere was weakening, allowing massive flows of solar wind to bombard its defences. Hot coronal plasma was being pulled along earth's magnetic field lines to the magneto tail behind it. The tail tore under the intense pressure of the flares, squeezing the solar wind back toward earth to feed the spectacular auroral display that Orrin now witnessed.

Orrin knew what it meant. The geomagnetic storms were rising. The earth's atmosphere was saturated with trapped particles, enhancing the current and warping the earth's magnetic field.

If it weren't for the unfathomable danger it represented, Orrin might have shed tears of joy. In all his life, from his stargazing enthralment as a little boy, to the endless hours he had clocked behind the lens of a telescope, Orrin had never seen anything as perfect.

The colours evolved and switched from one to another, constantly changing in a dance of electrons spiralling around the magnetic field lines that travelled the atmosphere down to the earth.

It's getting stronger.

Orrin stood staring for a long time. He knew there was logic somewhere, buried beneath the dirt and riddles and empty spaces. Whatever was causing the magnetosphere to decay was somehow related to Ivy's disappearance. Ivy's disappearance was somehow related to *Homo floresiensis*. There was a link, but no matter how hard he sought it, it eluded him. It was infuriating.

The storms were getting worse. Orrin knew it, not only from his own calculations, but from the blatant indication now illuminating the Melbourne sky.

It's only a matter of time... GPS signals will go - navigation, oil drilling stations, flights and transport. Satellites will be dead in the sky; the International Space Station will drop. Power grids won't be able to handle the storm's massive currents- they'll catch fire or explode. Hundreds of millions of people without electricity during months of repair- they'll starve or freeze to death. Nations will take years to recover. If mother earth will let them.

Orrin buried his face in his shaking hands.

"I have to fix this. Jaysus Christ, I have to fix it."

He dropped back to the couch, scouring the internet for more information, more clues. Hours later, Orrin was jolted from his thoughts by a shrill ring. He dropped his laptop back onto the coffee table. His latest search results reflected onto the glass windows that were still haunted by an auroral glow. *'Homo floresiensis - Beyond the protests: the benefits and ethics of proto-human experimentation.'*

Exhausted, Orrin fell back onto the couch as he tapped the mobile screen.

"Orrin James." His voice cracked in resistance.

"Orrin? It's me, Jayne. I'm sorry to call, I know it's 3am, but I found your number on that paper -"

He sat straight, weariness forgotten.

"What's happened?" Orrin's chest swelled with desperation for news.

"It's bad Orrin. Really bad." Jayne's voice tremored.

He deflated back against the leather, pushing his fingers into his closed eyes.

"Just say it."

"They've found more remains. At Liang Bua. An almost complete skeleton dated to fifty thousand years before present - on the same stratigraphic level as previous hobbit finds."

"And? They've found others before haven't they? What's the problem?"

Jayne's breathing paused for a moment. Then she let it out, all in a rush, as if trying to evict the words from her mouth.

"The skeleton is a modern Homo sapien. It's *not* a hobbit, it's one of us. And it's female. *It's a modern Homo sapien woman.*"

The tiled room rushed toward him. Orrin's vision blurred and sweat pricked his neck.

"It's not Ivy," he said. "It can't be. If she is dead there, how can I bring her back? How can I possibly bring her back?" His throat felt tight and the words broke high and frantic as they spilled from his lips. "I can't bring back a dead woman - I need more time!" Orrin clawed for an explanation. "It's - it's a native. A woman from Flores. Prehistoric. It has to be."

Jayne's breath faltered down the line.

"But there are no other remains of modern Homo sapiens at the cave until the Holocene. They begin thousands of years later. This skeleton was found at the back of the cave, beside the remains of a hobbit child, about three years old. I've been running tests. The stratigraphy is definitely Pleistocene and -" she paused again, taking a deep breath. "Orrin, I think it may be of European origin."

The words crushed him. *European origin.* Orrin had read enough to learn that the first European colonists, Portuguese traders and missionaries, had not arrived in Flores until the 16th century, conferring the island its name, 'flowers'. There was no one else it could be. *It was Ivy.*

Jayne tried to supplicate his silence. "I'm running the DNA tests again, but my initial results have set the dig team into a spin. To find a European skeleton in Pleistocene Flores - it just makes no sense to them. They think it might be evidence of this 'Hiranah' deity."

"Ivy *is* the Hiranah deity, Jayne."

She sighed. "I'm really sorry Orrin. God, you don't know how much I want to be wrong about this. I'm still at the genetics lab now. I've pulled in a favour with a friend and we'll stay here as long as we have to. As soon as I have confirmation, one way or the other, I'll call you." Her defeat was palpable.

Staring into the inky water far below, Orrin fought the darkness rising within him. *After everything I've done. I failed her.*

Finally giving in to it, his shoulders caved. And the tears fell.

CHAPTER 51

IVY

The music came to her slowly. It wove and whispered in broken notes in her head until finally the haunting melody fell together and Ivy listened. *Le Cygne. It's me.* The tone and timbre of her own cello were unmistakable; she knew its voice as well as her own. Ivy ached for it to be real. To feel the vibrations under her fingertips. To drown in the memory of polished maple and pine-scented rosin. But it couldn't be real.

Because somewhere deep behind the music, Ivy remembered the stegodon hunt. She remembered the karathah fight. To be hearing her cello, in this place, on the edge of death, meant she must be losing the battle. *I'm dying then. Or am I already dead?*

The music closed softly with a melancholic note. Then it started again. She listened through it, unable to rouse more than a curious wonder that it was there, in her head. The world was dark but she wasn't entirely sure that her eyes were open. She struggled, trying to fight off unconsciousness, however futile the effort might be. Then she remembered Rinap.

The weight of grief and loss crushed her. Death, once again, began to feel like a reprieve and Ivy felt herself drifting on the music.

No!

No, god damn it. Not again.

Ivy struggled to clear her head, pushing the temptation away. *Not this time. I have to fight.* She willed her body into consciousness. But with clarity, came pain.

First was her thigh. It throbbed, deep into the bone and Ivy's breath hitched as it hit her full force. Her fingers twitched in the darkness and with a groan she lifted them, blindly seeking the open wound, but instead finding a poultice bound in hide strips. Ivy shivered despite herself, wishing her mind was clearer. She guessed she owed her life to Lahstri and Shahn, both of whom must have tended to her, while they grieved themselves. She widened her eyes; they were definitely open now. Hearth coals glowed nearby and the soft light of a full moon diffused the darkness of the cave.

There was a soft grunt near her head. Warm fingers grazed her forehead. Ivy struggled to pull herself upright.

"Kyah!" She turned, burying her face in the bonobo's arms. They closed around her, as if they had been waiting forever. Kyah hooted a soft greeting, letting Ivy loose and then pulling her close again as Ivy's eyes strained to make out her friend's face in the shadows. Ivy's head pounded and her sight was blurry. The faint noise of her own movement amplified terribly in her head, conflicting the soothing cello that still dominated her mind. The perfumed candlenut oil that Shahn had used to fight her septic fever reeked too sweetly, bringing bile to the back of her throat. Le Cygne finished and started again.

I don't understand. I'm alive and the music is still playing?

The song had played numerous times now, beginning again as soon as it ended.

I'm losing my mind.

Ivy lifted her face away from the suffocation of Kyah's fur.

I need air. She pulled herself up on the bonobo, wobbling

precariously on her injured leg. Sparks of pain swam before her eyes.

With Kyah's help, Ivy limped to the front of the cave, bypassing the sleeping bodies by their hearths. She was greeted by a perfectly round, ivory moon.

And then she heard him.

"Bleeding Christ! What am I doing wrong?" A muffled thud.

"You can't be dead. You're not dead."

It was like a whisper behind her. The same sort of whisper she had heard once before, in what seemed like a lifetime ago, only that time, Ivy was in a different world, and it was Gihn who was calling to her through time.

"I'll find you. I swear to God, Ivy, I'll get you back."

Ivy's neck stiffened. Adrenaline flooded her heart. Her fingers twitched with desperation as it pulsed through her body. *Could it be?* She forced herself to slow down and breathe.

One breath. Two. Three breaths, and with the last, came courage.

"Orrin?"

She squeezed her eyes shut; too scared to see the world outside, in case it took away his voice.

Silence. Ivy's heart pounded. Every nerve and cell in her body was screaming. Memories came flooding back to her. Dark flecked eyes and the soft taste of coffee and spearmint. That beguiling Irish lilt on his tongue. Curls she longed to twist her fingers through. The scent of oak moss and fir.

Losing herself.

Please.

"Orrin?"

She heard a sharp intake of breath and something crash.

"Orrin! It's me! It's Ivy! I can hear you!"

Orrin spun around, sending another stack of papers and leads flying from his desk to the floor.

What the hell? Her voice! It was beside him. But there was nothing there. A cold sweat raced the adrenaline to his palms. It was right there, Ivy's voice, just as real and solid as it had been in the beginning.

"Ivy?"

"Orrin! I'm here! I can hear you!"

"Where? Where are you? I can't see you." Orrin spun around, his eyes frantic. It was midnight. Another frustrating day had passed in the laboratory and Phil and Dale had long since left. His monitor shone with iridescent light. Articles and reams of data were scattered across the floor and the music dock blinked its low battery light sporadically as it played Le Cygne on repeat. Tools were scattered nearby on the floor where he had been making some adjustments to the Tesla coil, which sat dormant.

"I can't see you either. But I can hear you."

"I can hear you!"

"This is what happened - I heard them, just like this - they were calling to me before they took us -"

"Who took you? What do you mean?"

"These people. The Hobbits - I mean Homo floresiensis people. They called me here somehow, to come to them -"

"Are you there? With them now? Are you in Flores?"

"Yes! They think I can – oh my god, they want the impossible from me." Ivy shuddered and let her knees buckle. She collapsed, stunned, on the lip of the cave under a full moon, clutching the amulet like a lifeline. The stone was hot in her hand - hotter than it should be in the cool night air. Kyah shuffled around Ivy, anxiously twitching her head. The music was still playing some-where - and Ivy realised - it was playing a world away.

"There's so much I need to tell you," she gasped. "I don't even know where to start – I just..." she took a deep breath. "I miss you. You don't know how much."

Orrin's trembling fingers found the bridge of his nose and his glasses fell askew. He swallowed past the lump in his throat, his reply barely a whisper.

"I miss you too." Understatement of the year. I love you, he wanted to scream. Ivy's voice, her words, they were everything. He had no idea how, or why he could hear her voice. Was it a miracle? Or had he finally gone insane? He wasn't asleep. But even insane, he couldn't risk not speaking.

There was a moment of silence and Ivy felt her heart stop until Orrin spoke again.

"I've been trying to find you. It's been murder. I don't know how to get you back," Orrin's voice was cracking. "I'm trying so hard, but there's something missing. I thought you were dead."

"I'm not dead! I'm here," Ivy looked across the moonlit forest below her, suddenly overwhelmed with the inherent madness of the situation. "I'm not dead, I'm just... prehistoric." She laughed, and heard Orrin hiccup the same, slightly manic response. There was another moment of silence between them.

Focus. Ivy snapped her thoughts back. "Listen Orrin - my amulet - it's important," she said. "I don't know how or why...but, do you remember the necklace I was wearing at that rally, it had a black stone on it - the chain broke when I fell -?"

"Sure," Orrin said. He pushed his hand into his pocket, pulling the amulet out and holding it in his palm. It was burning hot. As always, it kept his gaze like a magnet. "Ouch. I have it here. The whole thing. The chain as well. Why is it hot? Something's wrong with it - something's happening to it -"

"You have my amulet? How?"

"I found the chain broken in my lab when you disappeared -"

"It always breaks," Ivy said, despairingly.

"- but Jayne had the stone itself. It was an artefact from the Flores dig," Orrin continued. "Buried 50,000 years in that cave. It's how I knew you were there."

"Okay." Ivy had no idea what to make of that. Her thoughts raced ahead, words stumbling to keep up. "Wait - an artefact? My amulet was buried in the cave fifty thousand years ago? Does that mean... I am too? I'm going to die here?" Resentment swelled inside her chest. "No!" She said bitterly. "I'm *not* going to die here, Orrin! I swear to you, it's not the end for me here, not anymore!"

Jayne's words spun in Orrin's head and he swallowed back his nausea. 'The skeleton is a modern Homo sapien. It's not a hobbit, it's one of us. And it's female.'

"Ivy..." Orrin began, his voice trembling.

"No, Orrin! I'm not – going – to – die here!"

"I'll do whatever it takes," Orrin said, through gritted teeth. "I know where you are, I just don't know how to get you back. But I'm trying."

"Just – help me. Keep helping me." Ivy squeezed her eyes shut, desperate to maintain the flow of thoughts. "The amulet changed when I disappeared, okay, it went really hot like it is now - this stone is part of the connection somehow. Across time."

"Mine's hot too," Orrin said. The stone was burning his palm but he didn't dare drop it in case the connection was lost. "Will it happen again? Is it happening now?"

Ivy looked hopefully at her amulet, hot in her own palm. "It's not enough," she said. She turned it over, willing it to do something. To make sense. She could feel her palm burning, but there was no swirling grey, no streaks of lightning. Her body, as broken as it felt, didn't feel as if it was being ripped apart the way it had. This time, she wasn't Falling. "No. I can hear you, but I can't see you. I'm stuck here."

"We need to make it work," Orrin said, desperately. "There's a catalyst. But I don't know what it is."

Ivy squeezed her eyes shut, trying to tame her desperation into rational thought. If she had any hope of going home, she had to find the missing piece of the puzzle.

"Last time," she said, "there was a big flash of blue light. Like lightning."

"The Tesla coil malfunctioned. It was electricity -"

"And the hobbits were singing," she added. "They were calling to me somehow. It's like a ritual they have - they call it a *Dusk*

Song. I just – I don't even know what that means, but I know it's important. They have to be singing for the Fall to work. That's what I did - I Fell. On a volcano nearly five days walk from this cave, *Kelimutu* - they saw me Fall from the sky as they sang. Like a streak of lightning to the earth." Ivy was rambling, trying to get as many of her thoughts out as she could, all at once. She didn't know which parts might help him, but she was desperate to give Orrin as much of what she had figured out as she could. "The harmonies- the music of their dusk song- *that's important.* They said that it's something about the energy from the moon? God, damn it! I don't know what any of this means. And the stars, I left you a drawing of it, just in case it helped -"

"I saw it. I saw the stars."

Ivy stopped abruptly. "You saw the stars?"

"It was brilliant. A perfect lunar calendar. I knew it was you."

"You did?" Ivy stuttered. "I didn't think you'd ever find it."

"I told you, Ivy. I've been searching for you. For clues. Everywhere."

Ivy couldn't help but grin into the darkness. She shook her head and drew her arms tight around her body. Seconds disappeared in silence.

"Orrin?"

"I did this," he said. *"I've made a mess of everything and I wouldn't blame you if you hated me for it. But I'll get you back, no matter what it costs me."*

"No. It's not your fault, please don't say that," Ivy implored in a whisper. "Sometimes the thought of you is all that keeps me going here."

"Really?"

"God, yes," Ivy admitted. "This life here, it's like a beautiful dream and a nightmare all at once. These people have the most incredibly rich life, and so much love *inside* their hearts, but there's so much *death* all around them. And I just - I've already lost so much." Her heart ached for Rinap and the hunters that she guessed were days buried while she lay unconscious. Turi. Krue. Emiri. And then there were the others. *Her own.* In another life-time, so many years ago. *I lost them too.* Ivy took a deep breath and looked to the night sky for strength. "But I have to make this right, Orrin. For them."

"You shouldn't be there," Orrin said. "It's all a terrible mistake."

"But that's just the thing, I think I should be here," Ivy implored. "I don't know how to explain it, and I resisted it at first. But now I think - that I'm meant to be here. I always was. I'm meant to help them survive. That's why they called me here. There's no other explanation - as crazy as it sounds."

"No!" Orrin's voice was shaking. "Their survival is not your problem Ivy-"

"But it is! It's everybody's problem!" Ivy cried out. Her voice echoed down the terrace below. Her hands shook and she forced herself to breathe. "They don't deserve this, Orrin. This isn't natural selection. It's genocide. It's deliberate and cruel and fuelled by greed alone! I can't just sit back and let it happen. These people are smart and kind and yes, different - but they have a right to fight back!" Kyah shuffled closer and dropped her chin gently onto Ivy's arm.

Orrin sighed. "But why do you have to be the one to fight for them?"

Ivy buried her fingers in Kyah's soft hair. "I think - because *no one else will.*" She looked across the black landscape before her. "I want to come home. *No,* I *need* to come home, but I don't know if it's even possible. I've been trying to figure it out but it's so complicated and - I need you to understand that no matter what happens; I have a job to do here."

"Ivy, please -"

"No, listen! These people, they need me. I *want* to help them. But I want..." Ivy's voice softened to a whisper. "My God, I just want to come home. I want to be with *you,* too. I want you, Orrin. *So much.*" The last admission fell from her lips like a prayer.

Orrin buried his face in his hands. She wants me. She wants me too. "You have me."

"You're playing my music," Ivy said. As trivial as it was, the realisation made her blush.

"On repeat." *Orrin looked to the music dock with its red flashing light. The batteries were nearly dead and the music was beginning to stutter. "It helps me focus."*

Ivy heard a shuffling sound and a deep breath.

"There's something I need to tell you Ivy, about what's happened here since you've gone. I mean... what you've done... to me and... and the way things are now here... you see everything's changed..." Orrin's voice cracked with emotion.

"Done to you?" Ivy breathed.

She waited. The rest of his sentence didn't come.

"Orrin?"

Silence. His voice was gone. The soft cello was gone. There were only the night sounds of the forest below.

"Orrin?!" Ivy tried to calm her panic. *Please don't be gone.*

"Orrin?"

Nothing. He still might come back.

"Orrin?" She stared up at the full moon, clenching her jaw. Tears slipping. "Please?"

I'll wait.

Ivy waited, all of her thoughts willing to hear his voice again. Her knuckles turned white as she held the amulet to her chest. The stone cooled within her grip. She waited until the full moon disappeared behind her and the dawn sun split over the valley ahead. But Orrin's voice didn't return. The connection was gone.

*

As the morning crept over her, a new, singular determination pounded in her heart. Orrin had said he had her amulet on his side of the time shift. How it came to be buried in this cave fifty thousand years earlier, *in her lifetime, here, now,* Ivy didn't want to know. But that stone was clearly the key to her coming here, and if Orrin had it in the future, then she had hope it could take her home. She squeezed it tight. *No matter what, I can't lose it. I need to guard this stone with my life. It's my only link to home.*

The hobbits needed her, now more than ever. But she wanted to do more than survive.

I'll live here. For now. But I refuse to die here.

Ivy closed her eyes, imagining the scent of lavender garden-beds, thick green lawns and the cool, stone lecture halls of the university. The forest noise left her for an instant, and the chatter of students filled her mind instead. She retraced the fading sand-stone cloisters in her memory, found her musty paper-filled office and the comforting forget-me-not blue kitchen of her little apartment. Would it all be waiting for her when she returned? Would she simply settle in, as if she had never left?

No, I'm done with settling. This time I want to *live. Really live.*

Ivy had exiled those precious memories from her mind. But now, she savoured every detail, like watching a black-and-white movie come to life in vivid colour. She remembered sprawling jacarandas snowing the earth in a purple drift. White daisies ushering her onto the street each morning. Lazy afternoons in the great court, rolling oranges through the grass with Kyah. The soft *swish* of starched coats hanging behind the lab door. Even the acrid smell of laboratory floors seemed suddenly appealing. Memories rushed through Ivy and bit her bones.

My cello. Coffee. Chocolate. Shampoo!

She allowed the banished faces to creep back. Tom in his tartan hat, tending the garden at a snail's pace. Liam and his fear-less energy. Late night gossip with Jayne over a microscope.

And Orrin. Heat flooded her every cell. His face was the most vivid in her mind and his voice so fresh in her memory. Ivy trailed her fingertips across the skin of her thigh below the poultice that Shahn had put on. She was left with a tingling whisper across her skin and a deep ache inside her that didn't feel like it belonged to the wound.

I've already let time steal too much from me. But no more.

"How am I going to make this work, Kyah?" said Ivy aloud. Possibilities were colliding in her mind.

"Home," Ivy signed. "Let's go home."

Kyah frowned and lifted her face to the trees, apparently searching for a response.

Home. Kyah signed back. *Liam. Jayne.*

"Yeah," Ivy sighed.

Cage. Kyah added.

Ivy had no response.

Trahg. Home. Kyah signed. *Stay. Trahg.* The bonobo dug her toes sullenly into the hard soil of the cave entrance. Then, with a scan of the dawning sky, she leapt with fluid grace into a branch, leaving Ivy alone.

No. Ivy wasn't ready for that possibility. She pushed it away, swallowing hard. *This is a cage too. For both of us. Kyah doesn't belong here any more than I do.*

Ivy wrapped her fist around the amulet. On the other side of fifty thousand years, she knew now that Orrin was holding same stone. There was still a connection between her old life and this new one. So there was still a chance.

Whatever obstacles are keeping me here; I have to break them down.

Behind her, the hobbits began stirring in Liang Bua Cave.

It was time for change, Ivy decided. It was time not just to survive, but to *live*.

She lifted her face to the morning sun, resolute.

They deserve to live. But so do I.

She was going to achieve the impossible.

Not only for her new family, but for herself as well.

Somehow, whatever it takes, I'm going to save them. And then I'm going home.

TO BE CONTINUED

Ivy's story continues in *EXTINCT*, book two in *the Ivy Carter* adventure series, to be released in 2022.

JOIN MY READER'S CLUB

There are more books to come!

HayleyCamille.com/subscribe

LOVE IT? PLEASE REVIEW!

Your reviews are vital to the success of each book. Each book takes me months to research and write, so I'd really appreciate a few moments of your time if you enjoy reading them.

HayleyCamille.com/human-novel

Become a part of **#IvysTribe** on Social Media to tell us what you loved, and what you think might happen next.

ACKNOWLEDGMENTS

Thank you so much for becoming part of Ivy's journey by reading this book. It has been such a joy bringing her to you. Ivy evolved from my passion for prehistory, combined with the habit of disappearing into my imagination. Her story is far from over.

There have been many who have inspired me in the writing of this book, but none more so than Alex, who has supported my passion for human evolution into the creation of this series over many years. His creativity and knowledge are woven into the storyline in countless ways and the beautiful musical composition of the 'Human' book trailer is his.

To my children, Finn, Orrin and Ivy - I love you. You inspire everything I do.

I am eternally grateful to my mother, Penny, for always reading early chapters when Ivy was just a shadow of the heroine she would later become, and being the first to read the story in its entirety. Most importantly, she taught me to love animals, to advocate and speak for the voiceless and has always been my greatest champion. My father Rob, with his vast knowledge of physics and nature, inspired me to love science and is an endless source of encouragement and support.

Clayton, the best brother a girl could have, offered his time, skill and creative genius in coordinating and directing the book trailer for 'Human', and has always been so supportive and an inspiring collaborator. Thank you to my sisters, Kellie and Jasmine, who never tire of my odd obsessions, and who keep me sane and laughing despite lack of sleep. Thanks for reading drafts and offering advice, there is more of you both in this story than you realise.

Much love and huge thanks goes to my writing group for their wonderful advice and editing for this novel, with extra special hugs to Ben Langdon, Kathryn Hall, Linda Bibby and Fleur Guenther who picked up Ivy whenever she was losing her way and threw her back in the jungle where she belonged. You guys are the best.

Mike and Mel Smith, Malcolm Fenton and Leanda Michelle beta-read the final book for me and offered valuable feedback, which I very much appreciate. Thank you also to Barbara, Teresa and Bill for reading early versions.

To the late Dr. Tom Loy, for being so kind to a young post-graduate in the residue lab and always so generous with his enthusiasm and knowledge in the field of molecular archaeology, of which he was a pioneer, I will always be so grateful we crossed paths, even for a short time. It changed my world.

Of course, the real-world subject of this fictional story is owed entirely to the archaeological discovery of LB1 and her fossilised *Homo floresiensis* companions at Liang Bua in Flores, Indonesia by the late Dr Mike Morwood and his collaborative team of Australian and Indonesian palaeoanthropologists, archaeologists and inter-disciplinary experts. This was a remark-able discovery that really shone a new light on the reconstruction of our hominid family tree and continues to astonish and inspire us as new details are revealed. Thank you to all these scientists who reconstruct our prehistory and expand our knowledge with such excruciating care and detail – I admire your work and passion greatly.

Finally and above all, I would like to recognise the animals in cages, laboratories, servitude and entertainment all over the world for the suffering, grief, imprisonment and sacrifice they continue to endure for the sake of our species. In a battle that seems sometimes hopeless, your innocence gives us the strength to keep fighting for you. One day, we humans will see you. A change is coming.

ABOUT THE AUTHOR

Hayley Camille is the author of the *Ivy Carter* adventure series and multi award-winning *Lady Vigilante* crime series, as well as *The Ultimate Players Guide to Skylanders* gaming guides for kids.

Hayley loves dinosaurs, jazz, animals and all things vintage. She loves to collect teacups, though oddly, doesn't drink tea.

www.hayleycamille.com

Connect with Hayley at:

ALSO BY HAYLEY CAMILLE

The Ivy Carter Series

HUMAN

Archaeologist Ivy Carter holds the fate of humankind in her hands.

Ivy Carter is no stranger to losing the people she loves. She keeps everybody at arm's length, even Orrin James, the brilliant young astrophysicist falling for her.

But when she is stolen through time, and trapped fifty thousand years in the past, Ivy is tasked with the greatest challenge of her life; to prevent the extinction of a primitive human species against overwhelming odds. Determined to save them and desperate to find a way back home, Ivy reaches out across time and space, to the only person in the modern world who remembers her.

As Orrin uncovers Ivy's trail of archaeological clues to prove she existed, the modern world around him spirals into destruction. Every move Ivy makes in the past, puts future Earth in danger.

Each alone, they battle demons, inside and out, to prevent a genocidal war that could change the course of human evolution forever.

In a thrilling adventure that flips between modern world catastrophe and primitive survival, Ivy Carter holds the fate of humankind in her hands.

Available at: HayleyCamille.com/human-novel

EXTINCT

Two species of Human. Only one can survive. The choice is hers.

In the stunning sequel to HUMAN, modern-day archaeologist Ivy Carter begins a perilous journey across prehistoric Indonesia, at a time when volcanic eruptions, mass extinction and a genocidal war are tearing it apart.

Available at: HayleyCamille.com/extinct-novel

The Shadows and Light series

Judgement

In the shadow of Mortwood Forest dwells the most prolific murderer of the Kingdom. The curse he carries, however, may also make him their saviour.

In a world where magic has been lost and innocence is stolen, a prophesy begins. The darkest intentions hidden within every man's soul are exposed, as Shadows and Light, and only one has the power to Judge them.

But he is not what you expect.

Free short story available at: HayleyCamille.com/judgement

The Lady Vigilante Series

Mrs. Betty Jones: Lady Vigilante is the award-winning crime series that readers describe as "An EXPLOSIVE laugh-out-loud story!" with the indomitable protagonist, Betty Jones, as "a female Jack Reacher", "powered as all hell" and "Sassy, Smart and Deadly!"

"Lady Vigilante takes on the tropes of femininity in the 40's- the dutiful wife, gals who just want to look pretty letting their man do all the heavy lifting and thinking - and flips them on their head." - *ScreenCraft*

If you love ruthless revenge, kick-ass action and unforgettable characters, then you'll love Betty Jones.

SEASON ONE

As WW2 rages, a lone vigilante takes to the streets of New York to wage war against a powerful crime syndicate. She's the antihero the city needs, hidden in plain sight, with the perfect double life. Meet Mrs. Betty Jones.

Betty Jones has a dark past, which she paints away each day with Avon cosmetics and a bright smile. She has created a new life with her picture-perfect family, but old scars are beginning to itch.

When a series of heists leave a trail of dead soldiers and missing military cargo, Betty recognizes the calling card of her past demons. Blessed with gifts that make her more than human,

Betty is unable to live with the continuing existence of the people who once ruined her, so she embarks on a cold-blooded vigilante mission to be rid of them once and for all. But the past is catching up to her, and Betty's perfect life is beginning to crack.

SEASON TWO

A gang war is raging in the underbelly of 1940s New York as a mysterious femme-fatale, known only as the Boudoir Butcher, leaves a trail of bodies between the sheets. When NYPD Detective Jacob Lawrence turns to Betty for help tracking down the serial killer, she can't refuse him. After all, Betty has always been drawn to old flames and open fire…

But will Betty's perfect life be engulfed in the raging blaze she stirs up?

Season Collections available at:
HayleyCamille.com/lady-vigilante-season-collections